EXCALIBUR

BOOK 1 IN THE ARTHUR CHRONICLES SERIES

PETER GIBBONS

Boldwood

First published in Great Britain in 2024 by Boldwood Books Ltd.

Cover Design by Colin Thomas

Cover Photography: Colin Thomas

A CIP catalogue record for this book is available from the British Library.

Paperback ISBN 978-1-83518-232-1

Large Print ISBN 978-1-83518-228-4

Hardback ISBN 978-1-83518-227-7

Ebook ISBN 978-1-83518-225-3

Kindle ISBN 978-1-83518-226-0

Audio CD ISBN 978-1-83518-233-8

MP3 CD ISBN 978-1-83518-230-7

Digital audio download ISBN 978-1-83518-224-6

Boldwood Books Ltd
23 Bowerdean Street
London SW6 3TN
www.boldwoodbooks.com

For Mike Duggan. Who kept a lad on the straight and narrow.

Now when his youthful strength had increased, and a noble desire for command burned in his young breast, he remembered the valiant deeds of heroes of old, and as though awakening from sleep, he changed his disposition and gathering bands of followers took up arms; [...] when he had devastated the towns and residences of his foes, their villages and fortresses with fire and sword, and gathered together companions from various races and from all directions, [he]... amassed great booty.

— FROM THE *VITA SANCTI GUTHLACI*, WRITTEN BY
THE EAST ANGLIAN PRIEST FELIX IN THE EARLY
EIGHTH CENTURY

BRITAIN, C. 540

N

PICTLAND
DAL
RIATA
LOTHIAN
GODODDIN
BERNICIA
RHEGED
DEIRA
ELMET
SAXONS
GWYNEDD
POWYS
DEMETIA
GWENT
Kingdoms of
DUMNONIA
KERNOW
Dumnnonia

THE GREAT SIXTH-CENTURY
KINGDOMS OF BRITAIN

After the collapse of the Roman Empire in 400 AD, the legions left Britain to descend into a place of constant, brutal warfare. By the sixth century, the island is ruled by fierce kings from behind crumbling Roman strongholds and menacing hilltop fortresses. The south-east and western kingdoms have fallen to marauding Germanic invaders known as Saxons. The Saxons are a warlike people from across the sea, first invited to Britain by Vortigern, a weak king of a small kingdom, to aid him in his wars against the rival kings of Britain.

Rheged – Located close to Cumbria in modern-day England. Ruled by King Urien from his seat at the Bear Fort. Warriors of Rheged carry the bear sigil upon their shields.
Gododdin – A kingdom in Britain's north-east, close to modern-day Northumberland and East Lothian. Ruled by King Letan Luyddoc from his fortress Dunpendyrlaw. Gododdin's warriors march under a stag banner.
Dal Riata – Kingdom on Scotland's west coast, covering what is now Argyll.
Dumnonia – Ruled by King Uther Pendragon. Dumnonian warriors

march to war with a dragon sigil upon their shields. Located in Britain's south-west, mainly in modern-day Devon, Somerset and Cornwall.

Gwynedd – Ruled by King Cadwallon Longhand. Located in north Wales and Anglesey.

Elmet – Ruled by King Gwallog. Located in the area around modern-day Leeds, reaching down south to the Midlands. Elmet's warriors wear the *lorica segmentata* armour and red cloaks of the Roman legions.

Bernicia – Lands lost to Ida, the Saxon conqueror. Covers what is now south Northumberland, Tyne and Wear, and Durham. Its warriors once fought beneath the proud banner of the fox.

Deira – Lands stretching along much of Britain's west coast, which fell to Saxon invaders in Vortigern's Great War.

Lothian – Ruled by King Lot, encompassing what is now southeast Scotland.

Powys – Ruled by King Brochvael the Fanged. A large and powerful kingdom in what is now central Wales.

Pictland – Lands occupied by the Picts in Scotland's north.

Demetia – Lands in the south-west of what is now Wales. Ruled by King Morholt and his Irish warriors who took the kingdom by force.

Gwent – A kingdom between the Rivers Wye and Usk, in what is now south Wales. Ruled by King Tewdrig.

1

540 AD, BRITAIN

A blood-coloured sun crept above jagged treetops as three mounted
warriors and twenty spearmen left the Bear Fort on a frosty spring morning. Long shadows crept through grasping boughs to dapple the land in
dark shapes and a shallow mist lingered on the forest floor. A wild storm
had thrashed the stronghold for a day and a night, howling across its
spiked walls to soak through men's cloaks, breastplates and tunics, so the
warriors marched in grim ranks with damp clothes clinging to their skin
like shrouds. Hooves and boots crunched through the undergrowth,
leather belts, bridles and armour creaked, and the men grumbled about
the early start as they marched with ash-shafted spears resting on their
shoulders and breath billowing from their mouths in great clouds to mist
the chill air.

'The next man I hear complaining gets a thick ear,' barked Ector, his
voice gruff and as menacing as the snarling bear painted upon his shield.
He was their *comitatus*, as the Rome-folk would have it, the leader of the
war band and King Urien of Rheged's champion. Ector was fearsome, a
huge man with hands like shovels. He wore a coat of shining chain mail
and carried a long sword in a fleece-lined scabbard strapped to his thick
leather belt. Ector's face was broad and as hard as mountain rock, his fore-

head jutted like a cliff, and his chin was wide and strong. Scars ran across his broken nose and cheeks, and he was as fearsome to look upon as a winter storm. His forearms were so thick with death rings that they tattooed his entire arms dark blue. When a warrior killed an enemy in battle, he tattooed a ring around his forearm in memory of the slain man's warrior spirit, and Ector had run out of room upon his arms many years ago.

Arthur shifted on his horse and lifted his spear for a moment to ease its weight on his shoulder. He rode because he was Ector's foster son, and the marching spearmen cast resentful glances at him, their judgement burning Arthur like a whip. This was Arthur's second march with Ector's war band. The first had come two weeks earlier when the war band had marched south to collect overdue render from farms on the southern edge of Urien's realm. Each hide, or farm, in Rheged owed Urien one tenth of their farm's surplus. If the render was not delivered, the war band would go to collect it, and Ector's visit was never gentle.

'We might get to fight this time,' said Kai, Ector's son, Arthur's foster brother and friend. He leaned over so that Ector would not hear and grinned at Arthur. Kai and Arthur had both seen seventeen summers, but Kai was both taller and wider across the shoulders. He had hair the colour of a rusted blade and green eyes like his father. Kai had his father's face, but it was as yet unmarked by battle, and his beard was as sparse and wispy as Arthur's. 'I will earn my first death ring today.'

'Hopefully,' Arthur lied, forcing himself to smile. Arthur and Kai had trained with weapons since the time they could walk. Ector and his brutal captain, Huell, taught them the thrusts of the spear, the cuts of the sword, knife fighting, the bow and the war axe. Arthur could fight, and he loved the sword, but he had never killed a man.

'Pick up the pace there, bastard,' Huell growled on Arthur's flank. He glanced down at the stocky warrior, whose scarred face was as wrinkled and hard as a boar's back. The grizzled warrior snarled at him and spat into the undergrowth. Arthur rode whilst Huell marched, and the veteran of countless battles hated Arthur for that. Huell hated that Arthur slept beneath warm furs in Ector's household, he hated that Arthur was an orphan who shared Kai's privileges. Arthur's legs hung loose at the horse's belly, so he dug his heels in and clicked his tongue to pick up the roan mare's pace.

They followed a mud-slick path through the thick forest. Wagon wheel ruts ran deep to either side and the track stank of horse shit and wet earth. Arthur's mare kicked up clods of mud and he stifled a laugh as Huell cursed behind him. Blackbirds sang in the boughs, and a robin trilled somewhere in the canopy of green and brown. Fresh leaves filled branches, and the sunlight punched through them in shafts of light to create shifting shadows in the mist. The forest smelled of the storm, damp and heavy like a wet dog. Bluebells and wildflowers spattered the sides of the path with a wash of cover.

By late afternoon, the war band rested on a high crag, a jutting cliff with a view into a sprawling valley where woodland gave way to fields separated by ditch and hedge. Farmers were busy finishing sowing their furrows, bringing animals to green pastures after long winters and shearing their sheep for wool.

'Bastards are down there somewhere,' said Ector, glaring down into the valley. A river cut through the lowland, meandering and glistening like a blue snake. Thatched farmsteads shone like gold amongst the fields, and Arthur looked across the valley with his keen hazel eyes but could see no sign of an enemy.

'There's no smoke,' said Huell, spitting as he so often did through his missing front teeth. 'Wherever there are raiders, there's smoke.'

'They are probably sleeping off a long night enjoying stolen ale and beef,' said Kai, and Ector grunted without taking his eyes off the shining river.

'A farmer in the fields said they were at the old villa. We'll be there before nightfall.'

'If they are still there,' said Ector. 'They'll know we're coming. All men know that to raid Rheged means death. Urien suffers no attacks on his land. Even the *bucellari* know that. If they have any cunning in their masterless skulls, they will be long gone by now.'

'If they had the cunning of a turnip, they'd not have raided Rheged.

Any *bucellari* this far north have come from Bernicia, or Deira. *Bucellari* bands of masterless men fighting for any lord who can pay them must have come from beyond that frontier. Maybe they've grown tired of fighting the Saxons in the east and fancy themselves some easier prey.'

'Bastards picked the wrong prey this time,' said Ector. He rested his hand on his sword's leather-wrapped hilt. 'We march to the villa and kill any man we find there.' He turned and the heat of his gaze fell upon Arthur and Kai. 'You are men now, full grown and ready to fight. Your place is with the war band, so today you'll fight and kill. You know how. This is what we do. We serve King Urien, fight his wars, and kill his enemies. We collect the render owed to him, and he provides us with land, men, silver and glory. If you can't fight, you can't stay in my service, son or not. So, kill and soak your blades with blood so the men can see it. Earn their respect. I gave you both spears and knives and horses to ride, so earn them, too.'

'Your father and I started with nothing. Everything we have, we won by the blade,' Huell snarled, and he slapped his sword hilt for extra emphasis. 'The first time I fought, I carried a rusty dagger. I killed two men that day and have been a warrior ever since. Don't let me catch you shirking, bastard. You'll fight today or I'll drive you out of Rheged myself.'

'Enough. They know their duty. Let's march.'

Arthur swallowed hard and glanced up at his spear's sharp point. Father Iddawg had told him it was not a sin to kill an enemy, to kill an innocent man was murder and God looks kindly on those who uphold the king's peace. Arthur worried about that. Father Iddawg was a pious man and Ector's priest. He lived on Ector's estate and ate his food and saw to the souls of Ector's men and their families. Arthur had prayed and asked God, and the old gods, for aid many times. Countless nights he had prayed to know who his mother and father were and why they had abandoned him, but God never answered his prayers.

'If I have to hear one more story about Huell and my father fighting for King Uther in the Great War, I'll gouge my eyes out,' said Kai once the two old warriors had left to join the men.

'Do you think you can do it?' asked Arthur.

'Do what, gouge my eyes out?'

'No, kill a man?'

Kai shrugged. 'We have no choice. That's our life now. Besides, these are wicked men. *Bucellari* are mercenaries without honour. You heard the farmer in Urien's hall. These men have killed women and children and razed farms to the ground. They deserve to die.'

Arthur nodded and followed his friend back to their mounts. Fear curdled his belly and Arthur did not share the meal of oatcakes and ale. All the men in Ector's war band were hard men, killers and professional warriors. Ector himself was the champion of Rheged. Many said he was the greatest warrior in all of Britain. Ector never lost, not even on the practice ground. Kai had come close the last winter, almost landing a strike with a wooden sword, but Ector had recovered and thundered a fist into Kai's belly to win the bout. It was time to become a man, and Arthur hoped he was brave enough. Kai could do it. He was fearless and a fine warrior with every weapon. He beat Arthur in most practice bouts, and Arthur himself was skilled with sword and spear. In his heart, Arthur was not a violent man. He liked to listen to the bards and their stories, to dream of heroes and legends and of the Rome-folk and their mighty empire. He enjoyed weapons, especially the sword, and the physicality of the practice yard. Every lesson Ector and Huell had taught told Arthur that to kill was his purpose in life, he would be a warrior and protect Rheged from her enemies. But to rip a man's life away, to pierce his flesh with cold iron and send him screaming to the afterlife, that was different to hitting Kai with a wooden sword or a spear.

The war band reached the villa as the sun set behind them, washing the land with a dim light the colour of gold. Their spears cast long shadows like the claws of a monster upon lush green grass as twenty-three warriors crouched behind a gorse thicket. They peered at the ruins of a sprawling villa, its white stone walls crumbled, and red tiles which once covered its sloping roof littered the ground. The villa was another remnant of the mighty Romans who had ruled Britain for hundreds of years and then left in the time of Ector's great-grandsire to leave the land littered with memories of their greatness and riven with violent anarchy without law or legion.

'How many?' asked Ector. He crouched with his sword drawn. Its steel edge gleamed, and its blade caught the twilight to reveal the strange smoke in its metal. It was a magnificent weapon, given to Ector by Uther Pendragon for his services in the Great War against Vortigern and the marauding Saxons. Arthur could not take his eyes off the sword. He hoped to own such a weapon one day, the weapon of a champion. Arthur carried a spear and a long knife, and he would continue to do so until he killed a man and gained better weapons, or his lord rewarded him with them.

'Thirty men,' Huell said, his flint-hard eyes squinting at the men lolling in the villa's courtyard. They had made a fire from rotting roof beams and lolled about it, laughing and drinking ale from clay jugs. They were rough men, bushy bearded, with dark eyes and darker laughs. Three women mewed and wept as the *bucellari* mercenaries passed them around the fire. The women, stripped naked, had terror-stricken faces drawn long by fear and suffering. A nest of spears and shields were neatly piled in a corner, while six tied horses stood beside the rubble of a fallen-down barn. The *bucellari* wore wool tunics and dark cloaks, a handful wore leather breastplates, and none wore the heavy chain-mail coats which separated the lords of war from the rest of the warrior caste. Ector and Huell each wore a heavy mail coat, made from tiny, interlocked rings of iron which protected them from neck to groin.

'We'll do them now whilst they're drunk,' said Ector, and Huell grinned wolfishly.

'A rider!' hissed a spearman. Arthur turned; spear lowered. He licked at dry lips, thoughts flashing through his head. What if it was enemy riders? Perhaps the enemy had surrounded them?

A figure approached from the treeline beyond a wild meadow, the same direction from which Arthur and the war band had marched moments earlier.

'Bloody fool, girl,' Ector cursed, but Arthur smiled because the figure was not the enemy.

It was Lunete, Kai's younger sister. She came with a bow slung over her shoulder and a quiver of arrows at her belt. Her dark hair fell about her slim shoulders, and she raised her chin in defiance as Ector and Huell waved frantically at her to duck down before the *bucellari* mercenaries saw her.

'I warned you, girl,' Ector said through gritted teeth as Lunete crouched between Arthur and Kai. 'I'll marry you off the moment we get home. You're going to get yourself killed!'

'I can't let you two have all the fun whilst I spin yarn and listen to the wives talk of weaving and babies,' said Lunete. She ignored her father, blue eyes prideful and her raven-black hair shining. Lunete unslung her bow and tested the string, and Arthur laughed at her brave impudence. She was Ector's favourite, the apple of his eye, and he doted on her wild savagery. Lunete's upbringing should have focused on spinning yarn, weaving clothes and tapestries and becoming a good wife. But she was wilder than either Kai or Arthur, and Ector indulged her, training her to fight with bow and spear and allowing her to ride and live with his men.

'Don't get in the way, pig-nose,' Kai whispered, and Lunete punched him on the arm. She hated that name, earned because of her snub nose, and Arthur laughed again at the fond rivalry between brother and sister. It masked his fear momentarily, but Huell readied the men and the gnawing heat in Arthur's belly returned.

'Strike fast, don't hesitate,' Lunete whispered, fixing him with her bright eyes. He nodded and swallowed the lump in his throat.

Ector stood and raised his sword to the heavens. 'For God, and Rheged!' he roared, and strode from the gorse like the champion he was. Orange light from the enemy's fire caught the links of his mail and the patterns of his sword blade, and the enemy leapt from the fallen masonry. Men dashed for spears and shields and Ector broke into a charge, flanked by Huell and his twenty loyal spearmen. Each warrior in Ector's war band was oathsworn to fight and die for him, and he led from the centre, brave and unflinching. The warriors charged like a flock of birds, Ector at the tip of the wedge, every man howling his war cry. Kai ran with them, spear lowered, his boyish face twisted in anger. All Ector's men carried spears in their fists and long knives at their belts. Some were lucky enough to carry shields, but only Ector and Huell had swords.

'Go, Arthur,' Lunete shouted, kicking Arthur in the leg. Fear rooted him to the spot like a tree, unable to move or breathe. 'You can do it. Go!'

Arthur clenched his teeth and gripped the smooth ash of his spear. He surged to his feet, held his breath, and ran. His heart thundered in his chest like a war drum as he followed ten paces behind Ector, spear lowered, the sound of men shouting and horses whickering churning in his ears. The enemy panicked, desperately readying weapons to fight off the men who came screaming from the fields like demons. Ector killed the first man with a sweep of his sword, and blood flew bright in the fading light as death came for the brigands who had raided King Urien's lands.

An arrow whipped past Arthur's head and slammed into a *bucellari* warrior's chest, and Arthur glanced over his shoulder to where Lunete nocked another arrow to her bowstring. He turned back, and his spear shifted off balance. The butt caught his trailing leg and Arthur sprawled on the grass. He cursed and scrambled to his feet, but a short man with a furious face swung an axe at Arthur's head and he thought he must die, but an arrow struck the enemy in the thigh, and he sank to the earth in pain. Arthur twisted around the fallen man and kept on running. The fight raged around him, and Huell drove his spear into a big man's throat and twisted the blade with a mighty roar. A *bucellari* disembowelled a Rheged man with a long knife. Arthur knew him and gasped at the terrible wound. The iron stink of blood, and the stench of shit as dying men voided their bowels, filled the air and Arthur ran. He reached the villa's crumbling walls and realised he was running to nowhere, caught up by fear and closeness to death.

Huell dragged his spear free of a dying man and roared his war-fury as he threw the spear to take another enemy in the chest. Huell spat and dragged his sword free of its fleece-lined scabbard. He parried an enemy spear and slashed open that man's throat with a vicious backswing. Hot blood spattered Arthur's face as he ran past Huell, and he gasped at the feel of another man's lifeblood upon his skin.

This is what you were trained to do, so do it. Fight! Arthur tried to convince himself, but his feet would not move, as though fixed to the earth by a druid's spell. Kai drove his spear into the belly of a young warrior, yanked the point free, and stabbed again to make his first kill. Arthur's mouth was dry, his tongue like old leather. He could feel eyes upon him, judging him, could imagine Huell's cruel rebukes if he failed to strike a blow in the fight. *I should have killed the axeman.* Lunete had saved his life, and all Arthur had to do was kill the wounded man and the deed would be done. He would be a warrior. But he had just run away like a dog without sense or courage.

A huge enemy with a thick black beard and wild curly hair burst from the ruins, holding a war axe in one hand and a shield in the other. He barged Huell out of the way with his shield, roared in defiance, and cracked the edge of his axe into a Rheged warrior's skull with a sickening crack. The bearded enemy yanked the axe free in a wash of dark blood and grey slime and grinned as his eyes rested on Arthur. He came at Arthur, his maw full of stubby brown teeth and his beard a mess of tangled hair, lice and filth. He swung his axe and bellowed with hate, and Arthur ducked beneath the wild swing. The shield came about and crashed into Arthur's shoulder, driving him backwards. Arthur stumbled under the impact and the axe came around in a blur. He raised his spear just in time to parry the blow. The big man kicked Arthur savagely in the groin and, as he doubled over, a knee thundered into his face. Arthur fell to the ground and scrambled over the dew-soaked grass. He was winded, gasping for air, and had dropped his spear. Panic flooded his senses as he tried to drag his knife free of the sheath at his belt. He closed his eyes tightly, expecting the axe to fall and chop into his skull, neck or back.

'Fight me, dog,' barked a familiar voice. Arthur sucked in a chest full of air and rolled onto his back. Ector had come, and the big *bucellari* left Arthur to face King Urien's champion. The two men circled each other, like great wolves eying the other's size and battle scars. Arthur scrambled to his knees and then stood, bracing himself against the rough edge of a broken-down wall. He found his spear in the grass, and humiliation washed over him. To drop a weapon in battle was shameful and Arthur looked around, hoping that nobody had seen him fall before the enemy warrior, and found Huell's cruel eyes boring into him, a smirk playing at the corners of his hard mouth.

The battle was over, and six enemy warriors knelt in submission. Only the bearded man remained. More writhed on the blood-soaked ground in miserable pain, whilst others lay dead amongst the ruins. Ector's war

band gathered about to watch their leader fight the fiercest of the enemy
and the big man spat at them, shaking his axe and daring Ector to come
and die. Ector dropped his shield and drew his long knife in his left hand,
his sword blade soaked with dead men's blood and held firm in his right.
Arthur stared at Ector, wondering how he could be so brave and so fearsome. The war band stared at Ector like he was a hero of old, one of the
giants who had lived in Britain before the Rome-folk came. Their eyes
blazed with pride. Ector's hard, flat face was implacable as he advanced
on the huge *bucellari* mercenary.

The fire crackled and spat, and its light danced on the planes of Ector's
face. He came forward, sword held in an aggressive stance and his knife
held low. The sword lashed out, snake fast, and the enemy warrior darted
away from its bite and swung his axe at Ector's midriff, but the knife
blocked the strike with a great clang of iron as the two weapons came
together. Ector stepped in and head-butted the enemy warrior savagely in
the nose, and then again. He sliced his sword along the bigger man's
shield arm, and the bushy-bearded enemy dropped his shield and staggered backwards. His face was a mask of blood around his ruined nose
and Ector stepped back and drove the point of his sword into the *bucellari*'s chest. The enemy tottered, staring down with horror at the blade in
his chest and Ector dropped his knife, gripped the sword hilt with two
hands and ripped the blade downwards so that it tore the enemy open
like a hunted deer, disembowelling him with fearsome strength. The big
man fell to his knees and the blue-red horror of his insides slopped out,
steaming, onto the grass.

The war band cheered, and Ector cleaned his blade on the dead man's
filthy cloak.

'Kill the rest of them, all but one, and mount their heads on the ends
of their spears as a warning to any other raiders who come this way,' Ector
ordered, and Huell saw it was done. All the *bucellari* died, save one sullen
warrior whom Huell tied to a post to wait for Ector's questioning. 'Arthur,
are you hurt?' Ector came close and draped a heavy arm about Arthur's
shoulders. He could not meet his foster father's eyes and stared instead at
the ground.

'No, spear-father,' he said, using the name he had used for Ector since he was a small boy. It was not right to call the man his father, for he was not, and spear-father had always seemed more appropriate.

'You must learn to be more ruthless, my boy. Kai made his first kill, congratulate him.' Ector placed a thick finger beneath Arthur's chin and raised his head so he could peer into Arthur's eyes. 'Your time will come, lad. There is a warrior inside of you. I can see it. Believe in yourself and master your fear.'

'But I was afraid, I...'

'A man can't be brave if he isn't afraid. What is bravery but the overcoming of fear? I was afraid today, and so was every man here.'

'You were afraid?'

'Of course. All men fear death. You must accept it, lad. Pretending to be brave and acting in the face of danger is still bravery.' Ector smiled and clapped Arthur heavily on the shoulder and then left to join his men.

Arthur sighed. The warriors gathered about Kai, and Arthur's friend and foster brother basked in their acclaim. He recreated his spear thrust, and the warriors cheered him. Huell grabbed Kai's forearm in the warrior's grip, and Arthur thought that was the thing he wanted most in the world, to be respected by Huell, to be offered the warrior's grip from so great a warrior. Ector went to his son and raised his arm in triumph. He stripped the weapons from the man Kai had killed and handed them to his son, along with a conical helmet the dead man wore. Finally, Ector placed his hand on the dead man's wound, stood, and wiped the blood down Kai's face. The men of the war band bowed their heads and then roared their acclaim for the newly blooded member of their brotherhood of warriors.

'I killed two men today,' said Lunete. Her lithe limbs bounded over rubble, and she stood beside Arthur, watching Kai's glorious moment. 'Nobody bloods my face.'

'Your father is angry with you,' said Arthur. 'You shouldn't have come.'

'If I hadn't, you'd be dead.' She crossed her arms and raised her eyebrow. Lunete had none of her father's harsh features and all of her mother's beauty, or so the women of Ector's hall said. Her mother had died when Lunete was a girl, and so she had grown up amongst the warriors.

'I would have killed that axeman if you hadn't hit him with your arrow.'

'No, you wouldn't.' She stood, teary-eyed with her lip quivering. 'A thank you would be nice. You are a horrible boy, Arthur.' She stormed off. Arthur wanted to go after her, to thank her for saving his life, but he just slumped against the ruined villa and pondered his failings.

2

The war band spent the night at the ruined Roman villa. The warriors kept the raiders' fire blazing in the courtyard and sat around it, drinking stolen ale and eating stolen meat. Arthur sat alone inside the crumbling walls, wanting to join in as the men became drunk and congratulated Kai for his kill and told old war stories. Huell took a bone needle and made the death ring on Kai's right forearm. He made myriad pricks with a needle the war band used to stitch wounds and smeared the bloody ring with a mix of soot from the fire and crushed plants mixed into a dark paste. Arthur's shame kept him away, and he sat in the darkness on a floor of tiny square stones which had once made a fine floor picture but were now as scattered and random as beach shale. The men told tales of the Great War, of how the kings of Britain had united to fight Vortigern, the Usurper of Deira, and the army of Saxon warriors he brought across the sea. They cheered the tale of how Ector and Ambrosius Aurelianus had fought and killed many Saxons in a great battle on the country's wild east coast. They told of Excalibur, the sword of Britain, which Ambrosius wielded to slay Saxons by the hundreds.

The roof was intact in its corners, and so the corner beams and surviving red tiles kept any rain off Arthur during the night. He wondered at the skill and craftmanship that the Romans used to make such buildings, which had crumbled and decayed across Britain. Men said that the Romans could heat the floors of their buildings, and that those floors were more beautiful than the finest tapestries. Arthur could imagine it as he toyed with the tiny square pieces, which felt like shards of a broken jug, each one painted with bright colours which had become stained and pitted by time. The skill to make such things had left with the legions, and now men built in timber, thatch and wattle which rotted and stank and needed constant repair. Arthur tried to block out the war stories and wondered what else the Rome-folk knew, what secrets they had of history, law, war and healing that were lost to Arthur's people.

Arthur lay down beneath his cloak and closed his eyes, unable to shake off the memories of the day's fight and how he had missed his chance to become a warrior. Lunete lay down beside him silently, and he felt her big blue eyes staring at him in the darkness but could find nothing to say to her. Even she had fought well, using her bow with devastating effectiveness. *Perhaps it is I who should spin yarn and she who should do the fighting.* Eventually, he drifted off into a fitful sleep, only to be woken by a big hand shaking his shoulder.

'Wake up, lad,' said Ector, his hard face peering at Arthur through the gloom. 'Follow me.' Ector held out his callused paw and helped Arthur rise. He followed the scarred warrior out into the courtyard, which was deserted, but the fire still blazed and warmed the sleep from Arthur's eyes. 'It's my watch, so I thought we could talk awhile.'

'Yes, spear-father,' Arthur said. Ector took a spit from the fire and offered Arthur a chunk of roast beef, which he took hungrily, blowing at the meat and his burning fingers before popping the juicy chunk into his mouth.

'We might as well eat. The beast is dead. It's no good to the farmer now.'

'Where did the raiders come from?'

'From the borders of Bernicia, just as we thought. They fought for landowners there against the Saxons until the enemy became too many and the fighting too hard. So, they thought they'd come to Rheged for easier pickings.'

'And now they'll never leave.' Arthur glanced around the villa at the spears Huell and the warriors had sunk into the ground with grisly heads spiked on their points. Firelight flickered on the dried blood and greasy hair of the severed heads, and Arthur looked away, the meat in his mouth suddenly losing its lustre.

'And now they'll never leave,' Ector agreed. 'They raped those three women mercilessly and killed their families. They cut a swathe of death and suffering across our lands, and it's our job to protect our people from wicked men.'

'Why does God not protect them?'

Ector laughed. 'That's a question for Father Iddawg when we get home, or a question for the old gods. But these are Urien's lands, and we are his warriors. The people look to us for protection, Arthur, so we must be every bit as brutal and savage as the men we face.'

'I let you down today.' Arthur looked away from his foster father and the severed heads and into the campfire, searching there for a reason why he couldn't live up to Ector's expectations, but found no answers in the red glow.

'I'm as proud of you today as I was yesterday, lad. Never doubt that. You'll be a great man someday. You are clever and brave. God only knows what goes on inside that thought cage of yours, but it's in your blood. You just need to trust in yourself, boy.'

'What blood? I'm an orphan, as Huell keeps reminding me. But he calls me a bastard. How can I be both a bastard and an orphan? I could have the blood of a peasant, priest, or a warrior. Who knows what I am?'

'Never mind that. Your fate is what you make of it. You have a brain inside that head of yours, and you fight well. Here, take this.' Ector passed Arthur a spear and picked one up himself. Ector had already wrapped each spear point in rags from dead men's clothes. 'We lost men today, good men. We'll lose more before the summer's over. The prisoner I questioned told of hordes of Saxons. Fifty ships landed in Bernicia this spring commanded by a man named Octha. We must tell King Urien and protect our borders. We must be strong and protect our people, Arthur.'

'Fifty ships!' Arthur gasped. Urien kept a captured Saxon warship at one of his western ports and Arthur had seen it once. Sleek hulled with a dragon-carved prow, it looked too flimsy to sail across the wild ocean to Britain's east, but the Saxons braved those dangers in increasing numbers and each ship could carry sixty warriors to Britain's shores. 'That's three thousand warriors.'

'See? It would have taken me days to work out such a number.'

'Why do they come here? What's wrong with their own lands?'

'They think we're weak? Our land is more fertile than theirs? They love war? Who knows? All I know is that we must throw them back. Bernicia and Deira are lost, as is Kent in the south. That's almost the entire east coast of Britain lost to the Saxons. If we want to stop them, we must kill them. Now, raise your spear.'

'Please, I am tired and we...'

'You are tired? Do you think Saxons give a turd if you are tired? They are coming for us, Arthur. They will kill, rape and burn until everything we have is gone, we are dead, and our lands are theirs. The Saxons are merciless, lad, and so must you be.'

Ector flashed his weapon forward and cracked the ash stave against Arthur's head. He staggered and then raised his own spear. Arthur shook his head and Ector hit again, this time striking Arthur in the ribs, and he doubled over in pain. Anger flared in Arthur then, anger at his shame, at his hesitation, at the way the men looked at him, at being an orphan, at being alone. He gritted his teeth and attacked, lunging at Ector with the forms he had learned from the old warrior every day since his memories began. Ector parried and ducked and smiled as Arthur's spear almost broke through his guard. The two men danced around each other, and the spear staves sang through the air, twisting, lunging and parrying with deftness and skill until Arthur's brow became wet with sweat. Their weapons came together, and Ector's left hand snapped out and grabbed Arthur around the neck, his huge hands strong and rough.

'You almost had me there,' Ector said, and released his grip. 'You have all the skill you need, lad. Just learn to be more savage, more brutal than the men you fight. The spear is not just the blade, it's also the stave. You have your hands, your head, knees, and feet. You have a long knife on your belt and your teeth. Fight like a bear, Arthur, fight like a wolf, and fight for our people who cannot fight for themselves. Follow the warrior's code as I have taught you, but show no mercy to the enemy, Arthur, for mercy is the dream of weak men who have not seen the face of war. The Saxons hate us, with a passion far beyond the rivalry between the kingdoms of Britain. They believe themselves superior, that their gods command them to take our lands from us, and they will show no mercy to a Briton. Hate and rage are powerful, son, but they can also be the betrayers of warriors. The temptation when fighting led by hate is to stab, hack and slash without control. A warrior must use his skill and his mind to remain calm and strike with determined force. A man's life is precious to him, and he will defend it with every scrap of strength in his body. It is not easy to kill a man. When you fight, you must fight to kill, full force. A man I thought I had killed and left lying on the ground once stabbed me in the leg. An enemy will fight like a demon from the Annwn underworld to cling on to life, so strike hard and without mercy. Rip them and rend them. You must harden yourself to it, Arthur, or you will surely die in this harsh world.'

Arthur could not sleep that night, listening to the whimpers of the three women the war band had rescued from the raiders who wept inconsolably at the horrors they had suffered at the hands of the bandits. Ector's words rattled around his head like mice in a barn wall, of how he must harden himself to the world if he was to take his place within it. Everything Ector had said Arthur had heard before from Ector, Huell and the warriors of Ector's war band on the training ground, but now that Arthur had seen battle, it all seemed more real, more relevant and more important to remember.

The war band rose early that morning and the three women rode captured horses behind Ector, Kai and Arthur whilst the war band marched in a silence punctured only by the cough or moan from a man suffering from too much ale the night before. The news of the Saxons and their fifty ships quietened them, and the men feared what that new army meant for them and their families, for it meant war, fear, death and suffering.

'Thank you for saving my life,' Arthur had said to Lunete the moment she awoke, and a broad smile creased her pretty face. He had helped her up from the broken-tiled floor and given her his last oatcake to break her morning fast. As the warriors struck camp and prepared litters for their dead, Arthur had found Kai and congratulated him on his bravery. Arthur marvelled at the dark blue death ring etched on Kai's right forearm, and his foster brother had grabbed Arthur in a warm embrace. Amends were made and Arthur rode with the war band back to King Urien's Bear Fort with Ector's words burned into his mind like a cattle brand. He had to steel himself to what must be done, had to be ready to kill and strike with his spear, and he promised himself that next time he would strike without hesitation.

The war band marched through the forests and hills of Rheged under a pale blue sky the colour of winter ice. The kingdom of Rheged sat in the north-west of Britain. Britain contained many kingdoms. To the north was Dal Riata, Gododdin, Lothian and Pictland, to Rheged's east were the lost kingdoms of Bernicia and Deira. South of Rheged lay Elmet, and then Dumnonia ruled by Uther Pendragon, the king of kings. To the south-east lay Kent and other lands lost to the Saxons, just as Deira and Bernicia were. Finally, the western kingdoms of Gwynedd, Powys and Gwent, and finally Demetia ruled by King Morholt and his wild Irishmen who had conquered that land a generation before Arthur was born. Each kingdom was distinct and fought to protect its borders, its woodlands, its cattle, salt, tin, clay, shale, jet, lead, iron and copper from jealous and warlike neighbours.

The Bear Fort stood high and proud atop its promontory looking down onto the River Eden as the warriors crested a heather covered hilltop. The Bear Fort was a timber hall built by King Urien's father, Cynfarch the Cold, perched on a steep-sided hill inside the River Eden's wide meander, which flowed out into the grey sea to the west. Cynfarch was a cunning old dog and had ordered every man in his kingdom to help build a mound atop the hill, and a hall atop the mound. Below the hall and mound, a wooden wall of sharpened timber stakes ringed the hilltop, encircled by a deep ditch. Inside the walls was a wide courtyard with thatched houses and room for blacksmiths, weavers, potters, craftworkers and Urien's courtiers. Many lords of Britain made their homes in the ruins left by the Romans. The neatly dressed stone walls were beyond the ken of any craftsmen in the kingdoms born in the fiery wake of the legion's departure. But Cynfarch built a new fortress, high and impregnable, or so he hoped. Marshland and reeds surrounded it on one side and the river on the other. Pastures and farmland swept away to north and south, and coppiced woodland to the east. The west led to the sea, to trade, fishing and salt pans. So the Bear Fort was both a snarling clifftop fortress and a rich hub for trade, silver and wealth.

Arthur stared at the pointed walls, the vast, lofty hall and its thatched roof. The hall appeared to be made of gold, shining in the sunlight, and the walls resembled sharp spears encircling the place, like a hall of an ancient god soaring high in the clouds. Smoke from a dozen fires hazed the hill and sat above the Bear Fort like its very own cloud, and as the war band marched up the worn path towards the fortress, a horn blared long and loud to announce their arrival.

Arthur and Kai secured the horses in a stable by the gate, and just as Arthur emerged from the stink of horse and fouled hay, he found Huell waiting for him at the stable door. The stocky warrior chuckled as Arthur approached. He had taken a shallow cut to his forehead during the fight, and his brawny forearms were thick with death rings.

'I saw you, bastard,' Huell said, his eyes narrowing. 'You've a coward's heart inside of you. Ector can't see it, but I can. Might be better for us all if you just left, rode off in the night and never came back. I don't want you beside me when we face the Saxons, boy. Your spear will drop, or you'll run, and our men will die. So, piss off when it's dark, run away. You know you want to.'

Arthur just carried on walking, pretending that the warrior's words hadn't affected him, even though they sliced into his heart like a sharp blade.

'What did he want?' asked Kai as they jogged to catch up with Ector.

'Nothing.'

'Ignore him. He's full of piss and wind. He had his eye on Lunete, and she's only got eyes for you.'

'What?' said Arthur.

'The men talk of it, that Huell will ask my father for Lunete's hand.

His own wife died in childbirth two winters back. Come now, you know
Lunete has loved you since we were boys. Don't play the innocent.' Deep
down, Arthur knew Lunete loved him, but it was the love of a child, of a
young girl for an older boy, and Arthur was a man now. He liked Lunete,
her wildness and ferocity and her bright eyes, but it was the love for a
sister, nothing more.

Kai punched Arthur on the shoulder and Arthur punched him back,
but they had thankfully caught up with Ector who strode towards King
Urien's hall, and Arthur could remain silent. The Bear Fort took its name
from a monstrous bear's skull mounted above the hall's wide oak doors. It
snarled down at Arthur, bone white with teeth as long as a man's finger.
Urien had killed the beast himself when he was Arthur's age, and as he
stalked beneath its snarl, Huell's words continued to sting him like a
whip.

Two burly spearmen guarded the door, and they frowned as Arthur
and Kai passed between them. A wall of heat hit Arthur as he entered
King Urien's great hall. The warmth was like the blast from a furnace, but
tinged with the acrid smell of sweat, leather and iron. The roof was high
and smoke-blackened. Torches flickered in iron crutches set high on
support posts which stretched from floor to rafters. Shields with Urien's
bear sigil hung on the walls, along with shields of men Urien and his
warriors had slain in battle. Warriors filled the place, men wearing hard-
baked leather armour, a handful in chain mail, and all peering over one
another for a glimpse of what occurred at King Urien's high seat. Arthur
shouldered through the warriors, past men he recognised and others he
didn't. Men with braided beards, some with blue-black tattoos on their
faces, others with scars and missing teeth.

'Why are there so many men here?' said Arthur as he sidled around a
broad-shouldered man.

'The king must have summoned his warriors whilst we were away,'
said Kai with a shrug. It would take over two days to bring all the warriors
of Rheged together. Even Ector's home at Caer Ligualid was a half-day
ride from the Bear Fort. Arthur had visited Urien's hall many times but
had rarely seen it so full of fighting men. A fire burned in a stone hearth
at the hall's centre and its smoke escaped through a smoke hole in the

thatch. The fire, combined with so many men, made the hall close and oppressive, and Arthur was glad when he reached the raised dais where Urien sat on his throne and glowered at the throng before him.

'Lord king,' Ector said. He stood below the king's throne and bowed his head.

'Ector has returned,' growled the king, his voice deep and as full of gravel as a riverbed. 'What news of the raiders?' Urien sat slumped on his throne, a wide and deep chair carved of oak adorned with the skulls of five warriors he had killed during the Great War. Urien was bald, and his braided beard was as grey as an iron spit, but despite his age he exuded power and strength. A scar ran from the top of his head down through his eye to his jaw. He was broad and thick necked, with a pugnacious round face and clever eyes. As a boy, Arthur had loved to sit by a winter fire and listen to bards talk of mighty Urien, Uther Pendragon, Ector, Cadwallon Longhand, Gorlois, Ambrosius Aurelianus and the other heroes who had fought against the evil usurper Vortigern and his Saxon horde.

'*Bucellari* from Bernicia's borderlands, lord king,' said Ector, and a rumble of voices swept across the hall. 'A band of masterless men whose heads we mounted on spears to warn others what happens to those who raid in Rheged.'

'Good. Perhaps I should have ridden with you. I could do with getting out of this cursed chair for a while. We should not call Bernicia and Deira by their old names any longer, for they are no longer part of our lands, no longer part of what was once Britain. They are Lloegyr, the lost lands, lost to pagan Saxons and their axes, shields and ships. Good land, rich land, all lost. By all the gods, but we must cast these bloody invaders from our shores.'

'The raiders were mercenaries forced out of Bernicia by a new force of Saxons, my lord. I questioned one of their number, and he spoke of fifty ships landed this spring. Three thousand Saxon warriors led by a man named Octha.'

More murmurs rippled across the hall as men whispered in shock at the huge number of warriors.

'There are already thousands of the scum in Bernicia and Deira, or Lloegyr, as you say, my lord. They swell Saxon armies to the size we haven't seen since Vortigern first invited the Saxons to our shores. And they do not come in peace, lord king. There will be war this summer, and it will take all our forces to keep them out of Rheged.'

'I know it, Ector. I heard tell of such a force. King Letan Luyddoc of Gododdin sent word days ago, which is why I have called my warriors and *comitatuses'* here to the Bear Fort. I have sent my son Owain ahead with fifty men to scout our borders. We must rally our army and march east to guard our borders. Rheged will fight the Saxon whoresons, and so will Letan. We march to war, my warriors, red war!'

The men in the hall stamped their feet and roared their approval at the king's command so that the hall shuddered with the noise.

'They are pagan scum,' screeched Dustan, Urien's priest. He was a pinch-faced man with a small mouth and close-set eyes over sharp nose, so that he looked like a sparrow. He wore a filthy robe, woollen, with a ragged hem and loose sleeves from which shook his thin white hands. 'Worshippers of foul gods, idolators, sinners and the enemies of God. They must be stopped, driven from this land like dogs. God wills it!' His voice grew in pitch until he screamed like a fox. Spittle flew from his mean mouth and his eyes rolled with pious fury. Urien, like Ector, allowed a Christian priest to live in his hall and preach to his people, just as he permitted folk to worship the old gods. Both men did so more out of fear of upsetting the nailed god than out of love for him.

The warriors reached for the crosses at their necks or touched charms and the iron at their belts for luck and to ward off the God-fury Dustan invoked. All men feared God, Jesus, the Virgin Mother and the priests who spoke their word. There were other gods in Britain, old gods spoken of in whispers or called upon at times of need, childbirth, sickness or battle. Arthur liked the tales of those violent gods, told by bards and scops, just as much as the tales of kings and warriors. But the word of God and his priests had power, and when Dustan screeched, the warriors echoed his cries for the slaughter of invading pagans.

Urien raised a ringed hand, and the hall fell silent. Only the creak of the hall's timbers and the sigh of men's breath disturbed the stillness. Such was Urien's command over his fighting men. Arthur wondered at Urien's words, for he must have heard of this new army of Saxons before he despatched Ector to deal with the *bucellari* raiders, which meant he sent Ector out close to the borderlands where thousands of Saxons massed for war because he cared little for his champion's life, or because he knew Ector would come back alive with the raiders punished.

'There is a messenger come to speak to you, lord king,' said Urien's steward, a thin man with a crooked nose and a bent back. He wore a finely woven tunic and a green cloak and waved his hand at a warrior in a helmet and with long moustaches who stood to the side of the high platform.

'Come forward and speak,' rumbled Urien.

'King Urien,' said the man in a strange accent. 'I come to you from your friend King Leodegrance of Cameliard. I have ridden far and crossed the sea, for my king has need of your help.'

'Leodegrance,' Urien said wistfully. The king sat back on his throne and smiled, his face creasing in a lattice of wrinkles across his broad skull. 'All men know of my brotherhood with your king, of how he sent men across the sea from Cameliard and Armorica in the dark days to help our cause. What can I do for my old friend?'

The warrior bowed deeply in recognition of Urien's respectful words. 'There is war across the sea, lord king. The Saxons continue to march westwards. They flee their homelands, a place of never-ending war, riven with violence since the Romans left so long ago. The Franks march eastwards and the Saxons' lands are a hell pit of slaughter and lawlessness.'

'Just as our lands were when the Romans left in my father's grandfather's time,' said Urien, and men in the hall nodded solemnly at the memory of those dark days.

'We are beset by war, lord king. Armorica and our once peaceful land are under attack from Saxon pagans and the warriors of Frankia. So, King Leodegrance fears for his family's safety and sent his daughter to you for protection, to be fostered by you until a suitable match can be found for her. She is of marrying age and ready for a good husband.'

'I would do anything for Leodegrance. His daughter is welcome in my hall.'

'He knew you would say that, my lord. Your legend burns as brightly across the sea as it does in your own lands. So, my king already sent his daughter to these shores on his fastest ship, guarded by his bravest men. But she has fallen foul of the very men your champion Ector spoke of. This Octha, a Saxon dog, has captured the princess and is demanding a monstrous ransom for her return amid threats of the worst possible kind.'

'The Saxons have Leodegrance's daughter?' Urien rose from his seat, huge and baleful and swathed in a bear-fur cloak.

'Aye, lord king. They have her in Bernicia, captured at sea, and your friend Leodegrance would ask you to free her from her captivity and bring her here, where our princess will be safe.'

Suddenly, the doors to Urien's hall burst open, and a gust of wind whipped through the rafters and made the hearth fire flare. Men turned and gasped as a tall man strode into the hall. He walked confidently and straight-backed with a black staff in his right hand. He came barefoot, with a head of wild white hair and a thick white beard. His face was drawn and wrinkled with a long, hooked nose above a cruel slash of a mouth. The strange man wore a black tunic and a cloak of purest white billowed behind him. Two great wolfhounds padded beside the stranger, tongues lolling, and their padded feet kept time with the slaps of the stranger's soles as he marched through the hall. The hairs on Arthur's neck stood up, and he shivered involuntarily.

'A druid,' Kai hissed in his ear, and Arthur gaped at the stranger, who exuded a strange, ethereal power which cowed every man in the hall. Even the great King Urien, so famed for his brutality and ruthless strength, sat forward in his chair, stricken by the stranger's dramatic entrance. The druids were the priests of the old gods, from the time before men worshipped God and Christ. They were men of great power who once held sway over all Britain, of similar standing and importance to kings. Arthur heard tell of their human sacrifices, their power, and the rumours of wizards and dark magic. The Romans had killed all but a few of the druids when the legions conquered Britain, but some remained upon their holy island of Ynys Môn, which some men called Anglesey, which was sacred to the old gods and their dead religion. Despite the growing Christian religion, all respected and feared the power of the old gods, of the demons and spirits of the forests, lakes, rivers, crags, caves and springs. So, though the druids did not hold the power or sway of ancient times, they were still feared and respected.

'Pagan!' screamed Dustan the priest. He pointed his finger at the stranger and rose from his bench, red-faced and furious. The stranger made the sign to ward off evil, stuck two fingers into his own throat and then pointed at Dustan, who promptly sat down. His face quickly changed from red anger to ash-white fear. The stranger marched past the hearth and tossed something into it, which made the fire hiss, and its flames turn blue-green. The warriors in the hall gasped. Some went to make the sign of the cross but stopped midway and sat upon their hands in fear of the druid's power.

'I am Kadvuz,' the stranger bellowed, his voice like the crashing of the sea. It filled the hall and echoed around the rafters like thunder. 'I come from Ynys Môn, at Merlin's behest.'

Men whispered and gasped at the sound of Merlin's name, the most powerful druid in Britain. Nobody had seen from Merlin since the days of the Great War, but all feared him, and bards told of his legends at hearths across Britain.

'You are far from home, druid,' said Urien, his mighty voice diminished by Kadvuz's harsh tone.

'War has come to Britain, and we have not faced such danger since Caesar himself came with the legions to rip our island asunder. We shall need the old gods' favour if we are to throw the Saxons back across the sea whence they came. You have abandoned the old gods. Many men here wear the nailed god's symbol, but will he protect you from the Saxons? Has he protected you from the Saxons?'

Urien glanced at Dustan, but the priest avoided his gaze and instead kept his eyes on the ground.

'Merlin demands that you hear his words through me,' said Kadvuz, after no man disputed the strength of his rebuke of God and Christ. 'We balance on a precipice and our footing is unsure. This task, this woman from across the sea we must rescue, is sent to us from the gods to test our resolve. Do this thing, and we can defeat the Saxons; fail, and our kingdoms and island will be lost.'

'Is the princess so favoured by Merlin and the old gods?' asked Urien.

'A band of warriors must march into Lloegyr, our lost lands, and recover her,' Kadvuz barked, ignoring the question. 'But those who take up the quest must be pure of heart and mighty of resolve. Merlin demands it.'

'We shall send our finest warriors, druid, have no fear,' said Urien.

'The gods must choose!' Kadvuz said, and he slammed his staff on the floor and cast his deep-set, dark eyes around every warrior in the hall.

Arthur noticed in the firelight that strange symbols etched the druid's staff, which seemed to glow and pulse in the half-light, and Kadvuz pulled a handful of bones and charms from a pouch at his belt and cast them upon the rush-covered floor. He knelt, and cast his long, pale hand over the knucklebones, tiny bird skulls, snakes' teeth and ingots of dark, shining metal. Kadvuz began to hum, the sound loud and undulating. His eyes rolled white in his head and the rumbling in his throat became as loud as a man shouting. Arthur glanced around the hall, and the druid and his fearful power transfixed every man, even the fiercest warriors. Every man hung on the druid's chanting and what his strange trance augured of the quest. Kadvuz shrieked, and Arthur and Kai jumped.

'Ten men will take the quest,' Kadvuz said, but not in his own voice. He spoke in a deep, slow, guttural tone as though somebody else used his tongue. 'Eight warriors of fair fame shall go, and two younger, untested boys who must be pure of spirit and body. Huell of Rheged shall lead, and he shall choose seven stout spearmen.'

'I am ready,' said Huell, stepping forward, his jaw set, and his chest puffed out with pride.

'And you two.'

Arthur rocked as though slapped, because the druid pointed his long-nailed finger at Arthur and Kai.

'You are the young warriors, pure of flesh and spirit, who will make this journey. The hope of Britain lies with you. Merlin commands you undertake this deed, bring back the lost princess, brave the Saxon hordes and return to us with the power of the gods in your hearts.'

Urien bunched his heavy fists and glowered down at the druid. 'It shall be so. These men will make the journey, so return to Merlin with my blessing.'

Kadvuz inclined his head slightly to the king, and then flashed a malevolent stare at Arthur and Kai, and Arthur was frozen to the spot as though turned to ice.

Urien pointed at Leodegrance's messenger. 'Go, friend,' he said. 'Return to your king and tell him that Merlin has spoken, and that Rheged will find his daughter for him. What is the girl's name?'

'In your tongue she is Gwynhyfar, but to us she is Guinevere.'

3

King Urien threw a feast that night for his warriors, and the most famous men in Rheged packed the feasting benches. King Urien invited only men with fair famed reputations into the hall, so Arthur and Kai had to settle for a meal of fish stew and hard bread outside Urien's pig hovel, while the warriors inside enjoyed mutton, cheese, honey, butter, duck and fine bread inside a fire-warmed hall. The hilltop hall roared with the noise of their boasting, laughing, gambling and tales of brave deeds, and the Bear Fort buzzed with the news of Kadvuz, how he had arrived unlooked for and had departed immediately, disappearing into the darkness with his dogs and his fearsome druid power.

'I still can't believe they chose us,' Kai said brightly as he mopped up the last of his soup with a chunk of black bread. 'Looks like we shall see lots of action this summer.'

'Why us?' Arthur said. 'How does the druid even know who we are? I understand why he would pick Huell, a famous warrior, but who beyond Caer Ligualid even knows our names?'

'Speak for yourself. I have killed a man. God save us, Arthur, but you are as miserable as an old fishwife. This quest means our chance at glory, time for us to make our reputations and have men tell stories about us like they do my father.'

'You are right, I'm sorry. We should find more ale before the warriors drink it all.' Arthur smiled, though he was full of fear. Not just of the druid and the hold he exerted over a hall of fearsome warriors, but also of the responsibility they carried with them. The very fate of Britain was in their hands, according to Kadvuz, not just the life of a princess, and Arthur had not even killed an enemy in battle.

The two friends searched the Bear Fort for a cask of mead and came upon a band of Ector's men sat around a small fire behind a blacksmith's forge. They were about to join them when Huell appeared, malevolent and smirking and with his thumbs tucked in his belt. 'No ale for you, pups. Ector wants to see you, Kai, and you, bastard. Up at the hall. He's outside the doors, so don't keep him waiting.'

Arthur sighed, and Kai shook his head, staring longingly at the men's mugs of mead. But they both knew better than to keep their father waiting. They trudged through the busy courtyard, churned muddy by so many boots and horses. They hurried around campfires where men huddled eating, drinking and casting envious glances up at Urien's hall, where bright firelight shone through the window shutters and the raucous shouts of men enjoying good food and ale rolled down the hillside. The warriors not invited to the feast gathered in the courtyard; they told stories and gambled on throwboards, and boasted about how well they would fight in the war to come.

Arthur found Ector leaning against the side of Urien's hall, staring at the stars. It was a clear night and the pattern of twinkling stars seemed low, as though heaven was that bit closer to the world of men that night.

'You asked for us, father?' said Kai, careful to keep the frustration at being denied mead from his voice.

Ector turned, surprised to hear his son, and snapped himself from his thoughts. His face was grave and pale, and there was a sadness in his eyes. 'Aye,' he said wistfully, a wan smile at the corner of his hard mouth. 'King Urien has called his men to war, and we march tomorrow towards our eastern borders to fight the Saxons. They have chosen you two for this venture into Lloegyr, and it is full of danger. I do not wish this for you both, my sons, for it has the cunning hand of Merlin behind it, and he is both betrayer and benefactor at his whim.'

'I am glad the druid picked Arthur and I, this is our chance to make our names,' said Kai, grinning and rubbing his hands together at the prospect of battle and the chance at glory and reputation.

Ector sighed, closed his eyes and raised a hand to still his son. 'I fear for you, my boys. There is a strangeness in this. No one has laid eyes on Merlin since the Great War, and I am reluctant to let you both become pulled into his perilous and cunning plans. But the king commands that it be done, and so you must go with Huell whilst I march with the army to meet the Saxon threat on our border. I know Merlin of old, and he had a hand to play in what our people lost in the war with Vortigern. Beware of him.'

'We are ready, father,' said Kai, and Ector sighed and cupped his youthful face in his huge hand.

'Do as Huell commands. Keep close to him and protect yourselves. Come back to us alive, my boys.'

'But spear-father,' Arthur said, the fear and shock of Kadvuz's arrival, and the impossible quest into Lloegyr, seizing hold of him. Talk of Merlin shook Arthur, a figure so revered by bards and scops at winter fires that he was almost legendary, a druid with ancient powers who had pulled Arthur and Kai into the warp and weft of his cunning. 'Can I not march with you and the army?' Huell was belligerent and cold with most men, but to Arthur he was cruel and malevolent, and Arthur could not entrust his life to a man who hated him, and he was still fearful of why the druid had selected him and Kai for this task.

'No, you must do this thing, there is no way out of it now. I must lead the army. That is my place. I trust you both. You are well trained and capable, and Huell will guide you. Kadvuz has spoken with the power of Merlin's tongue, and Urien will not go against that. So, you will do this thing, and I will pray every day that you return to me alive.' Ector turned to Arthur and his eyes bore into Arthur's like hot coals. 'There is reputation in this, boys. Rescue a princess from across the sea and men will sing of your deeds to their children's children. I will not be here forever, and this will be a hard war. You need reputations of your own. If you are to serve Urien and be warriors or a *comitatus* like me, you must earn it. This is my will, the will of the old gods, the new God and the will of the king, and you will see to it.'

'Yes, father,' said Kai, and when Arthur opened his mouth to protest again, Kai stamped on his foot to silence him.

Ector nodded, pleased that his sons accepted his orders. It was a strange order, Arthur thought. Why not just send Huell and a band of his trusted warriors to rescue the princess? Marching beyond the Saxon frontier was beyond dangerous, surely more dangerous than the war itself, where Ector and Rheged's army could protect Arthur and Kai. Who cared what the druids said about anything? Their gods were dying, and when Ector said he would pray for his sons, he would pray to God and to Cernunnos, The Morrigan and Manawydan. Arthur searched Ector's face but saw no guile there, nothing hidden. Arthur and Kai were men now. Many lads took up the spear two summers before the age Arthur was now and so he decided that Ector had spoken true. Ector saw in this quest a chance for his sons to earn a reputation beyond many of the greatest warriors in Urien's kingdom. Ector thought like a warrior. It was the very essence of his being. To Ector, reputation and warrior prowess were everything. He had earned his fair fame during the Great War and saw a chance in this dangerous expedition for his son and foster son to do the same. Ector knew the dangers, but the life of a warrior was to live amongst danger, violence and death.

'Queen Igraine is ill,' Ector said, leaning close with his voice lowered. 'The queen and I are old friends, and I would see her before we march. You will accompany me.'

Arthur glanced at Kai and then back at Ector, and then followed as Ector led them around the edge of Urien's great hall. The sounds of the warriors laughing and feasting wafted through the window shutters with the smell of roasted meat and logs burning on the great hearth. They reached the rear of the hall, and Arthur peered out into the river valley below. They were high on the Bear Fort's raised mound, and in the darkness the river glistened like melted silver, reflecting the half-moon in its shining water. The woodland, marshes and fields appeared as dark shapes, smudges beneath the cloak of darkness and Ector led them to a large, barn-like building built on to the rear of his hall. Two spearmen guarded its door, and they nodded as Ector approached, shuffling sideways to let him enter the small, low doorway. Leather hinges creaked as Ector pushed the door open. Arthur and Kai followed him in, ducking under the low lintel. Inside, a fire burned in one corner and its smoke collected in the roof, where it seeped slowly through the thatch. The room was ten paces wide, at its centre was a raised bed draped in warm furs. Two women knelt beside it, their hands clasped together in prayer. They were Igraine's handmaidens, and Urien's queen lay beneath the furs, her head propped up on a linen pillow stuffed with duck feathers.

'My lady,' said Ector, and he bowed deeply, lower than he had to King Urien. Arthur peered at the queen, but it was hard to see her clearly. A single rushlight lit the room, burning on a table beside the queen, and the three logs burned in the fire to cast shifting shadows across the timber walls. Igraine's silver hair splayed on the pillow, and from the doorway all Arthur could see was a thin old woman, her breath coming in short, wheezy gasps.

A veiny hand raised slightly on the bed and beckoned them forward, the back of her hand skeletally thin and dotted with yellow spots. Ector stepped forward, and Arthur followed. Kai pushed the door closed and stood at Arthur's side.

'This is my son, Kai, and this is my foster son, Arthur.' The two young men bowed, and the queen made a cracked, croaking sound. Ector smiled at her, and for a moment Arthur thought he saw wetness in brave Ector's eyes. 'I first knew Queen Igraine when I was not much older than you are now. She was queen of Kernow, then, before the Great War. Igraine was the most beautiful woman in Britain, and she is a good and kind friend. Men fought wars over her beauty, and I am proud to have known her. Pay your respects.'

Arthur knelt to the queen and made the sign of the cross. He clasped his hands before his chest and whispered a prayer, as did Kai beside him. Arthur said the words, but without conviction. He had seen nothing in the world to convince him that God or Lord Jesus helped anyone in need of their grace. As he prayed, Arthur closed his eyes and thought of the warriors who had died at the Roman villa, or the three raped women and their families, and wondered how the one God or the old gods could allow such cruelty in the world. Why did the gods not simply cast the pagan Saxons back into the sea and keep Britain safe and whole?

The two handmaidens wept as Ector knelt beside the queen and kissed her fragile hand. When their father rose, Arthur and Kai followed him from the room and out into the night. There was a strangeness hanging over the Bear Fort that night, a night filled with druids, kings, queens and quests. Arthur's head swam with the shock of it all and he stayed quiet, his eyes fixed on Ector's hard face.

'Kai, find Huell and prepare for tomorrow's march,' Ector said without turning to look at them. 'Arthur, wait here. I have a different task for you.'

Kai left to find Huell and Arthur pulled his cloak about his shoulders against the night's chill.

'Igraine is an old friend and a symbol of a lost time, of the days before Vortigern laid Britain low.' Ector spoke into the night with his back to Arthur, though he knew the words were meant for him. 'Her first husband, Gorlois, was a great man. He was the warrior-king of Kernow on our island's south-west corner, and Igraine was his love. I served Uther of Dumnonia in those days, as you know. The Great War tore us all apart, and eventually I was the one to bring her north to wed Urien after Gorlois died fighting Vortigern and his Saxons. Urien did not treat Igraine well. The first part of her life was all happiness and hope, but since Gorlois' death, it has been suffering, hardship and sadness. It was not my place to challenge that. Urien is the king and has my oath.' Ector sighed and shook his head, inclining his head towards his foster son. 'How I miss those old days, Arthur. Ambrosius, Gorlois, Merlin, Igraine. It feels like a different world, a different time.'

Ector sighed and pulled himself from his melancholy. He set his jaw and turned to Arthur.

'I want you to sit with the queen for a time, Arthur. I will send her handmaidens away. She needs company, but not the company of weeping maids, and I must return to the feast and spend the night making plans for tomorrow's march to war.'

'But spear-father?' Arthur said, stepping forward, desperate not to be left with the dying old queen. 'I can help you, or perhaps Kai can sit with the queen. Don't leave me up here.' The warriors were feasting, drinking, sharpening blades or preparing supplies for the march, and Arthur was to play maid to an old woman.

'Do as I command,' Ector barked, his face suddenly hard and angry. 'I must organise supply lines, give orders to the different war bands, plan a route to our borders. I must count spears, shields, horses, and make sure we have enough food and ale to feed our warriors for a week. But I would not have Igraine alone this night. Urien will not come to her. There is no love there and her son Owain is away fighting. So, do this thing for me, son. Keep my old friend Igraine company and her fire warm.'

Arthur nodded, but his shame rose to new heights. He stared at Ector's back as he stalked off, trailed by the weeping handmaidens he'd called from the queen's chamber. Arthur kicked a loose stone off the hilltop and had never felt so low. He had started the march from Caer Ligualid hoping to become a blooded warrior, his forearm tattooed with a death ring, but had instead returned from the march as a failure, scorned and mocked by the war band behind his back. Huell thought him less than a piece of cow shit on his boot, and Arthur knew Huell stirred bad feeling about him amongst the men. They thought him a spoiled lordling, given a horse, spear and knife without earning them, and he wasn't even Ector's true-born son. Arthur could only imagine what Huell would say when he learned Arthur nursed a sick queen through the night whilst the men prepared for war and a druid's sacred quest.

A rattling cough came from inside the small room, and Arthur cursed and ducked inside the door. He closed it behind him and trudged to the queen's bedside. The logs in the fire had burned down to glowing embers, so he grabbed two freshly cut logs from a stack next to the wall and threw them on the embers. Arthur sighed, took a milking stool from the corner and sat next to the old woman. The logs crackled and dry bark popped; the wood caught fire and brightened the room, and for the first time Arthur saw Queen Igraine's face. Her pale skin, drawn tight across high cheekbones, gave her the look of a fetch, or ghost from Annwn, the old gods' underworld. Her breath rattled in her chest, made louder by a still quiet broken only by the fire's crackle and hiss.

Arthur settled himself on the stool, leaning back against the wall, and wondered if Huell was laughing at him now, joking with the war band at

Arthur, the spoiled orphan bastard playing maid to a dying queen. His eyes grew heavy in the fire's warmth and time passed slowly, Queen Igraine still and unmoving. His thoughts turned to Lunete and whether Ector would really marry her to Huell. She was far too good for the brutal warrior, and Arthur imagined her subjected to a long life of suffering and sadness, whelping Huell's brats, taking his beatings, grinding his grain, spinning his yarn and sewing his clothes. That could not be Lunete's destiny, just as this could not be Arthur's.

An idea occurred to him as he stared into the orange-red flames. He should follow Lunete's example and do as he wished, rather than as Ector ordered him. Why should he play nursemaid to a queen and go on a dangerous quest deep into Saxon lands? Ector always forgave Lunete for her wilfulness. Had she not ridden to join the war band when her father ordered her to stay at home with the womenfolk, the children and the elderly? Lunete did as she pleased. She carried a bow instead of a distaff, and Ector and his men loved Lunete for her wildness. Arthur could leave, he could take his spear, his knife and his horse and ride away. He could go south to Elmet and join King Gwallog's service, or north to Gododdin, or even further south to Uther Pendragon in Dumnonia.

Dreams filled Arthur's thought cage. He saw himself becoming a famous warrior in Uther's ranks and returning to Ector as a champion or joining Gwallog's legions and becoming a hero. The men of Elmet followed the Roman ways, wore their old armour and carried their weapons, and Arthur imagined himself riding to war from Elmet in a red cloak and segmented armour with a short sword and a reputation for battle prowess. Arthur put another log on the fire and decided that he would leave. He wasn't even sure that he was a Rheged man. Nobody knew of Arthur's parentage or from where he hailed. They had only ever told Arthur that he was left outside Ector's hall as a baby, wrapped in an old cloak. If Huell and the men cursed him for a bastard orphan, an unwanted and unworthy thing, he could take to the road and forge his own destiny, prove Huell and the rest of them wrong. Fewer and fewer folk worshipped the gods of the druids any more, so why should Arthur care for Merlin or Kadvuz's commands, or for a lost foreign princess?

'Boy?' croaked a whispery voice, startling Arthur from his dreams. He started and leant forward on his stool. Queen Igraine's eyes were open, and they were the grey of a winter sea, but bright and fierce. Her head turned to the side and her eyes locked with his. Arthur swallowed and leant closer to her.

'My queen,' he stuttered. 'Ector asked me to stay with you, but I can fetch your maidens if you need food or drink?'

'You are Ector's boy?' Her pale tongue licked at dry lips, and her hand trembled where it rested on the bed furs. Igraine's voice was as dusty and dry as old thatch. Her words crept out of her throat as though they were reluctant and wanted to get back inside her.

'Not his son, no. I am his... foster son. Arthur.'

'Of course you are. You have grown into a fine young man.' She smiled at him, a slow, dry smile which wrinkled the thin skin of her face.

'Thank you, my lady,' he said, the strangeness of the situation making him uncomfortable.

'I must sleep again, but talk to me, lad. Just to help me sleep, tell me about yourself. Of your life at Caer Ligualid, of Ector and his children.'

Arthur wanted to say no. He was a warrior, trained for war, not talking to sick old women. But the look in her sea-grey eyes softened him, crushing his pride, tugging at his heart. So, he spoke to her of Kai, and Ector and Lunete. Igraine closed her eyes, but her smile remained. He added more logs to the fire and told her of his training, of the time when he and Kai had put nettles in Huell's boot, and he had thrashed them with his belt. Arthur told her about Lunete's wildness, and how Ector's wife had died from the coughing sickness. The night waned, and a sliver of light poked through the closed window shutters to cast floating dust motes in pallid yellow. The sun was coming up, and it was time for Arthur to pack his meagre belongings and leave the Bear Fort before Urien's warriors woke.

'It is time for me to go now, my queen,' he whispered, not wanting to wake her. 'I am sorry if I talked too much, but I hope you recover soon.'

'Wait,' she whispered. Her pale, thin hand rose slowly, trembling as it went to her chest and searched beneath the furs. 'Thank you for the tale of your life. Perhaps one day, Ector will tell you the tale of my life. We are of similar age, he and I, though my sickness has made me old before my time. Perhaps he will tell of what I was like in those long-ago days, which seem so bright and golden against the grim twilight which Vortigern, Merlin and Uther brought upon us all.' Igraine coughed, and her face twisted in pain.

Arthur reached to her table where a wooden cup of milk sat beside the long-gone-out rushlight. He lifted it carefully to her lips and Igraine drank a sip, which seemed to give her peace.

'Here, boy,' she said, and her stiff fingers suddenly gripped his hand with a strength that belied her frailty. 'Take this as a token of mine, a gift from the time before the Great War. Keep it with you, for luck.' She pressed something cold and hard into his hand. Arthur pulled away, and her token was a bronze disc half the size of Arthur's palm. A dragon with mighty wings and raking claws snarled on one side, and a small hole punctured its top. He bowed in thanks but struggled to find the right words. It was a fine gift, too fine for him, who hardly knew her. But Queen Igraine had closed her eyes again, and he did not want to disturb her, or insult her by refusing the fine piece of jewellery. Arthur closed his hand around it. He could use it to buy food or ale on his journey, or trade it for a better knife, perhaps even a helmet. He left the chamber and found the handmaidens waiting outside with the door guards. The sun crept over the horizon, and Arthur hurried from the hall's mound. It had been a long, strange, sleepless night, but it was time for Arthur to find his destiny on his own terms.

4

Arthur pulled the cloak of his hood up and kept his head low. Overnight, dark clouds had filled the sky, churning and malevolent above whistling winds which shook the thatch and blew strands of hay across the Bear Fort's hilltop. He reached the courtyard below King Urien's hall and walked quietly around burned-out fires and snoring warriors. Men slept in hovels, sties, barns, or out in the open beneath cloaks and horse blankets. A dog barked and ran across Arthur's path, and he cursed the animal as three men sleeping beside a fire's charred remains grumbled and rolled over. The warriors would soon be up, taking a morning meal and preparing their weapons. Ector would lead long lines of spearmen out of the Bear Fort and east across Rheged's rugged countryside to fight the Saxon invaders and keep Rheged's borders safe. Arthur wanted to be long gone by then, south, he thought, to Dumnonia. As far away from Rheged as possible.

Arthur still held the queen's bronze disc in his hand, his fingers running over the etched dragon, wondering if he would get in trouble for accepting it. A big man in a leather vest vomited behind a drystone wall, and the reek of ale made Arthur's stomach turn. A wind-whipped rain surged from the heavens and Arthur pulled his cloak closer about his shoulders. He hurried through the mud, darting in and out of the snarl of passageways and lanes between buildings until he reached the stables. He found his mare and stroked her nose; she bobbed her head and Arthur scratched her ear. He tossed a thick blanket over her back and fitted the bridle.

Arthur wondered if he should find Kai. They were brothers, and Arthur knew Kai would be hurt to find out that he had left without even saying goodbye, and the same would go for Lunete. But they would try to talk him out of what he must do, and Arthur must go. It was time to become a man, a warrior on his own path. The mare whickered as Arthur led her through the courtyard, each sound making him wince for fear of waking and being recognised by one of Ector's war band. But he reached the wide oak gates without challenge. One side was already open as a line of Urien's slaves made the morning trudge down to the river for fresh water. Arthur led the mare through the open gate and kept his head down, ignoring the spearman there who did not challenge him, huddled as he was beneath a heavy, hooded cloak. A loud clanking sound made Arthur jump, and he clicked his tongue to urge his horse on down the winding path away from the Bear Fort. Priests rang a bell, clanked a pot or sang to call folk to the first prayer of the day.

The path levelled out as the forest loomed up ahead. Arthur winced at the sound of the rain thrumming against the fields and treetops and the howling wind. He leapt upon the mare's back and grabbed the leather bridle. He carried his spear, long knife, a bundle of flatbread, some dried fish and a half-empty skin of ale. Arthur dug his heels into the mare's flanks and rode away from his quest, from the Bear Fort, King Urien, Ector and his brother and sister with a heavy heart. He reached the forest's edge where silver birch and elm twisted together like a brooch of silver and gold, and just as he was about to enter the woodland, the sound of hooves beat above the rain. Arthur reined his horse in and glanced over his shoulder and was surprised to see two riders approaching. They galloped along the pathway, their horses throwing up great clods of earth and grass as they splashed through the rainwater. Arthur peered into the sheeting rain, which had become heavier as the morning light vanished into a stormy gloom.

Lunete's crow-black hair streamed behind her as her horse galloped through the rain, and Arthur cursed his luck. Kai rode beside her, his brown cloak billowing behind him. Arthur glanced at the forest and for a heartbeat he considered trying to outrun them, riding east and then turning south. He could lose them in the woodland and escape to freedom. Again, the idea of returning with a reputation built on the skill of his spear burned bright in his thought cage, and then died as the wind ruffled his hair and he realised his naivety. It was a foolish, childish dream. So he waited, head bowed for Kai and Lunete to reach him. He had failed again and was sure now that he would never amount to anything, never be a great warrior or leader of men. It was time to join Ector's war band, to take the mockery and scathing barbs from Huell and get on with life. That image of riding south to become a famous warrior, arm thick with death rings, wrists heavy with silver and gold, was dead. He would marry a warrior's daughter, live in a hovel in Caer Ligualid and see out his days just like everybody else.

'What are you doing?' Lunete shouted through the rain. She reined her horse in, and it wheeled around in a circle, her rain-soaked hair flicking about her shoulders as she turned her head to keep her angry eyes on Arthur.

'Please tell me you aren't running away, brother?' said Kai as his horse slowed and stopped next to Arthur's mare. His eyes bore into Arthur's, and he looked so like his father in that moment that Arthur felt like the great champion was judging him through his son's gaze.

'I was...' Arthur began, but Lunete laughed mockingly.

'You were running away. How could you?' she said, her face twisted in disgust. 'I saw you leaving and woke Kai.'

'I'm not running away. It's just time to strike out on my own. Make my way in the world.'

'Strike out on your own?' said Kai. He shook his head in disbelief, rain pouring down his face in rivulets. 'After all my father has done for you? We have a chance here, Arthur. They have entrusted us with a glorious task – to ride deep into Lloegyr and rescue the daughter of King Leodegrance. There will never be a better chance for us to make our names.'

'I know that, but Huell will lead, and the men look down on me. They mock me, and surely there must be more to my life than mockery and failure.'

'The only way to shut Huell up is to earn his respect. The men won't look down on you once you've earned your place in the war band. This is not the way. It looks like you...'

'It looks like you are afraid,' Lunete shouted above the wind and rain. 'It looks like you are running away because you are frightened to ride into Bernicia and face the Saxons. Are you afraid?'

'No!' Arthur shouted back at her. 'I do not fear battle...'

'What is it then? What are you running from?'

Arthur wiped the rain from his eyes with the back of his hand, his hood was soaked through, and he pulled it away from his head. He reached down and took the queen's bronze disc from the pouch at his belt and passed it between his fingers, rubbing the dragon, its wings, fangs and claws.

'Are you a coward, brother?' Kai said, anger turning his face hard.

'I am no coward. I just want more. More than being a simple warrior, more than a life lived as an unknown destined to die old and withered in a shit-stinking hovel in Caer Ligualid.' Arthur realised he bellowed those words which had come from deep within him. Now that he had given voice to his ambition, a lightness fell over Arthur. He wanted more. He felt it stirring within him like burning desire.

'Well, earn it then,' said Lunete, and her blue eyes searched Arthur's own. He held her gaze, and she nodded, seeing the fierce determination there.

'What life do you think there is for us in this place? You married to Huell, forced to meet his every whim, suffer his brutal embrace and whelp his pups? Is that what you want?'

'Huell?' She looked from Arthur to Kai and shook her head slowly. 'I will not marry him, although he is a man of honour and reputation. My heart lies with another.'

Arthur sighed and Lunete's face became etched with sadness. Her look confirmed that she held a dream that she and Arthur would marry, and though he loved her, it was the love of a brother for a sister and could be nothing more. He had hurt her, but Arthur wanted her to see the bleakness of what lay before them.

'Our choices are not our own. Ector decides where we go, who we marry, and what our destinies will be. Why should we not try to take charge of our own lives?'

'You talk like a fool,' Kai spat, his voice dripping with scorn. 'That spear you carry was a gift from my father. As was the knife at your belt. That horse you ride is my father's, and most men would give anything to be so honoured by Ector. The clothes you wear came from my father. You cannot just ride away and pretend like you are free. My father took you in and raised you when you had nothing. How many other men would have done so? He treated you like his own son, and Lunete and I have always looked upon you as a brother. If you leave like this, you will break Father's heart and I will never forgive you. Repay the debt you owe, earn your spear and the life of privilege Father has given you. Don't forget, someone left you at our door without a pot to piss in.'

That hit Arthur like a slap across his face, a shocking blow of hard truth. Arthur just nodded at his brother and friend. There was nothing left to say. He owed Ector his life and realised how his leaving must seem to Kai and Lunete. They cantered back to the Bear Fort in silence, riding up the pathway which ran with little rivers of water as the rain kept falling. The three riders dismounted as they reached the gate and led their horses through the Bear Fort's courtyard, which was as chaotic as a kicked wasp's nest. Warriors shouted, ran, and hurried between buildings as they prepared to march. The rain stopped and men looked up and laughed as cauldron-grey clouds gave way to bright sky and the morning sun peeked through the grey to warm their soaking faces.

Arthur tied his horse off beside the stable. He turned to Lunete and pulled her into a warm embrace. She held him tightly. He had come within a whisker of leaving and seeking a new life. Everything Kai had said was true, how could he leave when he owed Ector so much? His life, family friends were here. Arthur stared off at the distant forest, wondering at what could have been, but realising that duty bound him to stay. Kai slapped Arthur's back, and Huell's roars lifted above the bustle to order his men to gather.

'I will see you when we return,' Arthur said, wiping wet strands of hair from Lunete's face.

'Not if I see you first,' she said with a mischievous grin. She would ride with Ector and return to Caer Ligualid, whilst Arthur and Kai rode with Huell and the war band to strike deep into Saxon lands and find a lost princess. Arthur and Kai went to muster with Huell and the picked warriors who would make the journey, and Arthur set his jaw to the task. It was time to become a warrior, to repay the debt he owed Ector and become the man he must be.

5

Ten warriors rode from the Bear Fort, Arthur and Kai on their own
horses, and Huell and the seven warriors on horses provided by King
Urien's stable. They pushed east, leaving Rheged's dense woodland and
entering the high mountains which ran across the middle of northern
Britain like the bent back of a mighty dragon. Oak, ash and elm gave way
to pines the higher they rose, and lush pastures and meadows became
heather and gorse as the war band rode into lands free of villages, road or
farm. Glass-surfaced tarns provided fresh water where they sat nestled
between lofty peaks, and the war band stopped to rest the horses wherever they found grass or water for their mounts.

Arthur rode with Kai, and Huell led from the front. Thankfully, the
grizzled warrior had so far left Arthur alone, preferring instead the
company of his warriors to taunting Arthur. Huell relished his chance at
command, leading the riders around foothills, ordering stops for rest and
then camp at the end of the first day. The men Ector sent with Huell were
all warriors of reputation. Rhys, Serwil, Nyfed, Merin, Kadored, Dunod
and Cynfan were veterans of the wars against the Saxons, men with
braided beards, each with a dozen death rings marked on their forearms.
Each man carried a spear, a long knife and a shield slung over his back. It
would take two days to ride from the Bear Fort to the border of Bernicia

and Arthur rode quietly for much of the first day. He and Kai rode in companionable silence and, thankfully, not a word was mentioned of Arthur's attempt to leave Rheged.

Huell called a halt to make camp on a rocky shelf facing west between two great mountains. Heavy rocks and boulders covered the slope, so the war band made camp among those cold, lichen-covered stones in order to hide their campfire from the east. Kadored told the tale of how King Uther had killed a Saxon king in single combat during the Great War, and the warriors shared their skins of ale. Nyfed had caught a rabbit with the bow he carried over his shoulder and so they had fresh meat to add to the supplies each man brought for the march.

'Bernicia is a big kingdom,' said Serwil, a thick-chested man with a broad nose and silver loops hanging from each earlobe. 'Where do we search for the princess?'

'Ida was the Saxon leader who took Bernicia from our people in the Great War,' said Huell. 'He made his fortress at Dun Guaroy on a high crag beside the island of Lindisfarne. We could follow Dere Street, the old Roman road north, but that would attract too much attention. So, we keep heading east until we reach the coast, and then follow the sea until we reach Ida's stronghold. If the princess is anywhere, she is there.'

'But didn't King Urien say that it is this new Saxon warlord, Octha, who captured the princess?' said Arthur, and then immediately regretted opening his mouth as Huell shot him a baleful frown.

'When I want the opinion of a lackbeard boy yet to blood his blade, I will ask.'

'Are Octha and Ida allies or enemies?' asked Serwil. He chewed on a piece of rabbit meat and eyed Arthur carefully.

'During the feast, Ector discussed these matters with King Urien, and all we know is that Ida and Octha have formed an alliance to conquer new lands and establish a new Saxon kingdom. Octha did not bring his warriors to our shores for nothing. He means to make himself a king.'

'They are settling here. Bastards want to breed us out of our own lands,' said Nyfed, and he stared around at each man, making sure they understood the weight of his words. 'Which is why the druids have stirred themselves from Ynys Môn, and why this quest of ours is so important.

We must strike at the Saxons; show them we can penetrate deep into their stolen lands. Whilst Ector fights them in battle, we strike at the very heart of their new lands like a spear thrust to the Saxons' hearts.'

'Saxon dogs,' said Rhys, a wiry man with corded muscle on his thin arms. He made the sign of Annwn with his fingers to ward off the Saxon evil, and then crossed himself so as not to anger God.

'We start at Dun Guaroy,' said Huell. 'Many of our people are slaves in those lands, so we will ask the folk in the fields and on the coast if they have heard of a captured princess from across the sea. Octha will want men to know that he captured Guinevere. It makes him famous, and men will know a ransom is coming his way. Warriors and *bucellari* flock to rich lords, war and silver to a warrior is like firelight to a fly. Slaves will have heard the talk from their Saxon masters, and that is how we shall find the princess.'

'You are more cunning than you look,' said Nyfed, and Huell winked at him and spat through the gap in his teeth. The war band laughed and talk shifted to more mundane matters, such as which of their wives was the worst cook, and then Cynfan tried to stump them with riddles. His father had been a bard, and so Cynfan was fair famed for the riddles he learned from his father and was often called upon to test the warriors' cleverness. Arthur watched Huell in the firelight and wondered if the brutal warrior was indeed more cunning than he seemed, for his plan seemed practical. There was little sense in following the Roman road, the principal thoroughfare linking Bernicia with Deira and the south. That route would be busy with folk travelling north and south, merchants trading furs, amber, iron, copper, bronze and even amphorae of wine from across the sea. News would quickly reach the Saxons of a Briton war band heading north, armed with spears and shields, and Huell's war band needed to avoid trouble before they found Princess Guinevere.

Talk dwindled once the meal was over, and it was a dark night with only a sliver of moon in the sky. The men lay back on their riding blankets and covered themselves with their cloaks to bed down for the night. Arthur lay with his spear next to him and just as he was about to close his eyes, he caught Huell glowering at him across the fire.

'There will be battle on this journey, bastard,' Huell said, pointing a thick finger at Arthur. 'When it does, we shall need every spear sharp and ready to strike. If you fail us, if you shirk or run, you leave us a man down. I did not want you with this war band, and I said so to Ector. If I catch you shirking when the Saxons come for us with their broken-backed blades, their wild savagery, their axes and their hate, I'll kill you myself.'

Arthur turned away and closed his eyes, under no doubt that Huell spoke the truth. It was a chilly night, but Arthur slept deeply, having not slept at all the previous night spent beside the ailing Queen Igraine. He woke early and took the strip of leather he used to tie his hair at the nape of his neck and cut it into two thinner pieces with his knife. Arthur used one piece to tie his hair again and threaded the other through the small hole at the top of his bronze dragon disc. He tied the leather thong around his neck and hid the disc beneath his tunic. At first it was cold against the top of his chest, but then there came a warmth from wearing the charm close to his skin and Arthur hoped it would bring him luck.

The war band rose before the sun crept fully over the sprawling mountains and they set off westwards, skirting the summit of a peak which seemed scorched by fire, black, bleak and devoid of trees, grass, heather or bracken. Huell led them around to the eastern side of the mountain and Nyfed believed they would see the sea before nightfall. Huell ordered a break to rest the horses when the sun reached its highest point on its westward journey and the war band stopped beside a babbling brook. The horses drank the cool mountain water, and the war band ate leftovers from last night's meal. Once the horses had recovered, they rode down the mountainside, avoiding scree and loose rock, and stayed in the areas where the land was dusted with bracken or heather.

A sparrowhawk soared above them on the breeze and Arthur followed its flight as the bird searched for prey on the high slopes. The sun began its downward journey and Huell searched for a place to camp for the night. He led the war band into a copse beside a broken-down timber shack which must have belonged to a shepherd or goatherd, but the wood was so weathered and its roofless walls so broken that it could not have been used for a generation or more. Arthur's horse shied as they entered the clutch of trees, and he patted her muscular neck. An animal rustled in the undergrowth and scampered away unseen.

'I have a riddle for you,' said Serwil, slowing his horse and ducking beneath a low bough. The men groaned because Serwil was not renowned as a deep thinker. 'At night they come out without being fetched, and by day they are lost without being stolen.'

'The answer is stars. My grandmother told me that one when I was still at my mother's tit,' said Rhys, to guffaws. They rounded a twisted hawthorn tree and suddenly went quiet. Arthur kept his horse moving forward, but Huell and others stopped dead, staring ahead with open mouths.

'God help us,' Kai whispered as he and Arthur came around the twisted hawthorn branches. Fifteen Saxon warriors sat in a clearing between the trees. They crouched around two men trying to light a fire with flint and steel. They were big men with fur at their necks and shoulders, some with golden hair and blue eyes and others with dark, braided beards. The Saxons were making camp in the trees, just as the Rheged men were about to. Two enemy war bands had, by some cruel twist of fate or fell-luck, stumbled across each other. The Saxons rose slowly, and their eyes flickered to a stack of spears resting against a tree trunk, surrounded by a dozen large shields covered with leather and bossed with iron. The Saxons outnumbered the Rheged men. They were filthy and smeared with dirt from hard marching. Arthur had never seen a Saxon warrior before, and they were not so different to his own people, save that they wore furs about them and strange amulets around their necks. They had come across the wild sea in their warships, braving the terror of high waves and sea storms to reach Britain's shores. They came for land, wealth, women and glory, and their brutal, ancient gods demanded blood and war.

A big Saxon with a milky eye dropped his hand to the axe at his belt and Huell snarled. Huell cocked his arm and threw his spear at shocking speed. The spear thumped into the Saxon's chest and sent him sprawling backwards into the undergrowth.

'Dismount! Arm yourselves!' Huell roared and leapt from his horse, drawing his shining sword in one fluid motion. A man cannot fight on horseback. There is nothing for his feet to grip or brace against, and so men always fought on foot. Arthur slid from his horse, already holding his spear, and in a heartbeat the forest's calm erupted into a welter of shouting, of iron, steel and wood clanking together. A Saxon threw an axe, a short-hafted thing with a curved blade. It turned head over haft in the wan forest light and chopped into Dunod's face with a wet slap. Dunod fell, his head a horror of blood, bone and mangled flesh. Huell charged at them, his bright sword held high and his war cry terrible. The rest of the war band followed him, and Arthur charged with them. He gripped his spear with two hands and followed Kai as he swerved to the right, towards the Saxons' left flank. The enemy had no time to retrieve their spears or shields and they met the Rheged men with axes and the wicked bladed seaxes, which gave the Saxon people their name.

Kai roared and charged with his spear levelled. He dashed towards the rightmost Saxon, a young man with a short beard and an axe in his fist. Arthur's boots crunched on fallen leaves and twigs and his heart thundered, blood rushing in his ears. He aimed for the next warrior over from Kai's man, another young Saxon with a golden beard and a hatchet-hard face. That warrior bared his teeth and spat a curse at Arthur in the Saxon tongue. He held a seax, a single-edged knife as long as a man's forearm, with a long tapering point. Arthur reached him without slowing and aimed his spear at the enemy's chest. The Saxon parried the attack with his seax, and as Arthur's momentum drove him forward, the Saxon tripped him, sending Arthur sprawling in the bracken.

Arthur turned, gasping with fear, just in time to see the seax swinging for his neck. He brought his spear up and caught the blade on the spear stave with a loud crack and kicked the Saxon's legs from under him. The fight raged around him, weapons clashing, men screaming and bellowing as each tried to kill the other. Kai fought with a Saxon, their weapons flashing as they moved around each other, seeking the killing blow. In the blink of an eye, Arthur remembered Ector's lesson at the villa. That savagery was as important as skill in a fight to survive. So Arthur surged forwards. He dropped his spear and dragged his long knife free of the sheath at his belt and leapt upon the fallen Saxon.

The Saxon scrambled to his feet and was in a half-crouch as Arthur slammed into him. Both men fell to the forest floor, rolling and thrashing in the leaf mulch and rotting branches. The Saxon grunted and his elbow cracked against Arthur's head. He ducked and drove his knee into the Saxon's groin and stabbed his knife upwards, but the Saxon blocked it with his seax. As Arthur struggled for space, the enemy pressed Arthur's head into his chest, forcing the stink of sweat and leather into Arthur's nose. The seax point flicked at Arthur's neck and drew a trickle of blood and, with his free hand, Arthur reached up and clawed at the Saxon's face. He yanked Arthur's hand away and Arthur bucked, raising his head to free himself of the suffocating stink, but the seax point ripped across his cheek and chin like a white-hot whip. *Be savage, you will die here unless you can kill this man.* Somewhere around Arthur, a warrior shrieked like a demon and another warrior roared his war-fury like a bear, or like Balor, the Demon King of legend.

A calm descended over Arthur in that moment, taking him into another part of himself, like sleep takes a man into the dream world. Ector's words were with him, burned into his mind. Arthur heard himself growling and shouting like a man possessed, and his heart pounded, filling his limbs with strength. Arthur planted his boots in the earth and drove his head upwards, cracking off the Saxon's chin, and he pulled his head back and butted the Saxon full in the face. He twisted to get away from the pain as Arthur's forehead crushed his nose into a bloody pulp and Arthur pressed his forearm into the Saxon's neck, leaning on it with his chest. The man choked and thrashed at Arthur with his free hand, and his seax sliced into Arthur's shoulder, tearing through his jerkin to slice his flesh. But Arthur's knife hand was free, his arm low at the Saxon's waist and Arthur drove it upwards, piercing the enemy warrior's side and pushing the sharp blade into the man's flesh. He felt resistance and pushed harder. He was above the Saxon, staring into his eyes which grew wide with horror as he felt cold iron slicing into his body. Arthur pushed again, and the blade hit the solid bone of a rib, so he twisted the knife, ripped it free and pushed into the Saxon's guts. He could feel blood warm and wet against his own midriff, but not his blood. The Saxon screamed, his breath stinking of milk and onions.

The Saxon's hand grabbed Arthur's face, an unnatural strength in the fingers as the man fought for his life. His nails scratched Arthur's cheeks like an eagle's talons, and he hooked a finger into Arthur's mouth, trying to rip his cheek open like a fish hook. Arthur twisted his head away and bit down hard on the filthy finger until he could taste blood. The hand came away, but grabbed his gullet, squeezing and choking Arthur. Arthur stabbed again twice in two short bursts into the Saxon's guts, and the hand fell away. It was a vicious fight, and Arthur stared into his enemy's eyes, which were wide and dilated. The Saxon's mouth contorted and his teeth ground together so hard that one of them shattered like rotten wood.

Arthur pulled himself free of the dying man, but the seax darted upwards and cut Arthur's forearm. Just as Ector had warned him, a man doesn't die easily and Arthur fell upon the Saxon again, stabbing him in the neck and chest repeatedly with his long knife until fiery blood splashed his face and the enemy lay dead. Arthur stood, caught in the grip of battle calm. Kai still fought his man, both circling each other wearily, sweat drenching their faces. Arthur knelt and picked up his spear and as the Saxon warrior parried a thrust from Kai's weapon, Arthur charged and sunk its leaf-shaped point into the Saxon's side. Kai turned in surprise, but Arthur left the spear and kept moving. Rhys lay on the ground with a bloody gash in his neck. Dark blood oozed there like a black pool, and his eyes stared lifelessly at the heavens. Huell fought against three Saxons, and two more lay dead at his feet. Arthur bent and picked up a fallen seax and dashed to Huell's side with a weapon in each fist. The first Saxon saw him coming and lunged a long spear point at Arthur's face, but he parried the blow, driving the spear across the man's body, and stabbed the seax into his heart without hesitation. The countless days of weapons practice made Arthur's blades move without him thinking. He was like water pouring over rocks, finding his way through the battle naturally, following its contours and shifting with its dangers.

Huell opened a Saxon's throat, the third Saxon licked his lips, turned and ran. Huell dropped to one knee, exhausted from the battle. Arthur took a spear from the man he had stabbed through the heart, took two steps, and threw it overhand at the running man. The blade took him between the shoulder blades, and he fell into a clutch of dark brown bracken.

'For Rheged!' shouted Huell between gasps, and the surviving members of his war band responded with three clipped roars.

The Saxons were dead or dying, but Rhys and Dunod were dead, Huell suffered wounds, and Merin rolled in the undergrowth clutching at a bloody gash in his stomach. The battle calm left Arthur as quickly as it came. It was as though he awoke from a dream. Suddenly he felt a pain in his face and shoulder where before there had been none. His hands were wet with blood and death had come to the woodland. Huell staggered to his feet, bleeding from multiple cuts on his arms and legs.

'You are a warrior now, bastard,' Huell snarled. 'Oh, you're a savage one. Found yourself, have you? I can see it in your eyes, boy, you are a killer. Maybe I was wrong about you.'

Kai crashed into Arthur and draped an arm around his shoulders. 'You killed the enemy today, brother. You are part of the war band now. Father will be proud.'

Arthur nodded and tried to smile. He had done it; he had killed and received praise from cruel Huell. The thing Ector had raised him to do, trained him to do, what Arthur had always wanted to do. But the achievement left him numb as the injured wailed and the dead lay soiled in the undergrowth, their bowels voided to leave the copse stinking of shit and blood. Arthur suddenly bent over and vomited into the leaf mulch. He wasn't sure if it was from the thrill of battle or the horror of taking a man's life.

'It will feel bad for a while, that you have taken a man's life. But it will pass. You have earned your death ring now, and more than one.' Kai ruffled Arthur's hair and grinned.

Arthur forced a smile. To look upon the torn and bloody bodies was gut-wrenching, fearsome because of the nature of their injuries and how close Arthur himself had come to suffering such blow. But he didn't feel bad for the slain. There was no guilt for the lives he had taken. It was life or death, just as Ector had said it would be. Arthur felt no pity for the men he had killed. They had come to Britain for war and had found their destiny. If they were not prepared to lose their lives, they should have stayed in their own lands and left his people in peace.

'Take anything valuable,' Huell ordered. 'Weapons, silver, food. Anything we can use.'

Cynfan and Nyfed tended to Merin. They propped him up against a tree and helped him take a sip of ale from a skin. He coughed and pulled his hands away from his stomach to reveal a terrible wound, purple coils visible beneath the bloody ruin of his tunic. Merin wept, and Nyfed held his hand to comfort the dying warrior.

'One of them got away,' said Kadored, emerging from the forest dripping with sweat. 'I chased him, but he was too swift. He's disappeared over the hills.'

'A pox on these Saxon whoresons,' said Huell. 'They'll be after us now. We'd better be gone from here soon.'

Merin died moments later, and Nyfed said a prayer over his corpse. There was no time to bury the bodies or provide any sort of send-off worthy of a dead warrior. Huell wanted to march through the night. If they stayed in the copse, they could awake to an army of Saxons descending on them, for they did not know how far the fleeing Saxon must run to find his countrymen. The Saxon war band was most likely a group of scouts, Arthur thought, ranging ahead of the Saxon army to scout the countryside and search for signs of the enemy, safe ways to march, places to camp and find supplies. But news of their slaughter would bring more Saxon spears searching for the Rheged men, and they must be as far away from the copse as possible.

Arthur took a hard-baked leather breastplate from a Saxon he had killed, along with a seax. Arthur strapped on the belt that came with it, and he placed the seax sheath at the small of his back. The seax sheath rested sideways so that he could quickly whip its antler hilt free and be ready to fight.

'We should find the horses,' said Kai, as they gathered weapons and silver from the dead. The horses had bolted at the sound of battle and the smell of blood.

'It will take too long,' said Huell, using a strip of cloth cut from a dead man's tunic to bind the cuts on his arm. 'Besides, they are too easy to track and will be heard for miles. We march on foot. There are only seven of us now, and half of us carry wounds.'

So seven warriors left the copse as darkness fell. Each man now carried spear, shield, knife and seax. They took skins of strong-tasting ale from the Saxons, and some scraps of hacksilver found in leather pouches tied beneath dead men's armpits. Arthur took a black cloak with fur around its neck and hood and followed Huell out into the wilderness. He was a warrior. Men had died under his knife, but Arthur's head swam with confusion. He had expected to feel guilt and sadness for taking another man's life, but all he felt was alive, and pride at living up to Ector's expectations.

6

Seven warriors left the woodland, half marching and half running eastwards with the mountains at their backs. No stars shone that night, and the sliver of moon showed itself sparingly beneath dense cloud cover. It was late spring, and a chill wind came from the south to sting their fingers, ears and noses, and Arthur pulled his fur hood close about him. He carried a heavy Saxon shield upon his back, much larger than the shields his own people fought with. The shield, made of linden wood riveted to an iron boss and ringed with iron, would protect Arthur from chin to shin if he crouched behind it with his spear. He carried his spear in his right hand and wore his long knife at his belt and the seax at the small of his back.

They ran through heath, cloying bog and splashed through shallow rivers, all the time throwing nervous glances over their shoulders in search of any pursuing Saxon forces. Arthur's face grew tight as the cut across his cheek clotted, and his shoulder screamed with fiery pain. There had been no time to wash or stitch the wounds in the woodland, but Arthur knew he would need to clean the wounds before the rot set in, and Nyfed carried a bone needle and gut thread in a pouch at his belt for such work.

'He can't carry on like this,' said Kai, who loped along next to Arthur.

Kai jutted his chin towards Huell's broad back, and the warrior stumbled once, righted himself for a few more steps and then veered to his right before Serwil caught him and kept Huell on his feet.

'He has to,' said Arthur. 'We must be as far from the copse as possible before the sun comes up.'

'We should have buried Rhys, Merin and Dunod so that they can pass to heaven.'

'I'm sure God will understand.'

A red glow lit distant clouds before the sun came up, and Arthur could taste salt on the wind as the war band stopped to rest beside a thicket which separated two tilled fields. Huell closed his eyes tight and pressed a hand to the small of his back. The hand came away bloody. Huell caught Arthur watching him and shook his head slightly, silently warning Arthur not to tell the rest of the warriors that he bore a serious wound beneath his mail. They finished what remained in their ale skins and consumed the last of their food. Arthur chewed on a piece of Saxon sausage taken from the dead, heavy with garlic and onion, and Kadored broke up a loaf of bread and shared a piece with each man.

'I can smell the sea,' Nyfed said. He took the bow from his back and rested it against the thicket. 'We should reach the coast soon.'

'Then to find this bloody princess before we're all killed,' grumbled Cynfan, dabbing his finger gingerly at a gash on his thigh.

'Maybe we should turn back,' said Serwil, and then looked offended as the others frowned at him. 'What? I'm only saying what you are all thinking. We have all taken wounds. Three of our brothers are dead. We don't even know this princess or her king. Let's get back home whilst we still can.'

'We go on,' said Huell through gritted teeth. 'We follow orders.'

'Even if we march to our deaths? Our spears are better served fighting Saxons with Ector than dying here for nothing.'

'We are oathsworn to Urien and Ector. Part of that oath is to follow his commands even if it means our deaths. I'll thrash the next man who questions that. We find Guinevere or we die.'

They rose slowly, creaking and groaning as the sun came up to warm Arthur's face. In the darkness, he hadn't realised how pale Huell had become. Sweat greased his skin, and the big man suddenly looked gaunt beneath his thick beard. Farmland turned to coarse grass, and the hills fell away to where gulls cawed, and a grey sea rolled beneath a bright spring sky. Kai laughed for joy as they clambered over high dunes and slid down white sand on to a beach which stretched away north in a wide sweep. The tide was out, leaving dark sand beyond the waterline where seabirds pecked and dug for worms and shellfish.

'Now to find a fishing village and news of Octha and his army,' said Huell. He limped along the sand, using his spear to brace his weight. Every man in the band saw his discomfort, but no one commented on it for fear of Huell's wrath. Their pace slowed to match his, and Kai pointed to a small boat bobbing in the surf at the beach's north end. Fishermen prepared for a day's work, and the war band marched towards them, hopeful of news or at least some direction for their quest. All Arthur knew was that they were deep in Lloegyr, in Saxon lands which had once been the proud kingdom of Bernicia. They did not know where Octha and his army landed or marched, only that the Saxon King Ida had a stronghold on a high crag which had once been Dun Guaroy, close to Lindisfarne Island.

A small man in ragged tunic and trews rolled up above his knees waded into the shallows. He worked at a fishing net, untangling a wicker basket from its folds and whistling a tune as the tide lapped at his small fishing boat.

'You there,' Huell barked. The fisherman turned, and wrinkles creased his sun-darkened face. He gaped at the war band, looked at his boat and then at their gleaming spear points.

'Please, lord,' the man said, lisping the words in a mouth containing a few stubs of brown teeth. 'I'm just a simple man.'

'Are there Saxons here?' Huell asked.

'Yes, lord. Have been since my father's time. These lands belong to Imma.'

'Who is Imma?'

'A Saxon, lord, who serves Ida of Bebbanburg.'

'Bebbanburg?'

'Dun Guaroy in our tongue, lord.'

'How far is Dun Guaroy from here?'

'A day up the coast, lord, no more.'

'Do you serve the Saxons?'

'Yes, my lord, but I have no choice. I was born under Saxon rule. I speak their tongue and my daughter married a Saxon.'

Huell spat and shook his head, and all the warriors' shoulders sagged because Bernicia was truly a Saxon kingdom, and it was as men feared it would be. The Saxons came with their ships and axes first, and then came their women and children. They ruled the land and took it for themselves. They lived on farms and in halls once owned by Britons and married their sons to Briton women, and so the Bernicians would become bred out of existence within a generation.

The fisherman's face changed, shifting from nervousness to fear. His jaw dropped open, and he shook his head, staring across Arthur's shoulder. Arthur turned and his stomach lurched, for a dozen Saxon riders rode down the beach towards them, the sound of their hoofbeats drowned out by the rolling sea and its crashing tide.

'Saxons!' Arthur called. The war band spun around and Serwil cried out, backing up into the sea until the surf broke around his knees.

'That bastard who ran set them on our trail,' said Nyfed. He unslung his bow from across his shoulders and pulled four arrows from the quiver at his belt, burying three head down in the sand and nocking one to the string.

The Saxons charged down the beach, howling an undulating war cry and swathed in furs. Nyfed loosed his first shaft, and it sang over the riders' heads.

'We cannot fight them and live,' said Serwil, shaking his head.

'So, we fight them and die,' said Huell. He gripped his spear and planted his feet in the sand. The fisherman scrambled in the water towards his small boat and Nyfed loosed another arrow. Its iron arrowhead hit a horse in the meat of its chest. The beast screamed and reared up on its back legs and tossed its rider onto the sand.

Arthur readied his Saxon shield, resting his spear on its iron rim, and Kai stood beside him, his spear held two-handed. Arthur had fought and killed, and the experience gave him confidence and belief in his ability and strength. Ector, the champion of Britain, had taught him to fight, and Huell, for all his faults, was a mighty warrior, as were the men beside him. The Saxons roared down the beach and tossed their spears whilst still on horseback. They had no purchase on their saddlecloths and three spears splashed harmlessly into the sea, and one smacked into the fishing boat's hull with a thud. Another slammed into Arthur's shield, and almost threw him off his feet. Arthur shook the weapon from his shield and set himself again as the Saxons wheeled their horses around and leapt from their backs to prepare to fight. A big man with close-cropped hair bellowed at the Rheged men and banged his axe upon his shield. The others fell in alongside him. They shouted guttural war cries, big men in furs and leather who hunted the Britons as though they were the invaders and the Saxons the natives. Each man carried a large Saxon-style shield, and they came in an organised line, shields overlapped with one another, and axes poised to strike.

'Kill the bastards!' Huell shouted, and he charged with his spear held low. Arthur followed him and his shield crashed into the enemy line with the sound of a falling tree. An axe blade swung at his face, and he ducked behind his shield, but the axe hooked over his shield rim and pulled it downwards, and then a spear flashed at his face, missing his eyes by less than the width of his hand. A seax came beneath the shield and Arthur had to dance backwards to avoid the blade tearing open his groin. He dropped his shield and stumbled backwards as Cynfan died with an axe buried in his chest. Huell ripped a shield from a Saxon's hands and tore the man's throat out with his spear. Blood spattered on the dark, damp sand and Kai caught an axe haft across his skull and fell to his knees. Arthur surged forwards, stabbing a Saxon with his long knife just as he was about to cleave Kai's head open with a two-handed axe swing. Arthur tore his blade free, and the Saxon toppled to his knees, gaping at the wound in his chest.

It was a slaughter on a Bernician beach, and Arthur was astounded at how the Saxons fought. They fought as a group, as a wall of shields in organised movements like a yuletide dance. Their shields were part of their weaponry, and of both attack and defence. It was a new way of fight-ing, and Arthur gaped at their efficient movements. Britons fought as single warriors, each fighting with his war-skill, his reputation and his bravery. Their shields were smaller and used only for defence, and Arthur understood in that moment why the Saxons were so successful in war. Nyfed loosed his last arrow, and many of the Saxons carried arrow wounds upon their bodies, or carried the shafts embedded in their shields. Nyfed joined the fight only to have his belly opened by the leading Saxon warrior. Huell jabbed his spear at the big man and the Saxon barked something in his own tongue, and his men fell back so that only he and Huell faced off. Arthur pulled Kai away from the fight into the shallows where Serwil and Kadored waited, staring open-mouthed at Huell and the broad-shouldered Saxon. They charged at each other, two champions, one Saxon and one Briton, and their blades flashed and clashed together. Arthur glanced over his shoulder; the fisherman also watched the fight from his boat. The ship bobbed in the gentle swell, and an idea struck Arthur like a blow to the head. He saw a chance to live, a desperately slight chance, and he took it.

Arthur left Kai, the grunt and clang of Huell's fight unfolding behind him, and grabbed the boat, hauling it towards the beach. The fisherman cried out, but Arthur grabbed his ragged tunic and glowered at him, the promise of death in Arthur's fierce gaze.

'Into the boat!' Arthur shouted, and Kai turned to him, glanced back at Huell and then at Arthur. Serwil didn't need asking twice and clambered aboard, rocking the ship so hard in his desperation that it almost capsized. Huell's spear shaft broke beneath his opponent's axe blade, but Huell recovered, spun around his foe, clutching the bladed half of what remained of his spear in his right hand. The Saxon crowed in triumph and lifted his axe for the killing blow, but Huell struck with the broken spear, driving the point deep into the Saxon leader's throat. He gurgled and flopped like a landed fish on the end of Huell's spear point and Huell let him fall dead to the sand.

'Huell, come now!' Arthur called. He charged out of the water and set himself on the shore whilst Kai and Kadored climbed into the fishing boat.

'We do not run,' Huell snarled.

'Run or die!'

Huell would not listen, and the Saxons came on in a wild charge. Arthur ran forward and swung low with his seax to rip open an enemy's thighs with the sharp blade. Huell killed a man with a brutal strike with his knife but there were too many, and even mighty Huell found himself driven backwards.

'Arthur, we must go now,' Kai shouted from the boat. Arthur couldn't risk a look backwards. The Saxons bayed before them like a pack of wolves, reluctant to strike at the man who had killed their leader but given confidence by their numbers. A squat warrior with bow legs lunged at Huell with his axe, and Huell parried it with his knife, but as he did so another axe sang through the air and chopped through Huell's wrist with a sickening crunch. Huell's hand and knife fell into the lapping sea with a splash, and Huell stared in horror at his wrist. Blood spurted from the wound, and Arthur grabbed him around the waist and pulled him deeper into the water. Huell made a strange mewing sound, just staring at the terrible injury, and the Saxons followed them into the shallows. Kai jumped back into the water from the boat and he and Arthur waved their weapons at the Saxons, who were still wary to attack after so much bloodshed. Kadored and Serwil dragged Huell into the boat, and the warrior still stared in shock at his severed right hand, a bloody stump where his sword hand should have been.

'Go,' Arthur ordered, and Kai scrambled over the side. Kadored shouted in alarm as the boat almost capsized again. A Saxon slashed an axe at Arthur, but he dodged the blow and sliced his own blade across the enemy's forearm. The Saxons fell back a pace, knee deep in the swell and wary of Arthur's bloody blade. Their leader was dead, and half a dozen other corpses littered the beach. The terror of battle and fear of death kept the Saxons back, but there was anger on their faces as they fought to find their courage once again. 'Pull me in!' Kai and Kadored grabbed Arthur and hauled him aboard. The Saxons roared and shook their weapons but came no further, and Arthur grabbed one oar and Kai the other. There were too many men in the boat, including the terror-stricken fisherman, but Arthur and Kai hauled for their lives and the boat surged away from the shore. Huell lay in the bilge, still gaping at his severed wrist and his blood sloshing with filthy sea water about Arthur's feet. A Saxon threw his axe, and it hit Serwil in the back with a thud. He screamed and fell overboard. Arthur roared with impotent rage as Serwil sank beneath the swell, his face staring up at Arthur beneath the grey-brown water.

'Pull, pull!' Kadored bellowed, and he threw his own knife at the Saxons and then gasped as a thrown Saxon spear took him in the chest. He looked at Arthur and Kai, his mouth flopping open wordlessly, and then slid over the side to splash in the rolling waves. Arthur and Kai rowed for their lives, and the boat soon went beyond the Saxons' reach, out into the heaving swell. It was a day of death, their war band all but destroyed by Saxon fury. Huell rolled in the thwarts, as pale as a midnight fetch, and he continued to make the same strange mewing sound as Arthur heaved on the oar. They had set out from the Bear Fort with ten men on a druid's quest to find a princess, but seven warriors were dead, their leader maimed and bleeding to death, and if their mission was a symbol for the future of Britain, then Arthur feared they were all surely doomed.

7

The Saxons, riding their stout ponies, followed the faering fishing boat along the coast until the headland rose into chalky cliffs and forced them inland. Arthur's arm and back muscles burned with the exertion as he hauled on the oars, glancing over his shoulder constantly to check their course. The fisherman guided them around sharp rocks which jutted from the headland and loomed underwater like the spiked walls of Manawydan's undersea fortress. Arthur and Kai rowed in silence, stricken by the war band's deaths and the utter failure of their journey to find Princess Guinevere. Arthur ground his teeth, the muscles of his face working beneath his beard, trying to block out the pitiful sound of Huell's whimpering.

'Tie his wrist,' Arthur said to the fisherman as the noise became too much. Huell's whines rose above the slop of the sea against the faering's bows, above the tide's crash against the cliffs and above the sea wind and scraped inside Arthur's skull like cat's claws. They came about the headland in a wide sweep, avoiding the jagged rocks and emerging into a crescent-shaped bay with a narrow shale beach and rolling sand dunes. The fisherman tore a strip of cloth from his jerkin and soaked it with sea water. He tried to bind Huell's wrist, but the big man batted him away with his remaining hand, shaking his head and babbling incoherently.

'He won't let me,' said the fisherman, staring up at Arthur with frightened eyes.

'Let him help you,' Arthur said to Huell as he splashed his oar into the sea for another stroke. 'Your wrist and back are bleeding, and you'll die.'

'You don't give me orders, bastard,' Huell spat. 'Let me die. You should have let me die on the beach, leave me. Throw me overboard or cut my throat. Kill me!' Huell began to roar and rock, his weight making the boat sway so violently that he threatened to turn the boat over.

'He's going to drown us!' Kai shouted, holding on to the side. Arthur and Kai had learned to swim in the rivers around Caer Ligualid, but they were so far out from shore in the sweep they had taken around the headland that Arthur doubted they could make the long swim to shore if Huell turned the boat over. The boat rocked, and the fisherman cried out because for a heartbeat it seemed the small faering would toss them into the deep. Arthur reversed his grip on the oar and crashed the shaft across Huell's skull, and the big man fell, limp and unconscious in the bilge.

'Now, bind his wound and his wrist whilst we go ashore,' Arthur snapped.

Kai stared at Arthur, surprised at his decisiveness, but to fall in the water was to die and Arthur had no choice but to subdue Huell before he killed them all, so he did not feel guilty for striking their leader.

The fisherman bound Huell's wrist tightly. They rowed the fishing boat towards the shore and Arthur leapt over the side when he could see dark, ridged, shallow sand beneath the rolling waves. Kai followed, and they dragged the fishing boat ashore.

'The Saxons will come around those cliffs soon,' said Kai, glancing up at the dark rock which loomed above them to the south. 'We should get away from this place.'

'We will,' said Arthur. 'Where is your village?' he asked the fisherman.

'The other way, lord, back around the headland.' The fisherman swallowed hard as Kai slapped the water in frustration.

'Where can we find shelter?'

'Follow this beach until you see a stream emptying itself on to the beach. Follow that inland and you'll reach my cousin's farm. They're Britons like us and will help you.'

Arthur and Kai dragged Huell out of the boat, and he came awake with a groan as he flopped into the bracingly cold surf.

'Let me die,' Huell whispered, but Arthur ignored him, and they dragged Huell to shore. The fisherman scampered back to his boat and rowed back towards the headland, keeping his large, fearful eyes on the bedraggled warriors.

'So, we push inland and find his cousin's farm?' asked Kai. He ran shivering fingers through his soaked curls and his thin beard.

'No,' said Arthur. 'As soon as he reaches shore, that fisherman will look for his Saxon lords and tell them where we are and where he has sent us. He's more Saxon than Briton now, and he'd sell our lives for a handful of silver. Get him up.'

They pulled Huell to his feet, and his hulking frame was heavy, too heavy for Arthur and Kai to drag across the beach and escape the Saxons, whom Arthur expected to come galloping over the dunes at any moment.

'Where do we go then?' asked Kai.

'Inland here, and head west. We keep away from farms and settlements. There are six Saxons left in the group we fought on the beach. Our quest is over. We cannot continue, and we must return to Ector.'

'We can't just abandon the druid's quest. What if Kadvuz curses us, or strikes us down with thunder?'

Arthur frowned at him. 'He can't conjure thunder. The Romans broke the druids' strength long ago, and what power can gods have if hardly anybody worships them any more? You and I can't storm a Saxon fortress alone and rescue a princess, especially not with Huell in this state. We return to Ector. Perhaps he will give us more men and we can return. If not, then we join his war band.'

Kai stared at Huell, as though he expected their leader to give an order, to disagree with Arthur or come up with a new plan, but Huell just sagged in their arms like a sack of meat and bone. Arthur wasn't their leader, and if anything, Kai had more right to decide things if Huell could not. Kai was Ector's son, and Arthur was an orphan with no say at all. But Arthur also wanted to live, and despite the hardship, the death of his comrades and their hopeless situation, he found he could think clearly. He could cut through the fear and the despair and see what must be done. They were deep in Lloegyr, and their men were dead, and he could see no other way for him and Kai to get out of there alive. Kai nodded, and they set off up the beach. Arthur's wet boots crunched on the shale, and despite it being late spring, the day had an overcast sky and a chilling wind from the sea, causing Arthur to shiver in his soaking clothes. He had lost his Saxon shield and spear, but still had his long knife and seax at his belt.

'We can't drag him all the way across Lloegyr,' said Kai after twenty paces. Huell was like a dead weight in their arms, dragging his feet on the tiny stones, and the two young warriors were out of breath before they had even reached the dunes.

Arthur dropped Huell, and the big man rolled onto his back, cradling his handless arm.

'Get up and walk,' said Arthur.

'He can't,' pleaded Kai, but Arthur ignored him.

'Get up and walk. How many times have I heard you say that we don't flee, or we don't surrender, or warn me to fight bravely? What kind of warrior are you to fall to the ground like a whimpering child?'

'They took my fighting hand,' Huell snarled, his face deathly pale from so much blood lost. 'I am worthless now, less than worthless. Just let me die.'

'So, you have given up? You are surrendering? All the years you have cursed me as a bastard orphan, believing yourself a superior, braver, better man, and here you are snivelling on the beach like a coward.'

'Arthur,' Kai raised a hand to warn Arthur that he had gone too far, but Arthur waved it away.

'They took my hand,' Huell shouted, his mouth turned down at the corners. His voice came as a half-shout and half-sob.

'Luckily for you, you have another. Now, get up and walk. You will heal and learn to fight with your left hand. We need you, Rheged needs you. Get up.'

Arthur held out his hand and Huell grabbed it with his left hand, his dark eyes blazing with anger. Anger was better than death, and Arthur needed Huell angry if that would force the warrior to live. So Huell rose, and he walked. When he stumbled, Kai caught him, but Arthur would not. Though wounded, Huell was still the man who had made Arthur's life a misery and so Arthur marched ahead, cresting the high dunes which rose like waves from the shale-topped sand. Coarse wild grass topped the dunes, and the three warriors left the coast behind as they marched across fields thick with purple heather and brush. Arthur headed west, constantly watching to the south for any sign of Saxon riders, but he saw none as they found a well-worn goat path which cut through a boggy heath of nettles, gorse and foul puddles.

A knoll rose from the flatlands, with a sickly elder tree at its summit. Arthur headed for the high ground to get a better look at their surroundings. They would need to make camp soon. Huell needed to rest, and the more they trudged around the coastline, the more tracks they left for the Saxons to follow. The three warriors climbed the knoll and Huell slumped down against the tree, grimacing in pain. Kai took off his cloak and ripped the wool into strips with his knife. He used one strip to make a sling for Huell, looping the sling around Huell's neck and forearm to take the pressure off the wounded limb, and to keep it elevated. Arthur scanned about them. The sea was to the east, beyond the dunes. To the south-west rose the clifftop where they had lost the Saxon riders. To the north, the land cut away long and flat, to where the coastline swept north-east. That way lay Dun Guaroy and the Saxons' stronghold, but Arthur must head west and hope to make it out of Saxon lands alive. Mountains rose in the west, black, shadowed and distant, and the border between Rheged and Lloegyr lay in their peaks and valleys, but to get there Arthur had to cross a swathe of open farmland. Green meadows, fields of crops separated by hedges and brown pathways, and clutches of woodland rolled over gentle hillocks to where the mountains seemed to touch a sky heavy with clouds the colour of curds.

'If we cross the fields, the Saxons will find us,' Arthur muttered.

'Perhaps they have given up on the chase?' Kai replied, tying off Huell's sling.

'After we killed six of their men? They won't give up.' Arthur ruffled his hair and beard with his hands to shake the itching sea salt out. His clothes began to dry and stiffen, and his mouth was dry. They had no food or ale, and Arthur had to find a place for them to rest. Daffodils and bluebells spattered colour across the brown pathways which ran between the fields, rutted by cart and wagon wheels. An oak tree grew tall and sprawling in a distant wheat field, and Arthur hoped perhaps they could find some shelter beneath its boughs. He could see no buildings, no thatch or any sign of the stream beside the fisherman's cousin's farm to the north or west. So the three set off towards the mountains and the oak tree in search of a safe place to rest.

Arthur's boots sunk into the bog, so that each step was a sucking, squelching drain upon his energy. Kai had to pull Huell along, and more than once the grizzled warrior fell shrieking as his bloody stump landed in the watery mud. Kai cursed as his boot came off in the mud, and he had to dig down to fish it out. As he rose, Kai's mouth dropped open, and he pointed to a raised bank to their south. Spear points wavered in the air like moving trees, and Arthur dropped to his belly, dragging Kai and Huell down with him.

They lay in the bog, its mud cloying, foul smelling and cold. Six Saxon warriors on horseback cantered along the hedge line bearing north. Cutting across the bogland where the three Britons crouched. Huell tried to rise, shaking his stump at the riders, and Arthur forced him down into the stinking bog water, fearful that Huell wanted the Saxons to find them and end his suffering. They waited in the muddy water until the Saxons passed from sight, and Huell sobbed silently, lying prone, his face covered in stinking mud.

The three warriors trudged through the flatlands, keeping to hedges and brush, crouching and moving with caution, eyes ever northwards in case the Saxon riders returned. The sun began to set as Arthur reached the oak tree, and as his hand touched the rough bark, it felt like a small victory over the Saxons. They had evaded the hunters twice, once on the beach at heavy cost, and again in the bog. They were no safer at the tree should the riders return, but to Arthur, the march to its wide trunk and sprawling boughs showed a change in his luck. And as he fell to his knees with exhaustion, he rubbed his forefinger and thumb on the bronze disc around his neck, hoping its dragon would bring him good fortune.

The oak was ancient and twisted, its roots gouged into the earth, thicker around than Arthur's arm. It cut into the land opposite the bog, its roots leaving deep culverts in the earth, and they huddled into its shelter, watching the sky, waiting for the sun to go down. Night meant the hunt would be over for that day, and they could rest. As darkness fell, Arthur and Kai gathered twigs and dry wood debris from around the great tree and stacked it around a pile of kindling. Kai fished into the pouch at his belt and found his flint and steel. He scratched at the flint with shaking, icy hands until finally the sparks caught in the crushed, dried leaves and crunched-up twigs and took light. Kai looked up and grinned, and Arthur smiled back. Though risky, the fire was another minor victory.

The flames crackled into life, and Arthur and Kai crouched around it, warming their hands and rubbing them together. Huell stayed back, curled into a ball, intertwined with the tree roots, silent and shivering with the stump of his severed hand clutched close to his chest. They kept the fire low, little more than a few fingers of dancing flame, fearful that its glow would be visible for miles and give their position away to the Saxon hunters.

Arthur and Kai lay down beside the fire's fragile warmth, warming their hands and aching muscles. Arthur silently rejoiced in his brother's survival, knowing that such sentiments were unspoken among warriors. He remembered how as children they would play together all day, climbing trees like the very oak they slept beneath, running wild in the fields around Caer Ligualid with Lunete and the other children of Ector's stronghold. He and Kai would play, practice weapons with their father, fight with each other, and had grown up as friends and brothers. They had faced death that day, and come through it alive, where other, more experienced warriors had perished and the mighty Huell himself had suffered a life-altering wound which might yet kill him. Arthur's eyes closed quickly, his body exhausted from running, rowing and fighting his way through Lloegyr.

Arthur woke the next morning with the fire still warm on his face, and a brisk wind ruffling his long hair. He had slept all night, a dreamless sleep where his muscles and his mind repaired and rested. Arthur stretched his stiff back and arms, sore not just from exertion but also from sleeping rough on the dirt and grass beneath the oak tree. Arthur rubbed the sleep from his eyes, and through the fog of sleep he wondered how the small fire had stayed burning all night long. He sat up and jumped backwards, shocked to see Kai sitting by the fire, which burned large and strong, with an old man. The old man was laughing, turning a rabbit on a makeshift wooden spit, and the smell of roasting meat made Arthur's mouth water.

'Ah, your friend is awake,' said the old man. He was a Briton and spoke the language with a bright, clear voice. He flashed a wide smile at Arthur. Despite his age, he had a perfect set of white teeth, and his grey eyes were bright in a face creased with age, wrinkled and worn. He was bald, but for a ring of white hair around his ears, which he had grown long and wore in tight braids. Strange tattoos covered the old man's scalp, faded symbols, writhing beasts and an arrow pointing down over his forehead. His beard was close-cropped to his chin, and he wore a long, dirty grey tunic belted at the waist with a hooded cloak the colour of burned bread. 'Eat. You must restore your strength.' The old man tore a chunk of meat from the rabbit and handed it to Kai, who glanced nervously at Arthur, but took the steaming meat and devoured it.

'Who are you?' asked Arthur, taking the offered meat from Kai. The old man had appeared from nowhere in the night and acted as though he was an old friend who should be welcomed. He showed no fear of the armed, travel-stained warriors and spoke to them like a scolding elder.

'Just a weary traveller who noticed three fools had started a fire in the land of their enemies and thought I would offer my help.'

'You are going to help us? And if we are fools, why have you kept the fire going?'

'Yes,' the old man said brightly and grinned. 'Well, the fire doesn't matter now that I have found you.'

'Found us?' Arthur asked slowly. Kai caught Arthur's eye and shrugged to say that he didn't understand the old man's presence, either.

'Yes, yes.' The man was becoming impatient and waved a long-fingered hand at Arthur to dismiss his question. 'Now, I must see to your man there, before his wound rots and he dies a long and painful death.'

The old man drew a short knife from his leather belt and thrust it into the fire.

'Keep away from me, old one,' said Huell. His voice croaked from within the tree roots, and he glowered like a red-eyed, white-faced demon.

'Now, now, Huell of Rheged, if I don't tend to your wound, you will lose your arm. So, no more complaining, if you please.'

'Who are you?' Arthur asked again, becoming annoyed with the old man's aloof tone and the surprise of waking to his strange appearance at the campfire.

'If we are going to travel together, I suppose someone should introduce us.'

'What makes you think we shall travel together?'

'Cut his skinny throat and be done with his meddling,' growled Huell.

'Many have tried that before, and here come your hunters. What a merry band of spearmen they make on their little ponies.' He pointed to the north and cackled as Arthur scrambled to his feet. Six Saxon riders approached in tied leggings and russet cloaks, their spears glinting in the early morning light. 'Your luck is in, young men. For I am Merlin and I have come to your aid.'

8

Saxon riders pounded along a raised bank which cut through the bog like a bridge, their spears shaking and points catching the morning sun. Arthur scrambled to his feet, grabbing his long knife and seax. Kai rose too, and the two friends glanced nervously at each other and then at the oncoming riders. Huell pushed himself to his feet, a shadow of his former self. Dirt and dried blood caked his body as he stooped, looking pale, with a face etched with lines of pain like a carved Roman pillar. Huell braced himself against the oak tree and staggered forward as though to join the fight. Merlin's presence at Arthur's campfire both baffled and awed him, and he had so many questions for the legendary druid, a man straight out of the stories told at winter hearths since he was a boy. But there was no time for that now. The Saxon war band had found them and came to kill.

'We cannot fight them,' said Kai, though he set himself for battle.

'Don't talk nonsense. You are the son of Ector,' said Merlin. Arthur wondered how Merlin knew who Kai was, but assumed the two had spoken whilst he was asleep. The old man stood with a groan and rubbed the small of his back. He was not a tall man, shorter than Arthur by a head, and was slight across the shoulders. Merlin reached behind the oak's roots and grabbed a long black staff, like that carried by Kadvuz when he had marched into King Urien's Bear Fort, but Merlin's staff had a fist-sized lump of polished amber at its top. The amber twinkled in the morning light like an egg-shaped drop of sun. Merlin pulled on a long white cloak and slung a large pack across his shoulders. He strode forward with his staff held before him like a torch on a winter's night, and the amber glowed as though it gathered power from the sun or from the earth itself.

Huell pulled a knife from his belt and stumbled past Arthur towards the oncoming Saxons.

'Stay back,' Arthur warned him, because the maimed warrior was in no fit state to fight.

'Let me die with honour,' he said, his lips cracked and pale blue. He grabbed Arthur's shoulder with his good hand, and there was some of Huell's old strength in the grip. Arthur stared into his glassy eyes and nodded. For all his cruelty, Huell deserved a warrior's death, a death in battle.

'Wait,' Merlin ordered with all the confidence of Ector or a great war-leader. The jovial tone was gone, and his voice was now as hard and sharp as flint. He waved his staff as though he wanted to catch the Saxons' attention, to make sure they had seen the Britons beneath the great oak tree. The Saxons whooped for joy at the sight of their prey and urged their horses into a gallop. The sound of their hooves was like thunder, and they shook their spears and let out an undulating war cry.

'They are trespassers on our land,' Merlin said, his voice low and fearsome, 'despoiling the soil of our forefathers with their malice. I call to you, Neit, god of war, grant us battle luck today, brighten our blades with your wrath and cast our enemies down to Annwn to suffer the horrors of the underworld for eternity!' Merlin shouted the last few words, the timbre of his voice grown low and powerful like Kadvuz's chanting in Urien's hall. Merlin brought his staff down, slamming it into the earth, and let out a mighty bellow, like the roar of a great beast.

Suddenly a score of men sprang up from beside the bank, men in leather, chain mail, black cloaks and iron helmets. They rose like demons from beneath the earth, and Arthur gasped, for it was like Merlin had raised warriors from the ground itself with the power of his druid magic.

'God, Christ, Maponos and Manawydan,' said Kai, almost dropping his spear in awe at the armed warriors who appeared from nowhere. They came howling from the earth like long dead Briton fighters from a lost war, risen again at Merlin's command to slay the hated Saxon enemy.

The foremost two men in black ran away from the ditch, dashing in opposite directions, and Arthur noticed that each carried one end of a hemp rope, braced over the hedge and a hawthorn tree on either side of the bank. They ran until the rope sprang taut, and the riders saw the trap too late to halt their horses. The first riders flew backwards from their galloping horses' backs as the rope bit into their chests. Their horses carried on thundering along the bank riderless. The next riders could not stop in time to avoid the rope, so what they thought was a gallop to glorious slaughter now became a ruin of shouting, panicked men, flailing horses and fallen warriors.

A Briton with a full-faced helmet clambered up onto the bank. He carried two shining swords and his black cloak billowed behind him. A Saxon tried to rise from where he fell, but the warrior in black swung his sword and the Saxon's head flew from his shoulders in a spray of bright blood. Another Saxon died with a spear through his chest where he lay on the bank with his leg twisted unnaturally beneath him. A horse galloped past Arthur and Kai, its eyes rolling white with fear at the smell of blood and the noise of clashing weapons and screaming men. Arthur leapt out of its way and then clambered up to rejoin Kai, using the oak roots as a ladder.

The warrior in the full-faced helm charged into the flailing Saxons, and his swords swung and struck as he danced into the carnage. His black-cloaked warriors joined him, and the Saxons fell beneath their spears, swords and fury. The attackers carried shields which bore a sigil Arthur did not recognise, a fox painted across their dark leather covers. They tore into the Saxons, stabbing and ripping with their blades. Two Saxons leapt from their horses. One fought with his seax blade, but the other set off running into the bog. He plunged into the heavy, watery sludge and tripped as he glanced over his shoulder at the slaughter. The Saxon struggled to rise in the cloying bog, and a black-cloaked warrior threw a spear. It arced through the air, leaf-shaped blade spinning, before it slammed into the Saxon's back between his shoulder blades.

'What are you waiting for?' said Merlin, scolding Arthur and Kai for their hesitation. 'Kill the Saxon dogs.'

Arthur raced along the bank with Kai alongside him, and the two young Rheged men charged into the fight. But by the time Arthur reached the rope and the screaming horses, the fight was over. Six Saxons lay dead beside a hedge, sprawled on the bank with bloody wounds. The warrior with two swords turned at the sound of Arthur's approach and brought a sword up, its blade coming level with Arthur's throat. He scrambled and stopped himself before he ran onto the bloody sword point. The warrior was fearsome in the full-faced helm, its closed cheekpieces hid his face so that only his eyes showed in the darkness beneath the metal helmet, giving him a demonic appearance. The warrior's head cocked to one side, his breath metallic and loud inside the helmet, but he let his sword fall to his side as Merlin strode along the ditch.

'Balin of the Two Swords, meet Arthur of Caer Ligualid, and Kai ap Ector,' said Merlin. Merlin introduced Kai as the son of Ector, and Arthur was pleased that he did him the honour of not introducing him as a man of nowhere and no father.

'I have fought beside Ector many times,' said Balin, and inclined his helmeted head slightly. 'Welcome to what was once Bernicia, my home, before we lost it to the Saxons and Vortigern's treachery.' He took off his helmet to reveal a lean face framed by a dark beard and close-cropped black hair. A jagged scar cut through the left side of Balin's face, from forehead to jaw. The scar caused his eye to droop, and the skin around the old wound looked puckered and tight, as though it had been stretched too thin across his strong cheekbones.

'Where did you come from?' asked Arthur. He realised he spoke in a whisper, still astounded at the warrior's emergence from the earth.

'We waited, crouched in the bog since before the sun came up,' said Balin with a grin. 'We've been tracking that war band for days. They were part of a much larger Saxon force raiding in the borderlands. They split in two. The smaller group went scouting in the hills, and this group was on its way back to Dun Guaroy. Who is that?' Balin pointed his sword over Arthur's shoulder to where Huell came stumbling towards them, his stump in its sling, the makeshift bandage around it filthy with dark, dried blood. 'I know that man.'

'Huell of Rheged,' said Kai, 'the Saxons took his hand.'

'Huell of Rheged, a champion of your father's war band?'

'Yes, a great warrior.'

'I know him. We fought together many times against the Saxons. Can you help him, Merlin?'

'Of course I can,' Merlin said with an impatient wave of his hand. He eased Arthur, Balin and Kai out of the way with his staff and peered at the fallen Saxons. Balin's men searched them for silver, weapons, food and ale. Three of the Saxons' horses had fled, but the remaining three stood in nearby fields cropping at the grass as though nothing had happened on that late spring morning. 'Are any of them alive?'

'All dead.'

'Warriors,' said Merlin with a sigh. 'Full of bravery and courage, but with heads as empty as a gambler's purse. I wanted to question one.'

Balin shrugged. 'We can find more, Lord Merlin. They are as thick in these lands as flies on shit.'

'Yes, well, thank you for that gentle analogy, Balin. Now, Huell, let's get you fixed up. Follow me.' Merlin strode back towards the campfire beneath the oak tree and beckoned Huell to follow him. Huell, however, just stood staring at Balin with glassy eyes, his skin shining white like wax. Kai took Huell by the good arm and led him after Merlin.

'It was as though you and your men appeared from nowhere, conjured by Merlin to kill the Saxons,' said Arthur as Balin took his forearm in the warrior's grip.

'That's Merlin's way, but we knew the Saxons would come for you. We saw them from the clifftop overlooking the bay. We'd followed their tracks from the hills but came too late to intervene in your fight on the beach. You had better help your friend.' Balin jutted his chin to where Merlin crouched by the fire, and Kai helped Huell sit against the oak tree's roots.

Arthur went to join them, leaving Balin and his men to search the dead for anything of value. As he walked, Arthur's head swam with the events of that morning. He had met Merlin, the most famous druid in

Britain, and had thought that Merlin had worked deep magic before his very eyes, when instead it was nothing more than a cunning ambush. The warp and weft of that ambush stuck in Arthur's throat like a fish bone. If Merlin and Balin had watched the Saxon war band since the fight on the beach, then they had used Arthur, Kai and Huell as bait for a trap. It was all too much to take in. A druid, a two-sworded warrior Arthur had never heard of, and a slaughtered Saxon war band, all before he had properly woken up.

'Hold him down,' Merlin said, pointing at Huell. Merlin wrapped the hem of his cloak around his hand and grabbed the handle of the knife he had placed into the flames before the fight. It came out glowing a fierce red, and Merlin nodded, satisfied with the red-hot blade. He shifted to Huell and reached for his bloody wrist, but Huell flinched away from the druid, and despite his weakened state, he was still too strong for Kai to hold alone. Merlin tutted. 'Grab him, I said!'

Arthur sank to his knees and grabbed Huell around the shoulder, but the big man understood what Merlin intended to do, and he jerked and thrashed, too strong for even Arthur and Kai together.

'Very well, then. I shall have to do everything myself. You two boys are as weak as kittens. We shall need to toughen you up. Try to keep him still.' Merlin shoved the knife back into the flames and came towards Huell slowly, his head and neck twisting like the undulating movements of a serpent. He made a deep humming noise in his throat, just like the chanting of Kadvuz at the Bear Fort. He stared deep into Huell's eyes, and the warrior tried to twist away. 'Hold him, I said!' Merlin roared, making Arthur jump. He and Kai wrestled with Huell and held him still, and Merlin's eyes locked with Huell's. The druid's eyes were grey, strange like the sky after a storm, and they went wide as he captured Huell's gaze. Merlin hummed his guttural rumble, and it grew louder, like a fearsome thundering song. After a short time, Huell went slack and lay back still, eyes still focused on Merlin's.

'You can leave him now,' said Merlin, breaking off his strange humming. 'Close your eyes, Huell, rest. You won't wake until I wake you. Do you hear me?'

Huell nodded and then his eyelids closed slowly as the warrior fell into a deep sleep. Merlin took the fisherman's coarse wrapping from Huell's wrist and tutted at the ragged stump. Arthur had to look away from the grey-brown flesh, which looked like rotten meat. It stank of foulness, and there was white bone amid the bloody, crusted filth. Merlin shook his head, mumbling under his breath. He took a small skin from his belt and poured water over Huell's wrist. Then he took a small knife and sliced away the corrupted flesh around Huell's wound. If Arthur hadn't been so hungry, he would have vomited, but Merlin worked quickly, confidently and efficiently. He seemed satisfied with his work and reached again for the fire-heated knife. Merlin took the knife, its blade too hot to look upon, and Arthur turned away again as Merlin pressed the searing iron to Huell's wrist. The wound sizzled and spat as Merlin sealed it closed. Arthur stood and stepped back from the foul stench of it, and Merlin slathered the burned flesh in honey and then wrapped it with a length of clean linen from a pouch at his belt. As Merlin searched beneath his cloak, Arthur noticed the druid carried many small leather purses tied to his black leather belt, and Arthur wondered what strange items the famous Merlin carried with him on the march.

Balin kicked out the remnants of the fire and scattered the embers into the bog. They eased Huell's unconscious body over the back of a captured Saxon horse and marched west towards the distant hills. Merlin strode at the front of the group with Balin of the Two Swords, whilst Arthur and Kai marched in the middle. Kai held the bridle of the horse which carried Huell. Ten of Balin's warriors marched in front of Arthur and ten behind as they left the slaughtered band of Saxons.

'I can't believe that's actually Merlin,' said Kai as they trudged through a field of wheat. A smile split his handsome face, and he shook his head in disbelief.

'For a moment back there, I thought he had conjured those warriors from the pit of Annwn,' said Arthur.

'I know. And then how he calmed Huell and put him to sleep. Lunete will never believe us.'

'The warriors weren't magic, though. Balin and Merlin tracked the Saxons, so they didn't just appear from nowhere.'

'Yes, but what were they doing in Lloegyr in the first place? Wasn't Merlin exiled to Ynys Môn after the Great War?'

'So they say. It was good luck on our part that they arrived when they did, anyway. Or we'd be dead on the end of Saxon spears by now.'

'Did Merlin tell you where we are going?'

'No, just that we would head west for now, before turning north. That was it.'

'We could ask Merlin and Balin to help with our quest. With their numbers, we have a chance of finding Princess Guinevere.'

'It was Merlin who sent Kadvuz to King Urien. So, Merlin knows of our quest, and he knew who we were with no introduction.'

'So, our quest hasn't been forsaken, after all. Nyfed, Kadored and the rest didn't die in vain if we go on and finish what we started.'

'Father warned to be careful of Merlin, that he is full of cunning and trickery. We must be cautious, Kai. We know nothing of this Balin and his warriors. What are they doing in Lloegyr? Why aren't they fighting along-side the army of Rheged and Gododdin against Octha, Ida and the Saxon horde?'

'I don't know, Arthur. But sometimes you worry too much. You over-think things. We were lost and defeated, but now we travel with brave warriors and a legendary druid. We should talk with Merlin and Balin about our quest and see if they will join us.'

'Aye, we'll see,' said Arthur. He marched towards the black hills with his thought cage full of conflicting thoughts. Kai was right in that it was lucky that Merlin and Balin had found them, but what were they doing so deep in Lloegyr in the first place, and hungered to know more of Balin and his war band.

Arthur remembered Ector's warning about Merlin the druid, and though the old man seemed friendly so far, he was steeped in legend, and many men blamed Merlin for losing so much of Britain during the Great War. Arthur wasn't familiar with the details and had never thought to ask. But all the old stories sang or chanted by the travelling bards and scops spoke of Merlin's magical cunning, of King Gorlois of Kernow, of Uther the Pendragon, King of Dumnonia, of Ambrosius Aurelianus, Ector, Igraine, Urien, and the war with Vortigern. Arthur let those worries rattle around and take form in his mind, and he followed Merlin the druid and Balin of the Two Swords across Lloegyr, understanding that his world had changed. The simple days at Caer Ligualid were behind him, and he marched into an uncertain future full of fear but wild with possibility and adventure.

9

The marching column reached the foothills just as the sun set beyond the high black mountains. Arthur had marched all day through pastures filled with freshly shorn sheep, and fields heavy with spring crops. A thin-limbed man in simple woollen clothes and hollow cheeks waited for them beside a shallow dyke, and Balin tossed the farmer a pouch which chinked as he caught it. The farmer nodded, clambered onto a sad-faced pony and rode lazily away.

'A local farmer. We pay him for his silence,' said a black-cloaked warrior when he noticed the puzzled look on Arthur's face.

They marched over an escarpment which rose sharply from the farm-land, its white rock stark compared to the lush greenery of Bernicia's fields and meadows. A deep cave lay tucked away behind the rocks and sharp inclines, hidden behind a ravine. The cave mouth was twice as high as a man is tall, and three times as wide. Merlin and Balin marched their war band straight into its cavernous maw, and so Arthur and Kai followed. Arthur shuddered as he entered the gaping mouth, which was as black as a moonless night, and its jagged lip dripped water into small, still pools. The high rocks above echoed with the sound of footsteps, making Arthur feel tiny, like a dwarf in a vast canyon. He sensed as though he had entered a different world, about to venture into the depths of Annwn itself. The gloom swallowed the sides and rear of the cave, while shad-owed alcoves opened wider inside.

Men lit fires using small stacks of firewood already prepared and set for their arrival, and soon the cave glowed with warm firelight, which cast strange shadows upon its glistening, damp walls. Balin's warriors brushed the cave floor clean of debris and stacked their heavy leather breastplates, furs, helmets, spears and other weapons against a wall. As the firelight spread, the cave lost its formidable air and seemed comfortable, almost welcoming. They laid out blankets around the fires and filled cauldrons and spits with chopped meat and vegetables. Soon, their chatter and laughter filled the open space, making it feel like a feasting hall. The smell of roasting meat swamped Arthur's hungry nose, and a man with a long face handed Arthur and Kai a skin of ale, which they shared thirstily.

'We'll rest here tonight,' said the long-faced man. 'Then march out again tomorrow. We use this cave to camp when in this part of our old kingdom. We are safe here in the hills, so eat, drink and rest.'

Arthur thanked the warrior and he and Kai pulled Huell from the horse's back and set his sleeping body next to a small fire. Huell was a big man, and it took both Arthur and Kai to carry his limp body.

'I almost forgot,' said Merlin cheerfully, striding to where Arthur and Kai sat with Huell. Merlin wore only his simple grey tunic and soft doeskin boots. He knelt beside Huell, removed the bandage on his stump, sniffed the wound and nodded appreciatively and then bound it up again. He rolled Huell over, cleaned the wound on his back, and smeared it with an oily poultice. 'Wake,' Merlin said slowly in the deep, rumbling voice he had used by the oak tree. Huell awoke as if someone had slapped him across the face. He stared at Arthur and Kai as though he didn't know them, and then seemed to find himself and sat up, looking around at their new surroundings.

'What happened?' Huell asked, his voice groggy.

'I have healed you, Huell of Rheged. You're welcome. Now, eat and drink because we march north tomorrow.'

'March where?' Arthur asked.

Merlin frowned at him, surprised at the question. 'We must find a Saxon who knows about this fortress Ida has built atop Dun Guaroy and put him to question. We can't rescue Princess Guinevere if we don't know precisely where to look. She is inside that fortress somewhere. The old fort on that headland was not in good repair, which I imagine the dead former king regrets now as he rots beneath the soil. Ida, however, is a cunning dog and so we can expect his new fortification to be formidable indeed. We must know what awaits us there. Don't be a fool, boy.' Merlin wagged a long finger at Arthur and raised one eyebrow. 'You must have your wits about you. We are at war with a fearsome enemy, and with their gods. The Saxons come to replace us, and their gods come to drive ours into oblivion, and by my beard the Christ God has already laid our blessed gods low. The road will be difficult and fraught with danger. So don't ask ridiculous questions and start using that empty head of yours.' Merlin tapped a long finger against Arthur's forehead.

Before Arthur could ask him any more questions, Merlin sprang to his feet like a man half his age and marched into the cave's dark recesses.

'He wears boots,' said Kai.

'What?'

'Merlin. He wears boots. Kadvuz came to Urien's hall barefoot, with two great wolfhounds.'

'What of it?'

'I don't know. Kadvuz seemed more fearsome somehow, more like a druid should be. Merlin is like any of the grandfathers back at Caer Ligualid, but with whiter teeth and a little pricklier. If one druid goes barefoot and had great wolfhounds, shouldn't they all?'

Arthur ignored Kai's question. His brother seemed quite taken with Merlin, Kadvuz and their druidic trickery. Arthur handed Huell the skin of ale, and the warrior took a long pull. Some colour had returned to Huell's face since Merlin had put him to sleep, and Kai gave him a strip of dried beef, which Huell ate hungrily.

'The Saxons who hunted us are dead,' said Arthur, and Huell looked across the cave as he chewed his food, staring at the black-cloaked warriors.

'I know Balin,' Huell said. 'How did he find us?'

'Merlin led Balin and his war band to us,' said Kai, shifting closer to

Huell with excitement in his eyes. 'They sprang from the undergrowth and cut the Saxons down just as they were about to charge into us.'

'I saw that much.'

'They were tracking the Saxons from the hills,' said Arthur in a flat tone, arching his eyebrow at Kai, who spoke as though Merlin had appeared in a puff of smoke and conjured Balin and his black-cloaked warriors from the earth itself. 'Though who Balin is, and what Merlin is doing with him, I do not know.'

'My hand,' said Huell wistfully, staring at his stump. 'What will I do now?'

'You have survived and must carry on. Learn to fight with your other hand.'

Huell stared at Arthur, surprised at his harshness. 'You should have let me die on that beach. I am not the man I was. I cannot return to Caer Ligualid like this.'

'Tell us of Balin?' asked Kai, changing the subject and trying to snap Huell out of his melancholy. A warrior approached with warm cloaks, and two plucked birds for the three men to cook and eat. Arthur thanked him, and Kai draped a heavy woollen cloak about Huell's shoulders as Arthur placed the spitted birds over their fire.

'Balin was a lord of Bernicia,' said Huell, pulling the cloak closer about his shoulders with his good hand and staring into the flames. 'He was a cousin to the old king and owned rich lands in Bernicia. He had a brother, Balan, but as so many in those dark days did, Balin fell afoul of Vortigern's treachery.'

Huell leaned into the fire so that it illuminated the planes of his face, and Arthur and Kai leaned in with him, keen to hear the story of Balin and his lost lands.

'Balin's is a tale of woe.' Huell whispered so that the black cloaks could not hear. 'Balin was a champion to the king of Bernicia, just as Ector is to King Urien. That fox upon their shields was their sigil, just as ours is the bear of Rheged. Deira shared a border with Bernicia and that is where Balin's, and all our sorrows, began. Vortigern was brother to the king of Deira and hungered for its throne. To kill his brother the king and usurp its throne, Vortigern brought ships filled with fearsome Saxon warriors across the narrow sea. He knew them, for Vortigern had fought in Frankia and beyond for the Romans and brought the Saxons back with him from his forays across the sea. Those first Saxons were Roman mercenaries, *bucellari*, and Vortigern brought them home to Britain to win a throne from his older brother, the king of Deira. Once Vortigern killed his brother and stole the throne, King Letan Luyddoc of Gododdin, our King Urien, and Uther of Dumnonia, rose against Vortigern, expecting to put the usurper down quickly. But Vortigern brought more Saxons to our shores to swell his ranks, and their leaders were Hengist and Horsa, names you have heard of and fear.'

'Horsa, who is now king in Kent?' asked Kai.

'The same. Vortigern fought back against the kings of Britain and so unfolded the Great War. Vortigern let his wild Saxons loose upon Bernicia, which they sacked mercilessly. They killed its king and all his family. The invaders put the lush lands of Bernicia to the sword, ravaging and burning them, and turned fair Bernicia into the front line of that war which so shook our island. Balin fought for his king and became a warrior of great renown. But his brother envied Balin's reputation and coveted Balin's fine lands, and so Balan joined with Vortigern. Whilst Balin was away fighting, Balan raided his home, a Roman villa with orchards, fresh streams and rich fields. Balin's own brother raped and killed his wife and butchered his children. He laid waste Balin's lands and when a truce was called at the end of the Great War, Balan retreated deep into Lloegyr to hide from Balin's wrath, and no Briton has seen him since.'

'His own brother?' said Kai incredulously.

'His own brother. So, Balin searches for Balan with a heart full of hate, vengeance and grief. Balin and these few men here must be the last of Bernicia's army, the last remnants of a dead king and his slaughtered people.'

'So, they fight and kill the Saxons where they can.'

'Aye, and forever entreat the other kings of Britain to help them recover what was lost.'

'But why do the kings not unite and lead their armies to recapture Bernicia, Deira, Kent and the rest of Lloegyr?' asked Arthur. The Saxons ruled in Lloegyr, which comprised old Deira, Bernicia and Kent, and had brought vast hordes of warriors across the sea from their homelands. But if each kingdom in Britain united and brought all of their warriors to Lloegyr, then surely, they would outnumber the Saxons and drive them back into the sea.

'Uther is the Pendragon, the king of kings, but so many men died, and there was such horror in the Great War that he and the other kings haven't had the stomach to start a new war. Even when the Pendragon called the kingdoms to arms in the Great War, not all brought their warriors. The men of Powys, Gwynedd, Demetia and more did not come. So, Balin fights on alone with what few warriors he has left. We are not one people. The Britain Merlin, Uther, Urien and others talk of is a dream, we are an island of small kingdoms, each one raids the other for cattle, timber, land and slaves and there are blood feuds stretching back to the dark days when Rome left. Without the empire and its legions, the strongest ruled and weakest suffered and died. The men of Demetia will not fight alongside the men of Rheged or Gwent, whom they hate as much as Balin hates the Saxons. So, you see, Arthur, the world is not as simple as it seems by Ector's hearth in the safety and warmth of Caer Ligualid.'

'And what of Merlin?' asked Kai.

'What of him?'

'Why is he here? Why was he banished? How old is he? The stories say that he was old and grey bearded at the time of the Great War, and that was before we were born.'

'Those are questions for men greater than I, Kai ap Ector. You should ask your father about those days of long ago. I did not fight in the Great War; it was before my time. But Ector was in the thick of it, and I would not talk of the druid behind his back.' Huell glanced at his stump and with his left hand made the sign to ward off evil.

'Merlin and Balin will join our quest for Princess Guinevere,' said Kai, smiling as though he expected Huell to be pleased.

Huell sniffed and raised his stump. 'This entire journey is cursed, if you ask me. Stumbling across Saxons like that in the forest, a princess and her ship captured by Saxons, all our men killed and me unmanned. Then we find Merlin and Balin in the middle of Lloegyr. There are other forces at work here, lads, believe me. We will be fortunate to survive this, or unfortunate in my case. What kind of life remains for me now?'

With that, Huell sat back, swathed in his cloak, and would say no more. Arthur and Kai ate fresh meat and drank ale, and they talked in whispered voices about all the things they had seen since leaving the Bear Fort and remembered the men of their company who had died. Kai was excited, talking as though they had already achieved deeds worthy of reputation and song, but Arthur brooded. All they had done was escape death by the skin of their teeth. The Saxon way of fighting had shocked him, how they formed a wall of shields and used their axes with blades shaped like a man's beard to pull down the Britons' shields, and then hacked at their faces and legs with their seaxes and spears. It was a new way of fighting, different to how the Britons fought with their smaller shields, where battle was more about individual prowess and glory.

Arthur wondered how the Romans had fought. What was it they knew that allowed them to conquer the world, a world which men said stretched far across the narrow sea beyond where Armorica and Frankia lay? He settled down and wondered at such things until his eyes became heavy. Why did the Romans who could build such wonders, and who had brought their laws and their legions to make Britain a glorious place of wealth and peace, leave it so quickly and, in their wake, left a land of rotting wood and thatch, of tribes and wars and suffering? No man had minted a coin since the Romans left, nor made a building of dressed stone or a straight, well-surfaced road. If the Romans were so powerful, what could have forced their withdrawal?

Arthur's thought cage wrestled over the deep matters which had never entered his mind until he had left the Bear Fort. Until the quest began, his life had been simple. Now that he had experienced war, Arthur felt as though a cloak had been lifted from his eyes, enabling him to see and think more clearly. He wondered if there were answers out there to the myriad questions he had and was sure that there were. The Saxon shield Arthur had carried for a time, though heavier than a Briton shield, felt easier to fight with. Just like Ector's description of how the parts of a spear could all be used for attack, the shield functioned in the same way. Its iron boss and rim could smash a man's nose and skull, its linden-wood boards catch an enemy weapon and rip it from his grasp. A wall of shields, each overlapping, and then the second rank overlapping the top edges, would present an unassailable wall to an enemy. Who would charge a wall of wood and iron bristling with spears, swords, axes and knives? His head buzzed like a kicked beehive with such thoughts, and there were more questions than answers in the discoveries he had made. Arthur tried to store his thoughts away, believing they were useful, but unsure what to do with them.

As Arthur and Kai lay down to sleep, Arthur listened to the black-cloaked warriors talk. They spoke, like all warriors did, of their deeds, of the dead and of old fights. They spoke of women they had loved and lost. One man sang a sad song, and the warriors stamped their boots in approval when he finished. Balin sat away from his men, running a whet-stone along the length of his swords, first one and then the other. The other black-cloaked warriors left Balin alone, and Arthur could only wonder at the rage inside a man who had lost his family to his brother's betrayal. Balin's men spoke of the hate they bore the Saxons, the warriors who had come from across the sea to steal their homeland away from them. The black cloaks spoke in memory of brave men who had died in the ceaseless war against the invader and drank to the memory of those fallen warriors. It stirred Arthur's heart to hear the men talk so, and he began to understand the hate they must bear against the invaders who had taken everything from them. He felt immersed in their world. Arthur had killed in battle and fought against Saxons who wanted to kill him. He had met Merlin, and Balin of the Two Swords, and as his eyes closed and sleep came, Arthur wondered what fresh wonders lay ahead of him.

10

Balin led twenty warriors out of the cave in a column of bristling spears, shields and shining helmets. Some of the black cloaks even carried the broad-bladed Saxon axes which Arthur had seen used so effectively by the enemy in battle. Merlin marched at the head of the column beside Balin, his white cloak flowing behind him, his long pack upon his back, and a broad-brimmed hat perched on his head. His amber-topped staff beat marching time on the ground, and they marched north from the cave's hidden safety into the rolling hills of Lloegyr, the lost lands which had once been the kingdom of Bernicia.

Arthur and Kai marched in the column's centre, and injured Huell sullenly rode his Saxon mare behind them. The sky broiled with dark clouds and a warm wind from the south, but no rain fell upon the war band. Gaunt-faced slaves stared at the warriors who traipsed through their master's fields. Men and women in tattered jerkins, with their hair cut brutally short to keep out the lice, busily spread dung across their lord's fields.

The first sign of the enemy came after Balin's men followed a broad river which came down from the mountains in a fast-flowing torrent through reed-banked meanders. The war band marched alongside the river until Balin led them up a gently sloped hill where they looked down upon a sprawling valley. A collection of huts and dwellings gathered about a babbling ford in the river where it slashed through the valley basin. Well-worn cattle paths to and from the river marked the ford, and Arthur stared down at the buildings which were subtly but clearly different to the buildings at Caer Ligualid, the Bear Fort and any of the other Briton settlements he had visited. The buildings in this valley were dug into the ground, high-gabled constructs of timber planking and pointed thatch, with side buildings tacked on to the side for pigs or goats. There were no smoke holes in the thatch, and smoke seeped through the rooftops as though the buildings inside were on fire. There were a dozen dwellings on the near side of the ford, and the place had no ditch, bank or stockade to protect it.

'This place used to belong to a man named Gwrien,' said Balin, standing tall on the hilltop with his shield slung across his back and his two swords set within it so that a hilt poked across each of his shoulders. 'He had a farm there, with a wife, a son, and a daughter who married a lad from the next valley. Their home is gone now, burned and replaced by these Saxon hovels. I do not know what became of Gwrien and his family.' The warriors joined Balin and made a long line across the hilltop facing the Saxon settlement. Arthur and Kai joined them.

'I knew Gwrien,' said a black cloak with a bushy black beard. 'My niece married his cousin.'

'Sound the carnyx,' said Balin. A warrior dropped what Arthur had thought was a spear but was, in fact, a long bronze tube the size and shape of a spear shaft. Another warrior took a leather sack from his back and pulled out a magnificent bronze wolf's head, its mouth agape and snarling. They fixed the wolf's head onto the bronze tube, and a burly warrior lifted the entire long construction above his head. He set his lips to the bottom of the tube and blew. Arthur started at the sound, and Kai grabbed his arm in shock. The carnyx blared fearsomely, undulating and high-pitched like the scream of a mystical beast. The sound filled the valley, and it imbued Balin's men with war-fury as they unslung their shields and readied their spears. Folk came from the Saxon dwellings to see what kind of monster could make such a stomach-churning sound. A line of warriors emerged, men in tunics and wrapped leggings with flaxen hair. They carried large Saxon shields, spears and axes, and Arthur counted fifteen men.

'Kill them all,' Balin bellowed at his men. 'They stole these lands and killed our people. Kill them all and burn their stinking hovels to the ground.'

'All but one,' Merlin yelled, shaking his rune staff. 'Keep one for me, keep one alive for me!'

Balin's usually calm face was now contorted into a rictus of hate. He drew his two swords from across each shoulder and let out a furious roar, almost as terrifying as the call of the carnyx. Balin charged down the hillside, and his men followed behind him like a spear with Balin at the point. They spread out like a flock of birds on the wing, and Arthur and Kai followed with weapons in hand. The Saxons made their shield wall and Arthur's stomach clenched as he raced down the hillside, uncertain about attacking a settlement which seemed so peaceful but caught up in the black cloaks' vengeful fury.

'For Bernicia!' the black cloaks called as they charged, and Kai took up their war cry, spear in one hand and a shield in the other. Arthur carried his seax and his long knife, for he had no shield. There had been only one spare at the cave, and Kai took it. Shrieking and cries of anguish from the buildings beyond the Saxon shields mixed with the din of the charge. The terrible sound came from howling women and children who saw a war band of armed, furious warriors charging at them, slashing through their peaceful day like a knife through flesh.

Balin did not break stride as he approached the line of shields. Where Arthur saw only an impossible obstacle, Balin charged fearlessly for the enemy centre. There was no delay in the attack, no time required for Balin's men to find their courage or become drunk with ale before the charge, as was often the case with Ector's warriors. It seemed the black cloaks must crash against that solid wall like the tide against rocks, smashed and ruined against impossible hardness. But at the last possible moment, when it seemed he would shatter upon the Saxon shields, Balin leapt into the air. He jumped like a spring lamb, high into the air, and crashed into the top of the Saxon shields and the men behind them with unstoppable force. It was breathtaking. Arthur had never seen such bravery or daring before, and as Balin disappeared behind the enemy shield wall, Arthur thought Balin must surely die. The black cloaks followed their leader, pouring into the hole he created in the shield wall like rats. They formed a wedge and punched into the gap, driving through the enemy, a vicious wedge of iron, leather and wood.

Steel blades rang together, iron crunched into wooden shields, men roared their belligerence and screamed in terror as the war band came together in a terrible crash. Arthur slammed his shoulder into an enemy shield and narrowly avoided a spear point aimed at his face. He danced backwards, expecting the seax which came snaking out beneath the enemy shield rim. Arthur had learned his lesson in his last fight with the Saxons, so he kept his shoulder pressed against the shield, but his groin was well away from the seax bite beneath it. Kai crashed his shield into the next man and shrieked as a spear slashed the edge of his upper arm. Arthur shoved with his shoulder, and when he felt the Saxon push back, he suddenly released the pressure so that the Saxon stumbled forward a pace. The enemy instinctively dropped his shield by a handsbreadth in case he fell, and Arthur glimpsed his blond bearded face, pockmarked and red nosed, and he slashed his knife at it, slicing through lips, teeth and skin. The Saxon fell back, and Arthur rolled across his shield to follow Balin's men towards the gap.

The Britons split the Saxon shield wall in two, causing their wall to crumble into the Britons' way of fighting as men squared off into individual combat. One war band filled with hate for the men who had invaded and stolen their land, the other maddened with desire to protect their families who cowered twenty paces away at the river ford. A bald man surged at Arthur with an axe, swinging the weapon so wildly that he was as much of a danger to his own men as the black cloaks. Arthur let the weapon sing past him, leaning away from its murderous scythe, and the Saxon ran onto Arthur's seax blade, the point punching hard into the man's stomach. Fiery blood pulsed over Arthur's hand, and he ripped the blade free, kicked the axeman in the groin and cut his throat with his long knife. Kai fought with a big Saxon, both men trading blows cautiously from behind their shields. Arthur sheathed his seax at the small of his back and picked up the dead man's axe. He ran to Kai, and without hesitating, he chopped the axe overhand. The bearded blade slammed into the big Saxon's shield rim and Arthur hauled it down, and the instant the shield dipped, he rammed his long knife into the Saxon's gullet. He stared at Arthur with surprised blue eyes and Arthur pulled his blade free. The battle calm had descended on him, the heightened sense of war pulsing through his veins like fire. He felt alive and strong. It was as though he was as fast as a hare and everyone else was slow like they fought in a bog.

A black cloak fell to one knee, beaten down by a Saxon shield, and Arthur threw his captured axe. The blade turned over and over in the air and then crunched into the Saxon's chest to send him sprawling on the grass. Balin fought with his two blades, seemingly uninjured or subdued by his wild charge, and his twin blades cut high and low, slicing legs, necks, faces, and slamming into shields. Arthur looked for a new enemy to fight, but the skirmish was already over. Four Saxons backed away towards their homes and families. They dropped their weapons and warily raised their hands to show that they surrendered. The rest of the Saxons lay dead or injured. Three black cloaks were down, one with his throat laid open, and two others writhing in pain.

Balin stalked amongst the Saxon wounded, stabbing down with his blood-soaked blades into their throats and hearts. 'Kill them all! Kill, kill, kill!' he roared and pointed at the settlement. His warriors set off again, streaming towards the houses, and Arthur took off after them. *I can't let them kill the women and children.* Ector had always told him that a warrior followed a code of honour, and never harmed women, children or the elderly. But what could he do? How could one man stop a war band from their slaughter? Arthur reached the surrendering Saxon warriors just as a black cloak cut one down with his spear.

'No!' Arthur said and blocked a thrust at a second Saxon with his knife. The black cloak snarled at him, his eyes as dead and hungry as a feral animal. 'Merlin said to let one live.' The black cloak grunted and set off towards the houses. Arthur guarded the remaining three Saxons; Kai joined him, and they turned away from the slaughter beside the ford. The screams and cries of that afternoon burned into Arthur's mind like the hot iron Merlin used to seal Huell's wrist. It sickened him, and the murder lasted ten times as long as the battle. Balin's men burned the houses, barns, and slaughtered everything that moved in the Saxon village, even the pigs and dogs.

'My father would never allow such a slaughter,' said Kai. The three prisoners cowered between Arthur and Kai, their eyes streaming with tears for the dead relatives, but unable to do anything for fear of Balin and the wrath of his black-cloaked Britons.

'Ector is not a killer of women and children, and nor are we,' said Arthur, and then set his jaw as Merlin came striding across the battlefield with his white cloak streaming behind him.

'You kept me one,' Merlin called cheerfully, 'well done, well done. Perhaps your head isn't as full of rocks as I thought it was.' He stared down at the three Saxons with a puzzled look on his face. 'There are three miserable Saxons there, Arthur, and I only require one.'

'We shouldn't butcher them,' Arthur said, his voice weak and unconvincing. Who was he to stand up to the mighty Merlin?

'Ha!' Merlin scoffed. 'You'll learn. Before you return to Rheged, you will see the face of war, young warrior. This is but one side of it. Had you seen what the Saxons did to Balin's lands, and to Bernicia, you would neither question nor deny their revenge. This is why we fight the Saxons. Before they came to our shores, Britain had not seen death and suffering on such a scale since the Romans left our land a pit of lawless desolation. War breeds slaughter. Balin is what the Saxons have made him. He is a child of war, an instrument of the war god. Balin's thirst for Saxon blood will never be quenched, not until all the Saxons are dead and gone from Britain.'

'You are no better than us,' said a heavily accented voice through gritted teeth. Arthur glanced down to see that it was one of the surrendered Saxons who spoke. He was young, of an age with Arthur and Kai with a fuzz of golden beard around a broad face. 'You *Wealas* are the baby killers, the rapers and killers.'

'Well, well,' said Merlin, scratching his beard. 'A Saxon who speaks our tongue. Mark him, Arthur and Kai, mark his words. *Wealas* is the Saxons' name for us Britons, but it is also their word for slave, which tells you what they think of the people whose land they have stolen. I'll take the sullen one.' Merlin pointed his staff at an older man who wore fox fur around his shoulders above a leather breastplate. 'The rest of them can die.'

'Let this man live,' Arthur blurted without thinking. He had no right to stand up to Merlin, but something inside him rankled at the impending slaughter, and he would save one life if he could.

Merlin fixed Arthur with an icy stare, a wry smile playing at the corner of his mouth. 'Very well, young warrior. Keep your pup, but the rest die.'

'You saved my life,' said the young Saxon to Arthur. 'So, my life is yours now. I must be your man until the debt is repaid.'

Merlin cackled. 'Your first follower, Arthur of Nowhere, watch he doesn't slit your throat in the night.'

'What is your name?' asked Arthur.

'Redwulf,' said the Saxon.

'How is it you can speak our tongue?'

'My mother was a *Wealas*.'

That surprised Arthur, but he beckoned the man to rise. First, however, he knelt and took Arthur's hand in both of his and swore a solemn oath in the Saxon tongue. Then he rose and fell in beside Arthur. Kai stared at the Saxon as though he had just crawled from the pit of hell, whilst Merlin dragged the sullen Saxon prisoner he had picked away by the hair. Arthur shuddered to think what Merlin would do when he questioned the prisoner, but thankfully, Merlin took him behind an as yet unburned barn and so spared Arthur whatever horrors he would use to extract the information he required.

Balin came striding from the burning settlement, his two swords held low, blades thick with dark blood and his face a mask of grim determination. Behind him, thatch caught fire and the Saxon buildings roared into towering bonfires, sending plumes of smoke into the sky. Balin had chosen not to wear his full-faced helmet for the slaughter, resulting in soot and blood smearing his cheeks, as well as splashes of blood across his arms and chest.

'These men have surrendered,' Arthur stuttered as Balin noticed the Saxon men and marched towards them. 'This one has sworn an oath to be my man.'

Balin didn't break stride and swung his two swords cross ways across one another and sliced the third Saxon's head clean off. Arthur jumped back involuntarily as the kneeling man toppled sideways and his head landed in the grass pumping blood, eyes open and staring straight at Arthur.

'All Saxons must die,' Balin said in a hard, bitter voice. 'You can keep your slave if Merlin allows it, but next time, do not hesitate. Any man left alive now will have a spear in his hand within days. So, kill them all.'

'Even the women and children? This is not the honourable way of the warrior,' said Arthur, and instantly regretted it.

'Last time I looked, Balin leads here, not Arthur. A child today is a warrior at manhood, and a woman can birth more Saxons. All Saxons must die. Do not speak to me of it, boy, until you have seen what I have seen. You speak of honour? Where was honour and the warrior's way the day my brother and his Saxons came to my home? Imagine, if you can, the love a man holds for his children. My children were my everything. The sun rose and set with them. They filled my heart with joy, and you will only truly understand when you have children of your own, but there is no greater bond, no feeling like the love of a parent for his little ones, they are part of man's very soul. The Saxons ripped that away with greed, malice and brutal savagery. They dashed my children's heads in and tore their little bodies with blades as though they were nought but sacks of meat. My wife, my most precious beloved, was raped and burned and left for me to find. That sight became etched into my skull forever, and not a moment passes when I cannot see their ravaged, dead bodies in the place I once called home. My hate for the Saxons is as white-hot as iron in a forge. They came here from across the sea and did that to me and my family, so I will kill as many of them as I can until they are gone, or I am dead. Never talk to me again of this. I talk only of war, only of where to march, which enemies to kill, where to find supplies and where to camp. Nothing else matters.' Balin shook with rage, and Arthur bowed his head, shocked by Balin's reasoning and cowed by his hate.

Balin left Arthur and Kai standing with Redwulf. The three young men exchanged nervous glances, unsure what to say in the wake of Balin's words. Arthur couldn't imagine the suffering Balin and his men had endured, their families slaughtered, and their lands stolen. The war with the Saxons was different for them. It was a thing of vengeance and hate, where for Rheged and the rest of the kingdoms of Britain it was a war to keep the Saxons out, to protect their borders and hope that the fate of Bernicia would not be their own. Arthur was ashamed to have challenged Balin about honour and the warrior's code, and saw then that Balin fought a different war, a war that all of Britain should fight if they wanted to avoid Bernicia and Deira's doom.

Merlin emerged from behind the barn. He walked with his hands clasped behind his back, deep in thought. Arthur peered over Merlin's shoulder but could see no sign of the Saxon he had taken to question. 'We must leave this place,' Merlin said to no one in particular. 'Dun Guaroy lies two days from here, and we must find more warriors on the way.'

'What did he say, Lord Merlin?' Kai called after Merlin.

'Who, the Saxon? He told me of a fortress of timber built upon a high crag. Not yet finished. Half the men from this village, along with the rest of the Saxons in Bernicia, were called in by Ida to help with its construction. He provided some useful information about the buildings and layout before the end.'

There had been no screams from Merlin's questioning, and Merlin showed no signs of blood upon his white cloak. Though Arthur saw a black cloak emerge from the same direction with a bloody axe in his fist. Arthur had more questions as they left the burning settlement behind. He could not understand the slaughter, though clearly Balin and his men thought it justified. Even Merlin seemed comfortable with the deaths, but the old druid was strange and hard to understand. Merlin was one moment jovial, and a heartbeat later terrifying and powerful.

The war band followed the river's meander through cattle pastures and Arthur turned to glance at the towering plume of smoke which twisted high into the sky behind them. It would surely be a sign, or a message, to all the Saxon warriors in old Bernicia that a Briton war band was loose in their lands, burning and killing. It was another mystery which Arthur chewed over as he marched with a Saxon shield slung across his back, his seax and knife at his belt and a leaf-shaped spear in his hand. If they were to get to Dun Guaroy alive, find a way into the fortress and rescue Princess Guinevere, surely it would be better to do so without a host of Saxons pursuing them? Balin and his men were both skilled and fierce, but they were only twenty warriors in a land full of Saxons. The Saxon King Ida, who had wrested the land from Balin's people, and Octha, the warlord with his three thousand warriors fresh from the Saxon homeland, were out there somewhere.

Arthur kept his eyes on the hills, expecting a wild Saxon horde to come howling from the east or north to crush him and his new companions, but they marched onwards, deeper into the heart of Lloegyr, where the vicious enemy waited.

11

Merlin led the war band northwards, and the river brought them to a farm with a large hall, a barn and a pen full of bleating sheep waiting to be sheared. Balin's men killed the Saxon farmer and set free four slaves who cowered in a cow byre. Two of those pitiful people were Britons, and they wept with surprised joy when Balin put a spear in their hands. They were not warriors, but simple men who had lived in Bernicia before the fall but seemed eager to strike a blow against their Saxon overlords. The remaining slaves were middle-aged women with lank hair and hands made raw by hard work. One was a Gododdin woman captured in a Saxon raid when she was a girl, and the other was an Irish slave who could not remember a time when she was free. Balin sent the women westwards, away from Lloegyr, with plenty of food and ale for their journey. The war band was no place for women, and though they were afraid of travelling alone in the wild, they scampered away from the farm and on into the fields beyond.

The war band spent the night at the farm. They shared a hock of ham found hanging in the rafters to dry, and there was plenty of wheat and barley, a wheel of strong cheese and a crock of goat's milk. Balin and Merlin talked alone in a dark corner of the farmhouse, and the rest of the black cloaks gathered around the hearth fire to take their evening meal. Arthur and Kai found a corner of their own, still not confident enough to sit with the war band, and not asked to do so. Arthur offered Redwulf a share of his food, which he accepted thankfully. Though one of the black cloaks cuffed the Saxon hard around the head as he left the barn to piss, and the blow was hard enough to make the Saxon dizzy. Arthur didn't complain about Redwulf's treatment. Balin's men were kind enough, and he knew better than to provoke their anger towards the Saxon. The black cloaks shared food and ale with Arthur and Kai and mostly left them alone, except for the hateful glances they shot at Redwulf whenever he crossed their path.

'When did you come to Britain?' Kai asked Redwulf. Kai drank from a skin of ale and passed it to Arthur, who took a long pull and then finished his share of the smoked ham. To drink water was to risk stomach sickness or worse, so all men drank ale or mead.

'I was born here,' said Redwulf with a shrug. 'My father came across the sea with King Ida, and when he settled, I was born to his slave woman.'

'Did you have a family at the place we burned?' asked Arthur.

'My uncle and his family. I helped with the farm work in spring.'

'Your uncle is not a warrior?'

'He was, but now he is, or was, a farmer.' A sadness came over Redwulf then, quickly replaced by a clenching of his jaw and a hard look which passed quickly.

'And you are a warrior, not a farmer?' asked Kai.

'Aye, with my father's war band. We serve King Ida but are not now at war, so I help with the farm.'

'Have you killed Britons?' asked Arthur.

'I have, but only raiders and murderers.' Redwulf cast a frown towards the black cloaks and then stared belligerently at Arthur. 'This is our land now. Woden made it so, and we shall hold it until the end of days. More of our people come, and soon we shall fill this entire island. It is the will of the gods.'

'Who says it's the will of the gods?' asked Kai, a tinge of anger in his voice.

'Our holy men. Woden and Thunor honour us with victory. How

could we have won so many battles if the gods do not will that it should be so?'

'Your gods are not our gods. How can you be sure yours are the most powerful?' said Kai with a deep frown.

'Many of you *Wealas* worship the nailed god. He is a god of peace, and that is why you lose. Ours are gods of war. They demand it, reward us for it. If I kill enough *Wealas* in battle, I shall earn my place in Woden's hall and live forever as a warrior in the afterlife.'

'And yet now you serve me,' said Arthur, 'so you won't kill any more Britons. If it comes to it, which it surely shall, will you kill your own warriors when we face them in battle?'

Redwulf shrugged as though the question was nothing to him. 'Yes. I have made my oath, and I will fight for you now. It matters not who I kill. Woden cares only that I fight well and die in battle. Then I can go to Woden's hall. We Saxons fight each other all the time. Perhaps one day Ida and Octha will fight each other to see who is the strongest and should be king.'

'We Britons fight each other too.' Which was a pity, Arthur thought. The kingdoms of Powys, Demetia and Dyfed fought each other, and they fought with Dumnonia, Kernow and Elmet in never-ending cattle raids, or fights for salt farms, woodland, copper and tin mines, even imported wine. Each kingdom alone was too small to defeat the Saxons, but how could they unite when such petty fighting erupted every summer across Britain? 'What do you know of Ida and Octha?'

Redwulf smiled and retied his golden hair at the nape of his neck. 'Ida is old now but was once a great fighter. He came to these shores as a mere warrior, called here to fight for your king Vortigern, and became a king. Octha, too, will make himself a king somewhere. He is the second son of a king in our homeland, but there is constant war there with the Franks and the Romans, so he comes here to make his legend.'

'Somewhere?'

'Here.' Redwulf cast his arm about the farmhouse, and shrugged. 'Perhaps west, north or south.'

'Vortigern is not our king,' said Kai, becoming increasingly annoyed with Redwulf and the lazy way he spoke about the Saxon conquest, which had caused so much suffering.

'He was king somewhere though, no? Now he belongs to Horsa.'

'Vortigern is dead, and no man mourned his passing.'

'Perhaps he is, perhaps not. But Octha is here, and so war is coming.'

'And we shall be victorious this time,' said Kai, daring Redwulf with his eyes, challenging the Saxon to contradict him.

Arthur left them at the farmhouse and went outside to piss. It was a clear night, and the sky shone with countless stars and bright moon as though the heavens peered at the world of men and Arthur went behind the building to relieve himself. No sooner had he started, than a figure came about the wall and surprised him.

'Apologies, young friend,' said Balin, raising his hand. 'I did not mean to startle you.'

Arthur said nothing and carried on, keeping his eyes down as Balin ambled further along the wall to relieve himself.

'Be careful what you say to your new Saxon friend.'

Arthur glanced at Balin, but the warrior stared straight ahead, and not at Arthur. 'What was that, lord?' Arthur did Balin the honour of calling him a lord, though the warrior no longer held any lands and was a mere war band leader. But the title seemed appropriate, given his fame and reputation.

'I said careful what you say to the Saxon. He might sneak off when we aren't watching and bring news of our location and intentions to his people.'

'He has sworn an oath, Lord Balin. I do not think he will flee.'

'An oath, you say? I have known many an oathbreaker, lad, and you have only known the Saxon for a day. He only gave you that oath to save his skin. So, watch him closely.'

'I will, lord.'

'It would be a shame if he slipped away. I'd have to bring the dog to heel.'

Arthur shuddered at Balin's bitter words and imagined waking to find Redwulf lying in the cow byre with his throat cut. The warrior finished his piss and made his way back to the farmhouse. But halfway there, he paused and turned back to Arthur.

'You fight well, lad,' he said. 'But if you want to be a leader of men in the war to come, you must harden your heart.'

'War?'

'Yes, the war with the Saxons. Why else do you think we are here? Merlin rouses Britain to take back what was lost.'

'I thought we were here to rescue a princess?'

'Of course we are. But in doing so, we must attack Ida's stronghold. That will stir the Saxons from their victorious slumber. So, you will need your skill with weapons, young Arthur, if you are to survive what must come.'

'But my father... I mean Ector and Owain ap Urien, march to protect their borders, not to fight a war?'

'Urien and Letan of Gododdin know what is coming. Ector and Owain guard Rheged's border in case the Saxons attack there. But there will be war, lad, whether it's in Rheged or elsewhere. Merlin is loose, and war drums beat across Britain. Why do you think Merlin and I march together if it is not to bring war and death to the Saxons? I hunt Saxons, and my traitor brother who fights with them, and Merlin wants the fight. Britain needs the fight.'

'We shall attack the Saxons in Lloegyr?'

'We shall draw them out, lad,' Balin said, and grinned wolfishly. He turned and continued to the farmhouse. 'We shall draw them out like wolves who scent an unprotected flock,' Balin shouted over his shoulder.

Balin woke them early the next morning, when the sun had just begun to warm the land and the war band stirred with groans and yawns. They each had a sup of ale and broke their night fast with leftover meat and cheese. Merlin led them from the Saxon farmhouse, striding with his amber-tipped staff, his pack slung over his shoulder, and wearing his wide-brimmed hat. He led them north-east towards a vast stretch of woodland, and they reached the edges of its ash and elm trees before the sun was halfway across the sky. Balin sent scouts into the forest, six men to spread out into a wide line and pick their way lithely through the trees whilst the rest of the war band waited for the scouts to return.

The first two scouts returned after a short time, red-faced and sweating from running through the forest.

'Saxons, lord,' said the first scout, a lean man with a single, thick eyebrow spanning the width of his face. 'Approaching the woodland from the north.'

The scout spoke to Balin, but the entire war band bristled with excitement at the prospect of battle.

'How many?' asked Balin.

'Two score,' said the scout, and the men instantly lost their brief thrill. 'The rest of our scouts are watching them.'

'Twice our number,' said Kai, shaking his head because it was too many to fight. Kai was always ready to fight, he always had been, and the son of Ector was as dismayed by the news as Balin's men, because only a fool would attack a larger enemy war band.

'So, our pyre of smoke worked,' said Merlin cheerfully. 'More Saxon war bands will come this way, mustering from their stolen farms, villages and strongholds.'

'But we are only twenty men, Lord Merlin?' said a black cloak named Dewi, giving voice to what every man thought.

Merlin leant towards Dewi and fixed him with a thoughtful stare. 'Then it's a good job you warriors have a druid to do your thinking for you then, isn't it? Inside that woodland is another force of Britons. They will meet us at the *dubhglas,* the black water deep inside the forest. A place of the old days, where our forefathers gathered in the days before the Romans came. The black water, where spirits live beneath the surface and elves stir in the trees, is one of the many places in our lands where the gods are close to us, where they hear our prayers and answer our call. Bors awaits us at the *dubhglas,* Bors the champion of Gododdin has come with thirty spears and we shall join our forces together!'

The black cloaks cheered and clapped one another on the back, for all men knew of Bors of Gododdin. He was a warrior, as famed for his prowess as Ector. Bors was the leader of King Letan's forces, who were at constant war with the Saxons and the Scots in Lothian and beyond. Gododdin was the kingdom to Bernicia's north and isolated from the rest of Britain. Rheged and Gododdin had been allies back to the days when Rome left.

Balin nodded to Merlin with stern determination, and he set off into the woodland with his men flowing behind him. Balin seemed like the only man in his war band not surprised by Merlin's words, and Arthur was sure that the druid and the warrior had this planned all along. The firing of the Saxon homestead, the march deep into Lloegyr, it all seemed clear to Arthur that it was all born of Merlin's cunning and as he ducked beneath boughs heavy with green spring leaves, he wondered how deep the warp and weft of Merlin's scheme ran.

The rest of Balin's scouts met the war band as they marched through dense woodland but reported no other sign of the enemy, though they confirmed what Merlin had said, that a force of Gododdin men waited for Balin beside a wide black pool. Kai hurried ahead of Arthur, so excited was he to see Bors and the Gododdin warriors that he left Arthur alone with Redwulf, who marched in sullen silence. Arthur expected the Saxon's usually easy manner had been shaken by the prospect of more Briton warriors in Saxon lands, and the chance that he might meet his countrymen in battle that very day. That chance had not bothered Redwulf in the slightest in the farmhouse, but now as he marched with Britons bristling with spears, axes, knives and swords it all became suddenly more real, and terrifying, Arthur thought.

The forest parted to reveal moss-covered stones, and a wide black pool the colour of jet. Its waters were eerily still, and around it willow trees stretched over the surface, reaching towards the still water like grasping fingers coated in green lichen. The clearing and the pool exuded a strangeness, with a thick gloom surrounding them. Ancient trees formed a dense overhead canopy, shielding the water from the sun, as their branches intertwined and mingled to create a roof resembling the highest hall. The small hairs on the back of Arthur's neck prickled as he emerged onto the *dubhglas'* bank. Reeds grew there, and lilies floated on the surface like a draped cloak. Lush green grass covered the bank and Arthur could almost imagine an old god like Maponos or Manawydan emerging from the pool to begin one of their adventures.

'Merlin!' boomed a deep, loud voice, and from the trees strode the biggest man Arthur had ever seen. He was head and shoulders taller than any man in the clearing and twice as broad across the shoulder. He wore a leather breastplate across his chest, and pieces of chain mail draped around his round shoulders and thick neck. The enormous man had a Saxon axe tucked into his belt, and a completely shaved head above a round, heavily scarred face. 'I told my men that if we were late, you would turn them into toads, or muck nuts hanging from a sheep's arse. I have never seen the stinking bastards march so fast!'

'Lord Bors, well met,' said Merlin with a mischievous grin on his face. A band of warriors emerged behind the monstrous warrior, and each carried a shield painted with the stag of Gododdin and a long spear. They bowed their heads reverently at Merlin, men in leather, padded woollen jerkins, grizzled beards and long, braided hair.

'We've been here for two days, and we ran out of food this morning. My belly thinks my throat's been cut and my men can't catch anything in this bloody forest worth eating. I hope you've brought some cheese with, or some meat. Cheese would be better. Ah!' Bors exclaimed and opened his arms wide. 'Balin of the Two Swords, you miserable bastard. I never thought I'd be so happy to see your serious face. It looks like a slapped arse, but by the gods, we need your sword.' For a moment, Arthur thought Bors would gather Balin into an enormous bear hug, but they slapped their arms together in the warrior's grip, each grasping the other's fore-arm. The black cloaks and the Gododdin men greeted each other warmly. Bors shouted constantly, greeting Balin's men by name where he knew it, calling out a brave deed or a memory of the man's relatives. He greeted Huell as an old comrade and made light of his lost hand. The warriors laughed and grinned at the huge champion and his brash warmth, his presence lifting their spirits like a barrel of mead.

'Why have the men of Gododdin come?' Arthur asked Merlin as the old man smiled mirthlessly at the warriors, who now numbered fifty.

'Because the Saxons captured Gawain, prince of Gododdin, and imprisoned him inside Dun Guaroy with our noble princess.'

'Prince Gawain is a Saxon captive?'

'Just so, young Arthur. King Ida captured him on a raid and plans to ransom him back to his father. Only I got to King Letan first, and so we shall free his son when we free Princess Guinevere.' Merlin winked at Arthur, and he wondered again at the druid's deep cunning, and how these events which had so shaken Arthur's life and awakened him to a world of war, revenge, druids and Saxons, seemed to shift in Merlin's palm like a weaver's needle. It was as though everything which had unfolded since Huell's war band had accidentally stumbled across the Saxons had been at Merlin's design.

'Like Ector said,' said Huell in Arthur's ear. 'Beware of Merlin and his trickery. We are up to our necks now, lad, up to our bloody necks in it.'

After the greetings, the combined forces of Balin and Bors wove their way through the tangle of trees, ferns and brush towards the approaching Saxon war band. They were fifty warriors, as large a force as Arthur had ever seen marching together. To him it felt an army, their boots crunched and rustled in rotting leaf mulch, the murmur of their whispers carried through the treetops like the wind. They reached the forest's edge, and Arthur crouched, watching the distant line of Saxons approaching from the lowlands.

'We need to lure the filthy whoresons to us,' said Bors, standing five men down from Arthur, towering over everyone.

'Send ten spearmen down to that brook there,' said Arthur quietly, speaking almost to himself. 'Act foolish, perhaps drunk. Horse around in the water and wait until the Saxons approach.'

'What was that, lad?' said Bors' booming voice.

Arthur's stomach clenched, and he could feel Kai's eyes burrowing into him from his right side. Arthur swallowed, his mouth suddenly dry. He wasn't sure why he had spoken; the idea had appeared in his mind like a painted image, and he spoke to himself as much as anyone else. Arthur's head had been full of marching, fighting and constant thoughts of war since his first fight, so much so that ideas and questions spilled out of his mind like an overfilled mead horn.

'Well... just an idea...'

'Speak up, don't stutter like a beardless boy tupping a whore for the first time. What is it?' Bors barked, and the warriors around Arthur laughed.

Arthur's face turned fiery, and he reached up and touched the bronze disc at his neck for luck. He cleared his throat. 'I said we should send ten spearmen down to that brook beyond the trees. The men should act like fools, as though they are drunk. Wrestle in the water or sit down for a rest. Make sure the enemy can see their shields bearing the fox of Bernicia or the stag of Gododdin and they won't be able to resist attacking. At the last minute, the spearmen flee towards these trees and then we can attack.'

'Like flies towards shit,' Bors said, grinning in his bush beard. 'You're not as stupid as you look, lad. You're Ector's boy?'

'No, lord, well, sort of...'

'Ha! Sort of? Did Ector rut with your mother or not?'

'No, lord.'

'What in Arawn's hairy arse are we talking about Ector rutting for?' Bors threw his head back and laughed, and the warriors laughed with him, except Arthur, who blushed. 'Never mind. It's as good a plan as any. Pick your nine men and get down there. Unless Balin objects?'

Balin shrugged and shook his head to show that he had no objection to Arthur's plan, but his hard eyes met Arthur's and held them for a moment, and Arthur wasn't sure if there was a flicker of respect there, or just a hard indifference. It felt like fifty faces all stared at him, waiting to see what he would do next, wanting him to fail or shirk from what he had committed to do.

'Kai,' Arthur said in a whisper, and Arthur blew out a small sign of relief when his brother nodded proudly. 'Redwulf, Huell.' The one-handed warrior rocked backwards in surprise at being selected, but he did not deny Arthur's request. Arthur picked seven other men at random, the youngest men he could find amongst the Rheged and Gododdin fighters, because he feared the older warriors with fiercer reputations would baulk at marching out of the forest under his orders. Arthur was young. He had killed and fought but was still untested and had never fought in a battle as large as the one about to unfold beyond the woods. If his ruse succeeded, then there was reputation in it, but if he failed, if the Saxons failed to take the bait or if he timed the retreat badly, then Arthur could face humiliation or even death if the enemy caught them.

Arthur's small party gathered about him, and he led nine warriors out of the trees, marching boldly towards the small stream which babbled its way through a sloping meadow.

'Remember,' Arthur said, making sure each man paid attention. 'We can't look at the enemy. They must believe we are fools who have raided deep into Lloegyr. They have seen the smoke in the sky from the burned settlement and will want revenge. We don't run until I give the order.'

'We are bloody fools,' grumbled Huell, though he seemed pleased enough to march beside Arthur. Becoming a one-handed, pitiful figure who rode whilst other men marched was humiliating and had stripped away all of Huell's brashness and warrior pride. So he marched with his wounded arm still in a cloth sling, but at least he marched with purpose.

'Who is Arawn?' asked Redwulf cheerfully. He held a spear taken from one of Balin's men, though the black cloak had been reluctant to hand his weapon to a Saxon.

'An old god,' said Arthur. 'Lord of Annwn, the underworld.'

'I hope this plan of yours works,' said Kai, ignoring the Saxon. He peered down the valley towards where the Saxon column marched in the distance. The enemy followed the valley's contours, and they were so far away, beyond a hill littered with rocks and boulders, that it was conceivable that Arthur's small band marching from the high forest had not seen them.

'It will work if we do it right,' said Arthur. 'The Saxons hate us. Their very name for us means slave. So, the Saxons believe themselves superior to us, that we are a worthless people. They believe their gods encourage them to take our land, that we cannot fight as well as they, and so they will attack us because they can't help themselves.'

Redwulf grunted at that truth, and Arthur shifted his grip on the fox-painted shield he had borrowed from Dewi in temporary exchange for his larger Saxon shield. They reached the brook, its water running fast down the hillside, leaping over slick rocks and pebbles. Arthur turned his back on the Saxon column, and his band did the same. They kept their shields slung across their backs to make them as noticeable as possible, and Huell dipped his left hand into the cool water and splashed it on his face. Kai scooped up a handful of water and threw it at Arthur, and the rest of the young warriors laughed and followed his lead, so that before long they were ankle deep in the fast-flowing water, kicking it at one another in huge splashes, laughing and chasing each other through the water.

Arthur risked a half-glance over his shoulder, and three Saxons pounded up the hillside towards them. They paused, staring at Arthur's men with hands over their eyes. The three men waited for what seemed like an age. He held his breath, worried that his plan would fail, but one of the Saxons turned and waved to the column so that forty Saxons in furs and leather marched up the hill towards the forest.

'Here they come,' said Arthur. 'Wait. Stay calm and do not turn around. When I give the order, we run for the trees as fast as we can.'

The men nodded and continued with their playful splashing. Arthur crouched by the brook's edge as though he filled a skin with water and glanced nervously over his shoulder. The Saxons were so hungry for the fight that they broke out into a run up towards the Britons. Arthur ignored the gnaw of fear in his belly; his plan was working, and as the Saxon warriors came on, they saw a chance to kill a band of raiders and if Arthur timed it correctly, then there would be a slaughter on a Bernician hillside. He waited until he could hear the clank of their axes and spears against shields, until the sound of their boots upon the wild grass rumbled like distant thunder. He stood and turned, feigned mock surprise at the Saxon approach, and stumbled backwards into the brook. The cold water sloshed about his boots, and Arthur grabbed Kai's shoulder as though alerting him to the enemy approach.

'Turn now, men,' Arthur said, 'look at them but do not run yet. We have to let them come closer so that when they charge, they do so in broken formation. Wait for it.'

His men followed Arthur's orders and stumbled about in the water, gathering their weapons and shields as though they were incompetent warriors. The Saxon scouts were closest and a warrior with a red beard stretched ahead of the rest with long, loping strides. He thought to make a name for himself, to be the first to strike at the inept Britons. Arthur hefted his spear, took two steps forward, levelled the point and threw it just as he had countless times on the practice field at Caer Ligualid. The spear soared high, and the red-bearded man slowed his pace, gaping up at the arcing spear point, but he could not react in time and the spear flew down towards him impossibly fast and its leaf-shaped blade sliced through his belly and dropped him to the grass. The Saxon wailed in pain, clutching at the weapon embedded in his midriff. His blood soaked into the grass, and the Saxons behind roared with anger, and their run turned into a furious charge.

'Now!' Arthur called to his men. 'Run for the trees!'

They turned and fled, but as Arthur ran beside Kai and Huell, he noticed one figure had not left the brook, and he turned and saw Redwulf running in the opposite direction.

Arthur paused. 'Redwulf!' he roared, and the Saxon turned to him. Redwulf spat towards Arthur, turned, dropped his trews and showed his bare arse. *Oathbreaker.* Arthur was stunned. He had protected Redwulf when Balin would have killed him, he had allowed Redwulf to live and march with the war band, Redwulf had sworn an oath to Arthur and to break an oath was to discard a man's honour, casting him as low as a beast in the ditch. But there was no time to contemplate that betrayal now, because two score wild Saxons hurtled up the hill towards him. They came for blood. They had seen the scar of smoke on their borders and knew that Britons had raided and killed a Saxon settlement.

Their fallen scout screamed in pain from Arthur's spear in his guts and they came to kill. Arthur ran as though he had wings, flying across the grass like a hawk. Huell had fallen behind the rest, struggling to run in his weakened state, and listing to his wounded side.

Arthur grabbed Huell around the waist and dragged him onward. 'We are almost there. Keep going,' he said. The trees were only twenty paces away, and some of Arthur's men had already reached the safety of the spears within the dense treeline. The Saxons bellowed with rage, and Arthur risked another glance over his shoulder. Two of the Saxon scouts were close, so close that Arthur could see the whites of their furious eyes and knew in that horrifying moment that he and Huell would not make the trees. The Saxons were upon him, axes in their fists and hatred twisting their bearded faces.

12

Arthur pushed Huell towards the trees where the war band lay hidden. Huell stumbled forwards and wrapped his good hand about the gnarled trunk of an elm tree.

'Go,' Arthur said. He swallowed the knot of fear in his belly, ripped his long knife free from his belt, and turned on his heel. If he was going to die, it would not be from a wound in his back. The two Saxon scouts were mere steps away from him. The first man came on with flowing blonde hair and a look of joy on his face as he brought his axe back in a wild, wide overhand sweep. Two steps and Arthur could smell garlic on the man's breath, and he ducked around the axe, dragged his seax free from its sheath at his lower back and in one fluid motion Arthur whipped the blade across the charging Saxon's stomach. The man tottered a few more paces and fell to his knees, but Arthur kept moving and he brought his knife up to parry the second warrior's seax which came for his neck in a wicked thrust.

Their blades rang together, and the Saxon barrelled into Arthur, his running weight driving them both to the grass, where they rolled together, grunting and gasping as each tried desperately to strike the killing blow. The seax blade sliced across Arthur's forearm, but his own blade found the Saxon's groin, and Arthur drove the seax home, twisting it savagely. The Saxon made a high-pitched mewing sound, and he stared at Arthur with watery blue eyes, and Arthur looked away as he ripped his blade free in a wash of thick blood. He sprang to his feet, heart pounding in his chest at the sight of the Saxon war band racing towards him. Arthur raised his arms out wide, a bloody blade in each fist, and he roared at the Saxons to come and die. The madness was upon him, the war-rage, and suddenly he felt no fear. His plan had worked, and two Saxons lay dead. Arthur saw Redwulf amongst the charging horde, the young warrior was gesticulating wildly at a shaggy-haired man with white fur around his shoulders, but the bigger man ignored Redwulf, though the oathbreaker did his best to warn the Saxons of the trap which lay ahead.

Arthur set his feet, believing he must die as forty bloodthirsty Saxon warriors charged at him, howling their hate. In those desperate heartbeats, he wondered if Ector would be proud of him, if they would bury him or leave him to rot on a hillside in Lloegyr where crows would peck at his dead eyes. Strangely, he wondered if Queen Igraine yet lived, and if Lunete was safe in Caer Ligualid. Screaming faces descended upon Arthur, bearded axes, spears and seaxes coming to tear open his flesh and slash him to bloody ruin. Arthur made ready to attack the first man, a tattooed warrior with an enormous axe held in two hands. But in that darkest of moments where Arthur thought death had come for him, warriors surged from behind. Howling men came hurtling past Arthur like a great tidal wave, crashing into the Saxons with a sickening crunch of steel, wood and flesh. The monstrous figure of Bors barged Arthur aside, as the champion of Gododdin tore into the Saxons. His shield threw two of the enemy from their feet and Bors' spear ripped a man's throat open with such force that it almost tore his head from his shoulders.

The battle was short and brutal. Arthur killed two more men in that fight, and the Saxons were defeated the moment Bors and Balin of the Two Swords emerged from the trees to meet the ragged Saxon line with their own controlled charge. A dozen Saxons escaped, fleeing down the hillside and into the valley beyond. Redwulf was one of those men, and his betrayal left a bitter taste in Arthur's mouth. The Britons cheered their victory, and Kai and Arthur celebrated together. Kai embraced him, and the two young warriors laughed at the sheer joy of killing an enemy who had come to kill them. Survival and victory were intoxicating, like too much ale drank at a feast, and Arthur's head swam with it. A large hand dropped onto Arthur's shoulder, and the giant figure of Bors stared down at him, his wide forehead spattered with blood.

'Well done,' he said solemnly, the usual loud joviality gone from his deep voice. 'What is your name again?'

'Arthur.'

'Who is your father, Arthur, if it was not Ector?'

'I do not know, I am an orphan, raised by Ector of Caer Ligualid.'

Bors nodded, and then the bronze disc at Arthur's neck caught the big champion's eye. 'Where did you get that?'

'It was a gift, lord, from Queen Igraine of Rheged.'

'A gift from a queen, and Queen Igraine at that. She is my cousin; did you know that? God help me, but that boar Urien treated her terribly. She deserved better, so fair and so kind. Take care of it, Arthur, for it is a fine gift from a noble woman.'

'Yes, lord,' Arthur said, resisting the urge to tuck the disc behind his jerkin so that nobody else would see it. The gift made Arthur uneasy. He did not know the queen and had only been in her company for one awkward night at Ector's request. Yet it brought him comfort, and more importantly, whenever he touched it, the dragon-etched disc brought him luck.

'You did well today.' Bors tapped Arthur's forehead with a thick finger. 'Cunning in war is as valuable as a hundred swords. If you have it, use it. Never be afraid to speak up. You killed those two Saxons where another man would have carried on running in fear. Men will follow courage, lad, they will follow a brave man into battle. Even if it means their death, a brave leader will incite them on to great deeds. Remember that, and I will remember your name, Arthur.'

'Yes, lord,' said Arthur again, unable to find any other words, so filled with pride was his head and heart.

'Now. You have the right to strip the wealth from those Saxon bastards you killed, so take their weapons, their armour and whatever else you can find on their stinking corpses.' Bors clapped Arthur so hard on the shoulder that he almost fell over.

Balin's black cloaks and the warriors of Gododdin busied themselves stripping the dead of anything of value, and they encouraged Arthur to take what he had won through combat from the men he had killed. Kai did the same, and grinned broadly at an ivory-hilted knife he took from a flaxen-bearded Saxon and a handful of chipped, thin Roman coins he found in the same man's belt purse. Arthur found the men he had killed, their faces still, flesh white and marked with crusted blood. Flies already buzzed about their eyes, and one of the dead Saxons had voided his bowels in his death throes and the stink, mixed with the iron stink of blood, was sickening. A pair of dead eyes stared at him, and there was innocence there, and fear. Arthur felt guilty then, ashamed that the dead men would never see their wives, children, mothers or fathers again. Then he remembered what Ector had said about mercy, and he thought of how many Britons must have died under the slain men's blades.

The other warriors watched him, and though he could hardly bring himself to touch the dead Saxons, he had to take his right. It was expected, and to not take what he had won in battle would show weakness, so he took some hacksilver and a new belt studded with copper buttons, and also a breastplate of hard-baked leather. The armour stank of stale sweat and horse, but it was armour, the precious sign of a warrior of reputation. It wasn't the chain mail of an elite champion, but it was armour, and Arthur shrugged it on over his jerkin. A commotion at the brook caught Arthur's attention, and he followed Kai down to where a knot of Gododdin men and black cloaks pushed and shouted at one another.

'What's all the bloody noise about?' asked Bors, striding into the midst of the disagreement and hurling men aside with his mighty arms.

'There's a half a dozen prisoners here, lord,' said a Gododdin man, 'and these black cloaks say they must wait for Lord Balin's command before they agree what can be done with them.'

'We don't take orders from Gododdin sheep shaggers,' said a black cloak with hard eyes.

'Set them free,' came the hard voice of Balin of the Two Swords. 'All men know I don't take prisoners, but these men are different.'

'Different how?' said Bors, sticking his thumbs in his belt and puffing his chest out. 'A Saxon is a Saxon.' The Gododdin men reared up at the black cloaks' insult, hands dropped to weapon hilts and the tension made Arthur shift his feet uncomfortably.

'We are going to set these men free.'

'Set them free?' Bors scoffed, so surprised that his big face turned red.

'Aye. They will serve a purpose. We'll tell them we are heading east and south to raid.'

'But we...' Bors began and then grinned, winked at Balin, and dragged his men away.

'They shall all go free as Balin says,' said Merlin, appearing at Arthur's shoulder. 'But not that one.' He pointed a long finger at a crouched, hooded figure amongst the sorry-faced Saxons. 'Stand.' Merlin commanded, but the figure stayed still, and so Merlin barked in the Saxon tongue and the figure rose slowly and removed the hood. The surrounding warriors took a step back from what lay beneath. It was a woman with the top half of her face smeared with black ash so that her eyes shone dark and powerful, and the bottom half covered in a white paste. She looked like a demon, like a horror from the pit of hell. She had set her hair into fearsome, stiff spikes with cow dung and around her neck was a necklace heavy with iron and stone charms carved into wicked faces, writhing monsters, a hammer, a phallus, and other pagan symbols. 'This one is mine.' Merlin beckoned the woman towards him. She was as tall as he, and she cast her fur-lined cloak back to reveal heavy breasts beneath a thin dress, and wide hips. The woman hissed at Arthur and the surrounding warriors, who leapt back in fear of her evil magic, and she cackled. She was a Saxon priestess, a holy woman who marched with their army to bring the warriors luck, to use her closeness to their gods to imbue the war band with luck and power. Arthur tightened his grip on his seax as she passed him, because she pulsed with a strange force, like being in the presence of a king, a fearsome warrior, or Merlin himself.

The woman followed Merlin as he strode away. She walked proudly, shoulders back and her fearsome head held high. Men made the sign to ward off evil as she passed them, and Merlin led her towards the trees. Balin spoke to the prisoners in their own tongue, told them what he wanted them to hear, and sent them scampering down the hillside. They would run back to Ida and Octha and tell them of the Briton war band heading east and south, and so drive warriors away from Dun Guaroy. They camped that night in the forest, Balin sent scouts out on horses captured from the Saxons, ranging north and west to watch for any other roving bands of Saxons hunting the Briton raiding party, and Bors had the men of Gododdin take shifts watching the forests edges and approaches. The evening was raucous with boasting and recounting tales of brave deeds, remembering the six men who had died in the fight. Those who had taken wounds grimaced and sweated. If the wounds were not treated properly, most of those eight men would die of the rot. Arthur took a cut of roasted rabbit from the campfire to a Gododdin man with a cut in his guts, and he would surely die without Merlin's attentions. But Merlin was ensconced in a vigorous conversation with the captured Saxon priestess at the camp's edge, and no man approached those two fearsome figures.

Bors congratulated Arthur again loudly on his successful plan and the men gathered around as Arthur, and others in the war band, had their forearms tattooed with death rings in honour of the men they had killed. The tattooing hurt, the tiny bone needle puncturing Arthur's flesh over and over and then the bloody marks smeared with a dark paste to make the ring permanent. Kai grinned with pride at the new marks on his arms, and Arthur and his brother wondered at how Ector would look upon their deeds since leaving the Bear Fort. Even Huell's mood lifted, happy to have been part of the ruse, and some of the burly warrior's melancholy lifted as he sat with the warriors and enjoyed their boastful stories.

Merlin stalked away from the Saxon priestess and marched back and forth amongst the trees, rubbing his palm over the strange patterns on his skull and pulling his braids. Arthur approached the druid slowly, and Merlin muttered to himself. Every so often he glanced up at the sky as though he searched for an answer, shook his head and carried on with his thoughtful pacing. Arthur stopped five paces away, and Merlin, keeping his eyes ahead of him, pointed a long finger at Arthur. The priestess sat against the trunk of a birch tree. Arthur caught her eye, and she smiled at him. There was an evil in her full-lipped, sharp-eyed face which made Arthur shudder. She could be beautiful, he thought, if it wasn't for the fearsome paint on her face and the spikes in her hair. She tapped a finger slowly to her cheek beneath her left eye, its nail was deep black like an animal's claw, and she pointed that finger at Arthur as if to say she was watching him. Arthur swallowed and forced himself to look away.

'What is it?' Merlin barked impatiently. 'Don't just stand there gawping at me. Spit it out if you have something to say. Don't look at her, lad, or she'll turn you into a horned toad, or worse.'

'Could she do that, lord?'

'She has power, I could do it, and perhaps she could too. So, mind yourself, even if you do fancy yourself a great general now that you have killed a handful of ragged-arsed Saxons.'

Arthur reddened at Merlin's hard words. 'They were Saxon warriors.' Arthur spoke defensively before he had time to consider his words and instantly regretted it.

'They were scouts and men of the Saxon fyrd. Farmers, potters, woodsmen and blacksmiths called up to fight by their lords. The real Saxon warriors are closer to Dun Guaroy, though they will no doubt march when they hear of the slaughter of this paltry force. The real Saxon warriors, the men who braved the wild sea, the champions and professional warriors, are a different thing entirely.'

'Does she have a druid's power?'

'Oh, she has power, not quite the power of a druid, but close and different. She is Irish, boy, captured as a girl by Saxon pirates. Her Irish name is Nimue, and the Saxons call her Vivien. She was raised in the old knowledge deep in the Irish heartland, at Tara, the home of Irish high kings. The Romans never went to Ireland, and though the nailed god is strong there, the old ways live on and those with that ancient knowledge taught her the secrets of their dark mountains, of dwarven smiths and elfish magic. The Saxons realised her power, and they taught Nimue the ways of their gods, of Woden, Thunor and the rest. She can converse with their gods, hear their commands, she can augur the fate of battle in the guts of a goat or the blood of a raven. She can speak Saxon, Irish, Roman Latin and our own tongue. Nimue knows the secrets of the stars, of the nine spells of Woden, of Manawydan, Maponos, Arawn, and has visited Annwn in a dream state. I must learn from her, Arthur, I must... think on these things. And more, for the very fate of our island is at stake.'

Merlin stared at Arthur for a long moment, his bright eyes searching Arthur's face as though he sought an answer there, or perhaps searched for an intellect with which to share his great problems. Arthur held his gaze until Merlin broke away with a disappointed shake of his head and waved Arthur away with a dismissive shake of his hand. Arthur nodded, not understanding half of what Merlin had said, but understanding enough to know that the druid needed to be left alone to ponder things that only he had the cunning to fathom.

The warriors continued their celebrations, Balin and Bors content to let their men enjoy the victory. Arthur warmed himself by the campfire and ate a thin flatbread which one of Bors' Gododdin men had baked on a hot stone. As the night drew colder and a shadow of cloud blocked out the moonlight, men fell asleep beneath cloaks and blankets. Kai had drunk too much strong Saxon ale and snored happily beside Arthur with his jerkin sleeve rolled up to the elbow, showing off his fresh death rings which, like Arthur's, were already beginning to scab over.

Arthur touched the cuts on his face and arms gingerly. Neither were deep, but both screamed of battle's risk. If he closed his eyes, Arthur could still see the blades scything towards him, the broad-bladed axes, blood-smeared spear points and the furious-faced enemy behind them. A handsbreadth deeper or lower and it would be Arthur lying cold and still on the battlefield in a glistening pool of his own congealing blood and the shit from his voided bowels. Arthur lay down and pulled his cloak about him. He was wealthy now, having won the accoutrements of a warrior from the men he had slain. Lunete would marvel at his breastplate, belt, death rings, weapons and silver. He closed his eyes and tried to busy his mind with thoughts of the march, of how his battle plan had worked, and what other ways he could use cunning to outwit the enemy. But no matter how much he tried to distract himself, the dead fought their way through his thought cage to haunt him. Arthur lay by the fire in a half-sleep, somewhere between sleep and wakefulness, and the fetches of the slain came for him with accusing eyes, bloody wounds, rotting teeth, ragged beards and grasping fingers. He knew that there would be more death before the quest was completed, more Britons and Saxons must die to rescue Princess Guinevere and Prince Gawain in the blood-soaked fight for Lloegyr.

13

The war band marched carefully, often taking circuitous paths through woodland and around the western slopes of high mountains to remain hidden from Saxon scouts. Balin of the Two Swords sent his own scouts ranging ahead of the column on horseback, searching for other bands of Saxon warriors and reporting back to Balin at regular intervals. The land was thick with Saxons, warriors mustering from farms and villages to gather to their lords' banners in response to the party of raiding Britons. Arthur and Kai watched, crouched in woodland or from lofty escarpments, as spearmen with heavy shields, golden hair and fur-draped shoulders marched along paths and byways.

Balin knew his business, Arthur thought. There would be no blundering into Saxon war bands in unscouted woodland on this march. He watched Balin and Bors, observing how each man led his warriors. They were very different men, Bors boisterous, always joking and laughing with his warriors, huge and fearsome, where Balin was quiet and assured, stern and grim-faced. Both commanders had the respect of the men they led but achieved it by different means. Arthur liked Bors. He kept the men in good spirits and was a brutal fighter. Balin was ever thoughtful, and there was a sureness and trust to be found in his calmness, and Arthur had seen Balin's ruthless savagery at first hand. Ector, whom Arthur had grown up following and learning from, was a great warrior. Ector's skill with spear, sword and shield was incomparable, and Ector was also a fair man, even gentle when necessary. *Men will follow courage*, Bors had said, and Arthur supposed that was true. Ector, Bors and Balin all had that in common. They were different men, but each an effective leader in his own way.

Balin led the march, for Bernicia's hills and dales had once belonged to him and his disposed band of black cloaks, and he knew the knolls, streams, caves, hedges and trees like the veins upon the back of his hand. It must be strange, Arthur thought, to wander a land where your ancestors had lived for generations beyond count, before the Rome-folk came, before men could remember, and travel through it like a hunted man. The Gododdin men grumbled at following the black cloak's leader until Bors slapped a few heads, and then his warriors followed without complaint. The black cloaks marched silently, grim-faced and determined, each man a reflection of their commander. The Gododdin men were rowdy. A loud fart brought peals of laughter. They told endless riddles, stories of brave deeds, and Arthur heard at least a dozen barbs from one warrior to another about the promiscuity or weight of the man's mother. Merlin marched at the column's rear, locked in debate with the intriguing Nimue. She walked free of bonds, her head held high and proud. Her hair was no longer spiked but flowed behind her like a raven's wing. The warriors eyed her broad hips and chest hungrily, but only when she was not looking, for Nimue's snarl was a terrible thing to behold, and all men feared her ability to turn their manhood to a shrivelled worm, to blight their bowels or curse them with black luck.

The column stopped for a midday rest, and men ate dried meat, cheese, and drank ale. Merlin strode alone to a hilltop which, he said, had once contained one of the tall druidic stones which littered Briton's high places. The Romans had removed many of such stones of power during their attempts to drive the druids from Briton, and so had the Christians who were ever resentful of the old gods. Nimue sat alone and Arthur went to her with his skin of ale. Kai grabbed Arthur's arm to warn him to leave her alone, but Arthur shook him off. He wanted to know about her. If the great Merlin learned from her knowledge, how could Arthur pass up a chance to talk with her and perhaps learn something for himself?

Nimue watched his approach, her dark eyes as deep and mysterious as the black pool where they had first met Bors and the men of Gododdin. She still wore the strange paint upon her face, but as Arthur drew closer, he noticed it was as dry and cracked as a dried-up riverbed. Nimue rose to meet him, and the strange charms about her neck jangled. Arthur held the skin of ale out towards her, and Nimue's head tilted to one side as she looked him up and down.

'Ale,' Arthur said slowly, and brought the drink slowly to his own lips to show her what it was.

'I know what it is,' she said in his language, her voice heavily accented and as silky as an otter's back. 'You are the boy of no kingdom.'

Arthur nodded, and she took the skin. He frowned at her, surprised that she knew who he was, and Nimue cocked an eyebrow. She smiled, and there were glistening stones set into her teeth, tiny rocks which shone like the stars, and Arthur wondered at this woman of such strangeness and power.

'Can you really turn men into toads or turn women's wombs to ash?' The moment the question left Arthur's lips, it embarrassed him. He had so much to ask her, but what tumbled out of his mouth was clumsy and not what he intended.

'Would you like to be a toad?' Nimue said with an evil smirk. 'I cannot change you into any animal, young warrior. But I could put you under my spell. I could speak into your eyes and make you think and dream whatever I wish. I can make a man love a woman, poison a womb, or kill a king with a tainted draught. There is magic in the world, but not what you common folk believe it to be. There is a spear in Frankia which is said to have pierced the body of the nailed god and whoever wields it can never be defeated in battle. Did the god's blood make it so, or is it the belief of the warriors who fight beneath its banner that makes it so? Men will believe the impossible if they wish to, or if a sorcerer can make them believe it.'

Her words surged in Arthur's mind, and he wondered at what she meant. Did she mean that magic was real, or that a druid or volva's power was based around the belief and weakness of men? Such things were too deep to contemplate, so Arthur pressed her on simpler matters.

'Where did you learn magic?' he asked.

'Merlin told me of you,' she said, ignoring his question. 'That it was your plan which laid my war band low. Men think war is about strength and skill with weapons, but men are fools. War is about cunning and trickery, about preparation, understanding the lay of the land, and knowing when to fight and when to retreat.'

'Then why did you charge?'

Nimue laughed and shrugged. 'I was not the commander of those men, I was merely their seeress, their volva. I used my *seidr* to bring them luck, that is all.'

'I hope you bring your next war band better luck,' said Arthur, and she frowned at him. Nimue spoke too confidently, as though she had won the skirmish rather than lost it, and that rankled Arthur. Had it not been for Merlin's protection, then her fate would surely have been terrible.

'The Saxons are not my people, young warrior. They took me from my people and made me their slave. But they taught me things, and I know their gods and what they want. I know what Ida and Octha desire and I know what Merlin wants. What do you know, young warrior who thinks to scold me with hard words?'

'What do the Saxons want?'

'Everything.' She threw her head back and laughed at that. 'They want your land, your women, your wealth and your future. They want to drive you Britons into the western sea or to Annwn, and their gods imbue them with the strength to do it.'

'Why?'

'Why not? The men who come here are nothing in their own lands, they are warlords and captains of mud huts and thin soil, here they can make themselves kings of rich land and all they have to do is kill a few weak Britons who cannot even unite as one people. You are Bernicians, men of Rheged, Elmet, Kent, Gododdin and Powys, and each of your chieftains hates the other, so the Saxons will defeat you one at a time and take everything you have until the memory of your people is as ruined as your old gods. Already they bring their women, children and their elderly to your shores. This land we walk upon now is theirs. The names of these hills are no longer in your tongue. The spirits of the forests, springs and marshes are Saxon spirits. Your world is crumbling around you like rotten timber, taken from your people by iron will and belief in powerful gods.'

'What does Merlin want?' Arthur stuttered the words, which tumbled from his mouth without him thinking. Her words shocked him. The finality of them, the surety about which she spoke of the Saxons' intentions, gave them an air of certainty which rocked Arthur. He had always thought of the Saxons as raiders, as temporary, violent men who would eventually be defeated and leave forever.

'Redemption,' she hissed, and leaned into Arthur, the sun catching in her dark eyes with a twinkle. 'He wants to make amends for the Great War that was lost and the part he played in that. He wants the return of the old gods and the old kingdoms, and he wants to rid the land of Saxons. Merlin wants much, young warrior, perhaps too much. He likes you, but beware that favour, for Merlin is a dangerous man. His gods are all but dead, there are few druids left on this island, there are more in Ireland, but few here. The nailed god is powerful and drives your old gods beneath his heel, but he is a weak god. He asks too much of his followers, and makes men shun war, death and the old ways. And that is why you will lose, young warrior, because your new god is weak and the Saxon gods drive them on to glorious slaughter, they demand it, and the rewards for Saxons who die in battle are an eternity of feasting, battle and resurrection. How can you defeat that with your nailed god?'

'What then of Dun Guaroy?'

'You are wise to shun such talk.' Nimue took a long pull at the ale skin, but kept her eyes fixed on Arthur's. 'For what difference can you make in a war between gods? Bebbanburg, as the Saxons call it, is a timber fortress upon a high crag. There are but two approaches, one from the sea, and the other up a slope towards where wall and gate are still under construction. What you seek is inside there, warrior, and you should make your attack before the high walls are complete, for then that place will be impregnable.'

'The princess and the prince are inside the walls?'

'They too are inside.' She cackled at the double meaning of her twisting words which confused Arthur. 'Ida has a hall and other buildings inside the walls. The Saxons built their feasting hall before they built the walls, so confident are they that you Britons could never march so far into their lands and attack the fortress before it is finished. Ida does not fear your people, young warrior, he scoffs at your warriors, whores your women, and uses the hollowed skull of a dead king as a drinking cup.'

'And what of Octha?'

'So many questions, young warrior.' Her eyes drank him in, flickering to the bronze disc at his neck and then staring deep into his soul. Her gaze made him hot. Sweat broke out on his brow and back and he shifted uncomfortably. 'Let this be the last. Octha is that most dangerous of men, come fresh across the sea with three thousand men who followed his promise of glory, land, women and reputation. He will carve himself out a kingdom or die trying. Octha is hard and ruthless, a champion in battle. He owes his men a debt, and that debt is your lands, your women, your children, and everything you hold dear. You should fear Octha, young warrior, like you fear the demons in the night. For he means to end your world.'

Balin barked the order to march, and men groaned as they rose from where they sat upon the ground. A Gododdin let out the largest belch Arthur had ever heard, and all thirty of Bors' men fell about laughing. Arthur nodded thanks to Nimue, he could have talked to her all day of the things she knew, and he hadn't yet asked her of the Saxon gods, of Ireland, and what she augured for the fate of Britain. He rose from his crouch, and Nimue rose with him, mirroring his movements whilst keeping her deep eyes locked to his. She moved like a hunting cat and Arthur stepped away from her, but as he moved, her hand shot out snake fast and grabbed his wrist. Arthur tried to yank his arm away, but Nimue's grip was as strong as a boar's bite. Her mouth turned in on itself, shifting into a flat, lipless slit as she forced his hand over. Nimue placed her own palm upon his and stared at his hand, tracing the lines upon his palm with her warm fingers. Her eyes glittered, and she smiled mirthlessly.

'What is it you want, Arthur, son of nowhere and no one?' Nimue said, and laughed as she released his hand and Arthur stumbled backwards. He left Nimue and returned to Kai, unable to shake Nimue from his thoughts. There was power in the volva. He felt it just being close to her.

Arthur glanced at his hand, wondering what it was she had seen there, and decided that he was better off not knowing.

'What did the *gwyllion* say to you?' asked Kai, using the old word for a witch, as he hefted his spear for the march. 'You look as white as a fetch.'

Arthur swallowed and shrugged as though the conversation had been nothing at all. 'She speaks nonsense, the desperate talk of a captured woman trying to prove her value.'

Balin's scouts returned as the afternoon drew long, and Arthur could taste salt on a brisk wind from the east. As the sun dipped, they reached sand dunes thick with coarse grass and heather, and Arthur laid eyes upon Dun Guaroy for the first time. Sharp timber stakes rose like monster's teeth atop a humpbacked crag in a wide tidal bay. The crag loomed, dark and foreboding in the distance with sharp cliffs and sheer sides leading down to the rolling grey sea and a sloping, grass-covered hillside on the landward side. A bleakly wicked wooden hall topped the crag, all sharp edges and threat. So far across the bay, its thatch was a dark brown, and there were gaps in the wooden palisade where men swarmed like ants across the pale rocks, working to complete Ida's fortress on a place where once Britons had lived. The new fortifications were jagged and sharp, like blades buried into the rock and pointing to the sky in defiance of the men from whom the Saxons had ripped the land. Gulls swooped over the dunes, gliding on the breeze, and the smell of the sea was thick in the air.

'Dun Guaroy,' said Balin with a sniff. 'And if the sight of the fortress isn't enough to curdle your blood, then behold the army of Octha.' Balin pointed a spear to the flatlands beyond the high fort, which no man had noticed, so transfixed were they by Ida's stronghold. There, on scrubland thick with short, rough grass and shallow hills, were a mass of leather tents and timber lean-tos set into holes in the ground. Countless camp-fires coughed smoke into a darkening sky, and Arthur gasped at the sheer vastness of Octha's warriors. He could not count the tents and hovels. Shadows of men moved in the smoke, tiny figures at that distance but as many as fleas on a filthy hound. Their camp was ten times larger than Caer Ligualid, and Arthur shuddered at the force required to fight and defeat so many Saxon warriors.

'Gods preserve us,' said Bors, his mouth agape. 'How can we approach the crag with such a force arrayed before us?'

'The tide will go out after sundown,' said Balin. 'The ebb goes far, and the wet sand will stretch from where we are now to the foot of Dun Guaroy.'

Bors clapped his massive hands and rubbed them together. 'So, we can cross at night, scale the rocks and get in through the gaps in the unfinished walls,' he said and clapped Balin on the shoulder. 'Turns out you men of Bernicia aren't completely useless after all.' Bors laughed so hard at his own jest that every man, even Balin's men, laughed along with him.

They settled down in the brush to wait for nightfall. There could be no fires and so Arthur huddled with his cloak gathered close about him against the wind which had grown chill as the sun fell beyond the western hills. Octha's horde was too vast to count, but Arthur believed their number could easily be the three thousand men Nimue spoke of. It was not a force come to Britain to hold Lloegyr for Ida, Horsa and the other Saxon leaders, it was a force come to conquer and Arthur feared for his people. He wondered how many men Rheged could muster to defend itself, but he had no guess. Ector spoke of hides, or farms, and how each hide must provide one fighting man if called upon by King Urien, but never of the actual numbers. Even if Rheged could summon three thousand men, which Arthur doubted, only a few of those were actual warriors. Only men like Ector, who kept a professional war band, and the king himself had warriors whose sole purpose was to train and prepare for war. They were the men who gathered tithes from the folk in the fields and farms, the men who marched to deal with raiders and men who broke the king's peace. Ector and Urien kept the warriors fed and clothed from the surplus gathered from the folk in Urien's kingdom. That render was the price of the people's safety. The rest of the warriors Rheged could muster were farmers and simple folk, and as Arthur stared across the bay at the Saxon camp alight with countless campfires, he wondered how many farmers it would take to kill one Saxon warrior.

Dun Guaroy glowed from fires within its palisade, and as the sun disappeared, a half-moon crept from behind sweeping clouds. The warriors watched the tide retreat and leave rippling wet sand which glistened in the wan moonlight. Merlin strode through the huddled warriors, his amber-topped staff held before him like a beacon. He called for Balin and Bors, and Arthur was surprised to hear his name called also by the old druid. Kai stared at him open-mouthed, and Arthur shrugged. He did not know why Merlin called for him. He didn't want to keep the druid or the leaders waiting, so Arthur scampered across the heather to join the three men who ambled over the dunes towards the retreating tide.

'It will soon be time,' said Balin, staring out across the bay.

'Nimue says the wall facing towards us is incomplete,' said Merlin. He spoke quickly as though he was in a rush to impart this most important of news. 'You can cross the tidal flats in darkness, climb the crag and slip in through the gaps in the palisade. There will be guards there. Ida keeps a force of fifty men inside the stronghold. Guinevere and Gawain will be in Ida's hall or held close to it. So, search there. And please, Lord Bors, go quietly. If the guards are woken or an alarm is raised, they will let no one leave that place alive.'

'I can be as quiet as a mouse's fart if I need to,' said Bors, jutting his bushy-bearded chin out in indignation.

'Well, that remains to be seen, doesn't it? Now. I must leave you this very night to travel east.'

'You are leaving us?' asked Bors incredulously.

'Just as we are about to attempt this most dangerous of tasks?' said Balin. He fixed Merlin with a fearsome stare. 'If there ever was a time where we need your magic, this is it, Merlin.'

'Magic?' Merlin waved his long fingers. 'I have cast a spell of good fortune across you all, and I will work a spell of concealment as you make your way across the bay. Beyond that, there is little I can do, anyway. It is stealth and blades you need inside Dun Guaroy, not a stumbling old goat like me.'

'The men won't like it, Merlin,' said Bors. 'They'd be happier knowing a druid was at their side when they climb that rock with an army on their flank and a guard of Ida's picked champions inside.'

'They have you and Balin and that should be enough to give any warrior confidence. Also, Arthur is with you.' Merlin paused, and Balin and Bors stared at Arthur like he was a lump of cow shit on the bottom of their boots. 'Arthur is a son of no kingdom, but a son of Britain. The land is his father, and the wind is his mother.'

'I am a Rheged man, lord,' Arthur stuttered, unable to meet Bors or Balin's hard stares.

'You are a man of Britain, Arthur, not Rheged. Nimue and I augured your future last night in the guts of a dog fox, and you are the one I have been waiting for. The one who must take up the sword.'

'Me? What sword?' Arthur took a step back, the conversation had changed too quickly, and Merlin's words were an unwanted surprise.

'This sword.' Merlin delved into his pack and pulled out a sword in a black leather scabbard. He drew the sword and held the blade aloft. There were markings on its silvery-grey blade and the hilt was wrapped in soft leather. The pommel was a ball of steel with a dragon carved into its centre. 'Caledfwlch, the sword of Ambrosius Aurelianus.'

'Excalibur!' whispered Balin and reached for the blade before Merlin shot him an angry frown.

'Yes, Excalibur is its name, but Caledfwlch was the name given to the blade by Neit, god of war, when the sword was forged in the distant mists of time. I gave this blade to Ambrosius during the Great War. With it, he was to crush the Saxons and drive them from our shores. Now, I give its power to you, Arthur ap Nowhere.'

'Please, Lord Merlin, I can't,' said Arthur, taking three backward steps. 'You are mistaken. I cannot wield such a sword. Give it to Balin, or Bors, or Ector. Ector is the champion of Britain.'

'He's just a boy,' said Balin. 'How can you entrust such a blade to him? Have you gone mad?'

'I have seen it, Balin of the Two Swords, as has Nimue,' shouted Merlin, his eyes bright and fearsome. 'Arthur is the one to take up the sword of our ancestors.'

'That witch has you under her dark *seidr*. I won't allow it. Our fate is at stake, Merlin. You were not here when Bernicia burned, when my family died, when my children were gutted like fish. Ambrosius did not save us then, and the boy cannot do it now.'

'Careful, Balin of the Two Swords,' growled Merlin, and he seemed to grow two feet in the darkness, his voice loud and rumbling. Arthur closed his eyes, wishing he was anywhere but there. 'Ambrosius was the brother of Uther Pendragon, and he led our armies well in the Great War. He it was who slew Hengist and brought us peace, albeit at great cost. We would have defeated the Saxons if not for...'

'For your meddling!' Balin said through clenched teeth. 'You it was who drew out Gorlois of Kernow so that Uther could steal his wife away. We were one until then, and then we were nothing. That disarray amongst the kingdoms united in a fragile alliance under the Pendragon shattered us. Then, in the night of the long knives, Horsa the Saxon slew King Gwyrangon of Kent, and Vortigern himself disappeared. We lost all lands east of Watling Street. Bernicia, Deira, Kent, all lost. You disappeared into exile on Ynys Môn, Ambrosius' peace meant the surrender of half our kingdom! Now, you would have me follow a beardless boy into battle against that?' Balin pointed across the bay at Octha's horde.

'I am Merlin! Druid of Britain and you will heed my words!' Merlin roared and brought his staff down hard into the sand. 'It is I who decides to whom the sword should pass, and it will pass to Arthur. All men know how we lost the Great War, and nobody regrets that more than I. Now is the time to make amends, to recover what was lost. We must trust the gods, Balin. We need their favour if we are to triumph. This time it will be different.'

Balin glanced at Arthur, a look of desperation etched on his scarred face. 'I hope you're right, druid, or our people will suffer like never before. On the souls of my dead wife and children, I hope you are right.' Balin stalked off to join his men, who had risen to their feet at the sound of raised voices.

'If you say it, Merlin, then so it shall be,' said Bors, and he laid a heavy hand upon Arthur's shoulder. 'I will stand with you, lad, but you must prove yourself if you want others to follow.' Bors followed Balin back to the warriors, leaving Arthur alone with Merlin.

Merlin stared out at the night-black sea, its distant waves rumbling on an unseen horizon. Arthur stood beside him for what seemed like an age, aware that the war band stared at them from the dunes, unable to understand why Merlin had spoken as he had, but not wanting to disturb the druid's thoughts. Merlin whispered something to himself which Arthur could not hear, and the chill sea wind whipped their faces. A single tear rolled down Merlin's face into his clipped beard and he smiled sadly to himself.

'Balin is right,' Merlin said eventually. 'It was my fault. Ambrosius could have led us to victory. We had Dumnonia, Rheged, Elmet, Gododdin, Kernow and Gwent allied and fighting as one under Uther the Pendragon of Britain. But it all turned to ashes when Gorlois of Kernow died in battle against the Saxons. I brought an injured Uther to Kernow, and I knew of his love for Gorlois' queen. Gorlois died, and Uther took Queen Igraine to Dumnonia and our alliance fell apart. I believed Uther and Igraine's union would birth a great king, a glorious warrior-king to return Britain to the old ways. The alliance of kings disagreed and forced Igraine to marry Urien of Rheged to keep the peace, and to spite Uther. Urien, who was and is a brute. Poor Igraine. Uther never recovered from that heartbreak. Then came the night of the long knives, Ambrosius died, King Gwyrangon of Kent died, even Vortigern who brought the Saxons to our shores was toppled from his throne. We had peace, but to get it, we surrendered half our island to Ida and Horsa.'

'I am not the man to wield the sword of Ambrosius, Lord Merlin.'

Merlin held the sword up and peered at its bright blade and ancient inscriptions, which Arthur could not read. 'This sword was forged in the days when the gods walked the mountains, rivers, glens and fields beside us, Arthur. Can you imagine that? Before the Romans came, before the nailed god. No man alive today can read what they etched on its blade. The words are lost to us. But you are the man to wield it. Trust me, both I and Nimue have seen it.'

'Nimue is a Saxon, and I...'

'Nimue is no more a Saxon than you or I. She is an Irish volva, a powerful *gwyllion* and seeress. She cares nothing for the Saxons, but not for us either. She craves only the chaos of war and the power it gives her over men, the elemental fury in it.' Merlin sheathed the sword and held it to Arthur, who shook his head and waved the blade away. Merlin sighed and his shoulders sagged. 'I do not know how old I am. I was old when Balin, Ector, Urien, Uther and Igraine were young. I was born into the wrong time, Arthur. There was a time when this land was great, when it was a haven of plentiful harvests, long summers and the people worshipped the right gods. Druids were powerful then, as powerful as kings. But then the Romans came, and they were clever. They saw the power of the druids and slaughtered all but a few who escaped to Ireland. They burned our sacred groves on Ynys Môn, and druids never wrote down our mysteries and so much of our old knowledge was lost. Now, the Saxons are here. We must fight, Arthur. I don't know how I have stayed alive this long. Perhaps it is the spectacles I produce, the tricks, the fearsome acts, the belief in the old ways. Take the sword. It is your destiny. The sword has the power of Britain in its steel. Men will follow and fight for the man who wields it. Take it.'

'I cannot, Merlin. It is not meant for me.' He didn't wish to refuse Merlin, but he was just an orphan. How could he wield such a sword? Perhaps the old druid had gone mad, or Nimue had entranced him and sought to ruin Britain with her Saxon *seidr* magic?

'It is for you, and you will take it. I must leave now, Arthur, but next time we meet I will tell you that which you crave, who you are and where you come from. Take the sword and fight for Britain, for our people. For me, for what was, and what could be again.'

Merlin thrust the sword at Arthur's chest, and he grasped it before it fell onto the sand. Merlin made to march away, but Arthur grabbed the druid's wiry arm.

'Wait, you know who my mother and father were?'

'Not now. Wield the sword. Fight, Arthur, and if you live, if you can return Guinevere and Gawain, then we will talk. I give you my word as a druid.'

Arthur let him go and watched Merlin march away to where Nimue waited for him across the dunes. They were gone in the blink of an eye, leaving Arthur alone with an unwanted sword, a head full of questions and a fortress to assault.

14

Arthur ran across the beach, wet sand slapping beneath his boots and his breath coming in short, cold gasps. The tide was out beyond sight in the deep darkness, leaving the bay a vast swathe of cold, ridged sand beneath Dun Guaroy's mighty crag. He wore Excalibur strapped to his belt, and the scabbard banged awkwardly against Arthur's leg as he ran, threatening to make him trip and fall amongst the war band, who eyed him with suspicion since Merlin's departure. Forty warriors ran across Dun Guaroy's bay under cover of darkness, their weapons clanking against their shields as they dashed across the sands. Earlier, Octha's campfires had been as numerous as the stars in the sky, but now all but a few had gone out as the Saxon army slept in the deep of the night. Fifty boots slapped on the wet sand. Men shushed each other if a spear clanked on a shield, or a warrior spoke. Three thousand Saxons lay across the bay, and more inside Dun Guaroy. To be heard or spotted was to die, so every man in the war band ran with fear in his belly and the hot thrill of danger in his chest.

The fortress loomed above them, the sharpened stakes of its unfinished palisade lit by burning torches at intervals around its perimeter. Arthur ran alone. He had kept his distance from Kai, Balin and Bors after Merlin's departure. They would have questions for him, and he did not have the answers. Everything Merlin had said roared in Arthur's head like the sea crashing against rocks in a storm, and he knew not what to do about it. All he knew was that Merlin and Nimue were gone, and he had an ancient sword, Merlin's trust, and the suspicion of a war band who had welcomed him so warmly into the ranks.

Balin and Bors took the lead, and the warriors stretched out behind them like a flock of starlings. Their best hope rested on the fortress not being closely guarded. Balin had spoken to that hope before they had left the dunes. Balin believed that Dun Guaroy was so deep within Lloegyr that Ida would not fear a Saxon attack on his new stronghold. Octha's army would only add to that hubris. That, along with Bors' utter fearlessness, brushed away some of the shock of Merlin's departure and imbued the men with courage once more.

Arthur gulped in mouthfuls of chilly night air as they reached the far side of the beach. The rock upon which Dun Guaroy stood loomed above him, much higher and more formidable than it had looked from the distant dunes. The war band leaned their backs against the damp, lichen-covered rocks that the sea would cover when the flood tide came. Each man took a moment to catch his breath, staring up nervously at the hard rock and grass-covered plateaus stretching above them in the darkness. The feel of the rock beneath Arthur's hand sent a shiver running up his back. It was a dark place, half sunken in the treacherous sea and linked to the land by its raised, sloping causeway. Dun Guaroy was a dread fortress, the centre of Ida's grip on Lloegyr, and the king himself was in there somewhere, looming like a monstrous beast in a cave. Arthur took a deep breath of sea air and calmed himself. He was about to creep into the lair of a vicious Saxon king and his brutal warriors, and if he considered it too closely, Arthur feared his guts would turn to liquid and his resolve would disappear like the ebb tide.

'Remember,' whispered Balin, 'we must be in and out before the tide comes in. Otherwise, we are trapped, the only way out then will be through Octha's army.' The men nodded, Balin had spoken that warning twice already as they mustered for departure, but to ignore his warning was to embrace death, so no man grumbled at the repetition.

'My men will skirt the north wall and make for the hall,' said Bors, also repeating what they had already decided. 'Balin's men cut through the fort's centre and meet us there. The five we have left in the dunes will sound the carnyx if the tide reaches the crag and we have not yet emerged. That will be our final warning. If we don't leave then, we die.'

Arthur dropped his hand to the iron ball on Excalibur's pommel, and its hard coldness felt comfortable, even reassuring beneath his touch. Mighty warriors had wielded Excalibur, it drank the blood of Britain's enemies and now Arthur would wield it, and he whispered a prayer to God, to the old gods, to the soul of Ambrosius Aurelianus and the warriors of distant past who had held the sword before him. He prayed for victory, for battle luck, and for the chance to live. He, Kai and Huell would go with Balin's men. Splitting the war band in two made the approach to Ida's hall less conspicuous, fifty men clambering through gaps in yet to be completed palisade would make a lot of noise, and fifty pairs of boots stomping through the lanes and pathways would wake even the soundest of sleepers. Balin's men were supposed to climb the rock first, and Arthur nervously glanced at one-handed Huell, who insisted that he would not be left behind. The rock was a monstrous mass of sharp planes, jutting buttresses, grass-covered knots, ledges and notches cut into the rock by crashing waves across millennia. The higher parts of the crag remained hidden in the night's gloom, and they had to climb it quickly if they were to find Guinevere and Gawain and get out before the tide came in.

'Time to go,' said Balin, and he leapt up from the sand to sink his hand into a rocky crevice. Balin hauled himself up, his boots skittering on the sea-slick face, and Dewi, the black cloak, thrust his shoulder beneath Balin's arse to give him a shove. The black cloaks followed Balin up the face, grunting and cursing in whispers as hands and nails scuffed and tore on the rocks. A man fell on his arse in the sand, but two others hauled him up again. Kai began his climb and Arthur pushed him from beneath to help Kai surge up to the closest buttress. Kai clambered over it, turned and lay on his belly. He dangled his spear shaft down to Huell, who gripped it with his left hand, and Kai hauled him up whilst Arthur gave him a push. The spear came down again and Arthur grabbed the smooth ash shaft and allowed Kai to pull him up whilst he sought purchase on the rock face with his boots. His left foot slipped on a layer of slimy bladderwrack, and Arthur's shoulder slammed into a jagged rock edge which numbed his arm. Around him men grunted and heaved, slipped and scraped their way up the crag.

Eventually, Arthur reached the summit. He, Kai and Huell were last. It took longer to help Huell make the climb than it took Balin and his men to scramble up the rocks. They paused for a few heartbeats to recover their breath and followed the tail end of Balin's twenty warriors into a gap between two high oak stakes and into the fortress. The palisade stakes were much higher close up, each three times as tall as a man and cut from stout oak sharpened to vicious points. When the palisade was completed, Arthur doubted any army could assault the place, so he placed his hand on the cold wood and slipped into the gap between the walls and thanked his luck that it was unfinished. A flaxen-haired warrior with fur at his neck and shoulders slumped inside the gap, open-eyed in the moonlight with a wide slash across his throat so that he seemed to have a second, gaping mouth below his open, dead one. Fresh blood pulsed from his wound, and its stink mixed with the smell of freshly cut wood.

They were inside Dun Guaroy, and all around Arthur were wattle and daub buildings cast in different shades of black and grey by the night. Thatch hung low from the old buildings built by the Britons of Bernicia before the Saxons came, and then higher, tighter-cut thatch on the Saxon buildings which sat lower to the ground like squat boxes with too-heavy roofs pressing down on their wattle walls. In the snarl of streets and pathways, the place stank of fish and piss, but the sharp smell of freshly cut timber masked the fouler stenches. Arthur followed Balin's men through the muddy lanes between the buildings. Dull torches glowed dimly behind window holes closed against the cold by wooden shutters. A dog barked from inside a house as Arthur ducked beneath an open window so as not to be seen and his breath came in quick, ragged gasps. The air grew heavier, as though the wet thatch and high walls closed in on him. There were Saxon warriors in the fortress somewhere, waiting and unseen. Ida slept in his hall, the peerless warrior and victor of countless battles, and as Arthur ran, he felt small, like a mouse trying to steal food from the lair of a great cat.

There was no sign of any Saxon guards as Arthur and the war band scampered through the fortress. He glanced through a gap between a blacksmith's forge and stable and saw the silhouette of Bors and his warriors skirting the northern rampart like ghosts cast in black against the night sky. Arthur ran into Huell's back and the big man cursed as he stumbled forwards. They had reached the edge of where the snarl of buildings led to an open square where three Saxons huddled around a burning brazier, warming their hands against the cold. Balin whispered to the warriors to wait, and he dashed off along the narrow space between two wattle buildings. Beyond the courtyard, the guards and the brazier loomed Ida's hall. It sat upon a higher part of Dun Guaroy's crag, with high, dark walls and a swooping lintel running across its top like the hull of a Saxon warship. Thick, fresh thatch covered the roof, which shimmered like silver in the moonlight, and a lazy column of smoke drifted from it to be snatched away by the sea breeze.

Moments later, Balin appeared from behind a long, pale building only ten paces away from the Saxon guards. Three chopped logs in their brazier crackled and spat with an orange glow. Balin tiptoed towards the Saxons, a sword held in each hand. He was black in the darkness, save the glint of his blades, and he moved lightly on the balls of his feet like a demon floating through the night. The Saxons did not hear or see the warrior approach and the first of them died with a swift lunge from behind as one of Balin's sword points punched through his throat to send a spatter of blood into the brazier where it hissed and bubbled in the fire. The two remaining Saxons turned, but Balin was deadly quick, and he cut them down with sword strokes so fast they came as a blur.

'Let's go,' whispered Dewi, and the black cloaks surged from where they crouched into the courtyard and up slippery stone steps carved into the rock towards the hall. Arthur, Kai and Huell followed, and Arthur winced as Balin dragged open a huge oaken door but, iron-hinged, it did not creak and Balin opened the hall doors only wide enough for them to slip inside one at a time. Arthur's breastplate touched the wooden door as he slid inside, and he slowly drew Excalibur to meet whatever horrible fate awaited him inside Ida's hall.

Arthur tiptoed along a timber floor through a corridor lit dimly by an almost spent rushlight further ahead, where the bobbing heads of Balin's black cloaks made shifting shadows on the walls. Men's breath steamed in the narrow space, the stink of garlic, sweat and leather thick in Arthur's nose. Kai glanced at him with large, fearful eyes and Arthur knew his face looked the same as they pressed ahead into the belly of Ida's hall. Arthur followed Huell's broad back into a vast black space. Their boots echoed as they scuffed on the hard-packed earthen floor scattered with floor rushes. Ahead, Balin held aloft a wood torch which cast firelight around him in wide circles. The light revealed high rafters and two floors of living platforms, then the light moved to show feasting benches pushed to the hall's sides and a huge hearth fire glowed like a sleeping dragon at the monstrous room's centre. Men and women snored at the edges, covered in furs on the raised sleeping platforms so that they looked like sleeping wolves as the torchlight passed across them.

'There,' Balin hissed, and his bloody sword point pointed to where two figures slumped against a great timber post which ran from the hall floor up to the high rafters. Arthur was closest to the figures, and as he dashed towards them, a broad face stared up at him, cheeks filthy and blue eyes fearful.

'Gawain?' he whispered, and the face nodded. Arthur sighed with relief and sawed at the man's rope bonds with Excalibur's blade. The sword cut through the hemp rope like butter, and Gawain rubbed at his rope-burned wrists in disbelief. Then Gawain glanced at the stooped figure next to him, and Balin came closer with the torch. The figure looked up at Arthur, and his breath caught in his throat, for staring up at him was the most beautiful woman Arthur had ever seen. Her hair shone like copper in the torchlight, her face was long and gentle with full lips, and eyes the green of a summer sea.

'Come with me,' Arthur whispered, and he cut her bonds. She took his outstretched hands, and her touch was like a warm nettle sting upon his flesh, shocking him with its intensity.

'Take them and go,' Balin hissed and then set off down the hall's length with his torch.

'Where are you going?' Kai whispered after him.

'To kill Ida,' Balin said, but just as he was about to turn and find the

Saxon king in his bed, a long sonorous sound broke the silence, like the wailing of a beast of legend beyond the sea.

'The carnyx!' hissed Arthur, an eyebrow raised in shock.

Balin cursed, glanced once more at the hall's higher platforms where he thought his mortal enemy Ida, the Saxon who had stolen Bernicia, lay abed. But the carnyx signal meant the tide had begun to flood the bay, and Balin knew his men would not leave without him. So, with a grim face, Balin took Gawain by the arm and dashed towards the hall doors.

'Princess Guinevere, stay close,' Arthur said, and the beautiful princess nodded at him with huge, fearful eyes. She wore a plain woollen dress with fur around its neck and sleeves, and she held Arthur's arm tight as they ran through Ida's hall. Dogs barked beyond the hall door, and Arthur heard voices in the hall behind him as he followed Kai and Huell back through the corridor and out of the huge oak doors into the courtyard beyond. The chill sea breeze hit Arthur's face, and then he reared up to stop as the sight before him hit him like a punch to the stomach.

Bors and his men of Gododdin stood in a half-circle before the hall with spears levelled and shields ready. Bors stood before them, huge and poised to fight. Beyond the Gododdin men, Saxon warriors thronged the courtyard. They held spears, axes and shields. Torchlight glinted off their helmets and blades and as Arthur peered out across Dun Guaroy, he saw blades and warriors also packed into the narrow pathways and streets.

'God help us,' gasped Kai, and he was right to pray, for the Saxons had filled Dun Guaroy with their might and trapped Balin and Bors' desperate war band in their hilltop stronghold. The sheer number of Saxon warriors was vast beyond count, big men with hard faces, bearded, scarred and made strong by war. They stood in eerie silence, staring malevolently at the pitiful number of Britons stood at the doors of Ida's hall. Balin tossed his torch to the rock-hewn steps and drew his swords, and he strolled down from the hall to join Bors before his men as though he had not a care in the world. Fear rooted Arthur to the spot, as was Kai beside him.

A figure shouldered its way through the mass of Saxons, a big man but bent slightly by age. He wore a shining coat of mail and carried a stone sceptre in one fist and a war axe in the other. He had long white hair and a braided beard, and next to him came a younger man of similar height and stature, but with flaxen hair, and then a hulking warrior with golden hair and eyes so blue they were almost white.

'Ida and his sons, Theodric and Ibissa,' said Prince Gawain through gritted teeth.

A third man joined the Saxon leaders, but this Saxon was a huge man, as big as Bors with muscled shoulders and a face so flat it looked as though a boulder had crushed it. He clutched a war axe in each of his enormous fists and came bare-chested so that his muscled torso shone in the moonlight.

'Octha,' whispered Guinevere.

Ida barked something in the harsh Saxon tongue and suddenly the throng behind erupted into a savage roar loud enough to shake the very earth. Arthur took a step back from that noise, and Guinevere clutched his arm even tighter. Ida raised his hand and the roar subsided. Another figure pushed his way to stand between Ida and Octha, and Arthur recognised Redwulf, the Saxon whose life he had saved in the fight at the brook, and the young man pointed up at Arthur and spoke something quietly to his king, who sneered.

'You *Wealas* scum come to my home,' Ida said slowly in Arthur's language. The words were guttural and heavily accented and scraped from Ida's throat like a blade from a scabbard. 'Come to kill me and steal my captives. Now, I will cut the skin from your bodies and hang you all from my walls. I will let the ravens eat your eyes and the women laugh at your flayed manhoods. I am King Ida!' He bellowed the last four words and his army surged forwards, seething with sharp weapons and malice. They came on like a great wave, surging around their leaders and charging towards the line of Gododdin spearmen.

'Make for the walls,' Balin shouted over his shoulder. 'Get Gawain and Guinevere out of this cursed place.'

Bors barged through his men and came bounding up the stone steps. At first Arthur thought the big man was fleeing the fight, but then Bors scooped Gawain in a brawny arm, almost dragging him from his feet.

'Come, my prince,' Bors growled.

'We can't leave the men to die!' Gawain protested, heaving against Bors' pull.

'I swore to your father, the king, that I would return you to Gododdin, and return you I shall.' Bors hauled Gawain with him and raced into a thin, dark space where the hall's south wall butted on to the edge of another long, thatched building. Arthur glanced at the charging Saxons, and then at Guinevere. He had a heartbeat to decide. Stand and fight, and surely die, or run and try to save the princess's life. Arthur turned and followed Bors. Guinevere ran with him, her hair flowing behind her. As he dashed into the darkness between two buildings, Arthur heard a sickening crunch as the Saxon horde smashed into the thin line of Gododdin men. Screams mingled with war cries, steel weapons clashed together, and Arthur felt guilty for leaving brave men to die whilst he ran away from the fight.

'How can we possibly escape this place?' Kai called over Arthur's shoulder, and as they burst out of the shadows to the hall's rear, Arthur glanced behind with relief to see that Kai and Huell followed him.

Saxons poured from the snarl of alleyways like rats, and Bors shoved Gawain away from him to strike down two Saxons with his spear. He threw the weapon at a third, and the force in the blow threw the Saxon from his feet. Bors bent and picked up an axe from one of the men he had killed and roared his defiance at the enemy.

'The walls!' Kai shouted, pointing beyond where Bors fought. A jagged line of sharpened palisade stakes rose behind a line of small huts. 'It must be the sea-facing wall.'

'Take her and get to the wall,' Arthur said, and he pushed Guinevere to Kai, and before his brother could question the order, Arthur charged down to Bors' side with Excalibur drawn.

'Are you ready to die?' growled Bors, grinning down at Arthur with a wild look on his brutal face.

'We hold them,' Arthur said. 'We back our way to the walls and jump into the sea.'

Bors sneered at the plan, jerked forward as if he would attack the Saxons again, and then remembered the oath to his king. He nodded and shuffled backwards to the line of hovels. Arthur went with him, and a bandy-legged Saxon carrying a spear charged him. Arthur parried the spear with Excalibur's blade and brought the point back with a flick of his wrist to slice open the Saxon's throat in a gout of dark blood. There was a score of them in the space behind Ida's hall, and they spat and cursed at Arthur and Bors, but they feared the Britons' blades and were reluctant to attack where four men had already died. Kai, Gawain and Huell ran around the hovels and Arthur's boot slid on a patch of grass. He could hear the crash of the sea above the Saxons' hateful shouts and knew that the walls were only steps away. The tide was coming in, and their only hope was to make a desperate jump into the churning waters. They could drown or smash like eggs on rocks beneath the waters, but there could be no surviving the mass of Saxon warriors come against them inside Dun Guaroy.

The Saxon host parted, and five big men marched through their midst. Each wore a coat of mail and carried a bright axe. They were broad-shouldered and strode with the confident air of champions. These men were the real Saxon warriors, the men who had won Ida a kingdom, and they did not flinch at the sight of their dead countrymen, or at Bors' vast frame. One of them broke into a run and Arthur lunged with his sword, but the big man batted it aside contemptuously with his axe and shoulder charged Arthur. The warrior's weight threw Arthur fully from his feet and he rolled on a patch of damp grass. As he came up, Bors and the Saxon traded axe blows, moving with terrible force and frightening skill. They hacked and punched at one another, each man parrying and striking with full force. The Saxon opened a cut on Bors' thigh, and for a moment Arthur thought the champion of Gododdin would die, and then Bors grabbed the Saxon's face in his hand and sliced his guts open with a sweep of his axe.

Arthur surged to his feet and ran to meet the four remaining Saxons, who all charged at Bors. He slashed open a man's shoulder with Excalibur's blade, but the man was already swinging his axe, and Arthur veered away from the shining blade. The big, bearded Saxon was fast, snake fast, and the axe opened a burning gash in Arthur's face. Arthur stumbled away, and another blow raked down his back. It felt like a horse had kicked him and Arthur crashed once more into the earth. The Saxons were unlike any man he had fought before. Too big, too strong and too fast. He scrambled in the grass towards the hovels, watching as Bors killed another man, chopping his axe into the Saxon's forehead with a wet thud. A blade slashed across Bors' shoulder and the Gododdin man reeled, and the three Saxon champions came for him with axes raised and teeth bared, and then died as five Britons charged into them from behind and cut them down with sweeps of sword and spear.

Arthur cried out with joy, because Balin of the Two Swords lived. He limped through the dying Saxons with blood-smeared swords in each hand, flanked by four of his black-cloaked men. Each bore terrible injuries and the Saxon horde chased them, howling and baying for blood like a pack of starving wolves. Arthur ran with them, Bors and Balin holding each other up and shouting at the other to live and run. A black cloak fell as a thrown spear took him between the shoulder blades. Arthur turned and slashed at a Saxon's face, but there were too many of them. The Saxons swarmed between huts like wild animals and Arthur tried to keep them at bay with his blade. They stabbed and grabbed at him in the narrow space between the shit-stinking slave hovels, and Arthur thought they must overwhelm him as he reached the palisade walls. Kai and Gawain hacked at the stakes with Saxon axes and there were huge gashes in the bright wood, whilst Arthur, Balin and the black cloaks desperately tried to beat at the Saxons with their weapons.

Bors roared and brought his own axe to bear, and in three great strikes two palisade stakes cracked and groaned as they fell backwards into the dark, churning sea. Rocks loomed there, dark and jagged. The flood tide heaved against Dun Guaroy's seaward cliffs, filling the wide bay with its tidal waters.

'We must jump!' Kai shouted above the crashing waves. Guinevere peered over the jaggedly chopped wood and shook her head with fear at the treacherous cliffs, and then dozens of Saxons flowed around the hovels to advance on the fleeing Britons. Bors pushed Gawain through the gap without hesitating and then leapt after him without looking at what lay beyond the palisade. Balin and his men hacked at the Saxons, keeping them back. A hairy Saxon arm grabbed Guinevere's wrist, causing her to shriek with terror until Arthur chopped the hand from the arm with a sweep of his sword.

'Go,' said Huell, and he hefted his spear. The one-handed Rheged man stepped in front of Arthur and Kai and stabbed his spear at the Saxons' faces, causing them to take a step backwards.

'We go together!' said Arthur, but Huell turned and snarled at him.

'I can never be the man I was. Let me die with honour. Tell men how Huell of Rheged died.' He charged at the Saxons with a mighty war cry, and Kai pulled Arthur towards the hole in Dun Guaroy's palisade. Huell stabbed and slashed with his spear in his left hand, its leaf-shaped blade tore out a Saxon's throat and slashed open the face of a bald enemy. 'Come and fight with Huell of Rheged,' he snarled, and a big Saxon in chain mail came at Huell from the horde. The Saxon roared his war cry and set about Huell with a long sword. Huell danced around the sword cuts and cracked his spear stave across the Saxon's skull and when the man stumbled under the blow, Huell stabbed his spear blade deep into the man's groin and tore it free. Huell howled with joy, and Arthur's heart soared because the maimed warrior had found a glorious doom. The Saxons came at him again. A seax cut Huell's thigh open, and a spear opened a gash upon his shoulder. Another axe swung for Huell's neck and just as it was about to strike him, Huell blocked it with his handless wrist. The axe chopped into the meat of Huell's forearm with a sickening crunch and Huell ripped the axeman's face open with a well-placed spear thrust. A sword pierced Huell's guts and the big man sagged in pain, but miraculously he found yet more strength in the well of his courage and drove his spear point into his attacker's chest.

'Go!' Huell roared, and as Arthur turned to flee from the carnage, a Saxon axe snapped Huell's spear.

Arthur grabbed Guinevere, put one boot on the chopped timbers and leapt with her into the darkness. Kai jumped with him, as did Balin and the last of his black cloaks. Air whipped Arthur's face and Guinevere clung to him as they plunged into the darkness. Saxons screamed as Huell made his legend inside King Ida's stronghold and the cold sea hit Arthur like a blow from a mighty war hammer.

15

Ice-cold water pulsed around him, and Arthur gasped and pulled at his
breastplate with one hand, panicking that its weight would drag him
down to drown in the murky depths. With the other he kept tight hold of
Excalibur. His cloak swirled about him, trapping his arms and cloying
about his face. Arthur screamed underwater and kicked frantically
beneath the ice-cold sea, fighting for his life whilst his mind roared at him
to take a breath. But if he did, the sea would fill his lungs with its grey
coldness. A hand grabbed his hair and forced him upwards and suddenly
his faced punched through the waves. Arthur sucked in a huge gulp of air,
and it was Kai, dragging Arthur out of the water until his thrashing boots
hit the sea bottom and he could stand. Spears and arrows launched from
the fortress walls, slapped into the lapping waves around them. Guinevere
shivered, holding her thin arms about herself as Bors, Gawain, Kai,
Arthur, Balin and two surviving black cloaks stumbled through the flood
tide. Every man save Gawain was injured, and they crashed through the
surf in grim silence, their blood mixing with the ocean to leave crimson
smears in its dark waters.

'We make for the men at the dunes,' said Bors, his voice strained. All
the Gododdin men save him had perished in the fight to escape from Dun

Guaroy, thirty brave men dead, but their prince Gawain of Gododdin was alive and free.

'They will follow hard on our tracks,' said Balin through gritted teeth. His men had to help Balin walk, and even in the darkness, Arthur could see cuts and gashes on the warrior's arms and chest.

'I'm tired of running from these Saxon turds,' said Bors, 'yet run, we must.'

Arthur could not yet see them, but he knew that thousands of Ida and Octha's men would come howling down into the bay at any moment. Arthur and his band reached the dunes where the five of Balin's black cloaks waited with four horses and dry cloaks. Those men turned pale when they saw how few had survived the horrors of Dun Guaroy, but Guinevere, Balin and Bors mounted the horses as the band sped away from the bay. The most severely wounded rode, and the rest marched. Guinevere also rode, on a bay gelding with an old cloak wrapped about her thin shoulders. The ragged band made their desperate escape in grim silence as a sickly yellow sun crawled over the eastern horizon. Arthur shivered in his wet clothes as he half walked and half ran across the coarse grass, holding a fistful of Guinevere's horse's mane to stop him collapsing. The cut he had taken to his face throbbed like a line of wasp stings, the wound on his back burned like fire, and every part of his body ached. So many of their war band had died atop Dun Guaroy, and though they had rescued Gawain and Guinevere, it seemed a high price for the brave dead to have paid. Images of Ida, Ibissa, Theodric, Octha became burned into Arthur's mind, but the overwhelming horror battering at his thought cage was the ease with which the five Saxon warriors had batted him aside as though he were a beardless boy without strength or skill. That had been a different fight, one he was ill-equipped for, and Arthur wondered how men would fare against hundreds of such Saxon champions on a battlefield.

Arthur travelled in a daze. He had survived the terror of Dun Guaroy and the forces of Ida and Octha, but Huell was dead. Brave Huell, who had always been so cruel to Arthur, and yet had given his life so Arthur and Kai could live. The treachery of Redwulf was sore to bear. The Saxon, whose life Arthur had saved despite Merlin and Balin's protests. Redwulf

had run to Dun Guaroy and alerted Ida and Octha of the approaching
Briton war band and their aims. That was why the Saxons were waiting
for them. Hidden and poised to catch the Britons deep inside their fearsome stronghold.

Arthur ran over rock, grass and heath, allowing the horse to drag him
through nettles, ferns and briars as the survivors fled for their lives. In his
half-dream state, Arthur realised he had been naïve and weak. There was
no room in this world for pity or mercy. Many had told him so, but Arthur
had always believed that he could live by a better standard, that folk
deserved mercy and kindness. Now, as his cut face burned, and the faces
of dead men rattled around his head, Arthur realised he must harden his
heart. He must become as cruel and fearsome as the men he fought. He
must use the sword Merlin had given him, and its legend, to strengthen
himself. The Saxons must be beaten for Rheged, Gododdin, Elmet,
Dumnonia and the rest of the British kingdoms to survive. If he was to
have any part to play in that struggle, Arthur needed to become stronger
in both body and resolve. The next time he fought Saxon champions, he
would match their strength. He would be every bit as ruthless and savage
as Ida and Octha.

The sun rose high in a clear sky and the survivors fled westwards
where the land turned in on itself in a deep bay, until they reached
another stretch of coastline, where Balin said a Roman fort called Olca-
clavis once sat at its southern tip. The bay swept westwards, hacking into
the coastline like a great bite out of the land. At its south-western tip, they
came upon a collection of stone-made buildings with earth-covered roofs.
Smoke billowed from great cauldrons boiling over charcoal pits and the
stink of that burning filled the narrow hills around the bay.

'Salt mine,' said Balin. 'We can find food and ale there.'

'It's a Saxon place. There will be guards,' Bors replied. The big man
slumped across his horse's back and his blood smeared its riding cloth
and flanks. Bors' face was white as the patch on the gelding's forehead
and if he didn't receive care soon, the champion of Gododdin would
surely die of his wounds.

'We must take what we need,' said Arthur. He straightened his back
and drew Excalibur. 'Bors and Balin are too grievously wounded to fight

again. Stay here with Gawain, Guinevere and the horses. Kai, Dewi and Aneirin, follow me.'

'Since when do you give the orders?' said Dewi. The tall, lugubrious black cloak glanced at Balin for support. Aneirin, the other black-cloaked survivor of Dun Guaroy, licked his lips and glanced from Arthur to Balin.

'Do as he says,' Balin whispered. His eyes were closed, and he grimaced, holding his elbow tight to his wounded torso. 'We need supplies and more horses. Be quick, for the enemy is surely on our heels. The rest of you also go.' Balin ordered his five warriors who had waited on the dunes to march with Arthur as well, so that eight men marched away from the beleaguered survivors.

Arthur followed a path with deep, rain-filled ruts worn by wagon wheels, down towards the buildings and boiling cauldrons. An overgrown hedge hid them from the salt farm, but Arthur could hear the harsh bark of Saxon voices as they drew closer. He came off the path and strode between two stone buildings and on to a shale beach where three Saxons in jerkins and carrying spears shouted at four men crouched in the shallows. The Saxons boiled brine in the cauldrons, and their slaves graded and strained the salt using deep buckets. Salt was valuable. Lords and wealthy men paid vast sums to buy it in sealed ceramic jars, and Ector always bought one for the yule celebrations in midwinter. The salt mine was precious to its owner, and so Arthur expected there to be more than the three Saxons guarding its production.

'Are you men Britons?' Arthur shouted at the four men who shook their buckets in the water. The Saxons and the slaves turned to him in surprise, and Arthur strode towards them. 'Are you Britons?' he repeated, but louder this time.

'Yes,' replied one slave, a thin man with hollow eyes.

'How many guards are there?'

'These three and three more inside.' He pointed a bony finger towards the buildings.

One of the Saxons shouted at Arthur in his own tongue, and all three levelled their spears. Without breaking stride, Arthur batted a rust-dotted spear aside and punched Excalibur's blade into the guard's stomach. He twisted the blade, wrenched it free and kicked the groaning Saxon on to the shale beach. The two remaining Saxons tried to run, but Kai and the black cloaks cut them down.

'I am Arthur,' he said, and held up Excalibur to the four slaves, who stared slowly, eyes flitting from the dying Saxons to the warrior who had come so unexpectedly. 'This is Excalibur, the sword of Aurelius Ambrosius granted to me by Merlin the druid, to free Britain from the Saxon invaders. You are now free. Will you pledge your lives to my cause and my sword?'

The four men looked at each other nervously. Kai, Dewi and Aneirin stared at Arthur as though he were a madman. But Arthur suddenly had clarity where before there had been confusion. He was a man where before he had been a child, and he knew what must be done. Merlin was a legend, perhaps the last great druid, and all men feared his power and knew of Ambrosius' sword. Arthur could use both the legend and the sword to bind men to him, to imbue them with confidence and belief in a magic which could become real if enough men believed in it. The belief in Merlin, Excalibur, the old gods and the power in the land itself could be enough to unite the kingdoms of Britain to fight the Saxon hordes.

'We will, lord,' said the hollow-eyed man. He threw his bucket aside and came from the water, linen rags hanging loose about his thin body. 'My name is Cadog, and I was a warrior once. I've been a slave in this godforsaken place for five winters.' He knelt and raised his hands to Arthur, and Arthur lowered Excalibur so that the man could kiss its bloody blade.

'You are now a warrior again. Do you swear to fight and die for me, to be my man?'

'Yes, lord,' he said. Though Arthur was not a lord, the man did him the honour of the title and the other three men followed his lead.

'What are you doing?' said Kai, staring at Arthur in disbelief.

'It's time to fight back properly,' Arthur said, and clapped Kai on the shoulder. 'There are more Saxons here to kill, and we need to find food, dry clothes and ale.'

They found the remaining Saxons asleep inside the stone huts, and Arthur let the four slaves kill them. They hacked at their former masters with spears and seax blades, took their clothes and weapons and became men again. Dewi found a wagon and two mules in a stable behind the stone buildings, which Cadog said the Saxons used to transport the salt in huge ceramic jars. Arthur took the wagon and the mules and filled it with supplies from the guardhouse. They had smoked fish, pork, butter, milk, loaves of dark bread and three jars of ale.

The survivors of Dun Guaroy ate the food hungrily, and Arthur handed Guinevere a loaf of bread for which she thanked him. Arthur overheard Dewi whispering to Balin of how Arthur had spoken to the slaves of his sword and of Merlin, and how Arthur had taken the freedmen's oaths, but Balin seemed not to care in his wounded state. They pushed hard westwards and as the sun set beyond the high peaks, they reached the foothills of the mountains which split northern Britain in two. Kai spotted spearmen in the distance, the first sign of their Saxon enemies pursuing them from Dun Guaroy, but the survivors reached the safety of the mountain passes before the enemy could draw close.

As night fell and washed the land in shadow, Balin led them high into the foothills to a sheltered cleft in a steep rock face. They risked a small campfire to warm themselves after the hardships suffered since the attack on Ida's fortress. Cadog and the freedmen kept to themselves, huddled tightly and thankful for their share of the food and ale. The warriors tended to each other's wounds. Prince Gawain bound Bors and Balin's wounds as best he could, but they would need to be cleaned and properly tended before the dreaded rot set in. Bors had taken too many cuts to his arms and body to count, but one gash across his side oozed dark blood and Arthur feared for the big man. His broad face was ghostly white, and he lay silently beside the fire, sweating from the pain, whilst Gawain gave him sips of ale to slake his thirst. Balin's men cleaned and wrapped his wounds as they huddled about their *comitatus*, remembering those who had died in the fighting with solemn words and vows to continue the fight for their lost kingdom.

Guinevere sat with Arthur and Kai, and with the fire to warm her, she seemed to awake from her shock at the rescue and escape from Dun Guaroy. Her copper hair fell about her shoulders, and she tied it back with a scrap of cloth to reveal her long face and high cheekbones. She shared one of the last remaining loaves with Kai and Arthur, and they each had a handful of food left from the provisions taken from the salt mine.

'I haven't thanked you,' Guinevere said. She spoke the language of the Britons, but with the strange accent of her people from across the narrow sea. 'You risked so much to enter that awful place. I shall forever be indebted to you all.' She smiled, and her beauty was almost painful to look upon. Her emerald eyes shone, even in the shadows beneath the rocks, and Arthur thought her smile was so radiant that it could dim the sun.

'Your father sent a man to King Urien of Rheged to ask for help, my lady,' said Kai. 'A druid came and ordered that we rescue you. Merlin was with us.'

'Merlin the druid marched with you?' she said, shuffling closer with excitement.

'Yes, but he left before we attacked the fort. We captured a *gwyllion* and Merlin took her with him.'

'You are brave men.'

'Any warrior would have done the same, and many perished in the attempt. Thirty men of Gododdin gave their lives to rescue Prince Gawain.'

'And he will feel the weight of their loss. Gawain was a prisoner far longer than I, and I fear he suffered at their brutish hands.'

'Did they hurt you, lady?' asked Kai.

'No, they paraded me and made me wear their stinking furs, but they wanted to ransom me back to my father and so Ida ordered his men to leave me alone. I sailed from Cameliard to join King Uther's court as a lady-in-waiting. I think my father hoped I would find noble suitors in Dumnonia or another powerful kingdom. The Saxons captured our ship off the coast and killed my father's warriors. They captured my two hand-maidens and I have not seen them since that fateful day.'

'We will take you to King Urien, lady,' said Arthur, 'then perhaps you can travel south to Dumnonia.'

'You are Urien's men?'

'We are,' said Kai, 'my father is Ector, champion of Rheged.'

'Then I am fortunate that the men of Rheged are so brave. Now, tell me of Merlin and this Saxon witch. I have heard tales of Merlin the druid since I was a girl, of how he defeated a dragon and trapped it beneath a mountain, of how he can see the future and turn men into beasts.'

They spoke deep into the night, even after the rest of the warriors had fallen asleep. Arthur could not take his eyes off Guinevere, and when she caught his eye, he looked away and cursed at the redness blooming upon his cheeks. As the conversation went on, mostly between her and Kai, Guinevere showed herself to be both clever and thoughtful. She knew of the events in Britain, of the kingdoms, their kings and the troubles with the Saxons. She spoke of her father's problems with marauding Franks, of how Cameliard and Armorica were hard-pressed with Franks from the south and east, battle-hardened from time spent fighting for the Romans. When at last they lay down to sleep, Arthur listened to her breathing and wondered if there was a fairer woman in the world than Princess Guinevere of Cameliard.

The Saxons did not pursue them across the mountain passes, and Gawain persuaded the band of survivors to turn north to Gododdin rather than continue south-west to Rheged. They were too few, Gawain argued, to make it through the borderlands between Lloegyr and Rheged, which were filled with bands of *bucellari* raiders and masterless men. Arthur saw no reason not to return Gawain and Bors to their kingdom before taking Guinevere to King Urien and marching from Gododdin to Rheged with a force of Gododdin spearmen to protect them on the journey seemed like a good idea after the dangers of their march to Dun Guaroy. They reached Gododdin after two days of slow progress. Gawain moved Bors to the wagon where he lay, sometimes shivering and sometimes sweating, and Arthur was glad when they spied the great hill fort of Dunpendyrlaw, home of King Letan Luyddoc of Gododdin.

The fort sat atop a huge, grass-covered mound which rose from the flatlands like a great hump. Balin had his men sound the carnyx to announce their arrival, and riders came thundering from the hill and were astonished to see their champion Bors laid low, and their prince alive and well. King Letan greeted them warmly at the fort's gates. He was grey-bearded, and his face lined with age, but he moved with the litheness and grace of a younger man. He clapped each man on the shoulder, thanked them for their bravery, and hugged Gawain so hard that he lifted the prince off his feet. King Letan had his finest healers take care of Bors and threw a feast to celebrate the return of his son. Gawain appeared at the feast in a fine tunic of green cloth and a bronze circlet upon his brow, his hair and beard cleaned and oiled, and looked no longer the filthy, thin prisoner of King Ida. The king honoured Balin, Arthur, Kai and the surviving black cloaks with gifts, and Arthur bowed in gratitude when King Letan handed him a finely woven russet cloak edged with yellow stitching and a fur-lined hood.

The men of Gododdin worshipped the old gods, for the further north a man went in Britain, the less fervent was Christ's grip. There were no priests in Gododdin, and King Urien tolerated their presence in Rheged more out of fear of their God's displeasure than because he favoured Christ over the old gods. In the southern kingdoms, like Dumnonia, all men worshipped Christ and priests and bishops were powerful men who spoke the word of God into their leader's ears. They obtained land for their churches and silver for their coffers. Druids kept no land, and their holy places were the groves, lakes, streams, dykes, mountains and marshes of Britain. Gododdin's shields bore the stag sigil, and a magnificent stag's skull with sprawling yellowed antlers hung above King Letan's high table, just as a bear did in Urien's hall. Arthur marvelled at the size of the antlers, and he and Kai argued over how big the beast must have been before it died. The men of Gododdin wore their hair and beards long, and they wove dyed strips of cloth into their hair. They wore woollen tunics dyed red, and each wore a russet cloak pinned at their left shoulder with cloak pins of silver and gold. King Letan wore a huge gold stag-shaped pin with silver antlers, and the younger warriors at the back of the hall wore faded cloaks with simple pins made of bronze or copper.

Guinevere came to the feast in a dress of blue wool, with her hair tied atop her head in plaited coils. King Letan presented her with a silver cloak pin in the shape of a swan, and her beauty captivated every warrior in the hall, including Arthur. A wise old woman with a wrinkled face and a milky eye had tended to Arthur's wounds before the feast. She had cleaned the gashes upon his face and back, sewn them closed with a sheep-gut thread, and packed them tight with a honey poultice. Arthur touched the wound on his face gingerly, hoping that Guinevere would not sicken at the stitching or cloth stuck to his cheek. King Letan wanted all the news of the march into Lloegyr, and there was much lamenting in the hall when Balin spoke of the number of warriors in Octha's army. There were not three thousand spears in all of Gododdin, and King Letan asked Arthur and Kai to talk to King Urien upon their return and ask him to send riders to Gododdin to plan for the inevitable wars to come. Balin also spoke of Merlin, and King Letan eyed Arthur carefully when he brought forth Excalibur and showed her finely wrought blade around the hall.

'Strange days indeed,' said King Letan when Arthur knelt before him to hand the king his blade. Letan turned it over and admired the weapon's balance and craftmanship. 'Excalibur has returned, and in the hand of a son of nowhere. Merlin's cunning is behind this, and none but a fool would try to understand the warp and weft of his plans. I fought beside Ambrosius in the Great War, lad, and I have seen this blade cut down many a Saxon. Wield it well, for doubtless you will need it when we fight the invaders.'

Arthur bowed to the king but said nothing. He shared a feasting bench with Kai, Cadog and the three men newly sworn to him. Frothy ale flowed freely, as did platters of meat, fish and honey cakes, and when men began to sing old battle songs with red cheeks and arms around one another, Arthur sought Balin of the Two Swords who sat alone at a bench below the high table. His men were on a nearby table, surrounded by Gododdin men as they told of the horrors of Dun Guaroy, of how well the slaughtered men of Gododdin had fought against the Saxon horde, and of how Bors had fought like a demon to free Prince Gawain from his captivity.

'Letan will send twenty spearmen south with you to Rheged,' Balin said as Arthur sat down opposite him.

'He is a gracious king,' said Arthur, 'and pleased to have his son returned to him.'

'Gawain might look every bit the high-born prince up there with his father, but he is a brave and skilled warrior. He will march with me and my men when we leave Gododdin.'

'Where will you go, now that...' Arthur didn't want to mention the deaths of so many of Balin's men. They were the last warriors of Bernicia and could not be easily replaced.

'I need more men,' Balin sighed, 'because the fight must go on. We must resist the Saxons, harry them wherever we can. For that, I need spearmen.'

'Where will you find them?'

'In the badlands. Amongst the roving bands of mercenaries, raiders and masterless men. I'll seek them out, try to have them join the fight.'

'I wish to come with you, if you'll have me.' Arthur stared into Balin's hard eyes, hoping the noble warrior would accept his request. Arthur was not ready to return to Rheged and Ector's service, not after he had been through and seen so much. The war was not within Rheged, but beyond in Lloegyr, and Merlin had entrusted Arthur with Excalibur, so Arthur must swing the sword against the enemy.

'Men will follow the man given the sword of Britain by Merlin himself. Men are fickle and strange. They would follow a legend where they would not fight for their own people. So, yes. I would be glad to have you with me, Arthur of Nowhere.'

'Men will follow Balin of the Two Swords, as will I.' Arthur bowed his head and left Balin in peace. He returned to Kai, who frowned in surprise when Arthur told him of his plan to march with Balin.

'But we must return to Rheged, with Guinevere, and to my father,' said Kai as though Rheged were all that mattered.

'Ector and Urien fight to protect Rheged's borders when we must take the fight to the Saxons. Balin does that, and I will join him,' said Arthur. He held out his hand for his foster brother to take in agreement.

'No, Arthur. Our place is at my father, our father's side. Balin fights for a lost kingdom and to find his treacherous brother. His path is a dark road full of death and defeat, there is bad luck and an ill doom woven into his fate, and we must defend Rheged. We are warriors now, you and I.' Kai lifted the sleeve of his tunic to show the death rings around his forearm. 'We can't even make enough rings to tell of the Saxons we have killed since leaving Rheged. Our country needs men like us, brother. Father needs our spears and our experience. Come home.'

'I cannot. I must fight, Kai, come with me.'

Kai picked up a horn cup of ale, drained the contents, and slammed it down onto the bench. 'Merlin has filled your head with nonsense,' he spat, standing and glaring down at Arthur. 'I don't know why he gave you that sword, but ever since that day, you have been under his spell, and that cursed Saxon *gwyllion*. I ride for home tomorrow with the spearmen of Gododdin to return Guinevere to King Urien, and then I will join my father's men. We leave at midday. If you are not there, I will know where your loyalty lies. Remember though, brother, all my father has done for you and what you owe him.'

Arthur let Kai leave the feast and brooded over his brother's words. He owed Ector everything, a debt he could never repay. But Arthur could see clearly that the way to fight for Rheged was to take the fight to Ida and Octha, rather than wait for them to attack and destroy each kingdom of Britain one by one. The kingdoms must be united, and Merlin had entrusted Arthur with the sword to make that happen. The choice Kai had presented him with was no choice at all. Arthur had to fight for Britain. So, before sunrise, Arthur packed his meagre belongings and met Balin and his seven black cloaks at Dunpendyrlaw's gates. He did not say goodbye to Kai, for he knew his brother would not accept his decision, but Guinevere found them at the gates, and she gave each man a kiss on the cheek for luck, and every burly warrior blushed like a small boy at the gesture. She pulled Arthur aside and pressed a cold metal object into his hand. It was the silver cloak pin given to her by King Letan.

'Carry this with you,' she said. 'I hope it brings you luck and keeps you safe.' She kissed him on the cheek and ran off towards the great hall, leaving Arthur dumbstruck. He held the pin in his hand as they left Dunpendyrlaw's hill but marched with a heavy heart. He would miss Kai. The two young men had never been apart. Theirs had been a life of brotherly friendship, training, fighting, playing together in the forests and orchards around Caer Ligualid. But that time was over. Now it was time for war.

16

Arthur, his oathmen and the black cloaks marched south-east into the dark lands that lay between Lloegyr, Gododdin and Rheged. Masterless men flocked to those border regions, which were not under the protection of spearmen or kings. There, they could raid, plunder, rape, murder and fight each other, and any who tried to stop them. *Bucellari* mercenaries camped in the dark lands when they could not find a lord to pay them to fight, and the folk who lived in the deep valleys, around its winding rivers, or in the mountain passes, lived in fear. In a continuous cycle, they paid the bad men to fight for them, to protect them from other roving war bands, with food, milk, butter, salt, cheese, slaves, women and what paltry silver they could muster. There were old families in the hills and even older blood feuds. The hills, springs, caves and trees bore ancient names and spirits and legends clung to landmarks with stories passed down by word of mouth across the generations.

For a year, Arthur and Balin roamed the bad lands, fighting vicious war bands whose members were both Briton and Saxon. Men who had lost favour with their lords, had committed a crime, or their lord had died in battle, leaving them with no one to fight for and nowhere to go. Balin sought such men, defeated them in battle, bound them to him with oaths, always seeking news of his dread brother Balan, and bound them to him with oaths. During the long months of skirmish and battle, Arthur also bound men to his service. He discussed with them the importance of Merlin, Excalibur and their role in the war that would determine the destiny of Britain. Hardened men swore oaths to serve Arthur, swayed by the legends, but also by the promise of spoils and glory in the wars to come. So it was that by the following summer Balin led a force of sixty warriors, and of those thirty were oathsworn to be Arthur's men. They were a ragged band of tough men with cruel faces, grizzled beards and flinty eyes. Each carried a spear, knife or seax, and wore a mixture of hard-baked leather breastplates, simple woollen clothing, and some even wore mail. One man, Hywel, a captain of five warriors, even wore a fantastic Roman cuirass of overlaying iron plates which moved together like a skin. He had lost favour with King Gwallog of Elmet and so he and his five men had become mercenaries.

Tales of Merlin, Ambrosius Aurelianus, the Great War and Excalibur entranced men, especially those who fought without cause or master. They bound themselves to Arthur and Excalibur's legend by kneeling and kissing the sword and swearing to serve Arthur until death. Any man sworn to Balin took to wearing the black cloak of his war band, and Arthur's men painted their leather shield covers with a white sword. Cadog was the first to daub that simple sigil upon his shield, and the rest quickly followed so that the sword became Arthur's recognisable sigil. There was no rivalry between Arthur and Balin, despite the Bernician's objection at Merlin giving the sword to Arthur. They fought for the same cause, to build a force to defend Britain against the Saxons, and Balin sought revenge against his brother, who lurked somewhere deep in Lloegyr amongst the Saxon enemy. Balin was a quiet, stoic man, and he and Arthur talked and agreed on plans together before marching to battle, and the two men rarely disagreed. Their war band was a formidable force and by the early summer following their departure from Gododdin, the badlands were all but cleared of masterless men. Balin and Arthur marched north into the mountainous river lands south of Dal Riata and found wild Irish and Scots warriors there who came into their service only after savage battles and crushing defeats. The surviving men joined Balin's ranks and swelled his numbers to forty men.

It had been a long year of ceaseless fighting against the odds, beginning with seven men and through brutal slaughter, shattered spears, broken shields, blood, wounds and suffering, Balin and Arthur had built a formidable war band. There were savage fights in dark forests, river fords and mountain passes where men sweated in leather, mail and furs to cut, stab and rend at each other, and Arthur lost count of the men he had killed and injured. His forearms were now entirely blue with death ring tattoos. Men with evil, scarred faces proved themselves loyal and brave, and men with soft beards and gentle faces who seemed good and honest proved themselves cowards or ran away in the night. Arthur came to learn the value of a man by his deeds, rather than by his words or looks. He trained his men to fight like the Saxons, using larger shields and practising shield wall tactics until their arms ached and their muscles screamed. They learned to advance, how to start a mock retreat before turning and reforming quickly, how to open a small gap to lure an enemy into the wall of shields before closing and trapping them. But the key strategy Arthur favoured was to pin an enemy with his shield wall and sharp spears, and then have ten riders encircle them on horseback before dismounting and attacking their rear. Fighting on horseback was a treacherous business which no warrior did willingly, with only a horse blanket across the steed's back and no purchase for feet or hips, so Arthur and his men used their mounts for speed but not for battle.

Arthur captured a white stallion which he named Llamrei, and ten of his men also rode fine mounts captured from defeated warlords in the wild borderlands. Arthur also wore a captured heavy chain-mail coat of interlocked iron rings which protected him from neck to knee, and a seax in a sheath at the small of his back. He still wore the russet cloak gifted to him by King Letan and wore Guinevere's silver swan pin on the inside of his belt behind Excalibur's fleece-lined black scabbard. He would hold the pin at night, rubbing his thumb over the intricately wrought silver, hoping to dream of Guinevere's beauty and wondering if she had remained with King Urien in Rheged or had travelled south to King Uther in Dumnonia. Word drifted north that Octha and his army marched south and fought the warriors of Elmet and Powys and were repelled at great cost of life to the Britons. Octha, or so said merchants and roving war bands fleeing north away from that war, had returned to Ida in Bernicia for the winter and now marshalled his Saxon forces again for a summer campaign to conquer the land he so desperately craved.

So Arthur and Balin marched their warriors south, skirting the borders of Gododdin and Bernicia, marching towards Rheged. Balin argued for a return to Bernicia so that he and Arthur could bring their spearmen against Ida and Octha's Saxons in Lloegyr.

'We are sixty against Octha's three thousand, and Ida's settled army,' Arthur had said as they spoke beside a marching campfire. 'Our men are battle-hardened, and we could harry the Saxons, burn their farms and kill their scouts, but we can't defeat them. We must march for Rheged, rally King Urien to war, and then on to Elmet and Dumnonia. To defeat Octha and Ida, we need an army to match theirs, an army with spearmen from every kingdom threatened by the Saxon invaders.'

'Uther is the Pendragon,' Balin had replied, 'and only he can unite the kingdoms. But you are right, we must do more than sting Ida and Octha's arses if we are going to return Lloegyr to its rightful people.'

Swallows and martins swooped above forests blooming with fresh, leafy boughs and cold, frosty mornings gave way to sunny days which warmed Arthur's neck as they entered Rheged's mountainous borders. Bees and butterflies hopped on carpets of blooming wildflowers, and gentle winds stirred violets and foxgloves in seas of bright heather. Arthur and Balin did not hide their force as they rode along goat paths and beside streams, and Arthur told the farmers and villagers he met along the road who he was and why his men came to Rheged. The war band bought meat, wheat, milk and ale from the common folk, but the news in the valleys and dales was of Saxon armies gathering across the mountains in Lloegyr, waiting ominously to pounce from their Saxon fastnesses.

A line of spearmen carrying shields painted with the Rheged stag appeared at midday on a rain-soaked day as Arthur and Balin marched along a lazy river thick with reeds and wild grasses. The men of Rheged greeted Arthur warmly, for they were scouts from Ector's stronghold at Caer Ligualid and Arthur knew most of them by name. Arthur was overjoyed to learn that both Ector and Kai were at home, and so he and his riders rode ahead of the war band, so eager was Arthur to be reunited with his spear-father and brother. Llamrei's hooves clopped along the old Roman road and Arthur's heart leapt as the stone and timber walls of Caer Ligualid came into view. The Romans had built a fortress of stone, oak and alder and much of their old work still stood, reinforced by a palisade, ditch and bank with Ector kept in good repair. The Roman aqueduct provided the fort and settlement with fresh water and as Arthur rode past woods, streams and outbuildings, memories of a childhood spent playing with Kai and Lunete came happily flooding back to him.

Arthur and his riders reined in before the gate and a gaggle of ruddy-faced boys took their horses to the stables. The gate banged and creaked as guards lifted the great oak spar and pushed open the wide gates. Arthur laughed for joy as the huge figure of Ector came strolling through. His bald head shone, and his long, braided beard hung thick upon his chest.

'Arthur?' said Ector with his huge, tattooed arms held wide in greeting. 'Is it truly you?'

'Spear-father!' called Arthur in greeting and ran to embrace the old warrior.

'By the gods, you've grown since you left.' Ector squeezed Arthur's shoulders and arms, thickened by a year of shield, sword and spear work. Arthur realised he was now as tall as Ector, the man who had always seemed so huge. 'Are you well?' Ector peered over Arthur's shoulder at the ten warriors who waited behind him. Their cloaks and boots were travel stained, but each man carried a sharp spear and large linden-wood shields bearing Arthur's sword sigil. Cadog and Hywel were there, the former no longer the thin man freed from the salt mine but now broad-shouldered and shaggy-bearded, and Hywel in his polished Roman armour.

'I am, Father. These are a few of my men. There is news of Saxon forces shifting in Lloegyr, so we have come south to fight.'

'Your men? Kai said you were with Balin of the Two Swords?'

'Aye, Balin follows on foot with fifty spearmen.'

'Fifty!' Ector exclaimed and blew out his cheeks. He brushed a finger across the deep scar on Arthur's cheek and stared down at the death rings on Arthur's forearms. 'You have been busy. And this must be Excalibur.' Ector pointed at the sword at Arthur's belt.

'It has been a long year, spear-father, and yes, this is Excalibur given to me by Merlin himself. But tell me of Caer Ligualid, of you and Lunete, of the Saxons and the coming summer campaign.'

'Lunete will be thrilled to see you. Come inside and take some food. Your men are welcome.'

'Thank you. Is Kai here?'

'He is, but we are preparing to march. There are Saxons on our borders again. They return like frogspawn each spring, stealing cattle, murdering our people.' Ector sighed and shook his head at the never-ending cycle of Saxon aggression.

Arthur followed Ector inside Caer Ligualid's walls, and he waved greetings to familiar faces, stewards, foresters and a gaggle of warriors' wives who sat in a circle, spinning yarn on wooden distaffs. Lunete came bounding from the stone fort and leapt at Arthur, hugging him as though he had been gone for years. He laughed and swung her around before setting her down.

'You look radiant,' he said, holding up her chin, and so she did. Her raven-black hair fell loose about her shoulders and her blue eyes shone like jewels. 'I have missed you.'

'You've changed,' she said.

'How have you been?'

'Bored. And now Father is sending me to the Bear Fort to join King Urien's court. He says he has a man in mind for me to marry, some coarse sheep lover from the northern mountains. I won't stand for it, that cannot be my fate.'

'It's time to find you a husband, you are a grown woman now,' Ector said, as he showed Arthur's men where they could find food and mead. 'A year in Urien's hall and suitors will flock around you like...'

'Flies around shit.' She laughed as Ector frowned at her coarseness, and Lunete led Arthur into the old Roman fortress. Arthur let his fingers drag on the cold, dressed stone and there was a happy familiarity in the place. Though it had only been a year since he had left, Arthur had seen and done so much that his time in Caer Ligualid seemed like a different life, and he a different person. Arthur and Lunete walked the narrow streets inside the fort arm in arm, and she told him stories of the long winter, of how Ector had brought in an old widow to help Lunete prepare for her time at court, but how she had instead hunted and ridden in the forests around the town. Arthur laughed, and for a moment he forgot the weight of Saxons and war. But the moment was fleeting, because Kai awaited them by the hearth fire inside Ector's great hall.

'Brother,' Arthur said, striding to Kai with his arms outstretched.

'Arthur,' Kai said, and he took Arthur's wrist in the warrior's grip. 'You are just in time, for we march to war this very week. Urien had despatched a hundred men to our borders, and we must join them. Saxons have crossed the hills from Lloegyr.'

'Balin is with me, and we bring seventy men. We shall march with you.'

'Seventy spearmen?' Kai said and folded his arms across his chest.

'Aye, thirty of my own and forty sworn to Balin.'

'And I thought you had returned to join us, not to gloat and boast of your time in the north.'

'I have not come to boast.'

'Whilst you were off wandering with Balin, I was here protecting our people.'

'Oh please,' Lunete interrupted. 'There was no fighting last summer. The Saxons fought in the south, and we had peace. All you did was scout the borderlands, hunt deer and guard the walls. Can we not be friends, like old times?'

'Come, brother,' said Arthur and clapped Kai upon the shoulder. 'Is there nothing to drink in this hall?'

Kai glowered at Arthur for a moment, and they both laughed as Lunete grabbed them around the neck and wrestled them to the ground. Arthur collapsed in a tangle of cloak, scabbard, seax and heavy chain mail. Ector found them rolling in the floor rushes and he bent double, laughing along with them. They spent the rest of that day drinking and eating and speaking of last year's harvest, of a wild winter storm which had torn the roofs from some of the Caer's homes, and then more sombrely of the increasing Saxon threat. They drank to Huell and remembered his deeds, and Ector lamented his lost captain.

Ector told the tale of Octha's march south, and how the men of Elmet and Powys had defeated Octha, but at great cost to their kingdoms. So many of their warriors had perished in the fighting that over half their fighting men were dead, leaving the two mighty kingdoms almost unable to defend themselves should Octha attack again. Eventually, they had paid him off with a horde of silver and gold and Octha had sworn to a year of peace, instead marching north to winter with Ida in Bernicia. But Octha could not stay there forever. Three thousand men eat a lot of meat and grain and Octha must provide land, glory and wealth for his ferocious warriors or lose them. So there would be war in the north before the summer was over.

Balin and the remaining war band arrived at the Caer later that day, and Ector welcomed him warmly. The two old warriors sat together and spoke of the Great War, and of the friends and family they had lost in the never-ending conflict. Arthur asked for news of Merlin, but there was none. Ector had heard from King Urien that Merlin was in the south, and that Nimue was with him. Balin and Arthur told Ector of their plan to march south and look for help from Uther Pendragon, but Ector gave no opinion of their plan. He only said that Balin and Arthur should visit King Urien at the Bear Fort after driving out the Saxon raiders from Rheged and ask for his support if they were planning to raise an army.

Ector's warriors marvelled at the sight of Excalibur, and Arthur passed the legendary blade around so that each man could hold and swing the famous sword. They rested at the Caer for two days, and then Ector led them west with thirty of his own warriors so that close to a hundred men left to meet the Saxon raiders. They spent a night camped by the old Roman villa where Kai had earned his first death ring, and Ector sat with Arthur as he ran a whetstone along Excalibur's blade.

'You have grand plans,' said Ector, jutting his chin towards where Balin and Arthur's warriors sat around a fire sharing a meal of hard bread and cheese. 'To defeat the Saxons, the kingdoms of Britain must unite. In that, you are right. But you have not met Uther, and many of the old kings are jaded and cruel, like Urien. They have not forgotten how the Great War ended and what was lost.'

'Somebody must try, spear-father. Merlin gave me Excalibur and his trust, and I must follow this road, no matter how hard or unlikely it may seem,' Arthur replied.

'Merlin's cunning weaves and dances across the land, and perhaps he has the right of it. No king of Britain will take orders from or follow another. They are too proud and are reluctant to align after what happened before. The memory of how hard their great-grandfathers fought to win their lands in the bleak days when the Romans left us in darkness still burns strong, and they have much to lose. Perhaps warriors like you and Balin, not oathsworn to any king, could unite us. The Saxons have taken Balin's home, and you were too young to swear an oath to me or King Urien before you left. But Uther could ignore you, or worse, he could see you and Balin as a threat and attack you. Without the Pendragon, you have nothing. Only the king of kings can muster an army of Britain.'

'The last time the kingdoms came together, Vortigern, Hengist, Horsa and Ida won. It must be different this time.'

'Aye, well. Things happened which drove a wedge between our last alliance. Love and betrayal cast us asunder, and men do not forget.'

'Uther, Merlin and Gorlois of Kernow? Men rarely talk of the details of that betrayal, as though its truth is lost in a fog. You were once Uther's man, Father, what happened?'

Ector sighed and placed his heavy hand on Arthur's arm. 'Now is not the time, son. But I will tell you the sorry tale one day. Of how we fought as one people and almost defeated Vortigern, and how lust and murder cost us everything, of how I left Dumnonia and came north with Igraine to serve King Urien.'

'Why do men not talk of what happened, and why are you so reluctant to talk about it even now?'

'Few know the truth, and for those who do, the wounds are still raw and bleeding, even after all this time. But I will tell you all, son, I swear it. But not now, we must sleep. Tomorrow, we hunt Saxons.' Ector rose and took a step towards his cloak and the warm campfire, but then turned as an afterthought. 'Do you still wear Igraine's gift?'

Arthur lifted the bronze disc from behind his mail and its leather lining and showed the dragon-inlaid treasure to his foster father. Ector nodded and went to his bed. Arthur wanted to ask Ector the tale of his birth, and how Merlin knew who his parents were, but Ector looked tired and in no mood to speak further. Such conversations were awkward, and even the sparse details Ector had just provided on the Great War were spoken with a reluctant tone. Arthur spent that night in a fitful sleep, wondering how the Pendragon would receive him, and if the Britons could ever form a united army capable of defeating the marauding Saxons. He rose early the next morning to brush Llamrei down and as he fed the horse a handful of oats, a warrior approached him wearing a deep hood and carrying a bow.

'Off to hunt for breakfast?' Arthur said in greeting and then shook his head in disbelief when the warrior threw back the hood to reveal a head of long black hair and piercing blue eyes.

'What?' said Lunete. 'I can't let you men have all the glory.'

'Father will lose his mind when he finds out.'

'Why shouldn't I march with you? I'm better with the bow than any of you, and better with the spear than half of these lackwits.'

Arthur laughed at that, not only because it was true, but because he had missed Lunete's wildness. 'Keep away from Ector,' Arthur warned her. 'Stay with my men if you wish, but watch them. They are rough men and not used to the company of women.' She grinned at him, and Arthur shook at his head as she bounded away in delight. Ector would be furious when he found out that Lunete had come with the war band, but Arthur could hardly send her back alone. He would have to tell Ector of her presence but hoped that another man would notice her and do the job for him, for Lunete would never forgive the man who gave her away. All Lunete wanted was to live the life of a warrior like her brothers, hunting, riding, fighting and practising with weapons, but that was not the fate for a daughter of a warlord like Ector. Her fate was marriage and the lethal dangers of childbirth. She was the daughter of Britain's champion, and a great prize for any ambitious man. King Urien would look for suitors for

Lunete, to bring him an alliance, land or wealth, and her marriage would also bring honour and wealth to Ector. But not if she died fighting Saxon raiders disguised as a warrior.

The next day, when sunlight shone through clouds shifting on a warm breeze, they found the Saxon raiding party. Balin's scouts picked up their trail from a burned-out farm, and Arthur's stomach turned as he rode Llamrei through the still smoking debris. Two little bodies lay curled up in a corner, surrounded by ash and charred timbers. Fire had shrunk their corpses so that they looked like babies, and the warriors made the sign to ward off evil. The Christians amongst them, like Hywel and his men from Elmet, made the sign of the cross and the war band marched on in silence, past the slaughtered mother who lay in a pool of her own dark blood. Her skin, where not darkened with soot and dried blood, had the pale complexion of death. Kai would not leave the dead in the open, so he and three men stayed to bury the corpses beneath the scorched earth. Arthur forced himself to take in every grim part of that ruined farm and its slaughtered people. They were common folk, good people trying to eke out their lives, battling the land, the seasons, storms and blight. They paid render to Ector and Urien each year, one tenth of their farm's surplus. It was a bleak and hard existence, but honest and simple, and now they were dead.

If Ector had more men, he would protect the entire border with Lloegyr, but that was not possible. So Arthur etched his mind deep with the memory of that farm and its burned, slaughtered family. That was the reason to fight the Saxons, if they had stayed in their own lands that family would still live in peace, the children would run and laugh in the meadows, the father would plough, reap and sow, and the wife would spin wool and care for her family. But the Saxons had come across the narrow sea with their weapons and their brutal malice, and Arthur must fight them before all of Britain fell to their blades.

A score of men marched lightly through Rheged as though they had not a care in the world. Saxons clad in leather and fur, carrying spears and goading a herd of twenty cows eastwards towards Lloegyr. Three of them rode small, swift ponies, and another sat atop of a mule wagon filled with plunder, behind which a line of five captured slaves trudged tied together by their necks and wrists. Their trail had been easy to follow, for they had not tried to disguise it. Llamrei crested a heather-topped rise, and Arthur watched as the Saxons marched down a rolling hill and away from Rheged. They laughed and joked and thought themselves great heroes, returning from Rheged with plunder and stories of raiding and slaughter.

Ector called Balin to him, and Arthur went too because he had thirty of his own warriors and had a right to be included in the plan of attack. Ector did not object to his foster son's presence, and Kai had not yet returned from burying the dead to disapprove. This was no battle, not even on the scale of the skirmishes and small shield-wall fights Arthur had fought in the dark lands. These were raiders, not Ida or Octha's picked warriors or champions.

'We'll just march down and kill them,' said Balin before Ector could offer a plan of his own. Ector nodded, because there was little point in guile or cunning when they outnumbered the raiders.

'I'll ride around their flank,' said Arthur, without waiting for Balin or Ector to agree. He knew what had to be done.

The Saxons cried out in alarm as they saw the Britons gathering above them, readying shields and spears. They formed a hasty shield wall around their wagon, and a squat man with a thick neck barked orders at them. He drew a short sword and waved it at the Britons, shouting insults in his Saxon tongue. Arthur led his ten riders down the hill and around the Saxon's right flank. Llamrei jumped over a thicket and the thrill of the ride quickened Arthur's pulse. The Saxons watched him, but there was nothing they could do. Their ponies were little use against the bigger horses and no man wanted to fight on horseback when they could fight with sure footing on land. So Arthur led his men behind the Saxons, and Hywel and his Elmet men tossed their light Roman pilum spears at the Saxons. The Saxons caught three on their shields, but one spear smashed through a man's rotting wooden shield and slammed into his chest to send him sprawling into the heather. The injured man screamed and twisted, his blood soaking the grass, and its smell caused their ponies to whicker and run away. Arthur dismounted and led his men forward with their Saxon shields and spears ready.

Ector and Balin's men charged down the slope, not bothering to keep formation or form a solid line of attack. Arthur clenched his teeth with pride as his own men stuck to the formation he had drilled into them every day in battle practice. They came on slowly, their big shields locked together and spears bristling like a hedgehog's back. The Saxons shouted at each other in panic, glancing from the larger force in front of them to Arthur's ten men in their rear. Ector's men charged behind their champion, and Ector smashed into the Saxons like a raging bull. The Saxons held their line at first, but once Ector's sheer size and ferocity set about them, it was as though their faces were too close to a burning furnace and they cowered before him. Ector killed one Saxon with a spear thrust of such savage power it punched through his chest and the leaf-shaped blade came out of the Saxon's back dripping blood. Ector released his spear, drew his sword and crushed the skull of the next Saxon with a terrifying roar.

Balin and the black cloaks swarmed the enemy, cutting them down with ruthless efficiency and in ten heartbeats the Saxons were overwhelmed and panicked for their lives. Their leader with the sword seemed to fancy his chances more against Arthur's men rather than face Ector's fury, so he charged with his sword held high in two hands.

'That bastard is mine,' Arthur growled. 'Kill the rest. No survivors.'

Arthur drew Excalibur, and the leather-wrapped grip was warm and comfortable in his hand. He raised the cold iron pommel to his lips and kissed it for luck and went to meet the murderous Saxon, a killer of women and children. Ector and Balin's men struck the Saxon line with a thunderous crunch. Men howled in rage and pain, weapons clashed and Saxons died. The Saxon with the sword charged at Arthur in an all-out run. He was a short man, but powerful across the neck and shoulders. Arthur lifted his heavy Saxon shield, tightening his hold on the wooden grip across its bowl and putting his shoulder behind the linden-wood boards and the iron boss and rim. The Saxon was mousey-bearded and as he came close, spittle flew from his rotten-toothed mouth. He screamed his defiance, and before he could bring his sword down to strike, Arthur smashed his shield into the man with full force. Arthur was a big man now, taller than most of his men and made broad by endless practice with shield, spear and sword. He grunted with the impact, and the Saxon flew backwards off his feet to land sprawling in the heather. Arthur's men ran past the fallen Saxon to kill the enemy who had begun to retreat from Ector and Balin's charge.

Arthur lowered his shield and strode to the Saxon leader, who scrambled to his feet. He came at Arthur again, stabbing his sword at Arthur's chest. His sword was short, and its hilt had no crosspiece, just a small bronze bowl above its grip. So Arthur drove Excalibur onto the Saxon's blade and slid the edge down the enemy's sword until it chopped into the man's unprotected fingers. He screeched in pain and blood sprayed bright on the light green heather. The Saxon fell to his knees, dropped his sword and stared open-mouthed at Arthur. But before he could speak, Arthur drove the point of his sword into the man's gaping maw and down into his throat, chest and torso. Arthur roared with hate and ripped the sword hilt back towards him, tearing the Saxon open from mouth to stomach. Blood and offal slopped onto Arthur's boots, and the butchered enemy died.

'Kill them all!' Arthur bellowed to his men and swung Excalibur at a fleeing Saxon's legs to trip him. The man fell and turned over, mewing in desperate horror as death came for his murderous soul. Arthur lifted his shield and crashed the heavy iron-shod rim into his throat to crush bone and gristle and leave the man choking to death. 'Kill the bastards!'

Ector and Balin's men were driven to rage by the image of the burned farm and its slaughtered inhabitants, resulting in the Saxons capitulating against the greater numbers and most of them being killed in the early exchanges. Ten of the Saxons surrendered, kneeling to beg for their lives. But Arthur ordered his men to kill them all, which they did with brutal efficiency. There was no room for pity in war. Arthur had learned that and would not forget it. He ordered his men to cut off the Saxons' heads and place them in a line facing westwards, as a warning to any other Saxon raiders who came that way from Lloegyr.

Arthur looked for Lunete as soon as the fight was over and was relieved to find her still on the hilltop with two of Ector's men who had hung back from the fighting to guard their cloaks, food and other marching equipment. Two men, one woman and two children were among the slaves who were freed. They were hollow-eyed folk from the raided, destroyed farms, and sobbed when Ector cut their bonds. Ector's men found them cloaks and clothes from the dead and told them to take the wagon filled with plunder and make their lives anew.

'You have become a warrior,' said Ector, laying a heavy hand upon Arthur's shoulder. And so he had, and now it was time to bring the war to the Saxons and punish them for the woe they had brought to Britain.

17

Ector sent ten of his men scouting across the borderlands for signs of any
other Saxon raiding parties. He would keep the rest of his spearmen
marching throughout Rheged, ready to strike if those scouts returned
with ill news. Arthur and Balin stayed with Ector and camped overnight
in a barn with high gables, which folk in the valley used to store their
surplus grain after harvest. The farmer, a portly man with bushy cheek
whiskers and a veined nose, gave them a cured ham to share, some bread
and freshly churned butter. Ector paid the man with a silver torc taken
from a dead Saxon raider and the war band huddled around a small fire
on a warm summer evening. The men were cheerful following their
victory and asked Balin and his men to tell them a tale of their battles for
lost Bernicia. Balin would not talk, and sat alone brooding at the barn's
rear, and Dewi told the Rheged men the tale of their attack on Dun
Guaroy, of Ida's impregnable fortress and the hordes within.

Lunete kept away from the huddle with her hood hiding her raven-
black hair; there were few places to hide in the barn and so she sat next to
Balin. Arthur brought them both a cut of pork and some bread. He eased
himself down beside her and she offered him an upside-down smile from
the shadows of her hood.

'What is it?' Arthur asked. 'Are you not happy that you are marching with the warriors rather than learning how to curtsey at Caer Ligualid?'

'It's nothing,' she said quietly, almost as a whisper. 'It's just... that farm and the bodies... The Saxons screamed as they died. There was so much blood.'

'One thing I have learned, sister, is that war is not the honourable test of spear skill we once thought it to be. The bards and scops sing of heroes, brave warriors and great deeds. But they do not tell of how a man clings to life, how he wails when it is ripped from him, how much blood a man's body holds, or the stink of battle.'

'Sometimes I wish we were young again, before all of this, before talk of marriage, and war. It all seemed so distant then, like someone else's world.'

'Ector fought and protected us from the harshness of the world, but now we are grown, and the world will eat us up like lost lambs unless we harden ourselves to it.'

'You have your sword, and your warriors and you are already forging a reputation as a warrior. Kai has the respect of every man in father's war band. But what of me? What is to become of me, Arthur? I don't want to go to Urien's court, and I don't want to marry some fat lord in a far-off land and have him whelp his pups on me. I want to ride and hunt and be free.'

'You must marry who King Urien and Ector say you must marry. I don't want that fate for you either.'

'Really?' Her pretty face stared up at him from beneath the folds of her hood, blue eyes shining hopefully.

'I want you to be happy, sister. But we cannot avoid our fate. Each of us has our own duty to fulfil.' Arthur loved Lunete, but the love of a brother for his sister. He had always known that her love for him was something more. Kai teased them both about how she would follow Arthur around, laughing at his jests and hanging on his every word.

'Perhaps I can stay at the Caer. If there is a man there, who would ask my father for my hand?'

'There is no man at the Caer worthy of you, sister. You are beautiful, funny, clever and will make any lord of Gododdin, Powys, Elmet, Dumnonia or Gwynedd a lucky man.' Arthur rose, not wanting to see the disappointment on her face. 'Balin of the Two Swords,' Arthur said, 'this brave warrior beside you is Lunete ferch Ector. Don't worry, Lunete,' Arthur said, waving his hand to soften the death stare she gave him from beneath her hood. 'I trust Balin as much as I do you, Kai and Ector. He will not give your presence here away to Father.'

'My lady,' said Balin, and bowed his head in solemn greeting. 'I am surprised to find you with the warriors, and shocked that none have recognised one so fair amongst the stink of their leather, ale and sweat.'

'Keep Lord Balin company whilst I talk to Kai,' said Arthur, and though both Balin and Lunete were uncomfortable and awkward left in one another's company, Arthur was pleased to see them talking together well enough as he searched for Kai amongst the warriors gathered around the fire. It was a small blaze, a few logs ringed with rock to protect the barn. It was a balmy evening, and the fire had been lit for light more than the warmth. Arthur found Kai supping ale and listening to Dewi talk of how Bors of Gododdin fought like a bear inside Dun Guaroy's walls, and Arthur touched his foster brother lightly upon the shoulder.

'Can we talk?' he mouthed silently. Kai sighed, but rose from his haunches to follow Arthur outside into the night air. It was a clear summer night and the stars twinkled around a crescent moon and its wan light.

'Fine evening,' said Kai, joining Arthur to stare up at the sparkling array of twinkling stars.

'I am glad to march beside you again,' said Arthur, and he held out his hand to his friend and brother. The manner of their parting after the escape from Dun Guaroy had stuck in Arthur's mind like a fish bone in a choking man's throat. Kai had been his closest companion for as long as he could remember, and he hated they had not departed as friends.

'Me too, even if you are carrying an enemy shield.' Kai frowned, but then chuckled at his mock gruffness and took Arthur's wrist warmly in the warrior's grip.

'The shields work well in battle; you should try one.'

'I'll stick with our own shields. Lunete joined us, I see.'

Arthur laughed. 'I thought no one else had noticed.'

'How could anyone not notice her? She has no beard and smells like a summer meadow. The rest of us smell like boars. Every warrior has noticed.'

'Even Father?'

'Unless he has become simple-minded. Nobody mentions it because Father would lose his temper, and who wants to face Ector's wrath? Father won't send her away because he knows he must soon break her heart when he packs her off to the Bear Fort. Even though she is in danger marching with us, he wants her close. Once she is married, he might never see Lunete again, and if he does, it will be rare enough. So, he turns a blind eye to her dangerous ruse and is comforted to see her content.'

'She'll never change.'

'She will when she's married. A husband won't put up with his wife riding with the warriors.'

'Everything changes.' Arthur spoke wistfully, sighing as he gazed upon his brother. Kai was a handsbreadth shorter than Arthur now, but he had become stocky, and his beard was long and braided into a thick plait. He wore a leather breastplate and a bronze torc around his neck. He was a warrior, they both were, and Arthur was relieved the tension between them had disappeared. There was no need to discuss why Arthur had left, and what he had done in the year since their parting. It was clear enough that Arthur wished to become a warlord and lead men in the war against the Saxons, where Kai was happy to fight for his father in the Caer Ligualid war band. There was nothing wrong with that. If he fought well and earned Urien's respect, then he would likely succeed Ector one day and become the lord of Caer Ligualid's Roman fort. He would marry the daughter of another lord, have children, and such was life. But that was not Arthur's destiny.

'Balin is as sullen as ever.'

'He is. One of the new men asked him about his brother and the fall of Bernicia one night at a winter fire, and I thought Balin would kill the man.'

Kai laughed. 'What happened?'

'Dewi and Aneirin warned the man off and told a different tale.'

'In all the days since we left Dun Guaroy, has he ever spoken to you of his brother or his family?'

'Never. And I have not asked. Balin will talk of planning, supplies, which route to take and where to camp. But he has never spoken to me of his past, and I have never asked. A man is entitled to his privacy.'

'So, where will you go now? Octha's army is back in Bernicia and Ida has rallied his forces for a summer of war. They could march into Rheged, and we could do with your sword and your men if they do.'

'Balin and I will go to Urien and ask him for support. We must build an army with spearmen from all the kingdoms in Britain if we are going to defeat Ida and Octha. Rheged alone does not have enough warriors to defeat the Saxons, and we can only keep the borderlands safe for so long before Rheged is overwhelmed.'

'We have enough to repel him, to drive him back across the mountains.'

'You do,' Arthur allowed, to soothe Kai's pride in his people rather than because he believed it. 'We saw the vastness of Octha's army with our own eyes outside Dun Guaroy. Rheged might repel Ida or Octha, but could you march into Bernicia and drive them out? Or what if Ida and Octha combine their forces?'

'Gododdin will come to our aid if we need them.'

'They would. But what of King Brochvael the Fanged of Powys? Or King Cadwallon Longhand of Gwynedd? Or King Gwallog of Elmet? There's as much chance of them attacking a weakened Rheged as of joining forces with Urien.'

Kai nodded sadly at that truth and said nothing to disagree with Arthur. The kingdoms held old grievances against one another, and frequently raided across borders for cattle, timber, salt, lead, clay, jet, copper or tin. 'So, you will try to build a vast army from every kingdom?'

'From every kingdom who will support our cause, yes. Otherwise, how can we ever destroy the Saxons?'

'Why would they follow you?' Kai stared deep into Arthur's eyes, challenging him with that hardest of truths. Arthur was a bastard and an orphan, and there was no reason any king would even admit him to his hall, never mind support him with warriors.

'They would follow Balin. They would heed Merlin's call, and they would follow this.' Arthur placed his hand on Excalibur's hilt. It was belligerent and arrogant of him to speak so plainly, but it was the best hope he had. That belief had come to him after witnessing the sheer size of Octha's army, and the realisation that so many Saxon warriors risked their lives sailing for Britain's shores to conquer. They came to take everything, and Merlin's words had rattled around Arthur's head for a year like a mouse in thatch, gnawing and scratching. Arthur had Excalibur, and Merlin could convince men to follow both the sword and the man who wielded it with no allegiance to any king. Arthur had escaped the horror of Dun Guaroy and come from its water ready for that challenge, understanding what must be done.

'And where is Merlin?'

'I had hoped to find news of him in Caer Ligualid, and of Guinevere.' Arthur still had the silver swan-shaped cloak pinned inside his sword belt, every night he would fall asleep thinking of Guinevere's green eyes and long face, hoping she had not yet found a husband, yet he knew that half of Britain would want her hand once men laid eyes upon the princess of Cameliard.

'Guinevere is at the Bear Fort still and has not gone to Uther's court. I think the old king has a hunger for our pretty princess, though her father wanted her to serve at King Uther's court in Dumnonia. Of Merlin, there is no news, but you will need him, brother. You are right about one thing. Men fear Merlin the druid and will take his advice.'

'And you?'

'I love you, brother,' said Kai, and he pulled Arthur into a tight embrace. 'And no matter how mad you sound, or what nonsense falls from your mouth, I will be here when you need me. There will always be a place for you in Caer Ligualid.'

'And if it comes to war?'

'Who else will watch your back if not me?'

Balin and Arthur left Ector's war band the following morning, and though Arthur was glad to leave Ector and Kai on good terms, Lunete would not say goodbye and kept herself away from the parting farewells. Ector held Arthur close and whispered in his ear to keep his shield up and told Arthur he would always be his son. As always with fathers and sons, there was much left unsaid between Arthur and Ector. Arthur wanted to ask Ector why he hadn't questioned him more on his plans, or why Ector hadn't tried to talk him out of it. To travel Britain and try to bring the warriors of each kingdom together with just Balin of the Two Swords and a small band of warriors wasn't just a risk, it was a dangerous quest, one most would think foolhardy, perhaps arrogant, but certainly a step above an unwanted orphan's station. But Arthur had Merlin's backing. He had Excalibur. He had men, and perhaps that was enough to convince even the mighty Ector that the goal was worth the attempt. There was a long look between father and foster son, a nod from Ector and smile from Arthur and though each man had much to say to the other, as it goes between men, they swallowed the difficult words and parted with a clap on the shoulder and a shake of the forearm.

The war band marched south-west into the face of a sudden summer rain. Arthur rode at the head of the column with his cloak pulled tight about him, its wool made heavy by the thumping, fat raindrops, and his hair lank about his ears. Arthur's large shield hung over Llamrei's back, Excalibur at his belt, and he carried a spear in his left hand. Balin rode beside him, silent and grim as ever, and sixty spearmen clad in leather, wool and linen marched behind them. Most wore leather or iron breast-plates, some wore bowl-shaped helmets, and all wrapped their trews with strips of cloth from ankle to calf. They carried heavy shields and followed an old Roman road whose stone still showed beneath the mud and moss of long years of hard use without repair. They reached the Bear Fort as the rain cleared, and the sea-grey sky parted so that shafts of sunlight burst onto the Fort's great hill as though the gods themselves showed the way to King Urien's hall. Ten spearmen dressed in leather, carrying shields painted with Urien's bear sigil, stalked down from the hill fort and emerged from the surrounding buildings to make a line across the path. Their leader wore a bowl-shaped, riveted iron helmet and had plaited his beard into two long ropes.

'Welcome, men of Bernicia,' said the helmeted warrior in a slow voice, eyeing the fox on Balin's shield with a puzzled expression. 'What brings you to the Bear Fort?'

'I am Balin of the Two Swords. Come to speak with King Urien. The Saxons mass on his borders, and I would talk to him of war.'

The helmeted man nodded gravely to Balin and then raised an eyebrow at Arthur and the sword painted on his men's shields. It was a new sigil, and not one of the familiar beasts of the great kingdoms of Britain.

'I am Arthur... of Britain,' Arthur said, not wanting to introduce himself as Arthur of Rheged or of Caer Ligualid. He was neither of those things now, and it would not do to ask King Urien for warriors as a man of his kingdom. Better to make the request as an unknown warrior who had yet to swear his oath to any king. Arthur was a new man, freshly emerged from the dread expedition to Dun Guaroy, and he was all too aware of the strangeness of his arrival and the request he must make of Rheged's famous warrior-king.

The helmeted man stared at Arthur for a moment, unsure what to make of a man who introduced himself as a man of Britain and not of a particular kingdom. A man who belonged to no king was masterless, an outlaw without honour who lived outside of the law, a *bucellari* mercenary and not worthy of admittance to a king's hall without invitation. But Balin was a lord and not to be kept waiting, and so the helmeted man tilted his head, quickly mulling over the risk of not admitting a lord like Balin to the Bear Fort, and the risk of incurring King Urien's ire. He scratched his neck beneath the two thick plaits, shrugged and beckoned them on. The helmeted man led them through the stables, smithies and other wattle and timber huts which dotted the Bear Fort's hill. Folk came from those houses, ducking beneath dripping thatch and stepping around brown puddles. Ruddy-faced churls in threadbare woollen clothes bowed their heads at Arthur and Balin, for both wore mail, carried swords and rode fine horses. They were warriors, men of that caste which sat above the laity and below only kings and druids in the order of Britain's peoples. Arthur rode with his shoulders squared and his back straight. It was strange to have people bow as he approached, but he followed Balin's lead and kept his eyes fixed on the road ahead.

The helmeted man had stewards take Llamrei and Balin's horse to the fort's stables to be brushed and fed, whilst their warriors were asked to rest outside the walls with a promise that bread, cheese and mead would be provided. That was no surprise, for no king would allow sixty grim-faced warriors inside his walls unless they were men sworn to his service. Arthur and Balin marched through the fort's gates, boots squelching in the mud. A thin dog ran across Arthur's path with its tail between its legs, and a woman with a goitred neck scurried between two buildings, carrying a basket of eggs towards Urien's keep. The fort rose from the hill with timber walls made dark by the rain, and the surrounding buildings smelled of damp, smoke and animal droppings. Faces stared at Arthur through window shutters, and doors held ajar by dirty nailed fingers. It was a long walk in Arthur's cloak made heavy by the rain, adding to the weight of his mail and weapons. Arthur's mail chafed his shoulders, and he was grateful when they eventually reached the hall, where the hearth thankfully burned high to fill the large, long, high-raftered space with warmth. Arthur's fingers were red-raw with wet cold, and he flexed his hands in the warmth to bring the feeling back.

Three hounds slept by the fire, filling the hall with the stink of wet dog, and a bandy-legged steward fetched Arthur and Balin each a wooden mug of strong mead. A door to the hall's rear creaked open, and King Urien strode from the doorway's darkness. His bald head shone in the firelight, and he walked with a stooped, rolling gait. Urien wore a leather tunic, stretched at the seams by his muscled neck and shoulders, and behind him came an equally muscled but younger man with long, dark hair framing a strong face. Their boots banged heavily on wooden steps, echoing around the high rafters as they mounted a raised platform to sit upon two thrones beneath the bone-white snarling bear's skull mounted upon the wall behind them.

'King Urien,' said Balin, dropping to one knee, 'and Prince Owain.' Balin clapped a fist to his chest, and Arthur knelt and copied the gesture.

'Lord Balin,' said Urien in his gravel-filled voice. 'Still alive, I see?'

'Still alive, lord.'

'I heard a rumour of your brother seen in the south, fighting with the Saxons against Elmet.'

'One day I will find him, lord king, and there will be a reckoning for all he has done.'

'This is Arthur... of Britain,' said the helmeted man, his words dripping with sarcasm.

'Arthur of Britain, is it?' said Urien. He coughed and sniggered at the same time, and squinted as his flinty eyes drank in Arthur's mail and sword. A line of courtiers hurried from behind Arthur. He glanced at them, and his stomach turned over when he noticed Princess Guinevere amongst them. She was radiant in an elegant black dress and her copper hair loose about her slender shoulders. She smiled at Arthur, and he flinched as his cheeks flushed red in response.

'Yes, lord king,' Arthur stuttered, turning back to face Urien's hard slab of a face.

'So not the Arthur of Caer Ligualid, raised by Ector as a son of Rheged?'

'Yes, the same Arthur, lord king.'

'So, it's Arthur of Rheged, then?'

'Yes, I am of Rheged, but I...'

Urien slammed a heavy fist onto the arm of his throne, startling Arthur. 'Every bastard with a blade thinks himself a lord these days. You are my man or a masterless man, boy. You were born and raised in Rheged, and you owe me your oath. That sword of yours is mine, should I wish it, along with the horse you rode in on, and your spearman at my gate. What does Ector think of your rejection of his hall and lordship? You owe me your oath!'

'Do you dispute the wishes of Merlin of Ynys Môn, King Urien?' came a shrill but familiarly accented woman's voice from the hall's entrance. Nimue came striding through the hall, her black staff held before her stout frame, and a white cloak billowing as she stomped through the hall. The people in the hall involuntarily took a step back from her strangeness as Nimue strode through, because Nimue had shorn her head of hair in honour of a druid's tonsure, painted the top half of her face as black as night to make the whites of her eyes shine like stars, and daubed the bottom half as white as bone. 'Merlin himself told you of Arthur's coming and of Excalibur, King Urien. He comes to talk of the great war to come, and his fight is the druid's fight, the fight for Britain.'

Urien snarled and spat, shifting uncomfortably in his seat. 'How much longer do I have to put up with this *gwyllion* in my hall?' he grumbled.

'I stay because Merlin orders it.' Nimue slammed her staff hard into the earthen floor. 'And you, King Urien, would do well to listen as these men speak.'

Urien gnashed his teeth and glowered at Nimue, but he was unwilling to argue with the powerful volva. Arthur was surprised to see that Merlin had anointed her with so much power that she could command her voice to be heard by a king. Nimue was a woman, and only men could become a druid. But Nimue had power. Arthur had seen how she had commanded a troop of Saxon warriors in Lloegyr, and how Merlin spoke highly of her knowledge and experience of the old ways. Owain placed a hand on his father's arm, and the gnarled old king nodded to his son and looked away.

'You are both welcome in Rheged, Arthur and Balin of the Two Swords,' Owain said brightly. He stood from his throne and opened his arms. 'Merlin has entrusted the Lady Nimue to protect Rheged with her power. She has cast spells of protection over our borders and sacrificed to the gods so that they will protect our people. Merlin himself told us of your coming. Times are changing. Merlin had emerged from exile, the Saxons muster for war, and Excalibur, the sword of Britain, comes unlooked for to our hall.'

Arthur waited for Balin to speak, but he stood as silent as a rock. Arthur gulped, feeling every eye in the hall upon him, judging him, making him feel as small as a mouse. His stomach clenched, and he wanted to turn and run from the hall rather than speak in front of so many important people. Guinevere was there, the woman who had occu-pied his head since the moment he had laid eyes upon her at Dun Guaroy, King Urien, Prince Owain, Nimue the volva and a dozen other noble members of Urien's court all waited for him to speak. Arthur's request was of the highest importance, but the words would not muster in his suddenly dry throat. Urien's eyes bore into him like daggers, disapproval and anger dripping from him like poison. The Saxons massed in Lloegyr and Arthur felt responsible for the fate of Britain, but the words he needed to ask Urien for men to support him in the fight against Octha would not come. Nimue turned and cast her fearsome gaze upon him. She urged him to speak with her blazing eyes, made fiercer by her black-painted face, and Arthur wanted to run. He felt like a boy in a hall full of great people, a boy dressed up like a lord who was nothing more than a jumped-up nothing. Arthur opened his mouth, but the words would not come.

18

A bead of sweat trickled down Arthur's spine, and he wished somebody would douse the hearth fire or open a window shutter. A man to Arthur's left coughed, and a burning log spat in the fire. One of King Urien's dogs yawned and stretched its paws, and Arthur thought the hall would close in upon him like a collapsing cave. He shifted his feet and rolled his shoulders beneath his heavy coat of chain mail. His hand brushed against Excalibur's pommel, and the cold iron sent a shiver up his arm. Arthur curled his hand around the leather-wrapped hilt and clenched his teeth. He had killed men in battle, led thirty of his own oathsworn warriors, and had raided the great fortress of Dun Guaroy deep in eastern lands lost to Saxon blades. Arthur squared his shoulders, set his jaw and told himself he had earned the right to speak in the Bear Fort.

'Merlin himself set me upon this task,' Arthur said, speaking loudly and clearly. 'The greatest of druids entrusted Excalibur into my keeping to wield against the ever-growing Saxon threat. Ida has almost completed his dread fortress atop Dun Guaroy and marshals his army for a summer of war. Octha, a warlord come fresh across the narrow sea, fought against Elmet and Powys last year and has wintered in Lloegyr with three thousand men and he must keep those warriors paid with silver, women, glory, land and battle. It is spring now, and Octha will march again, perhaps west to Rheged, to take our lands, our women and our children. There will be war. So, I come to you, lord king, to ask for spears to bind to our own so that we may...'

'Our lands?' barked King Urien, interrupting Arthur just as he found his stride. Owain slumped into his high seat and stared at the floor whilst his father took command of the hall. 'What land do you own, Arthur of Nowhere?'

'No lands, lord king, no hall and no crown. But when the Saxons come, they don't just come to kill kings, but all our people. They will kill every farmer, woodsman, smith, weaver, mother, grandmother and daughter until they make our lands their own. Octha has fought in the south and not found the kingdom he craves, so now that summer is coming, he will march again. I saw his horde at Dun Guaroy, three thousand warriors ready to strike out from Lloegyr and take everything we have. Not settlers, women, old folk or children. Every man in Octha's army is a warrior who braved the wild sea in search of land, women and glory. They come for our lives, lord king, to take everything from us. We need to unite the forces of every kingdom in Britain if our people are to survive.'

'This Octha won't come for Rheged. There are mountains between us and Bernicia, and he would need to get through Ector and the men of Caer Ligualid first. There are passes and valleys there which a hundred men can hold for a week against thousands of shit-stinking Saxon swine. If the Saxons attack in the north and I send my warriors to protect Gododdin, who will protect my borders from Gwynedd, Powys and Lothian? They would raid my lands all summer, mercilessly stealing my cattle, cutting my coppiced wood, killing and enslaving my people, and stealing my silver, tin, salt and copper. Where will you be then, Arthur of Nowhere? Where will my warriors be? Have you asked Powys, Gwynedd or Lothian to give you men, or do you come to me first because Merlin thinks me weak? Does the Pendragon order us to fight? I think not. Though I like him not, Uther is the Pendragon, our king of kings. I will not call my spearmen and march away to your and Merlin's war in another man's kingdom. The Saxons will go south again to Elmet or beyond, or perhaps to Gododdin on their northern border. But not Rheged, and I am Rheged.'

'With all due respect, lord king, but that is what the men of Bernicia, Deira and Kent thought when Vortigern first brought the Saxons to our shores.'

'Don't talk to me of the Great War, boy!' Urien roared like an old bear. He stood from his throne and wagged a thick finger at Arthur, his bald pate wrinkling under a thunderous frown. 'I was there. I fought against Vortigern and his Saxons, Hengist and Horsa. I saw Bernicia and Deira burn, so don't talk to me about Saxons as though you know them better than I. Have you ever fought a battle, pup? Not a skirmish of a few hundred spears, mind, a proper battle with thousands of warriors on each side, where the cries of the dying and the clash of arms shakes the very ground.'

'No, lord king, I have not. If the Saxons take Elmet, or Gododdin or any other kingdom, word shall travel back to their homeland and more Saxons will come across the narrow sea, forever more until the kingdoms of Britain are but memories, a shadow of a lost people. Merlin believes...'

'Merlin?' Urien shook a fist at Nimue, who growled at the king's tone. 'Where was Merlin when Deira fell? Or when they took Lord Balin's home? Where was he when my Queen Igraine died this winter? Merlin brought Igraine to me. Years ago, when his grand plan failed. Merlin wished to take Igraine from her husband King Gorlois when the king of Kernow's corpse was yet warm and deliver her to Uther, to sate the Pendragon's lust. Merlin came to my door when the other kings rebelled against his plotting. The great druid stuck with a whore princess and no whore master to marry her. I took her in at his request, and then Merlin disappeared into exile on Ynys Môn. His plotting failed and left Britain half in the hands of the Saxons and the rest of us alone again. The kingdoms of Britain grew suspicious of each other once more. The alliance failed, and we lost the Great War. Now, Merlin rouses himself like a beast from winter's slumber to leave his *gwyllion* here in my hall, and my queen died without care or aid from the druids. Merlin does what pleases Merlin. He once made Uther Pendragon and I his puppets, but never again. You have Excalibur, you say? I saw the sword when Uther's brother Ambrosius wielded it, and it didn't do him much good. It's nothing but another of Merlin's tricks. An old sword dug up from a barrow somewhere and imbued with legend by Merlin, the master of shadow and deep cunning, travelling the land telling men at every fire in every hall of its power and the gods who once wielded it. If Merlin says it is the sword of Britain and that men should follow its power, men believe it, will even fight for it, for who would not believe the great druid? Merlin tells folk that the sword will restore Lloegyr to us Britons, and they want to believe it so much that men would die following the man who wields it. I say the Saxons cannot conquer Rheged, not whilst we have the mountains, Ector and my son Owain, to throw them back. Let other men send their young warriors to fight for Merlin's cause and die in Lloegyr. Begone with you, Arthur of Nowhere and Balin of a fallen kingdom, and take Merlin's hag with you.'

Owain shifted uncomfortably in his seat at Urien's hard words about his mother, the queen, Merlin and Nimue. A murmur passed across the hall as folk whispered fearful surprise at Urien's disrespect for the powerful and feared druid and Nimue the volva. At a nod from the king, the helmeted warrior and his ten men marched from the hall's rear to stand between the throne, Arthur and Balin. Urien stalked from his high seat with clenched fists and out of the hall's back door. Balin took a step forward as though to address King Urien, but the warriors lowered their spears and Balin held his tongue.

What struck Arthur more in that moment was not the king's refusal of support, but that Queen Igraine was dead. He reached for the bronze disc beneath his chain mail and held it for a moment. Arthur remembered the queen in her sick bed, and the strange night he had spent at her bedside. He didn't know Queen Igraine, only the words they had exchanged that dark night before his life turned upside down, and yet her death saddened Arthur. There was much to consider in Urien's tirade about Merlin, about Excalibur, Uther, Igraine, Gorlois, Ambrosius and Merlin, and the words banged around Arthur's skull like a rat in a trap. He noticed now that Guinevere and the other courtiers were all wearing black in mourning for the dead queen, and Arthur had hoped to call upon Igraine again whilst he was at the Bear Fort, to thank her for the gift which he believed had brought him luck and good fortune since the moment he had worn her charm.

'Never point your spears at me again,' Balin warned the helmeted man and his warriors, and his voice was as cold as a winter storm. Their spears came up and Arthur followed Balin, stalking from King Urien's hall with a heavy heart. He exchanged a glance with Guinevere on the way out of the great doors and was surprised to see her follow him outside.

'Lady Guinevere,' Arthur said, stopping and smiling at her. 'I had expected you to be in Dumnonia by now, as your father wished.'

'So did I,' she said with a sigh. 'But King Urien keeps me here, even though I have asked to go.'

'Why? Prince Owain is married and there are no other men in Rheged worthy of your hand?'

'Queen Igraine is dead, and I fear Urien wants to wed me.' She shuddered, and Arthur resisted the urge to reach and hold her. 'He called me to his chambers, said he would send a messenger to my father, that I would be his queen and bear him sons. My father needs an alliance. We are under threat from the Franks who raid our borders and make open war against our neighbours in Armorica. Urien is old, fierce and looks at me as though he can see me undressed. They say he was cruel to the queen, that he beat her, treated her roughly and took many lovers without a care for her pride or honour. He is a beast.'

'He is a king, and a friend of your father.' Balin went to get their horses and left Arthur alone with Guinevere on the hall's steps. A breeze blew eastwards from the coast and ruffled Guinevere's hair, and her green eyes were pools Arthur could stare into all day. Arthur longed for her, dreamed for her when he slept under the stars, clutching her swan cloak pin in his hand. But he could never be with her, could never even give voice to that foolish dream. Guinevere was a princess, and Arthur was a simple soldier without lands, silver, title or hope of ever winning her hand. He did not intend to speak so bluntly, but against the power of King Urien, what could she do? Her father was also a king in distant Cameliard, but what king wouldn't approve of his daughter becoming a queen of a land which could provide trade, wealth and warriors?

'Nimue says you will go to King Uther in Dumnonia now, seeking men to build an army. Take me with you to Dumnonia, Arthur. Don't leave me here in this awful place. Cameliard is bright and airy. My father's court had bards, poets, libraries full of scrolls etched with Roman and Greek thinking. There is music and dancing, where here there is only this grim, cold hall and its cruel king. It is always cold, even though it is supposed to be summer. My father sent me to Britain to find suitors at Uther Pendragon's court in Dumnonia, where the sun shines and fields of wheat sway like gold beneath the summer breeze. Take me there, Arthur.'

'I would if I could, lady,' Arthur said. He stared into the green pools of her eyes, and looked for the courage to tell her of his longing, to grab her hand and run for his horse and ride away from the Bear Fort. 'But King Urien would send warriors after us, and I am trying to unite the kingdoms, not drive a deeper wedge between them.'

'Will you at least tell King Uther of my plight and of my father's wishes? Perhaps he will send for me, and he is the Pendragon after all, the king of kings. Urien will have to let me go if Uther commands it.'

'I will, princess. I hope you find the happiness you are looking for.'

'We don't have time for you to gawp at the princess of Cameliard,' said Nimue in her clipped accent, striding from the hall's rear, staff held before her, her cloak pulled tight about her neck, and a cloth sack for travel slung across one shoulder. 'We march for Dumnonia, where Merlin awaits us. If Urien will not fight, then the Pendragon must order it.'

Arthur glanced at Guinevere, wanting to say more, but Nimue was not for waiting and he left Guinevere staring after him from the Bear Fort's steps. He followed Nimue to the stables where Balin waited with his own horse and Llamrei, and they left Rheged's fortress under a cloud of failure. Balin, Arthur and his ten horsemen led the way south, with sixty spearmen marching behind them. Nimue strode next to Arthur's horse, and the men kept well away from her fearsome appearance. Many made the sign to ward off evil as she came from the fort, and others the sign of the cross, but Nimue either did not notice or did not care.

'We march for Elmet,' Nimue barked, pointing her black staff southwards.

'We decide where we go,' Balin said, leaning across his stallion's neck to glower at Nimue. 'Not a Saxon witch. Even if you have Merlin's ear.'

'You don't need to fear me, Balin of the Two Swords. I am an Irish volva, a *gwyllion* as you call it, and am every bit as powerful as your druid.

I marched with the Saxons because they captured me, but I have no loyalty to them, though they worship the old gods. If I wanted you dead, you would be a corpse already. We fight for the same cause, to restore this country to its people.'

'And what is that to you? You are not a Briton?'

'I swore an oath to Merlin after I met you in Bernicia, Lord Balin, a solemn oath beneath an ancient oak tree whose saplings first burst forth in the time of the Romans. The gods bore witness to that oath, and they hold me to it. So I am on your side, Balin of the Two Swords, and if I break that oath, then my soul will writhe in the fires of deepest Annwn for eternity.'

'Merlin awaits us in Dumnonia?' asked Arthur. He must question the druid on Urien's words about the truth of Excalibur and what had truly divided the kingdoms at the end of the Great War. Ector had a part to play in those dark days. He had brought Igraine north from Dumnonia to Rheged and left his place as Uther Pendragon's man. If Arthur was going to heal those old wounds and gather men to fight the Saxons from across Britain's kingdoms, he must know what happened.

'I did not say he awaits us,' Nimue said. 'He prepares the path for you, Arthur. He goes to Elmet, Powys, Gwynedd, Demetia and Dumnonia to tell men of Excalibur's return and the man who wields the sword of Britain.'

'Prepares it how?' Balin growled.

'So that men will welcome you, that they understand that the time has come to fight against the invaders. Your legend grows, Arthur. Merlin plants the seed and tends it, growing it so that when you ask, men will come to your banner.'

'Merlin plays a dangerous game. The kings will not like this news of a new man wielding an old sword who seeks to unite the kingdoms. Why should they welcome a man who threatens their rule?'

'These are high matters, Lord Balin. You do the fighting and let Merlin and I worry about the deep cunning. We have a war to fight, and we each fight in our own ways. You have your swords, and we have our minds and our power.'

'Aye, well. Let's hope Merlin's cunning doesn't cost us our lives.' Balin

spat over the side of his horse, clicked his tongue and cantered ahead of
the marching column, leaving Arthur to brood on Guinevere, Urien,
Merlin and the knife-edge on which his own life perched so precariously.
He left Rheged under a cloud with Urien's disapproval. Much of what
Urien had said was true. Arthur was a masterless man, he was no longer
the foster son of Ector of Caer Ligualid, he was his own man and
oathsworn to no king or kingdom. Arthur's future rested on Merlin's
dream of defeating the Saxons, and if it failed, Arthur's future would die
with it.

The war band reached Elmet and the king's stronghold at Loidis seven
days after their departure from the Bear Fort. King Gwallog's hill fortress
sat within ancient Roman walls, repaired over the years since the empire's
departure with stone taken from crumbling Roman buildings so that the
entire town was ringed by stone walls an arm's length higher than a man
is tall. It was a mixture of old, dressed stone, wattle and thatch, a melding
of the old world and the new. As Arthur looked upon gleaming stone and
rotting thatch, he wondered how it could be possible that the further time
went on, men's ability to build, carve and set stone had diminished? He
wondered why his people had not learned the skills to cut rock, chisel
marble, build straight roads and aqueducts from stone. All that knowledge had left the island with the Romans, leaving the Britons with rotting
wood and crumbling memories of the empire's greatness.

A guard of six warriors came from the walls to meet Arthur's war
band. Each warrior wore a red cloak faded to light pink by weather and
use, and Arthur marvelled at their armour, for each wore the segmented
cuirasses of the Roman legions, metal bands fixed to leather straps which
traversed their torsos above iron-studded leather kilts. Each wore a bright
Roman-style helmet with an iron peak at its top and oblong shields
bearing the Christian cross. They wore short swords on their right hips,
and carried Roman-style pilum spears with long, thin shafts of half ash
and half iron. Hywel and the men in Arthur's company who had once
been warriors of Elmet kept to the rear of the column with their heads
bowed, and their own Roman armour hidden beneath their russet cloaks,
for fear they would be recognised by their old comrades and their dispute
with King Gwallog reignited.

A big man with a red horse plume crossing the top of his helmet welcomed Arthur and Balin to Loidis, and brought them into a cold stone building which served as King Gwallog's hall. The big man named himself as Primus Pilus Idnerth, the commander of King Gwallog's legion of warriors, but King Gwallog himself was away fighting on Elmet's western border against raiders from Powys. The king left Idnerth and most of Elmet's warriors at Loidis in case the Saxons attacked from the east. Merlin had visited Loidis before Gwallog marched and warned him of the Saxon hordes massing in Bernicia, and Idnerth chewed his beard when Arthur told him of Octha's vast army which lingered in Lloegyr. Elmet had fought the Saxons last summer, and Idnerth told the brief tale of a savage battle where they had lost many brave men and only repelled the Saxons at the last. Arthur and Balin's war band stayed the night in Loidis, and Idnerth and his men were generous with a feast of boar meat, mead, bread, cheese and even a flagon of wine. Arthur had never tasted luxurious Roman wine before, and he found it bitter on his tongue, though Balin enjoyed it well enough, even though he ate in silence and left Arthur to answer Idnerth's questions.

Idnerth would not commit warriors to Arthur's cause in the absence of King Gwallog, but if it came to war Elmet could muster six hundred spearmen from its hides, even after the war with Octha, and the king's hearth troop was a cohort of eighty warriors equipped and trained in the Roman ways who stood ready to fight. Idnerth lamented the dangers on all of Elmet's borders, and his men told tales of their fight against Octha late into the night. Stories of bravery, warriors who died with honour, and brutal Saxon fighters who came with snarling war dogs. They told of wicked wizards capering before their battle line, and of how Gwallog himself fought in the front line like a champion. Nimue slept outside the stone hall with the war band, for the men of Elmet were all Christ worshippers and shivered at the sight of her pagan face paint, shaved head and carved black staff.

Arthur and Balin agreed not to wait for King Gwallog's return, and Nimue was impatient to march to Dumnonia and follow Merlin's path. So Arthur thanked Idnerth for his hospitality and left with the hope of Elmet's support when it came to war with the Saxons. They marched south, crossing Powys and Gwynedd but avoiding their towns and forts. Nimue persuaded Arthur and Balin to march hard for Dumnonia on Britain's south coast without stopping to talk to King Cadwallon Long-hand of Gwynedd, or King Brochvael the Fanged of Powys. Merlin was in Dumnonia, which was the most south-westerly of the British kingdoms, she said, and if they could return north with Uther Pendragon's blessing and a force of Dumnonian warriors, the other kings must obey the Pendragon's command.

They marched hard through deep forests of old oak, spindly beech and sweet-smelling pine, camping beneath the boughs and hunting for their food. The moon shifted from wax to wane as the war band reached south-western Britain and came to the old Roman town of Durnovaria, where Uther Pendragon kept his summer court at its fortress known as the Fist of Dumnonia. A ring of Roman stone walls circled the Fist, with a high stone gate with two arched entrances gated with stout oak doors. The walled part of the Fist could hold one hundred warriors and their families, but a sprawling settlement of wattle houses spread around the fortress on all sides and a cloud of dirty smoke sat above it, hanging still on a warm, early summer's day. A ditch surrounded the walls, and spear points glinted in the sunlight as warriors patrolled the fighting platform inside the high Roman walls.

A tanner's yard on the edges of the settlement stank of stale piss, and the warriors grumbled at the stench until they came to an awning beside the road, covered with an old, yellowed sailcloth where a woman with black teeth and curly red hair provided whores and ale for shards of hack-silver. Arthur, Balin and Nimue left the men happily spending what remained of their silver as they approached the Fist's high gates.

'State your business,' said a gate guard. He glanced at Balin's fox-painted shield and both men's chain mail before raising an eyebrow at Nimue's strange face paint and travel-stained white cloak. The guard wore a heavy wooden cross at his chest, over a stuffed and hardened linen breastplate. He wore two long plaits at either side of his head framing his narrow face, a silver ring about his wrist and the back of his head shaved high to leave the back of his skull stubbly and bald.

'Lord Balin of Bernicia,' said Balin, 'Nimue, follower of Merlin the druid, and Arthur of Britain here to talk with High King Uther Pendragon.'

'Is that the sword?' asked the guard, and Arthur nodded, sliding Excalibur's blade an inch from its black scabbard so that its steel shimmered beneath the sun. The man marvelled at it and then looked Arthur up and down. 'Yannig is my name. Wait here and I will let the king know you have arrived.'

'Is Merlin here?' asked Nimue before Yannig could turn away.

'He was. There were two druids here, Merlin and Kadvuz. They spoke with King Uther and left three days ago on the north road.'

Nimue sagged for a moment, and then straightened herself, gripping her black staff so hard that her knuckles whitened. They had expected to find Merlin waiting at the Fist to help them persuade Uther to send warriors north, and to talk with them, to ask how the druid fared with the other kings on his journey south through Britain's kingdoms. On the long road from Loidis to Durnovaria, Nimue had pulled the men's aching teeth, wrapped twisted ankles, cast enchantments on spear blades, stared into darting flames and told men if their wives remained loyal whilst they were gone, and told men's futures by the lines on their hands. She stared at the stars and told the warriors tales behind each constellation in the black night sky, stories of magical bulls, giants, heroes and old gods. Nimue filled their nights with stories of Lleu Llaw Gyffes, Gwydion, Bran the Blessed and other legendary heroes, and the men shared their meat and mead with her in return. She also told them of the Saxon gods, of Woden, Thunor and Týr, all harsh gods who urged Saxon men to war, gods of thunder, foresight, ravens, cruelty, with halls in the sky where the dead slain in battle could live forever. Now, she tried to keep her air of aloof power and confidence, but Arthur saw the waver in her at the news that Merlin had already left.

Yannig returned with two similarly clad warriors, and they led Arthur, Nimue and Balin through the gates and along Roman cobbled pathways towards Uther's hall. Limewashed buildings topped with thatch sat between perfectly straight streets. The warriors inside the walls all wore the same linen breastplates, and two braids hung on either side of their faces. Each man wore a green cloak, and all eyed Nimue with barely concealed fear. A small priest in a dirty brown tunic came running from a long building with a high cross on its gable end. He snarled at Nimue, making the sign of the cross and cursing her as the spawn of Satan until she hissed at him and threatened to turn him into a goat, and then he ran away with his skirts hitched around his knees.

Uther's hall was like nothing Arthur had ever seen before. It was a lofty building held up by glaringly white pillars along a sheltered, open walkway. Red tiles completely covered the roof, and Arthur couldn't determine if they were wooden or clay. However, they gave the building the angular and sharp appearance of a drawn sword. Supporting timbers painted red criss-crossed the gable end and stood between the bright white walls. It looked like something built by men from a different age, with skills long forgotten. Arthur stepped inside the doorway and a picture of fish leaping around a man in a great chariot sprawled across a floor made up of tiny tiles. The place was airy and clean with no hearth fire at its centre, but two fireplaces on each wall. Tall windows and square holes cut into the whitewashed walls cast bright sunlight into the room in stark contrast to the dark, smoke-filled halls of other kings and lords, and Arthur understood why Guinevere longed to escape the Bear Fort. Servants fussed at round tables, setting out jugs of mead and loaves of bread.

'It's as if the Romans never left,' whispered Balin, staring up at the high walls, and at a finely woven tapestry on the far wall above a throne inset with gold and silver. A metallic-sounding horn blared, and six warriors tramped into the hall carrying spears and a tall man came before them holding forth a long-handled axe tied about with wooden rods. The other five warriors wore green cloaks and carried shields bearing the red dragon of Dumnonia. They stiffened, stamping heavy, nailed boots on the floor, and then a broad-shouldered, hunched figure came from a side door, shuffling into the light. He was as wide as two men, with a huge bull-like head atop boulder shoulders. There was a power about the man, and the hall fell to a hush as he entered. It had to be Uther, Arthur thought. The figure shuffled because he limped and grimaced each time his left leg touched the floor, an injury from some long-ago battle. He had long white hair tied back from his face and a white beard. His skin was sun-darkened like seasoned wood and cracked like old tree bark. One eye glared fiercely at Arthur, and the other was an empty, cavernous hole surrounded by heavy scars. The big man shuffled to the throne and eased himself into it with a groan, and Arthur noticed that three fingers were missing from his left hand. He had never seen a man so ravaged by war. The little priest who had spat at Nimue scuttled in behind the old man, carrying a large cross completely covered in gold leaf. He set it down on the tiled floor, made the sign of the cross and glowered at Nimue.

'King Uther Pendragon,' shouted the warrior holding the axe wrapped in rods. 'Son of Madoc, grandson of Constantine, King of Dumnonia, High King and Pendragon of Britain.'

All in the hall bowed to Uther Pendragon, including Arthur; even Nimue bowed her head in respect to the battle-scarred old king.

'My lord king,' said Balin, and his voice rang around the hall.

Uther raised his right hand, a gnarled thing of bent, twisted fingers and purple veins. 'I know who you are,' Uther said, his voice a deep, dry croak. 'Merlin came before you and told me all about you, the sword, and the Saxons.'

'Then you know what we must ask of you, lord king,' said Arthur, finding the courage to speak by clutching Excalibur's hilt.

'I know, pup. And I see you carry my younger brother Ambrosius' sword in your soft hand. Merlin gave him that sword, long ago. He believed Ambrosius was the man to drive the Saxons back into the sea, a man who was not a king, but a fearsome and respected warrior, a man all kingdoms would rally behind. This woman can only be Merlin's volva. I've heard all about you as well. A daughter of the Irish, captured and raised by Saxons now joined to Merlin's druid magic. We are a God-fearing kingdom here in Dumnonia, not like those heathens in the north, so don't cast your spiteful frown at me, woman, or I'll have you flogged in the square. Your shaved head, face paint and staff have no power over me, so look away before I give you to my men.'

Nimue straightened her shoulders, but Arthur noticed she looked away from Uther, her eyes fixed on the hall's far end, beyond where the king's bulk squatted on his glittering throne.

'You come to me for men,' Uther continued in his harsh tone, 'and

Merlin believes that a clap of his hands commands me to give you two hundred spearmen to die fighting Saxon dogs in lands already lost. Well, life isn't that simple, and I am king here. The Pendragon of all Britain. Many had to die for me to become Pendragon. Nobody ever gave me two hundred spears without a fight. Proud Lord Balin here has already lost his country, his men and his family. Why should I support you two impudent, untested and unproven pieces of toad shit with my spearmen?'

'Merlin, lord king...' Arthur began, but Uther shook his monstrous head so violently that Arthur held his tongue.

'A pox on Merlin, his druidic cunning, and your hopeless war.' Uther coughed and rubbed his shovel-sized hand against his temples. He seemed to wrestle with himself, grumbling and mumbling softly so that Arthur couldn't hear. 'But Merlin had power, once, and messengers have come to me from Gododdin, Powys, Lothian and Elmet to warn of the Saxon threat, and so I have granted his request.'

Arthur let out a gasp of relief. Two hundred Dumnonian spearmen wasn't enough to fight three thousand Saxons, but it would encourage the rest of Britain to provide warriors once they saw the Pendragon's dragon banner at Arthur's side.

'On one condition,' Uther cackled, and leaned forward, his dead eye seeming to stare at Arthur from its cavernous hole. 'You, pup, must fight a man of my choosing. If you live, you shall march from Dumnonia with two hundred of my best spearmen. If you lose, you die. So, what say you, wielder of Excalibur, Merlin's last great hope?'

'I'll fight your man,' said Arthur, having no choice but to accept the high king's challenge. Uther laughed and roared at the priest to show his picked warrior in, and Arthur's stomach twisted as a monstrous warrior ducked beneath the side door's lintel and strode into Uther's hall. He carried a long sword, and a buckler strapped to his left arm, he was stripped to the waist and his chest and arms writhed with thick, corded muscle.

'Then you will fight Mynog the Boar, the undefeated killer of twenty men in single combat,' Uther crowed, enjoying the fear on Arthur's face. 'Defeat him and prove your mettle. My men will follow a man who can best Mynog the Boar. No need for delay, let's have the fight here, now.

We'll see if Merlin's power holds. If you die, pup, I'll let my men whore your witch here until she begs for death. I'll take your men into my service. Your sword will be mine and nobody shall remember your name. You will be lost to memory forever, nothing but a shit-stain reminder of Merlin's failure.'

Mynog the Boar raised his sword and let out a blood-curdling war cry, and Arthur dropped his hand to Excalibur's hilt, staring at the killer he must fight for his and Nimue's lives.

19

'Arthur,' Nimue hissed, the shining stones glittering in her teeth as she flashed a malevolent grin. Nimue unslung the pack from her back, and Arthur recoiled as she drew from it a yellowed skull painted with dark swirls and strange symbols. 'Remember, you have Excalibur's power, and I will cast a spell of speed and strength to imbue your limbs with the strength of the gods.' She capered to the hall's rear, her eyes rolling in her head as she chanted dark words in a language Arthur did not understand. Nimue stroked her hand around the skull, fingernails scratching over its *draíocht cailleach,* its Irish witch-magic. Uther's priest roared and spat towards Nimue, and folk around her scuttled away from Nimue's dark power. The priest shrieked in protest again, but Uther ignored him, his one eye fixed on Mynog who advanced to the centre of the great hall, making huge sweeps with his longsword.

Arthur shook off his cloak and drew Excalibur from its scabbard, the hilt and shining edge scraping upon its iron throat. The blade shimmered in the sunlight and the grip felt warm and comfortable in his hand. Arthur touched Igraine's disc with his left hand and then lowered it to touch Guinevere's pin at his belt. He closed his eyes for a moment and prayed for luck, to the old gods and the new. Mynog was an enormous man with bright blue eyes and his muscles shifted beneath his skin like trees in the wind as his sword hissed through the air, waiting for Arthur like a caged animal. Arthur reached behind him and checked that his antler-hilted seax sat in its sheath, and it was there, flat and secure across the small of his back. His heart pounded in his chest, and Arthur did his best to ignore the churning twist of fear in his guts. He suddenly needed to piss, and his mouth was as dry as old bones. Arthur gripped Excalibur in both hands and advanced. He had always loved the feel and balance of a sword, preferring it to spear, knife or bow. As a child, he had practised endlessly with Huell's wooden training swords, exhausting himself with lunge, cut, parry and the combinations Ector and Huell had drilled into him and Kai from the time they could stand.

'Fight!' Uther bellowed from his throne. Mynog roared again, and the men in the hall cheered their hero. Uther's warriors banged their spears against their shields as one to create a throbbing, drumming sound.

Nimue's undulating chants filled Arthur's head. He had the sword and his lucky charms, and Arthur hoped that would be enough to help him defeat Uther's monstrous warrior. To lose meant not only his and Nimue's death, but losing two hundred Dumnonian spearmen. Balin would leave Dumnonia without the Pendragon's support, and they needed the Pendragon's banner to gather men from the rest of Britain. So Arthur clenched his teeth and braced himself to fight in single combat for the first time. As he drew closer to his adversary, Arthur was surprised to find himself as tall as Mynog, their eyes on the same level which gave him a burst of confidence. Across the hall the bare-chested man had seemed hugely tall and broad, but up close they were of similar size, though the Boar was much broader across chest and shoulder. Arthur rolled his shoulders and flexed his hands around the sword's grip, loosening himself, trying to shift into a state of calm readiness.

Mynog darted forward with a quickness belying his vast frame, his sword lashed out point first, aiming to tear out Arthur's throat and end the fight quickly in one wicked lunge. Arthur stood firm and parried the strike with the flat of Excalibur's blade. The two swords rang together like a bell causing the people in the hall to gasp in awe at the sound. Mynog held his sword there, pushing against Excalibur, testing Arthur's strength. The stink of his sweat filled Arthur's nose along with a wash of rank, cheese-stinking breath, and he heaved back against the muscular man's strength. It was like pushing against a horse, but Arthur held him, the two men straining against each other, muscles tense and faces grimacing.

Mynog snarled, and followed the lunge with his elbow. Arthur barely ducked beneath the blow, turning as he came up so that he could dance away from his foe. Mynog kept moving, spinning on his heel to bring his mighty sword around in a great sweep to cut Arthur's head from his shoulders. Arthur ducked again, and the blade sang over his head. It came so close to his skull that the force of its passing ruffled his hair. Mynog drove his knee into Arthur's chest, throwing him from his feet. Arthur's boots slid on the floor tiles as he gasped for air, the pain in his chest like a hammer blow.

The Boar came on again, swinging his sword overhand with a mighty roar as though he meant to cut Arthur in two with one terrible stroke. Arthur brought Excalibur up and caught the sword on the downward stroke. He winced as the blades came together, fearing for Excalibur's sharp edge. Mynog leant on his sword, his chest and shoulders over the hilt, trying to drive Arthur's sword down. Spears beat on shields, mixing with Nimue's other-worldly Irish dirge to fill the hall with blood-curdling death music. Arthur grimaced, the muscles in his shoulders and arms burning as he desperately tried to hold the warrior's bulk above him. The longsword pressed close to within a handsbreadth of Arthur's face, but he held the big man through gritted teeth.

Suddenly, Mynog whipped his sword away and punched Arthur in the face with the buckler fixed to his left arm. The iron smashed into the side of Arthur's head, making his skull ring and his ear burn with pain. He fell, and Mynog kicked him savagely in the stomach. Air whooshed from Arthur. He rolled away, dizzy and gasping for air. Mynog tried to stamp on Arthur's head, but the boot crashed into the floor tiles barely a finger's width from Arthur's eyes. Arthur tried to scramble to his feet, but his opponent grabbed a fistful of Arthur's hair and tossed him across the hall like an old rag.

Arthur landed at Balin's boots, his scalp burning like fire, and Balin hauled him to his feet.

'Use your speed,' Balin hissed into his ear. 'You don't need Nimue's charms, or Merlin's sword. I have seen you fight, lad. You can beat this man. He's a brute, over-reliant on his strength. Be fast and sure and be brutal. No mercy.'

Air filled Arthur's lungs. He nodded at Balin, standing straight and setting himself to resume the fight. Mynog marched around the hall as though he had already won, his sword aloft, basking in the adulation from Uther and his warriors. Arthur returned to the hall's centre, pain ringing in his head and body, but Balin's words were clear and hard in his mind. Brutal. No mercy. Just as Ector had taught him, just as battle with the Saxons had taught him. So far, he had tried to fend off Mynog's attacks rather than trying to kill the muscled warrior. Arthur took a deep breath. He was as tall as Mynog, and had killed men in battle. He was a warrior. If he wanted to lead men into war, he had to kill the Boar and wash Uther's hall in his blood. It must be so, for Arthur's life, and for the fate of Britain.

Arthur ran at Mynog the Boar and unleashed a flurry of cuts and slashes. Mynog fell back, catching the first two of Arthur's blows on his sword and then a third on his iron buckler. Arthur realised he was screaming incoherently, that he had given himself over completely to war-rage. Mynog tried to grab Arthur's mail with his left hand and Arthur laid open the forearm with Excalibur's tip so that bright blood spattered the tiny floor tiles for the first time since the fight had begun. Mynog cried out and Arthur leapt away from a wild sword swing and danced around the Boar, slashing his blade along Mynog's bare back to open a wide cut.

The Dumnonians in the hall groaned as Mynog staggered and crimson blood flowed from his back and arm. Grimacing in pain, he swung again at Arthur, but his wounds had weakened him. Arthur swiftly stepped in and used all his strength to parry Mynog's sword with Excalibur's blade close to the hilt. The two swords rang again, but this time, Mynog lost his grip and his sword skittered across the tiles. The Boar stepped back, stiffened, mastering his desperation, and gestured for Arthur to let him retrieve his blade. It was the honourable thing to do, to let Mynog rest for a moment and recover his fallen sword so that they might resume their fight on an equal footing. But Arthur had been kind before, had shown mercy to Redwulf the Saxon, and it had cost men's lives. Arthur shook his head and Mynog's face dropped as he saw the implacable, ruthless look in Arthur's eyes.

In a last, desperate attack, Mynog threw himself at Arthur, screaming like a madman. He dived underneath Excalibur and crashed into Arthur, driving his shoulder into Arthur's chest, shoving him backwards. Fists hammered into Arthur's sides. A massive hand came up to claw at his face. Arthur kicked Mynog in the groin, but the muscled man grabbed his sword arm and savagely twisted Excalibur from his grip with a triumphant cry.

Time slowed, death was close, hanging over the fighters with evil intent. Arthur let go of the sword. His heart drummed in his ears in time with the thumping shields but slowed to a dull echo. Arthur reached behind his back and whipped his seax from his sheath. Mynog rose, his face grinning with impending victory as he tried to bring Excalibur around to strike at Arthur. Arthur snarled, grabbed Mynog's ear with his left hand and ripped his head back, tearing the ear from Mynog's skull and in one quick, savage movement, Arthur thrust upward with the seax in his right fist. The wicked, long knife slid up the Boar's blood-soaked belly, its broken-backed blade sleek like a pike in a surging river. Arthur drove the point into the soft skin beneath Mynog's chin. It punched through his beard, slicing through skin, gristle and up into the Boar's mouth. The seax cut through Mynog's tongue, and the warrior stiffened, blue eyes staring with horror into Arthur's face. Arthur grunted, grabbed the antler hilt with both hands, and ripped the weapon sideways. He tore Mynog's jaw from his face. Teeth and jawbone skittered across the fine Roman floor tiles like pebbles and Mynog fell to the ground, quivering as he died. Blood pulsed from the ruined face to form a dark pool, and the men in the hall turned away from the horrific death blow.

Arthur slid his seax back into its sheath and plucked his sword from Mynog's dead fist.

'I am Arthur, a warrior of Britain,' Arthur roared, his voice louder and more confident than it had ever been. 'I am a killer, a warlord, and I hunt Saxons. I go to war, and King Uther Pendragon vowed to give me two hundred spearmen if I killed Mynog the Boar. The Boar is dead, and I will march north with three hundred Dumnonian warriors, not two.

Dumnonia has the finest, most feared warriors in all Britain. If we march with your dragon banner, the rest of Britain will follow. I kill for Merlin, for our people and for Britain.'

Arthur stalked around the hall, letting Uther's court drink in his blood-spattered mail and his bloody sword blade. Nimue's chanting ceased. She held the skull up high and hissed at Uther's priest, who cowered behind the great king's throne.

'Everybody out,' Uther growled, and the courtiers, the priest and the king's warriors all marched out of the old Roman building. 'Not you, warrior,' Uther said to Arthur as he turned to follow Nimue and Balin out of the door.

Arthur faced Uther Pendragon, he slid Excalibur back into its black fleece-lined scabbard and stood straight, despite the throbbing pain in his head and body. Imbued with confidence from the brutal fight, Arthur met the old king's flat, one-eyed stare.

'Mynog was a great warrior,' Uther said wistfully, staring up at the high windows from which light flooded the hall. 'We shall miss his sword.'

'And now he is dead,' Arthur replied, puzzled at the king's melancholy because it was he who had suggested single combat.

'There had to be a test, young warrior. Your worth had to be proven if my men are to follow you into battle.'

'So, you will send men north to fight the Saxons?'

'You shall have the three hundred you asked for, Arthur of Britain, which is a hundred more than promised. Two hundred are mustered in a field beyond Durnovaria, I will add one hundred more and my man Malegant will lead them.'

'If the warriors are already here, then...'

'Merlin came to me and spoke of the Saxon threat, so I ordered my spearmen to prepare for war three days ago.'

'But Mynog?'

'Had to die so that you could prove your worth.'

'What if he had killed me?'

'Then you would be dead, and Malegant would march north with Balin of the Two Swords. I am the Pendragon, and if Saxons threaten our kingdoms, I must send men to fight, or the other kings will challenge my authority, and another will seek to become the king of kings. Now men know you are the slayer of Mynog the Boar, and you have their respect. Such is the world of men, lad, if you want to be a warlord and men to risk their lives marching into battle under your orders. They must believe in you, they must see your strength. Now, you have the sword, the witch, the warriors and the reputation.'

Arthur sighed and was suddenly exhausted after the fight. His mail was heavy about his shoulders and his arms ached from matching the Boar's enormous strength. He could have died in Uther's Roman hall, but Mynog was dead, and for a fleeting moment Arthur wondered if the warrior had a wife, children or a mother who would mourn for him. He swallowed those hard thoughts like a wolf eating a lamb, because there was no place in the world for such sentiment. Mynog would have snatched Arthur's life away without pity and danced on his corpse, so Arthur forced himself to accept the man's death as a necessity. Mynog knew the risks when he picked up the sword, and Arthur doubted Mynog the Boar gave a care for any of the men he had killed in such fights for Uther before.

'I thank you for the lesson, for the opportunity of reputation, and for your men.' Arthur bowed and pressed his fist to his chest in salute.

'Where did you get that?' asked Uther, rising slowly from his throne like a bear from its winter sleep. His finger pointed at Arthur's chest, and he glanced down to see the bronze disc had slipped out from behind the leather tunic which sat beneath his mail during the fight. Arthur rubbed his thumb over the metal charm and its dragon.

'It was a gift, lord king.'

'A gift from who?' Uther limped down from the raised platform, his one eye glassy and his bottom lip quivering.

'From Queen Igraine of Rheged, my lord. She gave it to me before she died.'

'She is dead?' Uther stumbled as though hit by a blow, and Arthur caught the old king's arm to steady him and helped the immense man sit on the lip of his throne's platform.

'She died this summer, lord, though she had been ill for a long time.'

'I did not know.' Uther stared off into the distance, as though he tried to catch hold of a distant memory lost to the mists of time. 'Did you know her?'

'My foster father, Ector, asked me to sit with Queen Igraine one night. We talked and then she slept. She gave me this talisman for luck. I only met her that one time, I am afraid.'

'Ector. He was my man, once, when he was young, and I could still hold a sword. A good man, a great champion. He took Igraine north, after the Great War, after Merlin's plans collapsed. I loved her, lad.' Uther whispered those last words, as though the memories whipped away the sound of his voice. 'God, how I loved her. Igraine was so beautiful that the mere sight of her would snatch your breath away. She loved me too, and that was our doom. I was wounded and Merlin brought me to Kernow to recover, and Igraine healed me. She was already wed to King Gorlois of Kernow, and he kept her in his dark keep at Tintagel, deep in Kernow, on the south-west tip of Britain. When Gorlois died in battle, I brought Igraine here to Dumnonia and would have wed her myself, but the other kings hated me for it. They said Merlin had arranged for Gorlois to die so that I could steal his wife. The fragile alliance of Britain fell apart, and the only way my brother could keep it together was to send Igraine away. I was the Pendragon, and to keep that title and maintain our fragile alliance was to let that happen. They sent her north to Urien, and I never saw her again. Ambrosius died fighting the Saxons, and we lost the war anyway, for our kings lost heart for the fight. They all returned to their hilltop fastnesses and left Deira and Kent to fight for themselves. Excalibur disappeared. Vortigern brought the bastard Saxons here, and now they have Kent, Deira, Bernicia and hammer at my eastern borders every summer. My sons are all dead, and I must marry again and sire a new heir for my line to survive, a line which harks back to the time before the Romans came to our shores.'

'I am sorry for your troubles, King Uther,' Arthur said. The king spoke in a hoarse whisper and Arthur wasn't sure why Uther, who had seemed so cruel when he first entered the hall, spoke so softly of his past and those monumental events which had shaped Britain.

'I gave Igraine that disc you wear as a gift to remember me by. It bears the dragon banner of my house. She wept as Ector took her north, and so did I. God forgive me, but I should have fought harder for her. I should have let the rest of the world burn and she and I could have lived out our days together.' Uther sighed and groaned at some hidden pain in his scarred body. 'A fool's dream. Our love cost us the war, cost us everything. Not a day goes by where I don't think of her eyes and her laugh. Look at me now. War has ravaged me, consumed me. That is your destiny, I think, Arthur of Nowhere. Merlin believes you can use that sword to unite the kingdoms and throw the Saxons back?'

'I must try, lord king.'

'Only the Pendragon can command the kings of Britain. The Pendragon is the high king, the lord of the rest, and the position can only be earned in battle. To be the Pendragon, a man must be a king first. Do you fancy yourself a king?'

'No, lord, I am just a warrior.'

Uther laughed mirthlessly. 'There is ambition in you, lad. I see it in your hungry eyes, it poured from as you slew my warrior. But why would Igraine give you such a gift, I wonder?'

'She wasn't herself, and I think perhaps her mind was not what it once was.'

'That woman was sharper than Merlin himself, and she did nothing without purpose. Ector is your foster father? Who was your father?'

'I am an orphan, left at Ector's door as a babe and he raised me as his own.'

'How old are you?'

'I have seen eighteen summers, I think.'

Uther stared into Arthur's eyes, his one eye rheumy and flecked with red veins. 'It's time for you to go. You can be halfway across Dumnonia before the sun goes down. Malegant will carry the *fasces* and the dragon banner of Dumnonia, the Pendragon's banner. The other weasel-shit kings will give you men, now that they know you have my blessing.'

'Thank you, lord king.' Arthur rose, bowed again and made for the hall door.

'Arthur,' Uther called after him. He held up the three fingers on his left hand. 'Destroy the Saxon bastards. Be as ruthless as you were today, be as cruel and savage as they are.'

Arthur nodded and strode out into the bright afternoon sun, where Balin and Nimue awaited him. He wondered at Uther's words and his tale of love, and again why Igraine had given him the disc. Arthur only recalled Guinevere's request as he left Uther's hall, but he could not turn and ask the king for another favour, having just secured three hundred of Dumnonia's best spearmen. Guinevere's request to join Uther's court must wait, despite the risk that Urien might force her into marriage. There were questions for Ector to answer. Arthur had to ask him again about the circumstances of his birth and how he came to Ector's care, and Merlin had promised to tell Arthur more the next time they met. He had to know. There were too many coincidences. First Ector leaving Arthur with the queen when she was sick, then her gifting Arthur Uther's dragon-etched disc, and now Uther's words.

'Are we ready to march?' asked a clipped voice, snapping Arthur from his thoughts. It was the big man from Uther's hall. He carried a long-handled axe wrapped in a bundle of birch rods resting on one shoulder. He was long-faced, with a short beard and his dark hair hung in two braids about the sides of his face. 'I am Malegant, captain of King Uther's spearmen. I have three hundred warriors, and twenty mounted scouts ready to go north.'

Arthur held out his hand and took Malegant's arm in the warrior's grip. 'I am sorry I had to kill your man, but King Uther commanded it.'

Malegant shrugged. 'Mynog was a great fighter, but he was a pain in the bloody arse, strutting about with his muscles as though he could churn milk to butter just by looking at it. I won't miss the bastard. You fought well.'

'We should march today with all haste. It's a long way north. Why do you wrap your axe in birch rods? Surely you can't use the weapon in that state?'

'It's not a weapon for fighting.' Malegant grinned, holding the rod-wrapped axe up for Arthur to see more closely. 'It's called the *fasces,* an old Roman tradition. When men see it, they know the holder comes with the empire's authority, or King Uther's authority, these days. When we march with the *fasces*, our orders carry the weight of the Pendragon himself. Bloody Romans, gone since before my grandfather's time and their ways still hold sway over us.'

Arthur, Balin and Nimue rejoined their war band and met Malegant in a wide field where three hundred spearmen rested around campfires, throwing dice and drinking mead. Malegant bawled at them, like only a captain of warriors can do, and they rose quickly to attention.

'Up, you lazy whoresons,' Malegant roared, strolling amongst the ranks, pulling at loose linen breastplates, frowning at a spear not held straight up. 'This is Arthur, the man who slew Mynog the Boar in single combat. That sword at his side is Excalibur. He fights for Merlin, and for all the kingdoms of Britain. King Uther has pledged your spears and your lives to his cause, which is to fight and kill Saxon bastards. Will you fight?' The warriors raised their spears and let out three clipped shouts in perfect time, the sound so loud that birds flew from a nearby clutch of trees. 'Pick up your dice, pack your food and a skin of ale, leave your whores and kiss your wives goodbye for we march to war, lads, red war.'

Arthur, Balin and Malegant led the marching column. They rode before Uther's three hundred, and their own force of seventy warriors. Arthur sent his ten riders and Malegant's mounted men ahead to scout the road and seek a place to camp for the night. They had close to four hundred men, but it was not enough to meet Ida or Octha in battle. Arthur still needed support for the other kingdoms if they were to mount any kind of fight against the Saxon horde. Arthur grimaced as Llamrei whickered at the sound of two dogs barking as they followed the column. Nimue had strapped his bruised ribs tight with fresh linen and spoke whispered spells over the swelling on his head. He was not sure if her skull and dark enchantment had helped him defeat Mynog, but he noticed how the Dumnonian warriors nudged one another and pointed as she marched along with them. Though they were Christians, they feared Nimue's dark magic and Arthur began to understand her and Merlin's power was as much about belief as actual magic. Men believed in their power, and that was enough to make them fear the druid and the volva. That fear gave their commands power. The men bowed their heads to Arthur and called him lord, and he enjoyed their respect, though he kept his face calm and serious.

They marched through Dumnonia's rolling fields of wheat and barley, alongside coppiced woodland and wide rivers. It was a rich land, swathed in green with thick, soft soil, and it was no surprise why the Saxons so coveted Britain's fertile lands. The first night's camp was a raucous affair, as men from Balin and Arthur's war band wrestled and raced against the Dumnonians. Ale and mead flowed freely, and it was late into the night before men finally went to sleep. Then, on the second day as they reached Dumnonia's north-eastern borders, a messenger came with tidings of war.

20

The rider came as Arthur and Balin watered their horses beside a swift stream in a valley with dark pine forest on one side and a hillside jutting with white rock and dense ferns on the other. He galloped from the pine trees, his chestnut gelding flecked with thick lather on both flanks as it thundered towards the shining waters. Malegant barked at his men to form a guard, and twenty warriors barred the rider's path with spear points lowered to prevent him from attacking Arthur and Balin should he prove to be a foe.

'I bring a message from Merlin,' said the man. He had tired eyes and wore a travel-stained cloak and mud-spattered boots.

'Let him through,' said Arthur, waving at Malegant for his men to lower their weapons. The rider's horse staggered, its forelegs quivering from the hard ride, and the rider slipped from its back, patting the beast's long neck. 'Merlin sent you?'

'Aye, lord, I come from King Tewdrig of Gwent. Merlin was there, lord, two days ago, and it was he who sent me with this message for you.'

'Merlin is in Gwent?' asked Nimue, striding from the stream with her dress hitched up about her knees. She had been searching the waters for elf stones, lucky rocks left there by the hidden folk which would bring warriors good fortune if they kept them close in battle, and she carried a clutch of them using her skirts as a basket.

'No longer, lady,' said the rider, stiffening at Nimue's strange appearance. 'He left the day the dark news came.'

Nimue frowned and let her stones fall to the grass. 'Where did Merlin go?'

'North, lady, to Powys.'

'What is your message?' asked Balin, keen to cut to the chase as always.

'An army of Saxons has attacked Gododdin, lord. There is war in the north. Merlin bids you return north with all haste, war is upon us.'

Arthur's heart quickened, and he glanced at Balin, who ground his teeth in anger. 'It will take us over two weeks to reach Gododdin from here,' Arthur said, clenching his fists.

'Then we need to force a fast march,' said Balin. 'Did King Tewdrig send men with Merlin?'

'Yes, lord,' said the rider. 'Eighty men marched north with the druid.'

Arthur's war band marched north with all haste, travelling through lands untouched by violence. It was summer, with warm days and balmy nights. In the fields sheared sheep capered with their young; farmers cut hay from meadows and fields coloured by wild lilies, foxgloves and honeysuckle. Malegant used his *fasces* and Uther's dragon banner to command food, ale and other supplies at towns they passed on the road north. Folk came to stare and bow at the army on the march. Arthur heard whispers on their lips of Excalibur and Merlin, and of his own name. Rumour, it seemed, travelled faster than spearmen on the march, and Malegant reported a swelling of the ranks as farm boys and runaways joined the column, eager to fight and make their reputation against the Saxons.

Nimue visited sacred places whenever the army camped. She sought springs, crags, caves, dark pools and gnarled trees and would chant prayers to the old gods, cut open the guts of goats, chickens and other animals to ask for the gods' favour. People came to her for healing, even Christians, and before they reached Elmet on the fourteenth day, she had delivered a baby trapped in its mother's womb, set a man's painfully shat-

tered thigh bone and expelled a dark spirit from a troubled child. Balin
and Malegant rode ahead of the marching column to Loidis to seek
Elmet's warriors, and when Arthur reached them with the army, Idnerth,
the Primus Pilus of Elmet, waited beside the stone road with a force of one
hundred and fifty warriors clad in Roman armour, with their oval shields,
short swords and pilum spears.

'It's all we can spare,' Idnerth said, removing his helmet crested with
bristling horsehair to glance back at his men. 'Saxons are loose on our
borders, and King Gwallog marches there with most of our army. But
these men are stout fighters, fifty of the king's own march with us.' He
gestured to a band of fifty tall men who all wore *Roman lorica segmentata*
armour and shining helmets. Beside them sat two wagons filled with
supplies for the march north. Arthur thanked Idnerth for his support,
though he had hoped for more men from Elmet to swell his ranks, and
after camping for a night outside Loidis' stone walls, they continued the
march north.

Idnerth spoke of messengers coming south from Gododdin and
Rheged with news of the Saxon advance. War bands of Saxon raiders had
struck along Elmet's borders not long after Arthur had passed through
the town, and for a while it appeared Elmet would be the target for the
massed Saxon forces. But when news came from Gododdin of thousands
of Saxons marching across their southern borders, it became clear that
the attacks on Elmet were merely a feint to prevent their warriors from
marching north to support the men of Gododdin. Idnerth could not say if
the Saxons who raided Elmet were men from Ida or Octha's war band,
only that they were Saxons clad in furs who enslaved the border-dwellers,
burned their farms and stole their livestock.

'Octha has struck his blow,' said Nimue, marching next to Arthur, who
rode Llamrei at the head of his warriors. 'He tried his hand at Elmet last
summer and was thrown back by its warriors and the men of Powys. His
men hunger for war, and Octha must give it to them. Without our men,
and support from Rheged, Gododdin will surely fall. Merlin must know.
He must march there along a different path.'

'We were too far away in Dumnonia,' Arthur replied, ruing the time it
took to reach Gododdin from Britain's south coast. 'Our men will be

exhausted by the time we reach the north.' He glanced over his shoulder. Already men marched with ragged boots and grumbled at the aches in their legs from long days marching through valleys, woodlands and bramble-covered fields.

Arthur hauled on Llamrei's reins and cantered along the column towards where Balin and his black cloaks marched as the rearguard.

'I must ride ahead to Rheged, to see if King Urien and Ector have marched already for Gododdin. Urien would not commit to support us when we met, but he cannot ignore an army of Saxons to his north. If they have not, then we shall need their spearmen. We are only five hundred men. It's not enough to fight Octha or Ida.'

'Or both,' said Balin, his hard face staring north into the wind. 'Octha wintered with Ida, eating his food and drinking his ale. So, they must be allies, and Octha will owe Ida a vast share of whatever he can conquer.'

Arthur paled at the thought of Ida and Octha's men united as one monstrous Saxon army. 'How many spearmen can King Letan of Gododdin muster?'

Balin thought for a moment. 'Three hundred warriors, and another three hundred from the hides in his kingdom. Go to Rheged. We shall meet you at Caer Ligualid.'

Arthur called his riders, and Malegant's scouts, to him, and they rode hard for Rheged. Their horses needed regular rest stops, and through the day and night it took to ride the Roman roads north, Arthur's mind churned with numbers of warriors, and how many men the Britons would need to stand against the Saxon army. With the men of Elmet and Dumnonia added to his and Balin's own men Arthur led an army of five hundred warriors, King Urien could march three hundred spearmen, and another few hundred farmers, smiths, weavers and tanners from the farms, or hides, in his kingdom, but that would still only swell the army to a thousand men. That, matched to King Letan's six hundred, was an army half the size of Octha's horde, and every man in the Saxon army was a professional warrior, come to Britain on fast ships to make war, capture land and win glory.

The riders reached Caer Ligualid to find the fortress heaving with men. Arthur led his riders from southern forests to join the Roman road, and warriors thronged the fields and orchards around the stronghold's palisade. Men stared at Arthur in his chain mail, flowing cloak and large Saxon shield hung across Llamrei's back. He rode with his own men who bore shields painted with the sword, and twenty Dumnonians who rode under their dragon sigil. Llamrei's hooves clattered on the wooden bridge which spanned the ditch, and the gate guards recognised Arthur and waved him on through the palisade's gate.

'Arthur?' shouted a familiar voice, and Arthur grinned to see Kai stood with hands on his hips, standing astride the pathway which led straight through the Caer and its stone, oak and alder buildings. He wore a leather breastplate, and his beard was grown long, hanging down to his chest. Kai wore the sleeves of his tunic rolled up and his forearms rippled with death rings. Arthur ran to Kai, and they embraced warmly, clapping each other's backs with heavy hands.

'Men are mustering here for war?' asked Arthur.

'Aye, there are two hundred men here. Owain has already marched north with the rest of Rheged's army.'

'So, Urien changed his mind. Is Ector still here?'

'Yes, we leave tomorrow. Riders came to Urien from Gododdin, and Ector pleaded King Letan's case at the Bear Fort. If Gododdin falls, Rheged will surely be next. Owain spoke in favour of war, and Urien finally relented. Look at you, brother, you went away a stripling boy and have returned a lord in your mail, cloak and sword.'

'Stripling?'

'Would you like to wrestle here, in front of everyone, so I can put you on your arse for the hundredth time? You might have grown tall, brother, but you still look as weak as piss to me.'

Arthur laughed and hugged his foster brother close again. Kai ordered men to care for Llamrei and the rest of Arthur's horses and for his men to bring food and ale. Then they strode together arm in arm to where Ector stood with his captains outside his hall.

'Spear-father!' Arthur called. Ector looked up from his deep conversation and a smile split his broad, hard face.

'Arthur, my lad,' Ector said, and met Arthur with a warm shake of his forearm. 'You return to us in dark times.'

'I know. That is why I have come. I rode with thirty riders ahead of my men, the rest march close behind. We have brought warriors from Dumnonia and Elmet. Balin marches with five hundred spearmen.'

'Dumnonians? So, Uther welcomed you?'

'I would not say he welcomed me, but he gave us three hundred warriors to help fight the Saxons. Word came to us they have attacked Gododdin?'

Ector grabbed Arthur's shoulder with his powerful hand. 'I must hear all about your travels. But time is now against us. You return just in time, and you've done well. We shall need every spear. There are three thousand Saxons marching deep into Gododdin as we speak. They are raping, murdering and looting their way north towards King Letan's stronghold at Dunpendyrlaw.'

'Octha?'

'We don't know yet, but it must be. He's the only Saxon warlord seeking to win a kingdom.'

'Have the men of Gododdin met the Saxons in battle?'

'Not that we know of, though the last message came here four days ago from King Letan seeking urgent aid. So, we march to war, son, and we are glad to have your men with us.'

'Arthur!' came a woman's call, and Lunete came bursting from Ector's hall with her dark hair flowing behind her like a raven's wing. She wore a blue woollen dress, and it was the first time Arthur had seen her wearing women's clothes, for she normally wore the jerkin and trews of a hunter. She jumped on him, wrapping her arms and legs about his body, her face pressed close against the cold iron of his chain mail.

'I have never seen you look so beautiful,' Arthur said, and she punched him on the arm.

'Lunete,' Ector growled. 'Back inside. We talk of war.'

Lunete frowned and pulled Arthur with her towards the hall. 'Father makes me dress like this now. He says I will go to join King Urien's court before summer's end. He says I must learn to be a lady if I am to be married.'

'I never thought I'd see the day. It suits you.' Her blue eyes shone, and any man would be lucky to marry Lunete, if he could manage her wildness.

'You must tell me of your adventures. Have you been far away?'

'To Elmet and Dumnonia, but now is not the time for tales, Lunete. I must talk more with Father, but I give you my word that we shall sit together and talk more when I have time.'

She frowned at him, and Arthur left her there in the hall's shadow where, even though it was not in her nature, she had to join the rest of Caer Ligualid's women, spinning wool on distaffs, weaving, and managing the hall's business. There was an unhappiness in her usually sparkling eyes, and as he went to Ector and his captains, he worried about Lunete and how she would cope in a world she was ill-equipped for. Ector had indulged Lunete, allowing her to hunt, learn the bow and spear with Kai and Arthur. Whenever she disguised herself to ride with the warriors, Ector would gently scold her, but all knew he was secretly proud of his daughter, who was a better archer than both Arthur and Kai. To change her now, expect her to wear a dress and become a doting wife to some lord in a distant hall was a challenge worthy of Merlin himself.

The army marched the following morning, Balin's black cloaks sounded the carnyx to summon the spearmen to war, and its metallic, sonorous song rang around Caer Ligualid and stirred men's hearts. They took a breakfast of cold meat, cheese and black bread, and each man packed enough food to last four days. Warriors marched with their war bands, Ector and the men of Rheged led the way with their shields painted with King Urien's bear sigil, then went the men of Elmet, and the Caer's folk marvelled at their Roman armour, bristled helmets, short swords, oval shields and long, iron-shafted spears. The Dumnonians marched next, led by Malegant who strode with the *fasces* rested on his right shoulder, and a warrior behind him carried a long spear tipped with the flowing dragon banner of Uther Pendragon. Arthur and Balin formed the rearguard, Balin's men in their flowing black cloaks and shields daubed with the fox of lost Bernicia, and Arthur's men with their sword-painted shields.

Columns of smoke smeared the horizon beyond sweeping forests as the army crossed the head of a steep valley which marked Rheged's border with Gododdin. The warriors had left Caer Ligualid in high spirits, men beating marching time with spears on shields and singing war songs to pass the long day humping their gear and supplies across Rheged's mountainous terrain. But the first signs of smoke sent the men into a sullen, silent trudge along a goat path as they descended into the valley basin. All men knew what those smears meant, and none more so than Balin of the Two Swords and his handful of survivors from lost Bernicia. Dewi led the black cloaks in a sad song to remember their fallen brothers and dead families, and the warriors of other kingdoms hummed along to the tune, all men fearing that Bernicia's dark fate could one day be their own.

They camped that night beside a glassy-surfaced tarn at the valley's northern end, where Arthur, Ector, Balin, Kai, Malegant, Nimue and Idnerth sat beside a fire with a brace of rabbits roasting slowly on the flames.

'This is where the march becomes treacherous,' said Balin, usually the last man to speak amongst the army's commanders. 'The Saxons are loose in Gododdin. That is the way they fight. They'll raid and ravage and then muster for battle once King Letan and his warriors emerge in numbers, seeking revenge.'

'Will they not make straight for Dunpendyrlaw and try to take the fortress?' asked Idnerth. 'Or lure King Letan out into the field to fight? If the Saxons want Gododdin, they must capture its fortress and kill its king.'

'The Saxons want to draw them out. They don't want to lay siege to Dunpendyrlaw or any of Gododdin's other strongholds. If they settle in for a siege, the Saxons must find food, ale or water for three thousand men. They want open battle where their greater numbers can deliver a swift victory. They will commit atrocities in the field, horrors whose tales will sail on the wind to Gododdin's warriors and its king and provoke them to leave their fastnesses to fight, to stop the rape, murder and enslavement of their people. We must scout the land ahead carefully, or we could come from a forest and stumble upon hundreds of Saxons baying for blood.'

'The Saxons owe blood to their gods,' said Nimue. 'Woden, Týr and

Thunor demand it of them. Balin is right, Ida or Octha, whoever commands, will let their war band loose on the people of Gododdin to slake their thirst for blood and plunder. Riders will scour the countryside in search of Gododdin warriors, and only when it is time to fight will the army become one. Then, they will look to crush Gododdin with one hammer blow, kill King Letan and Prince Gawain and Gododdin becomes a Saxon kingdom.'

'How do you know this, *gwyllion*?' asked Malegant, making the sign of the cross across his chest. All the Christian warriors feared Nimue with her shaved head, the oddly glimmering stones set into her teeth, her black staff and painted face, though many of them now carried her elf stones for luck.

'I know because I sailed across the narrow sea on their ships, I once healed a wound in Octha's thigh, and I sacrificed beasts to the gods for battle luck. So, though I am an Irish servant of the old gods, I know the Saxons well.'

'You are a Saxon sorcerer?' spat Malegant, rising to his feet in anger.

'I am no Saxon. I serve the gods and Merlin. I can weave a charm to bring you battle luck. Should you wish it?'

'I'd rather roast my balls on that fire, *gwyllion*.'

'I don't want to see your balls,' said Kai, and the others chuckled, breaking the tension, 'so let's carry on with the discussion.'

'So, we march carefully,' said Ector. 'No man here is new to war or fighting. We are in lands where an enemy could wait for us at every turn. Gododdin is as mountainous as Rheged in these parts, but it changes to lower plains and meadows in the east. So, we stick to valleys as we march, but keep to the slopes so that we do not yield high ground to the Saxons should they come upon us. Valleys give us access to water and grass for the horses. We do not camp on high hills, but on hillocks and knolls which give us a view of the surrounding country.'

The leaders all nodded at the sense of Ector's words, and then Balin stood, staring out into the northern night. 'They are out there,' he said wistfully. 'We must combine our forces, or the Saxons will pick off Owain's warriors, then King Letan's forces, and then our own. Alone, we cannot win. We must bring them to one decisive battle.'

'But they outnumber us?' said Kai.

'We either fight them in battle, yield Gododdin to the Saxons, or let them destroy us as we march.'

'Balin is right,' said Arthur. 'We must find Owain and get through to King Letan. No doubt Prince Gawain and Bors are readying for battle, somewhere in Gododdin's hills and valleys. I will ride out in the morning with my ten men and head for Dunpendyrlaw. Malegant, your riders should scout ahead of the army and look for signs of Owain.'

Arthur realised they all looked to him, and none of the captains disputed his plan. He had spoken more to suggest what to do than as a command, but the only responses were respectful nods. The time had come for war. All Arthur had worked and strove for since the day he had left Caer Ligualid in what seemed a lifetime ago led to this moment. The fate of Britain hung in the balance. If he failed, if Britain failed, then it would become a land of Saxons, his people slaves or worse. He looked out into the night. A few of the brightest stars fought their way through a dusting of dark cloud to shine in the heavens beside a low crescent moon, as curved and sharp as a blade. Arthur returned to Llamrei and fed the horse a handful of oats before bedding down for the night under his cloak. It was a long, sleepless night filled with fitful tossing and turning as he pondered the ride through enemy-infested Gododdin, where he could run into the savage enemy at any turn. He remembered the dread strength of the Saxon champions he had faced at Dun Guaroy, their brutal size and skill and the ease with which they had bested him. Arthur could not close his eyes without seeing Octha, Ida and his sons Ibissa and Theodric, their cruel faces dripping with malice and violence. Redwulf too haunted him. It was time to find them and face them, and the thought made Arthur shudder.

21

Llamrei picked his way through dense bracken, and a covering of fallen twigs and rotting leaves crunched and cracked beneath the horse's hooves. Arthur ducked his head between creaking boughs as he rode through a dense woodland of oak, rowan and birch trees, a day's ride from Ector, Balin, Kai and their army of spearmen. Arthur's ten riders trailed behind him, and five riders who had joined his forces on the road north swelled their numbers. Young men eager to be part of the fight against the Saxons. They rode in grim silence. Earlier that day they had passed through a ravaged farm, corpses bloated and stinking in the ruins, yet more evidence of devastating Saxon raids. A bloated cow had lowed painfully in the farm's pasture, its belly distended and in desperate need of milking. It had hurt Arthur to give the order to leave the slaughtered folk as they lay, but there was no time to stay and give the dead the respect they deserved. Arthur had to reach Dunpendyrlaw and bring the disparate Briton forces together before Gododdin fell.

A clearing opened up where the forest rose steeply to the north and fell away to a broad meadow with high, wild grasses to the east. A flock of birds burst suddenly from the treetops in that pasture, where an ancient oak sprawled in the bright space, and beyond it a clutch of birch trees reached for the sky with spindly, grasping limbs. Something spooked

Llamrei, and the horse reared a little, and then veered to the right. Arthur leant forward and shushed soothingly into the horse's ear and stroked his muscular neck to calm him.

'There's something in those trees,' Arthur said to his men. 'Hold here.' The forest canopy hid them from the bright clearing and its high grasses swaying on a gentle summer breeze. Llamrei bobbed his head and snorted, and Arthur stroked his ears. Undergrowth cracked, branches shifted and a line of warriors emerged from the northern woods, men with long hair and beards, and strips of dyed cloth woven into their braids. Each carried a shield bearing the stag of Gododdin, and at their head stalked a huge man, shaved head glistening, and a long-handled Saxon war-axe resting upon his shoulder.

'It's Lord Bors, and the men of Gododdin,' Arthur said warmly, happy to see the big warrior healed and hale after the wounds he had taken in the escape from Dun Guaroy. Arthur's men laughed with relief that the force was Britons, and not the dreaded Saxons. Arthur clicked his tongue and was about to ride from the trees and greet Gododdin's champion, when a voice from behind checked him.

'Arthur, wait,' said a woman's voice in alarm, surprising Arthur. Lunete's voice. 'Look, there are warriors in the trees.'

Arthur's head swam. He wanted to turn and rage at Lunete for sneaking away from Caer Ligualid again, but she was right. Shadows shifted in the trees across the clearing from where the birds had flown moments earlier. More of Bors' warriors trudged into the clearing until there were fifty spearmen in the open. A dog burst from the eastern trees, a hugely muscled beast, barking and slathering as it hurtled towards the men of Gododdin. Llamrei shook his head, the dog's bark and stink unsettling him.

'Saxon war dog. It's an ambush,' Arthur said through gritted teeth. A clearing surrounded by dense forest was the perfect position to launch an attack. 'Lunete, do not move from this position, or I'll send you back to Caer Ligualid in chains. The rest of you, on me.'

An arrow sang past Arthur's head, loosed by Lunete from the back of her horse, its white goose feathers whistling as it tore through the air and vanished into the distant trees. A man cried out in pain from those shaded eastern boughs, and then a blood-curdling war cry sounded. A Saxon war cry. Lunete slid from her saddle, hooded cloak still drawn up about her raven-black hair. She stuck a handful of arrows into the earth before her, knelt, and loosed them one by one towards the enemy. Arthur dug his heels into Llamrei's flanks, and the horse set off, cantering through the trees while Arthur's men followed.

Saxons burst from the woodland, howling as they charged towards Bors with seax blades drawn and spears in their fists. More war dogs bounded towards the Britons, and as Arthur rode between the trees, Bors killed the first Saxon with a mighty sweep of his war axe. Arthur nudged Llamrei right and led his men deeper into the woods, as the crash of iron, wood and bone cracked from the clearing like lightning as the two war bands came together. The hooves of his men's horses clattered through the leaf mulch, and Arthur turned again, driving his horsemen to where the Saxons had burst forth. Figures moved between the trunks. A Saxon holy man pranced with two long-haired scalps in each fist, bawling at the Saxon warriors in their harsh tongue. Arthur leapt from Llamrei's back, dragged Excalibur from its scabbard and pulled his shield from the horse's back.

'Attack the bastards from the rear,' he growled at his men and set off through the trees at a flat run. He clattered the holy man across the head with the flat of his sword. To kill a man beloved of the gods, even Saxon gods, was to invite their ire and so Arthur knocked the shrieking shaman to the ground instead. As he ran, Arthur quickly touched the bronze disc at his neck, and Guinevere's silver pin at his belt for luck, for all warriors need luck in battle.

'For Britain!' Arthur bellowed, and a tangle-haired Saxon hanging at the rear of the fight turned, eyes wide with horror to see a tall man in chain mail, carrying a bright sword and an iron-shod shield, charging at him. Arthur crashed his shield's heavy iron boss into the man's face and heard bones crack. He left the man to fall and swung his sword across the skull of another Saxon and then he was amongst them. A sharp-toothed war dog leapt at him, its jaws wide and poised to crush his bones to ruin, but Arthur battered it away with his shield and the beast squealed and ran away. In the chaos of battle, Arthur could not tell how many Saxons ambushed Bors' war band. His only aim was to take them by surprise and induce panic with an attack on their rear.

'Shield wall,' Arthur ordered as the Saxons grew thicker about him. Many had turned, hearing the shrieks of the two men Arthur had attacked, and they howled to see an enemy force behind them. They had thought to ambush Bors' men and have a great slaughter but found themselves surrounded instead. Arthur paused until his men formed up around him. Hywel overlapped his shield with Arthur's, and another warrior did the same on his left side. They advanced using the Saxon tactics Arthur had learned in the north and drilled into his men until it became second nature, an organised shield wall with spears bristling. The Saxons themselves had abandoned any sort of organisation, so hungry were they to charge into the ambush and spill Gododdin blood.

A big-bellied Saxon hurled himself at Arthur's shield and died with Hywel's Roman spear in his throat. More Saxons turned to attack Arthur's small shield wall, but as they did so the Gododdin men found gaps, and the roar of Bors the champion rose above the din of battle as he killed his enemies with his mighty war axe. A war dog tore out a Gododdin man's throat in a gout of dark blood, and men shrank away from its ferocity. A Saxon hooked the tip of his axe on the lip of Arthur's shield and tried to yank it down, but Arthur braced his knee against the shield's lower edge and the seax which came for his undefended throat instead rang off the shield's upper iron rim. Arthur slid Excalibur's blade across the shield rim and punched its tip into the axeman's eye, twisted the blade, and as hot blood splashed across his face, he swept the sword down to cut open the seax wielder's arm. He was a golden-bearded man, and his blue eyes clenched tight shut as Hywel drove his spear point into the man's belly.

Resistance before Arthur's shield wall vanished as the Saxons broke and ran for their lives. One Saxon fell with one of Lunete's arrows in his back, and the men of Gododdin were before Arthur, hacking and slashing at the fleeing Saxons.

'Arthur!' came Bors' deep voice. 'Is that you? By great Maponos' hairy balls, but I thought they had us there. Well met, lad, well met.'

Arthur dropped his shield and took Bors' brawny arm in the warrior's grip. The fight broke up around them as the Britons chased down the

routed Saxons. Three war dogs ran across the meadow beyond the fighting, sniffing the grass and barking at the carnage. One group of four
Saxons remained, shields locked around a tall man who wore a shining
helmet topped with a plume of black raven feathers. The helmeted man
wielded a sword and snarled at Bors' men, who surrounded him and the
last of his warriors.

'We have brought men to fight the Saxons,' Arthur said, catching his
breath after the skirmish. 'I'll tell you more when this is over.'

Arthur marched towards the man in the helmet and Bors ordered the
Gododdin men to stand down. The tall Saxon strode out from behind his
men's shields, glanced at Bors and then Arthur. He drank in Arthur's
expensive chain mail and his sword. Only the wealthiest lords and most
successful warriors went to war so richly garbed, and he levelled his
sword towards Arthur in challenge. He saw a chance to kill a warlord, and
so earn the favour of his brutal warlike gods before he died.

'I'll kill the Saxon turd,' said Bors and hefted his bloody axe.

'He challenged me, and the men saw him do it. I'll fight him.'

Bors nodded and shrugged, and men moved aside to let Arthur and
the Saxon fight. He was clearly their leader in his fine helmet, white fur-
lined cloak, and his sword had silver wire wrapped about its hilt. He
snarled and launched himself at Arthur with a flurry of wild slashes, but
Arthur easily parried them. The man was no swordsman, and Arthur
swayed aside from a wide chop and punched Excalibur's pommel into the
Saxon's nose, stunning him. The Saxon paused as blood squirted from his
ruined face, and Arthur drove Excalibur's point into his stomach, twisted
the blade and wrenched it free. He dropped to his knees, holding in his
entrails with his left hand. The stricken Saxon lifted his chin and Arthur
slashed his throat open in a swift cut.

'Kill the rest. No prisoners,' Arthur said coldly. He wiped Excalibur's
blade clean on the dead man's cloak and realised that the men of
Gododdin were all staring open-mouthed at him. It has been a quick,
ruthless fight, and Arthur supposed that shocked the spearmen. He took
the helmet from the dead man's head and held it aloft. Bors and the
Gododdin men cheered and set off to slaughter any Saxon survivors they

could find in the woods, beginning with the men who had stood at the end with their leader.

Arthur picked up the Saxon's sword and tossed it to Hywel. 'You earned it today,' he said, and the Elmet man bowed to him, grinning with delight at his prize.

'Lord Arthur,' said one of his men, running across the clearing with an anguished look upon his face. He carried a broken bow, its stave hanging from the string in two shivered pieces.

'What is it?'

'Your sister, lord, the archer.'

Arthur's heart sank. 'What of her?'

'She's gone, lord.'

'Gone where?'

'I saw a gang of Saxons bustling her away into the trees. I went after them, but they're gone and her with them.'

22

Arthur searched for Lunete until Llamrei could ride no further without rest, and then he doubled back, leading the horse on foot upon a different path, searching for any sign of Lunete and her captors but unable to find anything other than the marks of hundreds of Saxon boots. Bors sent his finest trackers into the deep forest, but they returned before nightfall with no sign of her trail. The woodland was too well trodden by Saxon war bands, as were the hills and dales. Their detritus was everywhere: camp-fires, bones from their food, pits filled with shit, broken spears and dead Britons. But no sign of Lunete.

After two days of exhausting, sleepless searching, Arthur came to accept the painful fact that she was lost. He wept for his sister, and cursed himself for not staying close to her once the fighting began, but to stay and search longer was to abandon the war. The decision ripped at his soul like sharp talons, but without hope of finding his beloved foster sister and with the fate of Gododdin upon his shoulders, Arthur eventually tore himself away from the forest.

Arthur and Bors led their men north. Columns of smoke in the south and east told of more Saxon war bands raiding Gododdin's countryside, and any of them could have taken Lunete as their prisoner, if she still lived. Arthur couldn't fight every roving band of Saxons, and so he camped a day's march from Dunpendyrlaw. His men cowered beneath their cloaks as a summer thunderstorm tore the sky and hammered the land with torrential rain. Ector arrived from the midst of that swirling storm, with Balin, Nimue, Idnerth, Kai and Malegant. Owain mab Urien rode at the head of their column alongside Balin and Ector and the prince of Rheged's men swelled their ranks with five hundred warriors, so that a thousand men trudged through driving rain and found what shelter they could beneath their cloaks and shields.

Ector, Britain's champion, its greatest warrior, shuddered like a spear hitting a tree trunk when Arthur told him of Lunete's capture. He told Ector of the dead Saxon found where she had been taken, an arrow driven into his eye at close quarters. Lunete must have fought like a bear, killing one of her assailants before the others could carry her away. Kai raged like a wild boar at the fell news, tearing at his hair and banging his fists against his chest. Ector's face trembled, and only the sheeting rain hid the tears rolling down his scarred cheeks. Kai wanted to ride off in search of Lunete and railed at Arthur for not searching harder for their lost sister until Bors calmed him and told of their desperate search.

'We must find her!' Kai cried, grasping fistfuls of Arthur's chain mail. 'She can't be gone.'

'We'll find her when the battle is over,' said Arthur, and Kai spluttered incredulously in his face.

'Battle? A pox on your battle. Saxons have taken our sister!'

'Arthur's right, son,' said Ector, pulling Kai into his massive arms. His face stretched, drawn, made long by unthinkable grief. 'She could be anywhere amongst a hundred Saxon war bands by now. She could even be in Bernicia. We must fight them first, and then, if we live and enough Saxons are dead, we'll find her. She's my daughter. I'll tear all of Britain apart to find her.'

'Why was she here? She should never have been allowed to ride with the warriors.' After spitting those last, cruel words at Ector, Kai stormed off and refused to be consoled. Lunete's disappearance was a knife in Arthur's heart. He wanted to weep, shout, rage and kill, to abandon the war, take his warriors and his sword and find his sister. But he could not abandon Gododdin, and he could not leave until the battle was fought. So

Arthur steeled himself, clenching his jaw and holding on to Excalibur's hilt until he mastered the grief, bottling it up like a sealed amphora of Roman wine.

The rain continued to soak Gododdin, coming from low sky, clouds dark and broiling like heated pitch.

'The gods prepare for battle,' Nimue said, raising her hands and staring up into the driving rain, letting it soak her through. 'Our gods do battle with the Saxon gods, and there shall be a great battle before the moon turns full. They say Kadvuz is here. I must find him and ask of Merlin. We must prepare ourselves to seek the gods' favour.' She strode off, calling to Arthur that she would make her charms, and use her Irish *draíocht cailleach* magic to bring luck to his men for the fight to come.

Arthur wanted to ask Nimue to use her powers to find Lunete, if that could be done, but before he could follow her with that request, Prince Gawain of Gododdin arrived with five hundred spearmen so that one thousand and five hundred warriors filled a sprawling dale, the sound of their chatter, footsteps, armour and weapons undulating like the sigh of the sea.

'The Saxons mass in a vale beside the mouth of the river Glein,' Gawain said later, as Arthur, Bors, Owain, Ector, Kai, Idnerth and Malegant sheltered from the incessant rain beneath a sailcloth tent.

'They have seen our forces marching,' said Balin, 'and now they seek to destroy us in one monstrous battle.'

'I thank you all for coming to Gododdin's aid,' said Gawain, tall and lean, wearing a bronze circlet upon his brow. He looked far removed from the tortured, battered prisoner Arthur, Bors, Balin and Kai had dragged from Dun Guaroy. 'We have men of Dumnonia, Elmet, Rheged and Bernicia here, united against our common enemy. But there is still no word or sight of Merlin.'

'They outnumber us two to one,' said Kai, his eyes red-ringed and his face drawn with grief for his lost sister.

'And yet we must fight,' said Prince Owain, 'if we don't stop the Saxons here, they will take each of our kingdoms one by one until they have everything, and we have nothing. We fight not just for our pride, or for glory, but for our people's very existence.'

'That river is but a day's march south from here,' said Bors. 'A wide, flat plain split by a river. We can make our fight there. A hard fight, a fight for the bloody ages.'

'They want us to meet them on ground of their choosing,' said Ector. 'If the land is wide and flat, they can use their greater numbers to outflank us. They want the fight on their terms.'

'Then let them have it,' said Arthur. 'Let them think we blunder onto land of their choosing. But we shall be ready. We will not march blindly into the shield wall. We can use cunning of our own.'

'We are princes and champions here,' said Owain, frowning at Arthur. 'When I want war advice from an orphan, and a masterless man to boot, I shall ask for it.'

'Arthur has proven himself,' said Ector, 'and he should have a voice at this council.'

'Why? Because he carries an old sword, and Merlin says we should all bow down to him? Where is Merlin? I do not think so, Ector. My father only agreed to this fight because he believed I would lead our men, not this pup.'

The council broke down into a shouting match, Bors growled at Owain, and Owain squared up to him. Balin stood back, arms folded, shaking his head, whilst Idnerth and Kai did their best to split up the champion of Gododdin and the prince of Rheged.

'Silence!' Malegant bellowed, and the men all turned to stare at the Dumnonian. He held up the *fasces,* the axe wrapped in birch bundles, and held it slowly before each man, letting them stare into its sharp blade so that the significance of the symbol sunk deep into their minds. 'Arthur speaks for the Pendragon, for the high king of Britain. So, we shall hear his plan. It was he who marched across our country, from Gododdin, to Rheged, Bernicia, Elmet and fair Dumnonia. How many of you have ever left your own kingdoms before, never mind marched the breadth of Britain?'

'Out with it, then,' said Owain, begrudgingly accepting that Uther's blessing gave Arthur the authority to be heard and to lead.

'Let them believe we blunder into their trap,' said Arthur, 'form up on the riverbank, and wait for them to make their shield wall. The Saxons believe they are superior to us, that we do not know how to make war. We can forge that arrogance to our advantage. Once they advance, we feign retreat across the water, then turn, form up swiftly and kill them as they scramble up our side of the bank. They won't be able to resist the advance. They need this fight decided in one battle, so they will attack.'

'What if our men do not turn? What if they become swept up in the feigned retreat and flee the field?'

'The men of Gododdin won't flee,' said Bors. 'I cannot vouch for the faint hearts of Rheged spearmen.'

'And what of our flanks?' asked Owain, rewarding Bors with a murderous frown.

'The river will slow them and protect our flanks for a time. We shall put our hardest men on those edges, Bors and Balin, the honour is yours if you will accept it. I will take my riders, and as many horses as we can muster, and ride about their flank before they can deploy their numbers. I'll come about their rear and attack, so that we pin them between our forces, fighting them in front and rear. My force will be smaller, but large and savage enough to create panic in their lines and allow us to break their shield wall.'

'Aye, I will fight where the fight is hardest. Their shirkers will be in the rear ranks,' growled Bors, nodding slowly as Arthur's plan formed a picture in his mind. 'The lovers of war, the killers, will be in the front ranks trading blows with me, you Balin, and you Ector. The braver the man, the closer to the front he fights. Those men in the rear want to kill, but only when the lines break, when one side flees, and the battle descends into a slaughter. They want to hack into fleeing men's backs and tell warped stories of their glory and bravery to their grandchildren as though they fought like Lleu Llaw of legend. They will break first, and when men start to fold, it spreads through an army like a pox through a brothel.'

'But we must ask one band of men to perform a brave deed, one from which they might not return,' Arthur said, and fixed each man with a dread stare. 'We must pin the Saxon centre in the river. A troop of our spearmen must advance into the river and engage the enemy line whilst the rest retreat to the bank. On the bank, my men will hold their centre using their own tactics, the shield wall. If one brave force can engage them in the water and, with that most dangerous of tasks, enrage them enough to make the Saxons charge the bank in fury, we can pin them on the bank. Then I can ride around their flank whilst they focus on the desperate fight on ground of our choosing, not theirs.'

'Their champions will be in the centre,' said Ector, his voice cold. 'Their king will fight there beneath his banner. That is where the fighting will be fiercest, where their pride and their gods won't allow them to take a backwards step.'

'Which is why that is where we shall draw them in, and where we must hold them. So, we must find a group of men willing to die, who can fight like starving wolves and entice them up the bank so that we can hold them there.'

'I'll do it,' said Ector. 'I'll hold the bastards and kill their champions, and I won't hear of any other man taking that honour. They took my girl, and she's probably dead now, or worse. So, I'll advance into those waters, and I'll rip their stinking hearts out, and dam the river Glein with their corpses.'

23

Arthur and the army marched to the river Glein on a morning where eldritch light seeped from a cold, pale sky, and a mist like steam sat low upon dew-soaked fields. Men trudged in tired silence, heads fogged from lack of sleep after a night spent fearing the battle to come. The river appeared as the sun crept from its slumber, a slow-flowing, rippling streak cutting through a level, grass-covered plane. Boasting and battle songs had filled yesterday's march, along with talk of brotherhood and oaths to slay the hated Saxon invaders. The night before the battle, however, had been grimly quiet, camped beneath the stars in rain-sodden fields where men's minds churned over the vast Saxon force awaiting them, outnumbering them two to one. This was a fight not just for their own lives, but for their wives, children, land and future.

The river, swelled by heavy rainfall, rose high upon its green banks, but scouts reported the waters were still only thigh high at their deepest point, and that the Saxons waited for them across the banks with an army beyond imagination. Countless campfires, men, spears, shields and seax blades waiting to crush the men of Gododdin, enslave its people and make it a Saxon kingdom. Arthur rode ahead of the army with Balin, Ector, Kai, Malegant, Idnerth, Bors, Owain and Gawain to examine the battlefield where the Saxons waited to destroy the army of Britain.

Sloping hummocks rose to the north and south-west, but the Saxons camped on wide fields of wild heather and grasses shorn short by cattle. The river's banks were shallow, without reeds, trees or gorse, which suited Arthur's plan. Had the banks been high, it would have impeded the mock retreat and allowed the Saxons to cut down his spearmen as they ran up the bank to re-from before the water's edge. Ector stared grimly at the landscape, chewing on his beard as he looked upon the place where he must stand and hold the mighty Saxon centre and buy time for the rest of the Britons to retreat and hold them long enough for Arthur to ride around the enemy flank.

Arthur had avoided his foster father the night before. Ector and Kai spent the evening together, father and son lamenting their lost sister and daughter, talking of the fight to come, and what Kai must do should Ector perish. Arthur spent the night alone, running a whetstone along Excalibur's blade and allowing the battle to play out in his mind. He thought of every possible outcome, trap, tactic and trick. Arthur thought about a British rout and how to stem it, and a Saxon rout and how to exploit it. He worried about Ector not holding, or the Saxons attacking too quickly and crushing Ector's centre, or the Saxons spotting his flanking manoeuvre and countering it before Arthur could strike. It had been a long, sleepless night, and now it was time to fight.

'There are so many of them,' Kai said, his voice quiet as though he spoke to himself.

'Stick to the plan. We hit them in front and rear, split them, and crush them,' said Arthur with a confidence he did not feel.

Owain shook his head. 'I march to war following a boy's battle plan. How has it come to this?'

Arthur ignored the barb, because their forces advanced into the plane and a war horn sounded from the Saxon camp, drifting long and sonorous through the mist. Three riders waited on the far bank: the Saxon leaders come to have the customary exchange of insults before battle.

'Let's see who we're fighting and what the bastards have got to say,' said Bors, and they all led their mounts to the river to meet their enemies.

'Ida and his sons,' said Balin of the Two Swords.

'Where is Octha?' asked Arthur, also recognising Ida and his sons, Ibissa and Theodric, from Dun Guaroy. He had no time to consider that concern, because Ida nudged his horse into the river's flow. The king of Bernicia rode a magnificent black mare, wore a coat of shining chain mail and carried a stone sceptre in his right fist. He hunched upon the horse's back, bent by age, and his long white hair hung loose down his back. Ida's was a hard weather-beaten face, as cracked and lined as the hull of an old ship.

'Come to surrender, dogs?' Ida said in the Britons' tongue. Ibissa chuckled, hulking with golden hair and bright blue eyes astride a bay gelding.

'Withdraw from Gododdin and swear an oath never to return,' said Gawain, shouting across the river's gentle sigh. 'And there is no need to fight today.'

'I want to fight today, so do my men. We shall kill your men and piss on their dead corpses. I want to flay the flesh from your bones, Prince Gawain, and take your mother as my bed slave. I will carry your father's head as a war trophy, whore your wives and daughters, and sell your sons into slavery.'

'Then it must be war,' said Gawain, and he turned his mount and cantered back towards his men.

'Octha is too scared to fight us?' asked Arthur.

Ida sneered. 'You are fools. Octha is in the south making his own kingdom. Did you think to find him here?'

Arthur fought to hide the surprise and fear from his face. If Octha was in the south, he could attack Elmet, Dumnonia, Gwynned or Gwent and there was nothing Arthur and his army could do about it. Octha could bring his massive army against an isolated kingdom and crush it with overwhelming numbers. 'We came here to kill Saxon warriors but are disappointed to find only an old man with a grey beard, his two stripling pups, and an army of sheep-shagging whoresons,' said Arthur, and Ida grinned.

'To battle then, turds. You shall all serve me in the afterlife. Your souls are mine until the end of days.'

'You will die without a blade in your hand, and your soul shall scream in the depths of the underworld,' Balin roared, trotting his horse across the riverbank and pointing at Ida and his sons. 'You shall regret the day you came to these shores.'

Ida laughed, a dry, cackling, humourless laugh, turned his horse lazily and rode away with his sons trailing him. Another war horn blared from their lines and warriors came from the mist, spear points bristling and voices shouting curses at the Britons.

'Octha has struck somewhere else,' said Malegant, his long face suddenly pale with fear for his people.

'But Ida can only muster two thousand warriors without him,' snarled Balin. 'So, let's kill the bastards, and then march to find and fight Octha.'

They rode back to the massing ranks, but Arthur wasn't so sure about Balin's guess on Ida's numbers. It was impossible to say from across the river how many warriors Ida brought to fight, but Arthur thought it at least matched Octha's three thousand. It was too late to worry about Octha now. Ida had invaded Gododdin and must be stopped. Arthur ordered his force of riders to him as the spearmen formed up before the riverbank. Arthur had his own riders, and another seventy horses gathered from the men of Gododdin and Rheged so that he would make his ride around the enemy with close to one hundred horsemen, each rider a spearman who understood their task, hardy warriors ready to fight and die against the hated enemy.

Nimue and Kadvuz the druid capered before the army, chanting and casting dark spells against the Saxons, and imbuing the Britons with the gods' favour. They held aloft strange charms, painted skulls, animal skeletons and a giant bone which can only have belonged to some giant beast long gone from the world. They spat and sang, and all the time Kadvuz's dogs whined and barked at the Saxon war dogs, who growled and barked in return from somewhere within the massing Saxon horde. Ector gathered his spearmen in the centre, opposite Ida's ragged battle standard of an eagle's wing on a high pole. That was where Ida's picked champions would fight, the big men, the lovers of war who Ida hoped would break the Britons' line and send them into rout and defeat.

Arthur slid from his horse and gave the reins to Hywel with a promise to return soon. He jogged across the grass, soil heavy from rain, pushing his way through the men until he reached Ector. Arthur laid a hand upon his shoulder and the big man turned and smiled sadly at him.

'It's time, son,' Ector said. His bald head shone beneath the morning sun, and he towered above his men, who shared around skins of mead, seeking courage in the warming drink.

'Spear-father, I...' Arthur began, but struggled to find the words he wanted to say. Warriors gathered close about, tightening straps, testing spear points and hefting shields.

'It's all right, Arthur.' A warm smile split Ector's broad face. 'I'm proud of you, lad. I have always treated you as my son, and you have done well. You have met kings, princes, champions and princesses. You have travelled the breadth of our country, and Merlin, I think, set you on that path so that you could march across Britain and become recognised amongst the great men of our people. Merlin has given you awe and power, weaving your legend throughout the kingdom, so use it wisely.'

'Was Igraine pregnant when you brought her north from Dumnonia?' Arthur blurted out. The thought had festered in his thought cage since he had met Uther Pendragon, and he had to ask his foster father the truth of his birth.

'She was.' Ector placed a heavy hand on Arthur's shoulder. 'I knew this question would come one day.'

'Is Igraine my mother, and Uther...'

Ector shook his head. 'Merlin would have folk believe that's the case. To build your legend and make you into a man men should follow. He wants to unite us, to restore Britain to our people, and he knows that the kings and warriors are more likely to follow a man of noble birth, but one with loyalties to no kingdom. But I'm sorry, Arthur. Igraine's baby died. She gave birth at Caer Ligualid. It was a boy, but he died not an hour after he was born. She married Urien the following week and never recovered from that loss. Merlin brought you to me after Igraine's wedding. He said you were an orphan, a child of nowhere who needed care, and so I took you in. But you are not Uther's son. Merlin wanted you raised in secret, so that he could claim you were the Pendragon's son once you reached manhood. But Merlin went into exile, and Uther lived on, and Merlin's plan drifted away like smoke on a windy day.'

Arthur's mouth flopped open, but he had nothing to say. The thought that he might be the Pendragon's and Igraine's son had grown secretly in his dreams, never quite forming, not allowed to blossom or grow, but always there. He had hoped that it might be true, that he was not an orphan after all, but something more, something better. But he was just Arthur, the orphan, son of a dead mother and forgotten father. He touched Igraine's bronze disc at his neck, hoping that its luck would still hold. The carnyx blared long and loud, sounded by Balin's men to signal that the army should form up for battle. Men glanced nervously at one another and took mouthfuls of ale or mead. Some pissed where they stood, and others closed their eyes, whispering prayers to the gods.

'Find Lunete for me,' Ector said, pulling Arthur into a tight embrace. 'Dead or alive, she must be brought home. If I die today... well, I love you, son.'

Arthur breathed in Ector's smell and pushed his face into his foster father's muscled shoulder. He wanted to tell Ector that he loved him too, to thank him for being such a good father, but as is too often the way with men, the words were left unsaid. They stared deep into each other's eyes, and Arthur pulled away to join his men. On the way, he grabbed Kai's arm in the warrior's grip and clapped men he recognised on the shoulder. His heart pulsed, heavy like a stone, hurt that it should be Ector and his men who must face the Saxon champions and pin them in the river, and Ector's words about his birth rang around his skull like a bell.

Nimue waited for Arthur, a goat held tight in her grip, and as he approached, she cut its throat with a curved knife and let the beast drop. The horses whickered at the smell of blood, but Nimue grinned, the stones in her teeth shining and her painted face bright with delight. The goat bucked on the grass, soaking it with arterial blood, and Nimue threw her hands up with malevolent glee at whatever she saw in the blood spatter.

'The augurs are good,' she crowed loudly so the men could hear. 'The gods are with us today!'

Men cheered, even the Christians, and Arthur climbed onto Llamrei's back. He strapped on the helmet taken from the Saxon he had killed, its raven feathers standing proudly from the helmet's crest. Arthur hefted his heavy Saxon shield and drew Excalibur. He dug his heels into Llamrei's flanks and cantered before the army of Britons. He recalled Dun Guaroy and the fear and terror of that terrible fortress, and how he had learned that pretending to be brave was bravery itself. Arthur held Excalibur aloft so that the men could see its shining blade. He was no fool, and knew the warriors of Dumnonia, Rheged, Elmet and Gododdin knew of its legend, and of his own, so finely crafted by Merlin. Arthur realised he could embrace that legend, use it and strengthen it. They cheered as he rode along the line, encouraged to it by Bors, Balin, Idnerth, Malegant and Ector, who each stood with their own warriors. The war cries rose like thunder, and Arthur let it wash over him, banishing all thoughts of Igraine, Uther, Octha and Merlin. There was no need for Arthur to talk, the leaders of each company bellowed at their men, and the army came together in a mass of shields and spears, men who came to fight for their loved ones, for their country and for freedom, and who readied themselves to face the horror of battle.

Arthur let them all see Excalibur and rode back to his own men. He sheathed the ancient blade and took his spear from Hywel and led his riders away from the army. The carnyx sounded again, metallic and monstrous, and the army roared. Llamrei's hooves threw up clods of mud, and Arthur rode in a wide arc around a hummock covered with bracken and coarse brush. The Saxons' horns blared, and though he couldn't see, Arthur hoped the enemy took the bait and marched to meet the advancing Britons in the river. A crunching thunder crackled across the rolling plain, and Arthur winced. The two front lines had joined in slaughter, shields coming together with murderous force as men stabbed, slashed, cut and tore at each other. The sound of battle raged, and Arthur drove Llamrei into a gallop, fear gnawing at his insides. What if Ector could not hold? What if the line broke? Arthur would find himself behind the enemy, alone, a battle lost, and his friends and family slaughtered.

His riders kept close about Arthur as they emerged from behind the hummock. Battle raged on their left and the sheer size of the Saxon army took Arthur's breath away. So many men, clad in fur, leather and iron, the number of spears so vast that their staves moved like a forest pushing inexorably towards the river. The Saxon flank stretched to the edges of the

Britons' line, protected by the stream's obstacle. Balin held the left and Bors the right, and Arthur trusted those two men and their warriors to hold. A Saxon pointed at Arthur and shouted, but his comrades ignored his warning, so intent were they on the battle's front.

Space opened up to Arthur's left, and he brought Llamrei about behind the enemy lines. A clutch of Saxon women screamed, huddled by leather tents as Arthur rode past. He galloped through smoking, ash-blackened campfires, broken shields and empty ale skins cast aside where the horde had camped. Then the enemy rear was before him, a broiling mass of spearmen, shouting and shoving at the men in front. Arthur reined Llamrei in and leapt to the ground.

'Kill!' he roared to his men as they dismounted and hefted their heavy Saxon shields and spears. 'We must smash them, crush them, show them how men of Britain fight.'

Arthur didn't wait for the shield wall to form up around him. His men would do that just as they practised every day. Arthur let rage overtake him. He let go of control and snarled, levelling his spear and charging at the enemy. He had always harboured a hope that his parents could be important people, felt that a secret destiny awaited him. Igraine's gift and Uther's revelations had only stoked that dream. But it was a dream made of straw, a castle made of sand, Merlin's creation. Arthur roared like a wild animal, and frightened faces turned, staring open-mouthed at his fury. Arthur drove into them with his shield braced against his shoulder. The Saxons cried out as the heavy iron boss smashed bones and threw them out of the way. Arthur killed a man with a spear thrust to the throat, and the iron stink of blood mixed with the cloying stench of leather, sweat, soil, ale, garlic and fear. Just as Bors had said, these were the shirkers of the Saxon army, the men who lurked at the rear, and Arthur killed them with contempt. He drove his spear into the small of a warrior's back, ripped it free, and lunged again into the back of an enemy skull. Arthur was amongst them now, surrounded by Saxons, who twisted and pushed to get away from his murderous anger.

More Saxons turned, and Arthur stabbed his spear into a warrior's belly. The man screamed in pain and the spear became trapped inside the dying man. Arthur let it go, drawing Excalibur and hacking into the

Saxons like a demon. His men came behind him in their organised shield wall, the tactic Arthur had learned from the Saxons. Their spears lanced out from behind overlapped shields and the Saxons fled before them like sheep. Arthur clove his way forward, until he was five ranks deep in the enemy lines, and then a big man turned to face him, a scarred-faced man with drooping moustaches. He caught Arthur's sword blade on his shield and lashed out with his spear, the tip scoring across Arthur's cheek and ear like a fiery whip. Arthur raised his shield to knock the spear away and slashed open the moustached man's throat with Excalibur's point.

More men turned to face Arthur's charge, and these were not frightened men. They were roaring, scarred warriors who organised themselves into a rearguard to keep Arthur's charge at bay. Three of them bullied Arthur back with their shields, and he shuffled in between Hywel's and Cadog's shields to join the shield wall. More Saxons turned, and there was confusion in their ranks. Arthur spied Ida's eagle standard only ten paces away from him as he cut a man down with a sweep of Excalibur's edge across his eyes.

'Forward!' Arthur cried, and his men obeyed. They pushed into the enemy, driving the line of men before them backwards, shields pressed together so that the fight became a shoving match. The Saxons backed into the men behind them, who faced the opposite way, and more men turned away from the front line. A cry went up from the Saxon front. Arthur felt their line buckle, and he hoped it was Ector carving into them like the champion he was. A big man bullied his way into the Saxons facing Arthur, his golden hair shining and his blue eyes as pale as a winter pool. It was Ibissa, son of Ida, come to see what disrupted the Saxon rear. Ibissa grimaced at Arthur, noting his fine helmet, mail and sword, and he pushed his men out of the way, gesturing for Arthur to come and fight with a blood-soaked axe in his fist.

'Don't do it, lord,' said Cadog in his left ear. 'We are driving them backwards.'

Arthur could not refuse the challenge. He marched out of the line and charged at the big Saxon, hoping that if he could kill their prince, the Saxons would panic and crumble. He lunged at Ibissa, but the big man caught the sword on his shield boss, the ring of it jarring Arthur's arm to the shoulder. Ibissa swung the axe, and it chopped into the rim of Arthur's shield, the force of the blow like a horse's kick. Arthur stumbled backwards and Ibissa hauled on his axe, which had become embedded in Arthur's shield, and ripped the shield from Arthur's grasp. It clattered to the earth: a field churned to mud by a thousand boots. Ibissa snarled, his axe trapped in the fallen shield, and Arthur swung Excalibur to rip the hulking Saxon's throat open and spatter his men with their dying prince's blood.

A great lament went up from the Saxons, and Arthur laid into them with Excalibur held in both hands, hacking and slashing like a wild man. Arthur had killed Ida's son, and the joy of battle pulsed through him, strengthening him, making him feel unbeatable. Arthur charged again, but more Saxons closed in about him, the press of their bodies making it impossible to swing his sword. A man's hot breath washed over Arthur's face, stinking of stale ale and fish, and a spear smashed into the Saxon's cheek, crushing his face and splashing blood over Arthur's beard. He could not move, and the enemy snarled and spat at him, stamping on the corpse of their fallen prince so desperate were they to strike at Arthur and his men. The eagle wing standard rose above Arthur, a voice cried out in anguish and rage, so loud that it rose above the din of slaughter. The Saxons about Arthur melted away, some cowering, others thrown aside by a dozen enormous men. They were battle-hardened Saxon champions in furs and mail and at their centre lumbered King Ida, the Saxon conqueror, come to avenge his fallen son.

24

'Sunu,' Ida sobbed in his own tongue, dropping to his knees in the mire of mud, blood, shit and piss of terrified men. Beyond him, the battle raged, but Arthur saw a hedge of Britons' spears edging closer, flowing into the gap left by Ida's champions and carving into the Saxon shield wall. Ida rose, his face trembling and his teeth clenched. He bellowed at his warriors, and Ida's picked champions came at Arthur with grim faces and sharp blades.

Cadog cried out as a seax stabbed into his chest, and the freed slave died and fell beneath the mass of warriors. Arthur lashed out at his killer, screaming in horror at the loyal man's death, only to have his blade parried by a Saxon shield. A dozen of Arthur's men remained. The rest had perished in his desperate charge. They were close to the front, had carved the Saxon army in two, and if he could reach Ector and the river, then the Saxons would be divided completely. But the Saxon champions were implacable. A spear sliced open Arthur's thigh, and an axe haft smashed into his head. Arthur's helmet took the blow but slid over his eyes to blind him. He shook his head, panicking, and the axe came again, its blade chopping into his chest. The press of men denied the axeman a true swing, and Arthur's chain mail held the blow. He gasped, death close, and set his helmet straight. The axeman died with Hywel's spear in his armpit and the battle suddenly changed, like the tide turning from ebb to flood, and the Saxons fell back from Arthur, granting him a moment of respite.

Ida stumbled, dragging Ibissa's corpse with him, and his champions shifted from attack to form a circle of shields around their king. Arthur gasped for breath, pain from his wounds and aching limbs throbbing around his body. He sagged, finding himself in open space as the Saxons fell back, and then shields bearing stags and bears were around him, roaring in triumph.

'We did it,' said Malegant, helping Arthur to his feet. Blood covered the Dumnonian's face, and his shield was a battered ruin. 'They're retreating.'

'Ector?' Arthur said, peering into the mass of men searching for his foster father.

'He held them. I saw him kill four of those big bastards in the front line, but then I lost him.'

'They aren't running,' shouted a voice above the din. 'They're forming up again.'

The Britons groaned, and Arthur saw that the man was right. Ida stood before his warriors, swinging his stone sceptre in great sweeps, shouting his hate, desperate for vengeance for his dead son.

'Back, back to the riverbank,' Arthur said, and shoved men backwards. Malegant understood what Arthur intended and roared at his men to move beyond the river. The Saxons had re-formed, and they would trap the Britons between their shields and the river, and so Arthur moved them backwards. Slowly they went, trudging through the water and over the corpses and writhing bodies of injured men. Arthur splashed into the chill river water and clambered up the bank, and there he found Ector, slumped dead in the mud, his face and body slashed to bloody ruin by countless wounds. Arthur cried out in anguish and knelt beside his spear-father, the guilt of allowing Ector to be the one to pin the enemy as heavy as a millstone.

'He fought like a demon,' said Kai, reaching down to help Arthur to his feet. A filthy mix of mud and blood sheeted Kai's face and armour, a testament to how hard he had fought in the front, where the battle raged most dangerous. 'Let's not let him die in vain. He gave his left so we could win, so you could win.'

Arthur's heart soared to see Kai alive amidst so much death. He nodded and took his place in the front line, exhausted from battle and grief. The Saxons came towards the river in their organised shield wall, a mass of overlapped linden-wood boards bossed and ringed with iron. Ida urged them on with hate, screaming at them, spitting at the Britons, and his warriors edged forwards.

'Do not charge,' Arthur called. 'Let them clamber up the bank and over the corpses, and we'll kill them as they come.'

'There are too many,' said Kai, 'and we are too few to fight, but too many to die.'

'Then we die together, brother,' said Arthur, and he readied Excalibur to meet the Saxon horde. There were still so many, and the Britons had lost many brave warriors in the fight already. He looked about him but could not guess how many men had survived to fight again. He hoped it was enough. It had to be enough.

The Saxons splashed into the river and big men came towards Arthur, spurred on by Ida, who knew that Arthur had killed his son. He pointed his sceptre at Arthur and his men charged. The champions burst from the Saxon shield wall, splashing through the river, and Arthur waited. He forced his fear away, demanding himself to be calm, to fight like a commander. A monstrous man with a beard covering his face to the eyes and an axe held in each hand reached Arthur first, surging from the river howling with anger, but his boot slipped on the riverbank and Arthur killed him, punching Excalibur through his gullet, whipping the blade free to let the big man drop dead to the mud. He killed another champion as he fumbled over the first man's corpse, and Kai threw his spear to kill a third. The river water turned red with blood, and even the Saxon champions fell back to wait for the shield wall to support their charge.

Then they came as one. An organised shield wall marching slowly and inexorably through the river and up the bank. They pushed the Britons back, shields overlapping, so that there was nowhere for Arthur and his men to strike. Arthur found himself pushed backwards, and then the spears darted between the Saxons' shields. A warrior to Arthur's left died with a spear in his groin, and another fell with a seax blade to the throat. Arthur stood on his tiptoes and peered left and right. His line buckled, the Saxons using their numbers to wrap around Balin and Bors on the flanks. Arthur struck at the enemy but found only shields to hit. In a fleeting moment, he saw Redwulf fighting in the Saxon rear ranks, but then lost sight of the traitor. Arthur's shoulders screamed with fatigue and his own blood dripped from wounds on his face, legs and arms.

Arthur fought on, as did the surrounding men, desperately battling to hold the centre and keep the army from breaking. More Britons died, his father was dead, and Arthur's strength waned, defeat seeming inevitable. There were simply too many Saxons to kill. His plan had worked, and they had broken the Saxon line, but Ida had simply re-formed and charged again. A blow struck Arthur's helmet, dizzying him, and Kai dragged him away from the front line.

'We are lost,' Kai gasped, tears running down his cheeks in filthy streaks. And in that desperate moment where it seemed the Saxons would overwhelm them all, a horn sounded, bright and clear from beyond the river, and then blared again. The Saxon shield wall gave way. Just as Arthur thought his army would break and run, it was instead the Saxons who fled. Men pointed and Arthur laughed for sheer joy, because from the west came a new army, bearing standards of Powys, Gwynedd and Gwent. Arthur's men cheered wildly, and Kai laughed like a madman. A figure strode before the new force, a man with a wide-brimmed hat and billowing white cloak, and a black amber-topped staff held before him. It was Merlin, come unlooked for with an army to the battle for Gododdin.

Imbued with strength by the sight of Merlin, Arthur elbowed his way to the front line, where hundreds of Saxons ran for their lives, splashing through the river, broken by the sight of a fresh army of Britons on their flank. A band of Saxon warriors remained, fighting with Malegant's Dumnonians in the blood-red river. Ida was there with his remaining champions, refusing to retreat and howling at his men to stay and fight. Arthur leapt into the waters and a Saxon champion came at him with his shield, trying to shove Arthur off balance. But Arthur was no longer the lad who had fallen so easily at Dun Guaroy. Arthur smashed his shoulder into the shield, and it was the Saxon who fell back under the impact.

Arthur swept Excalibur through the water and cut the man's legs from under him, then stabbed down into his throat as he fell. Ida swung his sceptre from behind his warriors' shields and its stone head smashed a Dumnonian's skull like an overripe fruit. Arthur swung Excalibur over-hand, and its sharp edge sliced through Ida's wrist. He felt resistance as the blade sliced through bone and gristle, and both hand and sceptre fell splashing into the river.

Ida screamed in pain and his warriors dragged him away to join his routed army as they fled the field. Arthur picked up the Saxon king's sceptre and held it aloft, turning to shout victoriously at his men. They jeered the Saxons, cheering the victory.

'Arthur, Arthur, Arthur!' the Britons cheered behind him, but Arthur could not meet their acclaim. He fell to one knee in the river, overcome by the emotions of victory, closeness to death and the loss of his father.

'What are you doing?' a chirpy voice said, snapping Arthur from his exhausted trance. It was Merlin, standing on the opposite riverbank, grinning down at Arthur, a puzzled look on his lined face. 'This is no time to take a bath. The Saxons are beaten, and in no small thanks to my impeccable timing, I might add.'

'Ector...' Arthur began, and Merlin bowed his head solemnly.

'Died like the hero he was and will take a place of honour in the halls of the gods. We do not have time to tarry here. Ida yet lives. He will retreat to Bernicia, and we must pursue him. Octha strikes in the south and the war has only just begun. I raised this army travelling through the western kingdoms, just as you did on your march south, and it's as well I came when I did. To war, Arthur, this is but the first battle. We must fight on and keep fighting until the war is won.'

Arthur hauled himself to his feet, Ida's stone sceptre in one hand and Excalibur in the other. Ector was dead and Lunete missing, and the pain of their loss cut Arthur deeper than any enemy blade. Dead men's blood soaked the battlefield, and the injured moaned and writhed amongst a field of corpses where ravens circled. Arthur had become a leader of warriors, and had won the battle of river Glein, but he shuddered at the fervour in Merlin's eyes, because the druid was right. Arthur's wars had only just begun.

ACKNOWLEDGEMENTS

With thanks and gratitude to Caroline, Ross, and the fantastic team at Boldwood Books.

GLOSSARY

Annwn – Celtic underworld.

Bard – Professional storyteller in Celtic culture.

Bucellari – Mercenary war bands, the name comes from Roman escort troops.

Caer Ligualid – Roman city in what is now Carlisle, Cumbria.

Cameliard – Brythonic kingdom in Brittany.

Druid – High-ranking priest or shaman in Celtic culture.

Excalibur – Arthur's legendary sword.

Fasces – Roman symbol of power, an axe wrapped in rods, used to symbolise a Roman magistrate's civil and military power.

Fetch – Ancient word to describe a ghost or apparition.

Gwyllion – Welsh word for a witch or spirit.

Hide – Farm or portion of land used to determine the render, or tax, due from the inhabitants of a kingdom.

Lorica segmentata – Type of Roman armour with overlapping plates riveted to leather straps.

Pilum – Roman spear.

Scop – Poet.

Seidr – Ancient word for magic.

Volva – Seeress or witch.

Wealas – Saxon word for Britons, which also means slaves.

Ynys Môn – Island of Anglesey.

HISTORICAL NOTE

Arthurian legends have fascinated us for centuries, beginning in medieval literature, and adapting to their current form in modern-day novels, films and art. This tale of Arthur takes place in a crumbling Britain. A country under a veil of darkness following the Roman departure in the first decade of the fifth century after four hundred years of rule. After so many years of law, trade, taxation, military protection, roads and aqueducts, the country fell into anarchy. Gildas, a British monk and historian writing in the early sixth century, lays down a picture of abandoned cities, civil war and invasions by Saxon tribes. It is into this world that Arthur is born, a semi-mythical figure who is held up to this day as one of Britain's greatest kings.

For the two centuries following the collapse of the Western Roman Empire in around 400 AD, only fragments of evidence survive to help paint a picture of those dark days, which must have seemed like an apocalypse to the people of the time. There are mentions of Arthur in early texts, such as a poem known as 'Y Gododdin', an elegy for warriors of the Gododdin tribe from a region in south-east Scotland. The early mentions of Arthur add credulity to his legends, and many of the characters in this novel are historical people, such as Ida, Octha, Theodric, Urien and Owain, while others like Ector and Uther come down to us through the mists of time, legends, fragments of texts and folklore. Ida, for example, is mentioned by Bede as the progenitor of the Anglo-Saxon Northumbrian royal family. Bede mentions that Ida reigned for twelve years and built an early version of Bamburgh Castle on a coastal hilltop known as Dun Guaroy to the Britons.

Bede, a monk writing in the eighth century, writes of the ravages of the Saxon peoples as a punishment for the wicked ways of the Britons, and names Ambrosius Aurelianus as the leader of the resistance against the Saxon invasion. Bede does not mention Arthur but does state that Vortigern invited the Saxons to Britain in 449 and names Hengist and Horsa as their leaders.

A chronicle known as the *Historia Brittonum* (History of the Britons), written by Nennius, also talks of Vortigern and Saxon invasion. It mentions Octha of the Saxons and gives Arthur as the leader, or *dux bellorum*, of the Britons who defeated the Saxons over a series of twelve battles. The first of those twelve battles is at the river Glein, and the last is at Mount Badon. This novel deals with Arthur's rise, and ends with his first battle, which I have placed at the river Glen in Northumberland. Historians believe the river Glein could be the river Glen in Northumberland, or the river Glen in Lincolnshire. I have opted for the former.

Arthur appears in a wealth of medieval literature, which helped Geoffrey of Monmouth and Chrétien de Troyes shape the legends into the stories more recognisable to modern readers. The surviving Arthurian Welsh prose tales were first edited and translated in 1838 by Charlotte Guest into a work she called the *Mabinogion*. That important work contains Arthurian stories such as 'Culhwch and Olwen' (where Llamrei is mentioned as Arthur's horse), 'The Dream of Rhonabwy', and 'The Birth of Arthur' (which contains the story of Kaletvwlch, or Excalibur, the sword in the stone). One of the greatest collections of Welsh verse is the *Book of Taliesin*, originally composed by a sixth-century bard named Taliesin, which is dedicated to Urien of Rheged and his son Owain and contains references to Arthur and his adventures.

Geoffrey of Monmouth, a teacher, cleric and bishop, wrote *The History of the Kings of Britain* in 1136 which is one of the most influential developments in Arthurian literature. Geoffrey gives us the prehistory to Arthur's life, which includes Uther Pendragon, Vortigern, Ambrosius Aurelianus, and Merlin cast as a powerful wizard. The Merlin of this novel is a druid: the pre-Roman shamans, priests, lore keepers, advisors and medical practitioners of Britain. The Romans all but wiped out the druids during their invasion of Britain, culminating in the destruction of their sacred groves on the island of Ynys Môn, modern-day Anglesey.

Later writers, particularly the romantic Arthurian writers of the Middle Ages, give us many more Arthurian legends and add colourful characters such as Lancelot, Guinevere and Perceval and the story of the Holy Grail. We shall meet some of those characters in future novels in this series, but Guinevere can be traced back to the histories of Geoffrey of Monmouth, where the original Welsh form of her name was Gwynhyfar.

Lloegyr is a medieval Welsh name for the region of Britain lost to the Saxons during their invasion or migration to Britain, though the origins of the term are uncertain and are the subject of a great deal of speculation. In this novel, I give its meaning as *the lost lands*, and it is generally accepted that the term refers to a foreign people in a foreign land, and the modern Welsh word *lloegr* refers to the country of England.

The world I have attempted to paint at the time of Arthur's life is one of violence, extreme wealth, and extreme poverty, and any mistakes in the descriptions or telling are my own. Following the Roman departure, Britain fell into a lawless state where strongmen prevailed, carving out kingdoms for themselves using war and subjugation, and living in hilltop forts with earthwork defences. They were cruel men, living in the shadow of a literate church and the ghost of an ancient Celtic religion, with Roman-style commands of infantry and mounted warriors to protect towns and trade. The ruling elite fought for precious resources, and to gather the render due from the farmers within their kingdoms. There were twenty-eight *civitas*, or Roman towns, which had begun to crumble and decay but remained inhabited by powerful men, and the country crawled with mercenary bands, or *bucellari*, who sold themselves to lords in need of warriors. Warriors of the time did not fight on horseback, according to the historical sources. They did not possess saddles, and stirrups would not arrive in England until the tenth century. So, just as the Anglo-Saxons did later in history, the Arthur of this novel uses cavalry as a means to travel faster and outmanoeuvre his enemies, rather than to charge and destroy enemy warriors.

For a brilliant insight into the world of Arthur's time, I highly recommend Max Adams' fantastic book, *The First Kingdom: Britain in the Age of Arthur*. Any of the texts mentioned above provide interesting wider reading, but the later Middle Ages tales veer more into the romantic, stylised world of Arthurian legend. In this novel, we see Arthur win the first of his twelve battles, but the Saxons are far from beaten and he must march again to fight the tide of invasion and become the leader of Britain's armies.

ABOUT THE AUTHOR

Peter Gibbons is a financial advisor and author of the highly acclaimed Viking Blood and Blade trilogy. He originates from Liverpool and now lives with his family in County Kildare.

Sign up to Peter Gibbons' mailing list for news, competitions and updates on future books.

Visit Peter's website: www.petermgibbons.com

Follow Peter on social media here:

facebook.com/petergibbonsauthor
x.com/AuthorGibbons
instagram.com/petermgibbons
bookbub.com/authors/peter-gibbons

ALSO BY PETER GIBBONS

The Saxon Warrior Series

Warrior and Protector

Storm of War

Brothers of the Sword

Sword of Vengeance

The Arthur Chronicles Series

Excalibur

WARRIOR CHRONICLES

WELCOME TO THE CLAN ✕

THE HOME OF
BESTSELLING HISTORICAL
ADVENTURE FICTION!

WARNING:
MAY CONTAIN VIKINGS!

SIGN UP TO OUR
NEWSLETTER

BIT.LY/WARRIORCHRONICLES

Boldw∞d

Boldwood Books is an award-winning fiction publishing company seeking out the best stories from around the world.

Find out more at www.boldwoodbooks.com

Join our reader community for brilliant books, competitions and offers!

Follow us
@BoldwoodBooks
@TheBoldBookClub

Sign up to our weekly deals newsletter

https://bit.ly/BoldwoodBNewsletter

Milton Keynes UK
Ingram Content Group UK Ltd.
UKHW042351010724
444980UK00001B/6